Fever Dream

Books by Dennis Palumbo

The Daniel Rinaldi Mysteries
Mirror Image
Fever Dream

Other Fiction
From Crime to Crime (short story collection)
City Wars

Nonfiction
Writing from the Inside Out

Fever Dream

A Daniel Rinaldi Mystery

Dennis Palumbo

Poisoned Pen Press

Poisoned Pen Press
6962 E. First Ave., Ste. 103
Scottsdale, AZ 85251
www.poisonedpenpress.com
info@poisonedpenpress.com

Printed in the United States of America

Again, for Lynne and Daniel
—with love

Acknowledgments

The author would like to thank the following people for their continued help and support:

Ken Atchity, who first got the ball rolling;

Annette Rogers, my editor at Poisoned Pen Press, whose guidance once again enhanced and improved my novel;

Robert Rosenwald and Barbara Peters, founders of Poisoned Pen Press, for both their editorial acumen and pragmatic wisdom;

Jessica Tribble, associate publisher, whose diligence, resourcefulness and patience undoubtably sets some kind of industry standard;

Nan Beams and Marilyn Pizzo, also at Poisoned Pen, for their enthusiasm and attention to detail;

My long-suffering friends and colleagues, too numerous to mention, but with special appreciation to Hoyt Hilsman, Bobby Moresco, Richard Stayton, Rick Setlowe, Bob Masello, Garry Shandling, Jim Denova, Michael Harbadin, Claudia Sloan, Dave Congalton, Charlotte Alexander, Mark Evanier, Bob Corn-Revere, Lolita Sapriel, Mark Baker, Mark Schorr, Bill Shick, Fred Golan, Dick Lochte, Al Abramson, Rich Simon, Bill O'Hanlon and Sandy Tolan;

And, as before, Dr. Robert Stolorow, for his profound and seminal insights on the nature of trauma.

"Ideologies separate us. Dreams and anguish bring us together."
—Eugene Ionesco

Chapter One

Treva Williams, the only hostage to be released, sat on the curb beyond the cordoned-off area, wrapped in an EMT blanket. Shivering, teeth chattering, though the afternoon temperature had topped 100 for the third straight day.

She looked up at me with dull, disbelieving eyes.

"They shot him." Voice strained, a whisper. She was dissociating. Half out of her body. In shock.

"*Who* got shot?" It was Detective Eleanor Lowrey, standing beside me. The implacable heat had raised beads of sweat on her smooth black skin, though her violet eyes maintained their focus. "How many were there?"

"They shot Bobby. Bobby Marks."

"The assistant manager?" Lowrey consulted a Xeroxed page tucked in her notebook. The cops had just gotten a list of all on-site employees at this branch from the bank's home office in Harrisburg.

A long way from where we were now. Downtown, the corner of Liberty and Grant. Normally a busy intersection in the business district. The cacophony of traffic horns blaring, harried pedestrians shouting into cell phones, street vendors hawking Italian ices as relief against the blistering heat. The Brownian motion of urban life.

But not today. With the streets blocked off, traffic halted, sidewalks emptied, there was only the crackling tension of a city block under siege. The smell of sweat, the buzz of adrenaline, the pall of fear.

I looked down and saw that Treva had buried her chin in the folds of the thick blanket.

"They shot Bobby in the head," she said again, her words muffled. "Blood everywhere. Blood and—"

She paused, touched her forehead with trembling fingers. Looked at the bits of scarlet and grey dotting her fingertips. Blood and specks of brain matter. Bobby's.

Treva convulsed then, doubled over under the blanket. Colorless bile splattered the pavement at our feet. Eleanor Lowrey gasped and took a step back.

"It's okay," I said to her. She nodded.

Lowrey was a good cop, one of the best I'd ever seen. A rare combination of steely competence and empathy. But right now, her awareness of Treva's emotional state was in conflict with her urgent need for information about what was happening inside that bank. Other lives were at stake.

I turned my attention back to Treva. Put my hand on her shoulder, felt it trembling under the coarse blanket. Her auburn hair, tangled and drenched with sweat, curtained her face.

"I'm right here, Treva. The police, too. You're safe. You're not in the bank now. You're far away from those men."

It took a supreme effort, but she finally straightened again. Looked up with blinking, vacant eyes first at Eleanor Lowrey, then at me. Then at the uniformed men and women positioned beyond us, behind a semicircle of black-and-whites, lights flashing. Weapons pointed from every conceivable angle at the First Allegheny Bank building.

Standard containment of a robbery-in-progress. With hostages.

My own eyes riveted on her pale, stricken face, I heard the sounds of frenzied activity taking place behind my back. The angry shouts ringing down the chain of command. SWAT teams in Kevlar jackets taking position. News vans choking the streets beyond the perimeter, reporters and camera operators scrambling. Overhead, the persistent clattering of the police choppers, and, just beyond, those of two rival TV news channels. The controlled chaos of a full-scale police action.

Treva barely registered any of it. She drifted in and out of conscious awareness of her surroundings, including Lowrey and me. Perhaps even of what had just happened to her.

"Tell us about Bobby Marks," Lowrey was saying, not unkindly. She squatted on the pavement to put her face at eye-level with Treva's.

"I told you, they shot him. They said don't move and he moved, and then they shot him in the head. Right there, in front of me."

She swallowed air, gulping it like a fish pulled from the sea. Her eyes shone, wet with grief.

Treva looked with sudden curiosity at her stained fingers. "He's *on* me, isn't he? That's Bobby on me."

Lowrey leaned closer and tried again. "How many men, Treva? Can you tell us? How many guns?"

I glanced over at Eleanor and shook my head. She sighed, rolled the kinks out of her neck, and sat back on her haunches. Giving Treva some space.

Moving deliberately, I sat next to Treva on the curb, shoulders touching. Letting her know I was there. Anchoring us in the here-and-now. Keeping her in the present.

The heat shimmered off the cracked, sun-bleached pavement. This section of Liberty Avenue was without trees, without shade. The air hung thick and unmoving as a shroud.

"Do you know where you are now, Treva?"

She stared straight ahead. "Outside. On the street."

Suddenly, an unmarked sedan screeched to a halt just beyond the perimeter. Two guys in jackets and ties got out. One was the assistant chief of police, scowling as he brushed past a woman reporter from WTAE-TV who'd rushed to intercept him. He waded into the throng of uniforms, barking orders, his subordinate at his heels.

Lowrey and I exchanged glances. Treva hadn't even reacted to the squeal of tires, the slamming of car doors. The upraised voices of the cops on the scene.

"Can you look at me, Treva?"

She nodded, then turned her head. A pretty, oval face. Muted makeup smudged, etched with tears. Deep brown eyes, gone nearly black as her consciousness kept trying to recede, to escape an unacceptable reality.

Treva Williams was a smallish, slender woman of thirty or so. Under the blanket, I saw her standard bank officer's pale blue skirt and jacket, collared white blouse, and appropriately tasteful pearl necklace. Only her earrings betrayed any individuality. Larger than you'd expect, loops with tiny green stones dangling. A personal statement. Saying to the world, *I'm not just some drone in a bank...*

A world she was drifting away from, moment by moment. Pulled as though by a powerful force into a different time and space. Someplace far removed from bank hold-ups, men with guns, sudden violence. A place where the blood and brains of a colleague didn't end up on your fingers.

"Are you still with me, Treva?"

Her "yes" was unconvincing.

I kept my face composed. No smile, no reassuring look of empathy and concern. Nothing to set off her warning bells, remind her that people were worried about her. That something bad had happened.

"What color is my tie?" I said.

"Blue."

"What about my shirt?"

"You're wearing one."

I had to smile. "Yes, I am."

She stared me. Waiting. Compliant.

"Am I wearing a jacket with my tie?" I said. "And don't forget to breathe now, okay?"

"A jacket? Yes, you are. You must be hot." A long pause. "Did you say something else?"

"Yes. I said, don't forget to breathe."

"Okay." As if to comply with the crazy man, she took a deep breath.

Eleanor leaned across then and tapped my knee. Hard. *We need real info, Dan,* she was signaling me. *Get her to give us something we can use.*

I stared back at her. Treva Willams was in no shape to be a star witness. She was barely holding it together as it was.

"Do you want anything, Treva? More tea?"

For the first time, she looked down at the cooling Styrofoam cup in her small hands. Unpainted nails. No rings on her fingers. Odd, I thought, given the earrings.

"Is this tea?" Her voice thin, a wisp of sound.

"Yes. Would you like another cup?"

She was about to answer when her hands, as though with a will of their own, opened, and the cup fell to the pavement. Tea splashed my trouser cuffs.

"Treva?" I brought my face closer to hers, which had turned once again away from mine. Staring with unseeing eyes past where we three huddled at the curb.

Her face was frozen, a pale mask. Her body slumped, folded in on itself, as though deflated. As though her spirit had fled.

She was alive, unhurt. Saved from her ordeal in the bank.

But Treva Williams was…elsewhere.

Chapter Two

Two hours earlier, I was in session with one of my regular patients. Mary Lewicki had been in therapy with me for over three months, the victim of an armed carjacking that had left her with recurrent nightmares and a frequent, debilitating anxiety.

Like many of my patients, she'd been referred to me by Angela Villanova, the chief community liaison officer for the Pittsburgh Police. *And* a third cousin of mine, twice removed. From the neighborhood, as my old man used to say.

When I first met Mary Lewicki, she was sitting nervously in my waiting room, kneading her chafed red hands on her lap. After we'd exchanged brief, careful smiles, she seemed momentarily confused, as though unsure what to do next. Then, reluctantly, she got to her feet and allowed me to usher her into my office.

Like most new patients, she took a few minutes to acclimate herself to the place. She sat up straight in the chair that faced mine, looking expectantly at the diplomas on the walls, my bookshelves holding both clinical texts and old copies of *Ringsider* magazine. My weathered Tumi briefcase was in its customary position against one leg of the marble-topped antique desk.

Finally, as though a wary animal slowly trusting to the safety of her new home, she settled back against the brown leather chair. Her shoulders relaxed. Then she took that long, acquiescing first breath and brought her gaze up to meet mine. The familiar ritual, enacted by almost every patient on his or her initial visit.

Mary was a heavy-set woman in her late fifties, a long-time employee of AT&T, and a recent widow. As she later explained during that first session, "I just buried my husband, God rest his soul, and two months later this other thing happens. I don't know, Dr. Rinaldi. Maybe somebody up there's tryin' to tell me something."

The police had managed to arrest a suspect in the carjacking, but Mary was unable to pick him out of the line-up. Her nerves, she said. But according to Angie Villanova, Mary had actually had a panic attack while looking through the one-way glass at the line of suspects.

Fearing she'd had a coronary, the cops drove her to the ER at Pittsburgh Memorial. An hour later, given a sedative and a clean bill of health—at least physically—she was taken home.

After which, an angry Assistant D.A. named Parnelli figured there was no sense pressing charges against the suspect, some career loser from Wilkinsburg. If Mary couldn't make it through a line-up, there was no way she'd be able to point out her assailant from the witness stand. At least, Parnelli figured, the odds weren't good.

Besides, nobody gets promoted in the District Attorney's office for clearing routine carjackings. Not unless somebody had ended up dead.

But Angie Villanova, exposing the bleeding heart she keeps hidden under that alligator-tough hide—as well as a similar middle-aged, blue-collar kinship—referred Mary to me anyway.

"You've gotta help this lady, Danny," Angie had said on the phone. "She's the walkin' wounded. And her husband just croaked, which don't help. Though if it were my *Sonny* who kicked it, I'd be bookin' a goddam cruise to celebrate. But don't quote me."

She knew I wouldn't. She also knew I'd take the case.

I'm a clinical psychologist, and people like Mary Lewicki are my specialty. Victims of violent crime whose traumatic experience has left them with residual anxiety, depression, paranoia and fear.

Feelings I know all about myself...

Years ago, my wife Barbara and I were mugged coming out of a restaurant near the Point. Coked out of his mind, the mugger lost it and started shooting. Barbara was shot twice, killed at the scene, while a stray bullet in my brain kept me in the hospital for months.

After being discharged, I went into a tailspin, both personally and professionally. The grief was searing, unendurable, like someone was peeling away my skin. The only thing worse was the survivor guilt. The knowledge that I had lived, and Barbara had not.

During those long, agonizing months, I replayed the mugging a thousand times in my mind. I'd done some boxing when I was young. Golden Gloves. Pan Am Games. I should have been able to stop the guy, I thought. I should have protected her. *Saved* her.

It took me two years to finally accept that *I* didn't kill Barbara, some hooded thug with a 9 mm did. Some guy who's never been found. And probably never will be.

I still carry the scar from that bullet in my skull, as well as other, perhaps deeper scars—which, though less painful with each passing year, can still ache during certain long, quiet hours of the night...

◇◇◇

It took a lot of time and therapy to recover from that experience. Part of that recovery, as it turns out, was signing on as a consultant to the Pittsburgh police seven years ago.

Over that time, crime victims of all types and ages have consulted with me in my cluttered office overlooking Forbes Avenue. From the mildest of symptoms to the most severe ravages of post-traumatic stress disorder. From the survivors of rape and armed assault to kidnapping victims and battered spouses, I've borne witness to their anguish and, often, unexpected courage. Ordinary people struggling to make sense of their experience and trying, somehow, someway, to move on.

Over time, I've come to believe that trauma victims live in a very different world than everybody else—a world where the tragic, the inconceivable, the horrifying can *and* does occur. They're denied the complacency, the normal assumptions of daily life that most people walk around with. But I also believe that, with help and luck, they can learn to cope with the reality of what's happened to them.

All I can provide them is the help, to the best of my clinical ability. As for the luck part, I'm afraid that's above my pay grade.

But against the odds, and for reasons I'll never fully understand, I'm still here.

Chapter Three

Mary's appointment that day of the robbery had been coming to a close when my office phone rang. As usual, during a session, I let the answering machine pick up.

It was almost one o'clock, and a fierce sun shone stubbornly through the window blinds. Even the Oakland traffic rumbling up from the street five floors below seemed strangely muted, as though sluggish in the heat.

As had been the case for weeks, the suite's AC was putting up a losing battle with another typical Pittsburgh summer.

Mary was dabbing her forehead with a tissue.

"At least today I'm just mopping up sweat," she said ruefully. "Usually it's tears. Does that mean I'm getting better?"

Before I could reply, my cell phone rang. Unusual. My friends and colleagues knew not to call that number during office hours, unless there was an emergency.

"I'm sorry, Mary," I said, reaching for where it beeped insistently on the side table.

"Dr. Rinaldi?"

It took me a few moments to recognize the throaty voice on the phone. Detective Eleanor Lowrey. I hadn't seen or spoken to her in almost a year, when she and her partner, Sgt. Harry Polk, had worked with me on the Wingfield case. Or, as Polk would probably put it, when I had gotten my lame-ass self mixed up in the Wingfield case.

"This is Dan Rinaldi, Detective. But I'm in session with a patient and—"

She briskly cut me off. "I need you to excuse yourself for a minute so we can talk. It's important."

I didn't hesitate. I remembered Eleanor Lowrey as a no-nonsense cop, with none of her partner's angry swagger, owning instead a cool, somewhat guarded determination. I'd never heard this much intensity in her voice before.

"Of course." I asked Mary to excuse me, closed my office door behind me, and stood in the empty waiting room. Without a window facing the sun, the room was a full ten degrees cooler than my office. Almost immediately, I felt the sweat starting to dry on my shirt.

"Sorry to bother you, Doctor," Lowrey said. "But there's a situation. Have you heard the news? The story just broke on TV."

"I've been with patients all morning. What's going on?"

"An armed robbery in progress. Midtown, the First Allegheny Bank. We've got uniforms, SWAT. Half the damn force. Looks like a couple perps. Somehow the thing went down wrong, shots were fired. Apparently somebody's dead in there. Probably an employee."

"Jesus."

"Tell me about it. The pricks are still in the bank, holding the four remaining employees hostage. Demanding safe passage out of town. Your basic cluster fuck."

Her voice changed then, the urgent tones softening.

"Look, Dan, we got our hostage negotiator trying to talk these mooks outta there, but so far nobody's playing ball. Sergeant Chester, the SWAT leader—"

"Let me guess. Chester wants to go in, guns blazing. Practically guarantees more dead hostages."

"Maybe, but the SWAT presence must've spooked the perps, because just five minutes ago they let one of the hostages go. Woman named Treva Williams. EMT guys are working on her now, but she's in bad shape."

"Hurt? Wounded?"

"Freaked out. She's falling apart on us, Dan, and we need some intel about what's going on in that bank. Stuff only she can tell us."

By now, I knew where this was going.

"Any police shrinks on site?"

"Yeah, one of the regulars." Again, a shift in her voice. Softer still. "But he's not *you*, Dan. I mean, Harry would kill me if he knew I was calling you, but we need you down here. We need your help with this woman."

"Does Biegler know you called me?"

Lt. Stu Biegler was her division superior in robbery/homicide. Another cop I met during the Wingfield investigation. We hadn't exactly hit it off, either.

Lowrey drew a breath. "No, this is off the books. But, hell, you're on the payroll. Makes sense I'd want to call you in." A wry, mirthless chuckle. "Shows initiative, right? Or something?"

"Shows balls." I knew Biegler would have her head for pulling me into this. Not to mention the grief she'd get from Harry Polk. "So, what do you need?"

"I need you on the scene. ASAP."

Chapter Four

After apologizing to Mary Lewicki for cutting our session short, I saw her out of the office and started making phone calls. It took five minutes to cancel the rest of the day's appointments and lock up the suite. Then another two minutes, tops, to get down to the parking garage, behind the wheel of my green reconditioned '69 Mustang, and out onto Forbes Avenue.

I'd promised Lowrey I'd be at the scene in twenty minutes. Optimistic, given the usual traffic snarl coming out of Oakland. But with most of the student body gone for the summer, I quickly passed William Pitt Union and the Cathedral of Learning, leaving Pitt's urban campus behind. Soon enough I found myself cruising fairly smoothly down Fifth toward downtown.

The gleaming spires of the "new" Pittsburgh—chrome and glass monuments to the city's many software and financial giants—rose into view, interspersed with the venerable turn-of-the-century buildings I remembered from my youth. The Old County Building, the brown-bricked courthouse, the once-proud arches of Kaufmann's Department Store where, as a child, I'd be dutifully taken at summer's end to get new school clothes.

As I headed toward Liberty Avenue, the fierce sun sheening my windshield with an eye-squinting glare, I thought about the tension between old and new that defined contemporary Pittsburgh. The beneficiary of huge endowments from the Mellons, Scaifes, and Carnegies, the home of world-renowned hospitals, universities, and museums, it was still a city whose foundations had been laid by the hands of working men and women. It was their sweat, their toil, that had kept the now-vanished steel mills going, the coal barges chugging the dark waters of the Three Rivers, the freight trains carrying the country's manufacturing needs to points east, west, and south.

Most of those folks—and the industries they worked for—are gone now. For one thing, their children have, with rare exceptions, exchanged blue collars for white ones. For another, the world itself has changed. And, after putting up a pretty good fight, the city finally had no choice but to change along with it.

Now, as I crossed old Bigelow Boulevard, already aware of the traffic slowing as we neared the crime scene twelve blocks ahead, I realized how much I myself was like my home town. A kid who'd grown up in the old Pittsburgh of deafening steel mills and smoke-belching factories, now an adult in a city of MBA's and CEO's. The son of an Italian beat cop and an Irish homemaker, I was the first in my family to go to college, be in a profession, wear a jacket and tie.

That same tension between old and new, between different worlds of experience, existed in me. Informed both my personal and professional lives. Helped explain, I guess, my quick temper, my stubbornness, what Barbara used to mockingly refer to as my old-fashioned sense of duty.

Whatever. Maybe psychologist Alice Miller was right when she said that our childhood is the air we breathe. At least now, with the city's industrial past a fading memory, that air is cleaner...

I turned onto Grant Street, into another slow-moving line of cars. I'd dialed the radio to the all-news station, hoping to learn anything new about the hostage situation. They had a reporter at the scene, but all she could do was re-cap the story so far.

The station cut away then for a commercial, and I reached to lower the volume when I heard a familiar voice. District Attorney Leland Sinclair.

The patrician, smoothly ambitious Sinclair was already well-known for his high prosecution rate when I first met him last year in connection with the same case that had introduced me to Harry Polk and Eleanor Lowrey. But that wasn't the only reason I recognized his voice now.

This was an election year, and—as almost every political pundit had predicted—Sinclair was running for governor of the state. For the past two months, his TV and radio campaign ads, extolling his record as a tough-as-nails prosecutor, had flooded the airwaves. Moreover, he'd hired some young tech geniuses who, following the model pioneered by Barack Obama, were building the candidate a huge Internet presence. His website had thousands of hits daily, and contributions from eager supporters had started rolling in almost immediately.

"I can beat the politicians and special interests in Harrisburg at their own game." His voice on the radio was earnest, yet self-assured. With just a trace of the Ivy League education he rarely alluded to in public.

It was a voice I remembered well from our heated exchanges, the fierce rivalry that had quickly turned personal, during that crazy time last year. How could I not? For a while, he'd actually considered me a suspect in the murder of one of my own patients.

I pushed those thoughts from my mind and focused on the campaign ad. He'd added something new at the end of this one. Something that made me sit up straighter.

"And if you send me to Harrisburg, my first order of business will be to get some tougher judges on the bench. Judges who won't listen to the appeals of monsters like Troy David Dowd and their high-priced lawyers. Dowd doesn't deserve to sit on Death Row, fed and clothed by your taxes. You and I *know* what this killer deserves."

Then the now-familiar swelling music, and Sinclair's clear voice once more. "I'm Leland Sinclair, and I approve this message."

I bet he did. Troy David Dowd, the notorious serial killer dubbed "the Handyman" by the media, had been sitting on death

row for years, his execution stayed repeatedly by appeals. Over an eighteen-month period, Dowd had killed and dismembered twelve people throughout rural Pennsylvania, using handsaws, pliers and other tools, before his eventual capture and conviction. Since then, his lawyer's repeated success in keeping his client alive had fueled a fiery public uproar.

I felt my jaw tighten. Leland Sinclair was as coldly calculating as he was ambitious. By jumping on the Dowd bandwagon with this latest campaign ad, he was pandering to the state's most conservative, blue-collar constituents. Though, given the heinous nature of Dowd's crimes, there were also plenty of liberal, white-collar voters who'd be just as happy seeing his death sentence carried out.

Sinclair knew this. Just as he knew that, with a mere three points separating him and his closest rival in the polls, he couldn't afford to lose a single vote.

Traffic had long since ground to a standstill, and I could see past the horn-honking semis and exhaust-spewing buses to where two patrol cars, lights flashing, were blocking the intersection up ahead.

Screw this. I pulled out of the line of cars and parked at the curb. I'd get there faster on foot.

Or so I thought.

Chapter Five

The uniformed cop had one huge hand on my forearm, the other gripping the head of his holstered nightstick. He'd come running over, shouting, when he saw me step across the intersection and between the two parked black-and-whites.

"What the fuck?—" He was about six-two, 280 pounds of third-generation Irish street cop. And sincerely pissed.

"Look," I began, raising my free hand in surrender, "I'm Doctor—"

"I don't give a shit who you are. See them patrol units blocking the street? See them flashing lights?"

I reached inside my jacket pocket. "Listen, officer, I'm Daniel Rinaldi, and I work with—"

He tightened his grip on my arm. "This whole area's cordoned off, asshole. Ya think that don't apply to *you?*"

Before I could respond, another voice—gruff, a hard-drinker's rasp—called out.

"No, he probably don't."

The cop and I turned at the same time to find Sgt. Harry Polk, burly and unkempt, lumbering toward us across the strip of lawn stitching the sidewalk to the edge of Liberty Avenue. Red-faced and sweating, Polk came up to where we stood and swatted the other cop's hand off my arm.

"Let him go, Haney."

"You know this guy, Sarge?"

Polk grunted. "Only too goddam well."

I swear, Polk was wearing the same wrinkled blue suit as the last time I saw him. And the same sour, world-weary expression. Which he now aimed at me.

"What the hell are *you* doin' here?"

I smiled. "I've missed you too, Harry."

Polk ignored me and turned to Haney. "I got this. Doc Rinaldi here is sorta on the job. *Sorta.*"

Haney gave me a suspicious look, then shrugged and trotted back to where another uniform stood listening to his two-way radio.

Watching Haney take up his position again at the corner, I had my first good look at the crime scene. The entire intersection had been blocked off and evacuated, the streets in all directions cleared of traffic. Every store, coffee shop and street vendor cart stood empty and ignored, except for the towering First Allegheny Bank building.

Like the hub of a wheel, it was the focus of the entire operation. A roiling sea of cops, SWAT teams, media vans. With all eyes, weapons and cameras aimed at the white-bricked bank's shuttered double doors and steel-reinforced windows.

Even from this distance, I could hear the constant, dissonant chorus of angry voices. Reporters shouting questions to the cops on scene. Cops shouting curses back.

"I gotta get through there, Harry," I said.

Polk pulled a handkerchief from his back pocket and wiped the sweat from his brow. "No shit? Mind if I ask why?"

"Lowrey called me. She's with the hostage they released. Wants me to give her a hand."

Polk stopped in mid-wipe. "Lowrey called *you?*"

"That's right. Seems you guys can't get anything out of the hostage and—"

"Bullshit. You don't go in the field, Doc. You sit in your nice cushy office and head-shrink the vics that Villanova sends to you. That's all. That's it."

"If you think *that's* true, Harry, you've got a short memory."

He scowled. "Don't remind me. And fuck Lowrey. We got a situation here. Christ, wait'll I get a hold of her."

I felt my own anger rising. There wasn't time for this. I got in his face.

"Damn right, you've got a situation. One hostage dead already. The only witness you've got falling apart. So why the hell are we standing here arguing? Get me in there."

Polk bristled, and turned away from me. I could see the back of his neck reddening, as much from rage as from the punishing sun.

Then, abruptly, he started walking toward the outer row of patrol cars, calling over his shoulder at me. "So, Sigmund. You comin' or what?"

◇◇◇

With Polk shouldering a path for us through the maze of uniforms and plainclothes, we soon arrived at a side street just off of Liberty. There, next to where a young woman sat bundled in a blanket on the curb, stood Detective Eleanor Lowrey. She gave a brief smile and came over to meet us, taking off her dark glasses.

She was as striking as I remembered. Tall, graceful. Sleeveless t-shirt and jeans accentuating her firm, ample curves. Lips and nails painted the same shade of burnt red. The only difference was her softly-ringed, blue-black hair, which she'd let grow out since the last time I'd seen her.

Meanwhile, Polk barely looked at her. "Doc here says you reached out to him." His voice held an edge.

Lowrey nodded carefully, her eyes on his.

"We got nothin', Harry. I called an audible."

"Uh-huh." He sniffed, loudly. "Just don't make it a habit, okay? Biegler hears about this, we're fucked. You know what he thinks of this guy."

"Biegler's a dickless bastard. With all due respect."

Polk shrugged. "I'm just sayin'…"

He squinted past Lowrey to where the young woman sat, oblivious. Shivering in the blanket. "That her?"

Lowrey nodded again.

Polk stared at Lowrey for a long moment. Then he turned to me: "Okay, Doc. I guess she's all yours."

Without another word to his partner, Polk strode off.

Lowrey let her violet eyes narrow for a moment, before a rueful smile played on her face. Then, touching my elbow, she took me over and introduced me to Treva Williams.

Chapter Six

Which is how I ended up, ten minutes later, with my hands on Treva's slumping shoulders, keeping her upright. Her eyes vacant, staring at nothing. Unmindful of the damp blotches on her blanket, wet from the spilled tea.

Lowrey crouched in front of her again.

"What just happened, Dan?"

I lifted each of Treva's eyelids, felt her pulse.

"She keeps going in and out of shock," I said. "She can't deal with what she saw, keeps shutting down…"

Lowrey rubbed her forehead. "Jesus, you've gotta *do* something for her…"

Suddenly, Treva blinked and made a strangled noise. Against the dark weave of the EMT blanket, her skin was chalk-white, glazed as porcelain.

I took her hand. So small. Almost weightless.

"Treva, are you all right? Can you talk to us?"

Lowrey straightened again, flipped open her two-way. "Shit, I'm getting the EMT cart back over here."

"Good idea. She could use more fluids."

I didn't take my eyes from Treva's ashen, panicked face. Though I noticed that her breathing had become more regular, measured. She focused.

"Are you the doctor?"

"Yes. Dr. Rinaldi. And here's Detective Lowrey, remember? You're safe, Treva. It's all right."

"Good." She took another deep breath. "Good. I…I'm sorry, I think I went to sleep. I had a dream."

"A dream?"

"It must've been a dream. I was in the bank…I work at the bank."

"Yes, I know."

Lowrey frowned down at me, but I just raised a warning finger. I couldn't take the time to explain what I thought was happening.

Treva was still in shock and unable to grasp the reality of what she'd witnessed in the bank. But unless I was wrong, she wanted—*needed*—to talk about what she'd seen. At the same time, she couldn't cope with it. *Not if it had really happened.*

So her unconscious was helping her cope. Making it seem as though what she'd experienced hadn't been real at all, but rather just a dream. Some horrible dream.

"You had a dream about the bank?"

"Yes," Treva said. "A bad dream."

"Can you remember the dream, Treva?"

"I think so." She shifted her shoulders under the blanket, sat up straighter. Readying herself for the effort. "We were all there, working. But it was quiet. No customers. Phyllis had just come back from lunch…"

"Phyllis?"

"Our head teller. Well, we call them associates now. She was showing me the watch her husband had gotten her for their anniversary. It had those fake diamonds…I forget what you call them…"

I waited.

Again her breathing grew shallow. Gently, so as not to alarm her, I laid my fingers on her wrist. Feeling for her pulse.

"Suddenly, the front door banged open and this man came in. Wearing something on his face. Some kind of cloth, wrapped around his head. Like a mask. And he had a big gun. Before anyone could do or say anything, he aimed the gun at the two security cameras and shot them to pieces."

"Both video cameras?"

"Yes. They're on either side of the main floor. Then another man came in behind him, wearing the same kind of mask. He— they both had the same big guns. Phyllis had started screaming as soon as the first man came in, and now we all were. Screaming, I mean. And crying and…"

She closed her eyes.

"You're right," I said softly. "It *was* a bad dream. What did the gunmen do next?"

Treva tilted her head up, but kept her eyes closed.

"They shouted at us to step away from our desks, to come around to the front and get down on our knees. Hands on our heads. And not to move. They kept saying that over and over. 'Don't move, don't nobody fucking move!' But Bobby…"

"Bobby Marks? The assistant manager?"

She nodded, and finally opened her eyes.

"Funny, he was the last one of us to get down on his knees. I mean, he was so slow about it, like he didn't want to wrinkle his pants. Bobby was always so careful about his appearance. He liked tailored suits. And pocket handkerchiefs. You hardly see them anymore, but…"

I paused. "What happened to Bobby?"

"He…did what they said, but when he went to put his hands on his head, his glasses slipped off. The first masked man yelled at him, told him not to move. But Bobby, I guess he couldn't help it, he reached down for the glasses, and this man…"

Her voice caught. "Then…this man—he was tall, I remember—he just steps up to Bobby and puts his gun next to Bobby's head and shoots. And there's blood and stuff everywhere, and I'm kneeling right next to him, and—"

Lowrey and I risked a quick glance at each other as Treva stopped abruptly.

"Treva," I began carefully. "What happened next?…In your dream…?"

"The other masked man starts yelling at the tall one, really mad, saying it was stupid to shoot Bobby…I mean, we're all weeping and moaning now, scared to death. Bobby's blood is spreading all over the floor, and these two men are shouting at each other, cursing...I was afraid they—"

Treva swallowed a couple times, hard.

"Then...I don't know how, but the alarm goes off, and the tall man waves his gun at the rest of us. Tells us we better shut the fuck up and stay put. Stay just where we are. Then he aims his gun at George—"

"Who's George?"

"The bank guard. Real nice guy. He's not doing anything wrong, he's on his knees like the rest of us. Hands on his head. But the tall man warns him again not to move. Not to do something stupid."

I could feel Lowrey leaning in next to me, holding her breath, as though any sound might break the spell. Might interrupt Treva's recounting of her dream.

"This part's kinda hazy," Treva went on, "but I remember the second man, the shorter one, the alarm really freaks him out. He starts yelling, 'Fuck this, man. Fuck this!' And then he runs out of the bank, through the rear emergency exit door. The tall man yells after him, you know, 'Come back, asshole! Get back here!' Stuff like that. But the guy's gone, and the tall man is just standing there. Then I—"

She stopped suddenly, took a long breath.

I forced myself to stay calm. Patient. "Then what, Treva? Do you remember what happened next?"

"Nothing happened next."

"But you got out of the bank. In your dream, didn't the tall man release you? Let you leave the bank?"

"Oh, I didn't get out of the bank...I mean, after the other robber ran away, I just...that's when I woke up..."

A faint smile played on her lips.

"That's when I saw you, looking at me. You have a kind face, Doctor. Even with your beard."

I didn't say anything, but just kept watching her eyes. They'd begun to go dull again, fading, as though the life were emptying out of them.

"Can I go to sleep again?" she asked wearily.

I stood up to find Lowrey staring down at Treva with an odd, unreadable expression on her face. Then, sighing, she very deliberately put her sunglasses back on. I couldn't see her eyes as she looked at me.

"She still hasn't given us much. But at least—"

Before Lowrey could say another word, a staccato volley of gunshots sounded from behind us. Hollow booms, like distant thunder.

I whirled to see a small army of uniforms and SWAT guys swarm toward the First Allegheny building, shouting and cursing. Service weapons at the ready.

The shots had come from inside the bank.

Chapter Seven

It was all over in less than a minute.

Even before the first gunshots had faded, we could hear answering fire from the cops as they stormed the bank. The angry *pop-pops*, the shattering glass.

Lowrey grabbed my arm and pulled me down next to where Treva sat, her mouth working furiously behind the folds of the blanket.

"Stay with her!" Lowrey yelled at me, unholstering her service weapon.

Before I could respond, another round of shots echoed sharply. Treva screamed, her hands shooting up out of the blanket to cover her ears.

"It's okay." I put my arms around her.

Lowrey gave us a last, alarmed look and ran in a crouch between the patrol cars, toward the bank.

Holding the blanket tight around Treva, I craned my neck up and around to see what I could.

At first, all I saw was the unfolding column of cops, moving at all angles, converging on the bank. Breaking down the doors, shooting the glass out from behind the broad barred windows. Splintered shards exploded, glittered like diamonds between drifting tendrils of gun smoke.

Then, out of the corner of my eye, I saw something move on the roof of the building across from the bank.

Still clutching Treva, I turned and squinted my eyes. Again, the blur of movement. Sunlight flashing off body armor. A SWAT sniper rifle, angled over the edge of the roof. Firing.

Treva's body shook with each round the sniper fired off. I ducked back down, huddled us lower, felt her tremors as she burrowed beneath the blanket.

For what seemed an eternity we braced against a continuous, ear-pounding roar of gunfire, guttural cries, and exploding glass…

Until, suddenly—

Treva stirred in my arms, sniffling, and I gave her a little slack. She peered up at me. A questioning look.

I'd noticed it, too. The silence.

No more gunshots. No raised voices. Just an eerie, sticky silence that poured through the oppressive heat like molasses…

I glanced once again up at the roof's edge where the sniper was positioned. Or had been. He was gone, too.

I looked back down at Treva, whose hand had come up to rub her forehead. "Was I dreaming again?"

◇◇◇

I was still helping her to her feet when an EMT guy wearing Kevlar over his medic blues came running up.

"You guys all right?" Shaved head, mustache. Both sheened with sweat. Name tag on his shirt said "Karp."

"Can you get Treva here in the ambulance?"

She shifted under my arm.

"I want to stay with you."

"I'm not going anywhere, Treva. I just want the medic to check your vitals. Maybe give you something else to drink."

She shook her head. "I don't like him."

Karp laughed. "Trust me, honey, I grow on people." He held out his hand. "C'mon, now. Nothin' to worry about."

I let her out of my embrace and turned to face her.

"Look, Treva, I'm coming right back. Just go get in the ambulance and I'll join you in a couple minutes. I'll even ride with you to the hospital if you want."

"You will? Promise?" Voice as plaintive as a child's.

"Promise."

Again, that faint smile played on her lips. As though the thin, tinny sound of her own voice had amused her.

She shifted uncomfortably in the thick blanket. Frowning, she pulled it off and gave it to the EMT tech. Ran her hands through her sweat-matted hair.

"God, it's so hot. I was roasting in that thing."

"I guess you don't need it anymore."

She nodded gravely, and the smile fled.

In just that single, simple exchange, we'd brought her back to the present. To the awareness, once again, of the horrors that she'd witnessed. And that she'd soon remember in all their cold, irrefutable reality.

After a long pause, she looked away.

"Is it all over?"

"I think so," I said.

The EMT tech gave her what he thought was a reassuring smile, complete with gold tooth. "Sure it is, hon. Looks like everything's secured."

He was right. Over his shoulder, I could see uniforms moving in and out through what was left of the bank's open double-doors. Plainclothes cops, including the Assistant Chief, were coming out from behind cover to assemble at the entrance. CSU techs had already scrambled out of their windowless vans, trailing spools of crime scene tape. News crews were hustling into position.

But when I looked back at Treva, all I saw was the color leaving her cheeks. Her breath coming in quick, shallow gasps.

"So it really…Bobby's really—"

I lunged forward and caught her as she fainted.

With a surprised grunt, Karp stepped to her other side and held her around the waist. "She's shocky."

"You think?" Taking my frustration and worry out on the poor guy.

He gave me a pained, embarrassed look, which I returned with what I hoped was an apologetic one.

Then we carried Treva over to the EMT ambulance. After helping Karp get her settled on one of the two gurneys bolted to the floor inside, I left.

Five minutes later, I took my first steps inside the bank, where the cops had just finished sorting the living from the dead.

Chapter Eight

The first thing I noticed was how cold it was.

In contrast to the baking heat outside, the bank's lobby was as cold as a walk-in freezer. The combination of air conditioning, marble floors and, no doubt, the familiar chill of staid, institutional respectability. A cool oasis amidst the turmoil of an uncertain world.

On any other day, perhaps.

Today, what I felt as I stepped carefully into the glass-strewn, bullet-scarred lobby was the claustrophobic encasement of a meat locker. The overwhelming stench of a slaughterhouse. The smell of blood and open wounds held captive by the frigid air.

At first, I didn't even register the cops on the scene. Polk and Lowrey. Uniforms milling around. CSU techs setting up their equipment. EMT clearing out, the medical examiner and his people coming in. Their wheeled beds, body bags, white sheets.

In that feverish flurry of activity, nobody seemed to register me, either.

I took another breath and found myself looking at the walls. Maybe to avoid looking down at the bodies. The walls spattered with blood, scarlet blotches that sprayed out in a curving pattern like thrown mud. That dripped slowly in rivulets to the floor like some living Pollock painting.

Bits of flesh and bone fragments pitted the teller's stations, the customer counters, the free-standing courtesy desk whose pen still dangled half-way to the floor from its silver chain.

The first body I saw lay beneath it. A young East Indian woman, the top of her head blown off. Her wounds oozed blood that pooled on the cold marble beneath her. Spreading in waves to mingle obscenely with the blood of another, older woman lying three feet away.

She wore a pale green blouse and gray pants, and had a gaping black hole where her face had been. Head thrown awkwardly back against a nest of blood-splattered hair. At the end of an outstretched arm was a smooth, manicured hand. An expensive-looking watch on her wrist. Was this Phyllis, wearing the anniversary present her husband had given her?

Not a half-dozen feet away, a man lay sprawled on his back, arms and legs at odd angles. His Hugo Boss suit was flecked with blood and bits of flesh, but what drew my eye was the perfect triangle forming the tip of his white linen handkerchief, still neatly tucked into his jacket breast pocket. The tip itself stained pink.

Bobby Marks, the assistant manager. Most of his face had survived the bullet that had cleaved off the back of his skull. Now it lay unnaturally flat against the floor, like a grotesquely comic theatrical mask, eyes and mouth opened wide with surprise.

Suddenly I was all out of toughness, or stunned curiosity, or whatever the hell I wanted to call my state of mind. The room began to spin. I put out my hands, like a high-wire walker, and tried to get my bearings.

"Hey!" A sharp, officious voice made me turn. I drew a couple more deep breaths. Reoriented myself.

It was Lt. Stu Biegler from robbery/homicide, striding purposefully across the floor toward me. Not even glancing down at the body of Bobby Marks, other than to step carefully around the blood spreading beneath him.

Thin and handsome in a useless, male-model kind of way, Biegler was easily forty but looked ten years younger. Though he carried himself in a way that seemed more callow than youthful.

Now, planting his feet as though to establish his authority, he glared at me. "What the hell are *you* doing here?"

Boy, I was getting tired of people asking me that.

Not for the first time, though, anger helped me get a grip. Seemed like I was never in Biegler's presence without wanting to punch his lights out. Not the kind of response you'd normally expect from your average mental health professional, but there it was. Sue me.

"I was called to the scene, Lieutenant," I said evenly. "Got a problem with that, take it up with the assistant chief."

"Don't worry, I will. Last thing we need is some civilian fucking up our crime scene."

I indicated the bodies strewn about the lobby floor.

"Looks like somebody already did that."

He was about to respond, when something he saw over my shoulder made his jaw tighten. Then, to my surprise, Biegler covered his mouth with his hand and brushed past me toward the opened double-doors. His body in a kind of half-crouch, I could tell he was trying very hard not to be sick.

I turned and got my first look at what Biegler had seen. Steeling myself, I came over to where Harry Polk stood, shifting his weight from one foot to the other. Staring down at what was left of the masked gunman.

"Who got our perp?" Polk addressed the assistant medical examiner who squatted next to the body. His name tag said "Reynolds." Middle-aged, balding, and bored.

"According to the witness," Reynolds said, "looks like *we* got him. I mean, SWAT did. Their sniper took him down."

Before Polk could stop me, I bent to take a closer look at the dead man. Most of his face had been sheared away by the sniper's bullet, and what was left was still hidden by the singed fabric of his mask. A kind of thin, woven scarf that he'd wrapped around his head. It clung in bloody shreds to his exposed cheekbones, torn fragments dotting the ugly pattern of flesh and brains that fanned out from beneath his head on the smooth marble.

Reynolds got awkwardly to his feet. "SWAT uses those nasty-ass hollow points. A head-hit pretty much turns everything into Hamburger Helper."

"Where's his gun?" Polk said, pointing at a spot just beyond where the dead man's outstretched palm lay still against the floor. "It was just here, right by his hand. A .357 Magnum. Musta dropped it when the sniper dropped *him*."

"CSU bagged and tagged it," Reynolds said. "Already on its way to the lab. Lieutenant gave 'em the go-ahead."

"Sure he did." Polk gave me a sour glance as I straightened up again. "Biegler can't get this scene cleared fast enough. He's probably hiding behind a black-and-white down the block, puking his guts out."

Polk turned back to Reynolds. "Tell me we caught a break and there was some ID on this guy."

"CSU didn't find squat. No wallet, keys. Nothin'. Maybe we'll get lucky when we run his prints. He could be in the database."

"Probably is. I can't see some fuckin' virgin trying a job this size. In broad daylight. Him and his partner."

"Maybe the partner's the first-timer," I said. "According to Treva Williams, the partner got spooked by the alarm and ran out. Left this guy on his own."

Polk scratched his nose. "We'll know more once we get a look at the surveillance video."

"What there *is* of it," I replied. "Looks like the first thing this guy did when he entered the bank was shoot out the cameras."

Polk gave me an irritated look. "You got any other good news for me, Doc? 'cause so far all you're doin' is pissin' me off."

I smiled. "Kinda like old times, eh, Harry?"

Reynolds very deliberately cleared his throat. "Look, can we bag this guy, Sarge? Doc Bergmann wants all the vics down at the morgue ASAP."

"This asshole ain't no vic."

"He's dead, right? Makes him a vic in my book. Just another slob on a slab."

"Enjoy your work, don't'cha, buddy?" Polk shook his head. "Speakin' of your boss, where the hell is he?"

Reynolds jerked his thumb in the direction of the far corner of the lobby. "Over there. With the witness."

Polk said nothing, just sort of grunted and stepped carefully over the body at our feet. Then he headed across the floor, avoiding the coagulating pools of blood, the sprawled corpses of the bank employees, and a couple desultory coroner's assistants unfolding body bags. I followed.

We found Eleanor Lowrey standing with Dr. Rudy Berg-mann, the veteran medical examiner whose lauded forensics expertise was somewhat undercut by his famously bad hairpiece. A video of it slipping from his forehead during an interview with a local news anchor had become a YouTube sensation a few years back.

Bergmann was stoop-shouldered, bespectacled, and probably nearing retirement. So at first I was surprised to see him here. Then I realized that with a crime of this magnitude, the assistant chief would want the heavy-hitters involved from the get-go.

That's why the distinguished Dr. Bergmann was reduced now to doing triage, attending to the badly bleeding left arm of the bank security guard, who sagged, obviously in great pain, against the wall.

His name, I recalled from Treva, was George. Tall, salt-and-pepper hair trimmed to a severe V at the middle of his forehead. He was in his mid-fifties, and, given how tight he wore his olive green uniform, maybe a bit vain about how fit he was. Skin tanned like leather, a strong chin. Hard grey eyes that had seen a lot.

As Bergmann wrapped a bandage around his wound, a tangled spool of torn flesh and splintered bone, George winced angrily.

"It was *your* guys," he said, aiming those ice-chip eyes at Polk. "Your fuckin' sniper shot me. I'm on my knees near the goddam window and the next thing I know my arm feels like a hot spear went through it."

"Wait a minute, pal." Polk leaned in to peer back at the guy. "First of all, what's your name?"

"George," I said helpfully.

Polk grunted. "I think I got this, Rinaldi."

Then, back to the security guard: "George what?"

Lowrey spoke up. "George Vickers. Works for a private security firm the bank uses."

Polk glared first at Lowrey, then me. "How 'bout we let the guy answer for himself, okay? Unless either one of *you* wants to ask the questions…?"

Eleanor Lowrey gave her partner a wry look. "Easy, Harry, okay? We'll all a little stressed here."

"Yeah, a *little*." George Vickers snorted. "I mean, one minute I'm standin' in the bank, like usual. Next thing I know, this guy comes in, starts shootin' out the cameras. He and his partner have us down on the floor so fast, I didn't even have time to draw my weapon."

Polk glanced meaningfully at Vickers' belt holster.

"Yeah, I can see that. Since you didn't discharge it, you can hang onto it. We won't need it."

Vickers reddened. "Hey, you weren't *there*, man. You weren't the one that got shot."

"Don't worry, George," Polk said evenly. "The perp got his, too. Head shot. Real pretty."

Vickers smiled crookedly. "I know. I saw him take the hit. Spun him clean around. Like a top."

"Great. Think we can get the story from the beginning, George?" Polk pulled a notepad from his jacket pocket.

"Forget it. I ain't got time. I'm bleedin' like a stuck pig. Hurts like hell, too. I need to get down to the hospital. Ain't that right, doc?"

Bergmann sighed. "Unless the sergeant here wants to add another death to the four we've got already, I'd have to say yes. This bandage is makeshift at best."

Then the ME signaled to one of his people, who trotted over. She seemed barely out of her teens, with a pony tail that bobbed as she ran.

"Get Mr. Vickers here in the ambulance before it leaves with the Williams girl," her boss told her. Cutting his eyes back at Polk. "Or before he bleeds to death."

The girl had just started reaching for the wounded security guard when Polk stepped between them.

"C'mon, George. I bet you used to be on the job."

Bergmann stared at him. "Sergeant, I just said—"

But Vickers answered, coolly. "The two-forty, yeah. Did my twenty and got out."

"Then at least give me the headlines, okay? Help us out here."

Vickers considered this for moment, then smiled grimly. "Ya want headlines? Two guys try to rob the bank, one of 'em panics and splits. The other guy freaks out, starts killing the hostages. Suddenly, SWAT's shootin' through the windows. I get hit, but before I go down I see the perp get popped. Then the good guys bust in and the next thing I know, the doc here is bandaging my arm. Now all I gotta do is get me a lawyer and figure out who to sue. End of story."

He got gingerly to his feet, then reached out with his good arm for the pony-tailed coroner's assistant.

"Now, c'mon, girlie. Walk me over to the ambulance. I'm feelin' kinda faint."

As the wounded guard went off with the girl, Polk grunted something unintelligible and snapped his notebook shut.

"Fuck it," he said to no one in particular. "I'm goin' outside for a smoke." Which he did.

Then Dr. Bergmann adjusted his wire-rim glasses, gave Lowrey and me a cursory nod, and headed off to supervise the bagging of the victims. I didn't envy him the brutal day's work he had in front of him.

Standing next to me, I heard Lowrey's long, weary sigh. She spoke without turning.

"Like I said, a real cluster fuck."

Chapter Nine

It was then that I remembered my promise to Treva. I mumbled a quick explanation to Lowrey and headed across the lobby. Behind me, I heard the detective flipping open her cell phone and asking for a number.

I strode quickly out onto the sun-baked street. It still thronged with police personnel and news crews, but the Assistant Chief's car was no longer on scene. I couldn't see Biegler, either.

As I crossed the intersection and headed toward the far perimeter where I'd left Treva, I also noticed that a half-dozen uniforms had been deployed to keep a growing crowd of on-lookers back behind the crime scene tape. At least a third of them had their cell phones raised above their heads, shooting video of the scene. Maybe the cops would be bringing the dead bodies out soon! Something to show the wife and kids. Or put up on their Facebook page.

When I reached the stretch of sidewalk where I'd helped Karp carry Treva into the ambulance, I found only the pony-tailed coroner's assistant. She was leaning sullenly against a trash can, wiping her brow with her sleeve. The heat poured down in waves, like invisible lava.

"Where's the ambulance?" I asked her.

"You just missed 'em," Pony-Tail said. She was noisily chewing gum. "Doc Bergmann said to get the security guard on his way ASAP. So I put him in the back with the girl and Karp drove like hell outta here. Pittsburgh Memorial."

"So Treva Williams was with them?"

Pony-Tail stopped chewing long enough to give me a surly look. "You're Dr. Rinaldi, aren't you?"

"Yes. Was Treva awake and alert?"

"Alert enough to ask me where the hell *you* were. She said you were supposed to ride with her in the ambulance."

"I was. At least, I told her I would."

"Yeah. She said you *promised* her." Pony-Tail smiled unpleasantly. "You're some kind of shrink, right? Shouldn't guys like you keep your promises?"

I took a moment before answering. I wasn't really in the mood for this. "She say anything else?"

Pony-Tail looked off. "Let me see. Oh, yeah. She said, 'Well, it isn't the first time I've been fucked over by a man. Won't be the last.' Somethin' like that."

"I bet it was *exactly* like that."

She popped her gum. "Yeah, I guess so."

Suddenly, I heard Eleanor Lowrey's voice behind me, calling out.

"Dan!"

I turned and saw her trotting between the angled black-and-whites at the intersection, heading my way. Even from this distance, I could tell something was up.

Pony-Tail spat her gum onto the grass. "I gotta go. Some of us *work* for a living."

She made her way over to where a young uniformed officer was arguing across a length of crime scene tape with a heavyset man hoisting a shoulder-cam. Pony-Tail gave the uniform a sly smile, which he returned with a broader one. I guess they knew each other.

I wondered for a moment what Pony-Tail's problem with me was. Father issues? Bad experience with a therapist?

She'd certainly bonded instantly with Treva Williams. Maybe saw herself as a similar kind of victim. Of men, of life.

Or else none of the above, and I was just dealing with the horror of what I'd seen in the bank by indulging my clinical curiosity. The classic therapist's defense mechanism. A way to keep the image of all that blood and carnage, all that gruesome death, at bay.

My reverie was interrupted by Lowrey's arrival. Her eyes were bright, charged with feeling. Her sunglasses hung from the deep V in her t-shirt, glinting in the sun. "Good thing I caught up with you."

"Make it fast, detective. I've got a five-block walk to where my car's parked."

"Where are you going?"

"Pittsburgh Memorial. That's where the EMT ambulance is taking Vickers and Treva Williams. I promised her I'd ride down with her, and…well…I didn't get back here in time."

"She'll be all right."

"We don't know that. Treva's in a traumatized state. Since her release from the bank, I'm the only civilian she's been in contact with. The first one she's told about what happened in there. What she saw."

Lowrey considered this. "Well, I know she trusts you. Made some kind of connection with you. I saw it."

"That's why I've got to get to the hospital. I've already violated that trust by breaking my promise. I've got to do what I can to repair that. For *her* sake." I paused. "The truth is, as of now she's my clinical responsibility."

"Sometimes you act like *everyone's* your clinical responsibility. Remember what you went through last year?"

"I'm not likely to forget it. But the fact remains, whatever happens to Treva from now on—at least psychologically—it happened on my watch…"

Lowrey paused, put on her sunglasses. "Look, I think I understand. And I wish I could let you go. But I can't."

"Why not?"

"Because I have orders from Lt. Biegler to bring you with me. There's an emergency debriefing that's taking place in ten minutes, and they want to see you. Both of us."

I didn't understand this. Unless they wanted some kind of statement from me. I'd been the one brought in to treat the sole hostage the gunmen released. The only person who'd survived the shoot-out in the bank. Maybe Vickers' threat of a lawsuit had made everybody nervous.

"Look, Detective," I said quickly, "if this is the usual departmental bullshit, tell them to send me all the forms they want and I'll fill 'em out. In triplicate. But Treva's the one who needs me now."

Lowrey shook her head. "No can do. He specifically wants to see *you*."

"Who, Biegler?"

"No. District Attorney Sinclair."

I stared at her. "Sinclair wants to see *me*? Why?"

She managed a brief smile. "Don't ask me, I just work here. Now come on."

She took my arm, exerting just enough muscle to signal that she wasn't kidding around. I raised my free hand in mock-surrender and went with her.

"Where *is* this meeting, anyway?" I gently pulled my arm free.

"You wouldn't believe me if I told you," she said. "And for Christ's sake, stop calling me 'Detective.'"

Chapter Ten

We walked three blocks south of the First Allegheny Bank, and then into a red-bricked, two-story converted appliance store. Instead of banners announcing ceiling fans and dishwashers on sale, the broad picture windows were plastered with bright blue campaign signs.

I gave Lowrey a stunned look. Another surprise on a day full of them. This was the downtown office of Leland Sinclair's gubernatorial campaign.

"You're kidding," I said, as we crossed the main floor. The former appliance showroom now displayed a dozen nondescript rented desks piled high with papers, stacks of banners, dirty coffee mugs, and crumpled cans of Red Bull. Each desk also had a computer, fax machine, and printer crowding its surface, and a ridiculously young, caffeine-fueled volunteer sitting behind it.

None of whom even glanced up as we maneuvered through the room toward the back, where an old, wood-banistered staircase led to the second floor.

"Why are we meeting here?" I looked at Lowrey.

"Apparently, Sinclair's on a tight schedule, and he happened to be here anyway. So his people figured it'd be easier to do it here than for Sinclair to detour down to his office."

"But why does Sinclair even want to get involved, especially at this early stage of the investigation?"

She paused with her hand on the stairway bannister. "Hey, he's still the DA."

I gave this some thought. "Good point. The last thing he needs while campaigning as a tough law-and-order guy is a blood-bath in the heart of town."

"That's for sure. Sorta like what you were talking about with Treva. This bank mess isn't the kind of thing Sinclair wants to have happened on *his* watch."

"Yeah. Dead hostages make for lousy campaign ads."

Before we went up, I glanced around me once more at the swirling activity on the floor. Phones were ringing constantly, faxes curling out of their holding bays. Images from various cable news stations flickered from the four wide TV monitors positioned strategically around the room.

And throughout all of this hustle and noise, a few slightly older, obviously veteran political types were moving purposefully among the maze of desks, like bees going from flower to flower. Your standard campaign soldiers. Ties askew, shirt sleeves rolled up. Sweating profusely despite the shiny new window AC units. Cell phones and Blackberries in hand, they either leaned down to squint unhappily at computer screens, or up to stare unhappily at one of the TV monitors.

At the top of the stairs, Lowrey and I found a series of office doors. Again, a nostalgic tableaux of dark-stained wood and frosted window-glass. Above each door there was even the proverbial transom. It was like stepping back in time to the urban Pittsburgh of the early Fifties, when black soot coated the buildings, electric trolley cars rumbled down cobblestone streets, and everybody wore a hat.

Lowrey knocked at the first door we came to.

I smiled. "What's this, the last actual smoke-filled room?"

She wisely ignored me and we waited in silence. But only for a few moments. Then we heard Harry Polk's gruff voice calling through the door.

"If that's you, Lowrey, come on in. And bring the doc with ya."

◇◇◇

Leland Sinclair sat behind a small, cherrywood desk, elbows on the blotter as he listened to the murmured voices of the men arrayed in chairs around him. This room also had a newly-installed window air conditioner, whose steady drone provided an almost lulling white noise.

I did a quick head count. Lt. Biegler. Harry Polk. And a squat, powerfully-built man I remembered from one awful night during the Wingfield investigation. The SWAT commander, Sgt. Chester—I'd never gotten a first name—was still wearing his Kevlar from the crime scene. His narrow-eyed appraisal of me as Lowrey and I came in was a carbon copy of the one Biegler was giving me.

The only face I didn't know belonged to a tall, sharp-featured man in his late thirties. He gave me a look that tried very hard to be cursory, but didn't quite succeed. Instead, I got the impression of a hawk-like intelligence that didn't miss much. Dark hair, trimmed mustache. Silk tie, Windsor knot, long sleeved white shirt with gold cuffs. No jacket.

"I'm Brian Fletcher," he said with a tight smile, rising to shake hands. "Lee's campaign manager. Welcome to the madhouse."

Hardly an apt description. Leland Sinclair's campaign office was as spare and orderly as the main floor below was cluttered and chaotic. I wasn't surprised. I remembered his office in the district attorney's suite from my several visits there last year. Pristine, elegant furnishings. Appropriately-placed wall hangings, lighting fixtures, decorative items. Family photos on the desk, also appropriately placed.

This office, though much smaller and more spartan, reflected similar qualities of judicious thought, banked emotions. The studied attempt at control.

As did the man himself.

"Dan Rinaldi. Nice to see you again."

Sinclair rose from behind his desk to grip my hand. Handsome, patrician face. Silver hair trimmed a bit shorter than I remembered. Tailored Armani suit. Manicured hands that belied the strength of his handshake, which he held firmly, and a beat too long.

Reminded me of my opponents in my Golden Gloves days. Trying to intimidate you in the first round.

"Congratulations, Lee. I hear you're still three points ahead in the polls."

His smile was theatrically pained. "Never trust the polls, Danny. Just ask my pollster."

Brian Fletcher laughed shortly, as did Biegler. The campaign manager looked at him.

"I'm on the payroll, Lieutenant. I *have* to laugh at his jokes. What's *your* excuse?"

Biegler reddened, and glanced over at Sinclair, as though for moral support. Apparently, the DA wasn't in a giving mood. He retook his seat behind the desk and gestured at me.

"Now that you and Detective Lowrey are here, we can get down to business. But make it fast. I have to give a speech on the North Side in less than an hour."

Lowrey and I found chairs and sat. As we did, Fletcher began scooping up some papers from the desk.

"You want me to step outside, Lee? Since this is police business?"

"Hell, stay if you want. Besides, don't you have this room bugged, anyway?"

The two men shared a knowing smile, excluding the rest of us in the room. They had that easy banter, the cool familiarity, of the select. The entitled. The best and the brightest, in Halberstam's famous words.

"Now, then." Sinclair massaged his knuckles. "Before we begin, let me get everyone's jurisdictional concerns out of the way. I think you'll be happy to hear, Lieutenant, that the Assistant Chief is going to run interference for us with Neal Alcott."

"Who?" I asked.

"FBI." Biegler's tone was flat. "Bank jobs are federal crimes. Though usually they leave us alone, unless we ask for assistance."

"But not this time," Sinclair said. "Not with a hostage situation that led to multiple casualties. Luckily, Alcott's a desk jockey who'd rather brown-nose his way to a promotion than get his fingernails dirty. As long as we keep him in the loop, we'll probably get to run this investigation ourselves."

"Until the manhunt goes nationwide," Polk pointed out. "Then it's the Bureau's ballgame."

"All the more reason to get on top of this fast." Sinclair turned to Biegler. "So, Lieutenant, what the hell happened out there today? What do we know?"

"Not much, at this early stage." Biegler consulted some files he'd opened on his lap.

"Here're the broad strokes: according to the statement given to Detective Lowrey and Dr. Rinaldi by Treva Williams, two masked men entered the First Allegheny Bank at approximately noon. To be more precise, *one* masked man entered and immediately shot out the video cameras. Then his partner came in."

He spoke to Polk without looking up from his files.

"Sergeant? Any word from the lab on the video?"

Polk stirred. "I just talked to them. They've looked at the tape, and it bears out the Williams girl's story. I haven't seen it myself yet, but it apparently shows the first guy entering the bank, taking out a big gun—we figure it's the .357 Magnum we recovered from the scene—and shooting the surveillance cameras, one at a time. That's all we have that's usable on the tape. After that point...well...nothin'. Obviously."

"Obviously," Sinclair repeated. Then he turned to me. "Which is why *you're* here, Dan."

"I was wondering about that myself."

"According to Detective Lowrey, it was you who managed to get Treva Williams to talk about what happened. From what I understand, she was in quite a state."

"Suffering from shock, yes. But without knowing anything about her personal history, or previous experiences of trauma, I can't say for sure how deeply all this has impacted her. I *can* say she was barely keeping it together. Sometimes lucid, but more often dissociative. I'll need to do a complete eval. Including mental status exam. Perhaps some projective tests."

Sinclair's voice was clipped. "All very interesting. The point is, can we trust her story? Her account of what happened?"

"Hard to say. I think so."

"Even though she said she dreamed it all?" He made no effort to hide his skepticism.

"Believing it had just been a bad dream enabled her to describe it. Gave her the illusion of distance. Protected her."

"And you went along with it?"

"Seemed like the right call at the time."

I could tell Sinclair enjoyed looking unconvinced. He glanced meaningfully at Fletcher, and then Biegler.

"I was *there*, sir," Lowrey spoke up suddenly. "I think she was telling the truth. And what little info we have from the scene seems to back up her story."

Sinclair took a long breath, then turned to Polk.

"What do *you* think, Sergeant?"

Polk squared his shoulders. "I never disagree with my partner, sir. Bad for the team."

"I see."

Sinclair looked as though he wanted to say more, but hesitated. What would be the point? Even though he saw the facetious gleam in Polk's eye, he understood the serious meaning behind it. He knew enough not to try to divide two cops who'd been partnered as long as Polk and Lowrey. Whatever conflicts they'd have in private, they would never express them in public. *Or* on the record.

At a loss, Sinclair turned back to Biegler. "Okay, Lieutenant. Where were we? The first gunman enters the bank and takes out the cameras. Then what?"

"Then he's joined by a second guy, who enters the same way, through the front door. He's also masked and carrying a gun. Now this was confirmed by both Treva Williams *and* George Vickers, the security guard."

"Vickers is the only other survivor, right?" Sinclair clasped his hands behind his head, levered back in his chair. "How many victims, total?"

"You mean, the bank employees? Three."

Biegler flipped through some pages in his files. "We haven't officially ID'd everybody. The M.E. just got the bodies. But we have a list of names from the bank's home office in Harrisburg. Plus personnel files."

Sinclair clucked his tongue impatiently.

Biegler blinked a couple times and continued. "First dead employee is Tina Unswari. Parents emigrated here from New Dehli before she was born. Twenty-six, unmarried. Lived with her sister in an apartment in Greentree. Graduated from Duquesne University."

Tina Unswari. The first victim I'd seen when I entered the bank. The image of her body in death was still with me. I found myself involuntarily closing my eyes, unmindful of the others in the room, as though that would erase the picture. It didn't.

"Next we have Phyllis Hopper," Biegler droned on. "Married, two kids. Senior bank associate. Kinda like the head teller, I guess. Then there's Robert Marks. Called 'Bobby,' according to Treva Williams. He was the assistant bank manager."

"So where was the *manager*?" Lowrey asked, sitting forward in her chair. "The one in charge?"

"Home, apparently. Called in sick with a bad cold. Guy named James Franconi. One of my people spoke to him on the phone. Told him to make himself available for questioning later today."

Biegler glanced up from his files and targeted Polk. "You make sure somebody talks to that guy tonight, okay? Given that this could be an inside job, it's pretty damn convenient. I mean, Franconi coming down with a cold the day the bank gets hit."

Polk grunted his assent, making a big show of jotting down a note in his little pad.

Meanwhile, Sinclair motioned to his campaign manager.

"Get the names and addresses of the victims' next of kin. I want flowers sent, and I think we should plan some kind of public memorial. For all three of them. I'll make some remarks."

Fletcher nodded gravely. "Good idea."

"But I don't want it to look like we're exploiting this tragedy for political gain," Sinclair said.

"Best way to do that," I said, "is not to exploit it for political gain."

Sinclair gave me an indulgent smile. Nobody else seemed to do much of anything just then. Including breathe.

"Not that you asked my opinion," I added.

Sinclair took a thoughtful pause. "You know, as district attorney, I genuinely believe it's part of the job to express my condolences, on behalf of the city, to the victims' families. If you think anything other than that, Dan, it's *you* who's guilty of cynicism."

"Nicely done. Makes it hard to believe you've been dodging debates with your opponent."

Fletcher bristled. "Not true. Lee will debate John Garrity any time, any place. We just have to agree on the terms. Hell, his handlers have been totally unreasonable since discussions began. Not that I blame them. Not with *their* guy. I mean, talk about charismatically-challenged. The guy's a fucking tree stump."

Sinclair raised a hand. "Cool it, Brian. This isn't a strategy session. Besides, Dan and I go 'way back. We're used to taking harmless little shots at each other. Right, Danny?"

"If you say so. Lee."

Then we just stared at each other, like two rival kids in a schoolyard, until I felt pretty foolish. I could tell that Sinclair did, too. Luckily, Biegler's mounting anxiety rescued both of us.

"Want me to go on, Mr. Sinclair? I mean, I know your time is limited."

"Indeed it is. Thank you, Lieutenant. Shall we continue?"

Chapter Eleven

Sinclair brought his hands forward, clasped them on the blotter. "Now, do we have any idea what actually happened during the robbery attempt?"

Biegler consulted his files again. "According to Treva Williams, it went down like this: the two perps have everybody on the floor, on their knees, hands on their heads. But this Marks guy drops his glasses, and when he goes to pick them up, the first guy shoots him. Head shot. Everybody panics. The two perps argue about it, and then the alarm goes off and..."

"Who triggered the alarm?" Sinclair asked.

"That's not clear yet, sir. The Williams girl just said they all heard it go off, and this apparently spooks the second perp like crazy. He says 'Fuck this, I'm outta here,' or words to that effect, and runs out the back way, through the emergency exit door."

"Leaving just the one gunman," Sinclair said. "The first one who came in."

"Yeah. Then..." Biegler swiveled in his seat to Polk. "What did the security guard report, Harry? We'll need something to corroborate the Williams girl's account."

A sidelong glance at me. "I mean, since she thinks it was all a *dream* or some shit..."

Before I could think up an equally dismissive reply, Polk dutifully answered his boss.

"Vickers didn't offer much. He was in pretty bad shape himself. Arm shot all to hell." He scowled. "And for a former cop, damned uncooperative. Says he plans to sue."

At this, Fletcher tilted his head up. "Sue? Who? The city? The department?"

"We didn't get into all the grubby details. But I'm tellin' ya, the bastard smells money."

Sinclair waved his hand in frustration. "Let's not get off the track, people. His statement, Sergeant?"

Polk sniffed loudly. "According to Vickers, after the second perp runs outta the bank, the first one starts freakin' out, waitin' for his demands to be met..."

"Yes, safe passage out of town. A plane at Pittsburgh International." Sinclair smiled without humor. "These clowns all watch too much television."

"Anyway, we won't know the play-by-play on this till we talk further with Vickers and the Williams girl, but *somethin'* musta flipped the guy out. 'cause he just starts whackin' the hostages. We all heard the shots comin' from inside the bank. That's when the assistant chief gave the order to move in."

"And *I* authorized appropriate use of force," Sergeant Chester spoke for the first time. "We had SWAT on the ground, as well as a sniper on the roof of the building across the street. He saw the perp and took his shot."

Polk laughed. "Musta took a *couple* shots, 'cause his first one hit Vickers in the arm."

Chester's eyes went small and black. "Fuck you, Polk. My guy did the job. He took out the prick through a goddam window, from a building across the street. Guy deserves a fuckin' medal."

"And I'll make sure he gets one," Sinclair said, rising stiffly from his chair. He began fiddling with his tie. "Is that everything?"

"Like I said, it's all pretty sketchy." Biegler tapped his closed files on his knees. "We have a meeting with Internal Affairs in half an hour. Then we talk to all our people who were on-scene. Uniforms. SWAT. Everybody. Especially the sniper."

Fletcher glanced up, brow furrowed. "Internal Affairs? Is there a problem?"

"Don't worry, Brian." Sinclair picked a piece of lint from his jacket lapel. "Standard procedure with officer-involved shootings. Especially in a large-scale police action like this."

"*Standard*?" Fletcher sputtered angrily. "What's standard about three dead hostages, a wounded security guard, and a Wild West shoot-out in midtown? Christ, we gotta get a handle on how to spin this—and *fast*. I mean, we're right in the middle of a campaign. The potential blow-back from something like this could be crippling…"

Sinclair spread his hands. "See, people? Brian is not only my campaign manager, he's chief executive in charge of buzz-kill. If there's a dark cloud anywhere on the horizon, he'll see it."

"That's my job, Lee. And I'm damned good at it. So, yeah, I see a dark cloud. A huge sucker. What I *don't* see is any goddam silver lining."

By now, Biegler was looking at his shoes and Polk was pretending to be fascinated by something outside the window. I was beginning to wonder myself if the rest of us shouldn't just excuse ourselves and let Sinclair and Fletcher confer in private.

Sinclair seemed to sense my thoughts. He reached over and clapped a hand on his campaign manager's shoulder.

"Easy, Brian. Like it or not, I'm still the DA with a job to do. At least until November. Which means dealing with bad guys and the bad things they do."

Fletcher gave a bitter laugh. "Somehow I'm not seeing that silver lining yet."

"*I* do," I said. The two men turned, surprised.

I smiled. "If Lee plays this right, he and the cops come out smelling like roses. A bank robber is killing hostages, till he gets stopped in his tracks by a SWAT sniper. A young female teller and a wounded security guard are rescued. Order is restored. And Lee's strong, take-no-prisoners approach to law enforcement has been vindicated. Meanwhile, what was City Councilman John

Garrity doing during the crisis? Sitting somewhere nice and safe, uninvolved, watching it on the news like every other citizen."

I looked at Sinclair. "At least, that's how *I'd* spin it. You were thinking something along those lines, right?"

"More or less." A thin smile. "Perhaps you'd like a position in my campaign…?"

"Hell, Lee, I'm not sure I'm even gonna vote for you."

Sinclair's laugh was almost genuine.

But Brian Fletcher was unimpressed. "Let's hope you're right, Doc. But I've been around long enough to know only an idiot assumes how some unplanned event is gonna play out. Like, for example, what if this Vickers prick *does* decide to sue? Pending lawsuits during the final weeks of a campaign don't do much for your poll numbers."

"The man's got a point," Sinclair admitted. He tugged on his jacket sleeves and came around from behind his desk. "We'll just have to see how it rolls in the next couple days. Track the emails, voter contributions. The usual suspects. Meanwhile, Lieutenant, anything on the second gunman? The one who ran off when the alarm sounded?"

Biegler shrugged. "Without an ID, it's a stone-cold bitch. He had a mask on, too, remember. But I got a dozen uniforms canvassing a four-block area. Maybe somebody seen the guy running out of the rear of the bank. Or some guy jump in a car and take off in a hurry."

"Probably a dead end," Polk said. "All the guy'd have to do is take off the mask, slip the gun in his pocket, and stroll casually down Liberty Avenue. Just another mook on his lunch hour, workin' on his tan."

Lowrey spoke up suddenly. She'd been strangely quiet during the whole conversation.

"I think Harry's right," she said. "We'd have better luck working our informants. Picking up what we can from the street."

"Yeah." Polk nodded. "Big-ass score like this, you get a lotta chatter. Even if it all goes south."

"I'm inclined to agree, Sergeant," Biegler said. "Get whoever you need and get on that." He handed his stack of files over to Polk. "And let's get the new murder book started with these."

Polk looked doubtfully at the files. "If the second guy's not *already* in the wind…"

Sinclair clapped his hands together sharply.

"People, we're going to need a much more positive, proactive attitude on this thing. I want the second guy found. I want the dead gunman ID'd. And I want the department's media hacks on all the local TV news channels this evening. Same upbeat sound-bite: An outbreak of violence in the heart of our city quickly brought to a halt, thanks to the courage and professionalism of our police department. Am I clear?"

Biegler, Polk and Lowrey mumbled their assent. Chester just sat, face unreadable, his arms folded.

Meanwhile, I noticed Fletcher flipping through the sheaf of papers still clutched in his arms. Somehow, a pen had made its way to his mouth, clenched between two rows of expensive white caps.

Soon he found the paper he was looking for. He pulled the sheet from the stack, leaned over it on Sinclair's desk, and started writing.

"Lee," he said, without looking up from his work, "I'm adding a few lines to your North Side speech. Similar to what you just suggested for broadcast tonight on the news. Great stuff. We still have a few minutes, enough time for you to get familiar with it."

"Good. I'll read it in the car."

The rest of us silently parted to give Sinclair room to cross to the door.

Pulling it open, he said, "Let's get back in contact by phone in two hours. I'll want a progress report, as well as a head's-up on how IA's planning to proceed. You never know with those tight-asses. Best way to keep control of this thing is to limit any unwanted surprises."

"Yeah," Biegler agreed importantly.

As we all started to file out, Sinclair put a hand on my arm to stop me.

"Could you stay for a moment, Dan?"

If Polk, Lowrey, or Chester had any reaction to this, they did a good job hiding it. Biegler, however, jerked his head around to glare suspiciously at me. As I remembered from my previous encounters with him, the lieutenant hated being out of the loop.

When it was just Sinclair, Fletcher, and me, the district attorney closed the door again.

"What's wrong, Lee? Did I speak out of turn?"

"Not really. Or else I'm getting used to it." He leaned against the doorframe. "Actually, I just wanted to ask a favor."

I have to admit, this was a bit unexpected.

"Okay, shoot."

"Look, I don't know if I have your vote or not. But there's a major fund-raising dinner tomorrow night at the Burgoyne Plaza, and I'd like you to attend."

"Me? I don't know if I can swing the $5,000-a-plate entrance fee."

Fletcher looked up from his writing. A placid smile. "It's only $1,000-a-plate. But don't sweat it, you're comped."

"But why me?"

Sinclair's gaze was direct. "Truth is, Dan, you've got a pretty high profile, thanks to your involvement in the Wingfield case. I think if you're there with me, the mayor, the chief...Well, it'd be a nice photo op for me."

"I don't know. I'll have to check my schedule."

"Do that." He sighed. "Look, I know we've bumped heads a few times in the past, but there's no reason we can't let bygones be bygones."

I was still weighing my response when Fletcher came over and handed his rewrite to his boss.

"Tell you the truth, Lee, I think this guy's a loose cannon. As in, more trouble than he's worth." Fletcher gave me a cautious grin. "No offense."

"None taken."

Sinclair folded the speech and put it in his jacket pocket. Then he put his hand on the doorknob.

"Give it some thought, okay, Danny? I'm not asking for an endorsement. Just some public face time."

He glanced at his watch, then past me at Fletcher. "Is the driver downstairs, Brian?"

"Waiting at the rear door. With the engine running, the AC blasting, and two Rolling Rocks in the cooler."

"Great. Just make sure we ride with the shades down. Don't want my future constituents getting the wrong idea. Now let's get moving."

Sinclair was about to turn the knob when the door suddenly burst open, knocking his hand away. He stepped back, startled.

It was Biegler, face white as a paper plate.

"Sorry to barge in." He sucked in air. "But Lowrey just got a call from the hospital. The ambulance with Treva Williams and George Vickers never arrived there."

"What?" Sinclair recovered quickly. "Then where the hell is it?"

"Polk checked with Highway Patrol, and they'd just filed a report on an ambulance found off to the side of Crawford Street. In a ditch, smashed against a tree."

I stepped quickly in front of Sinclair. "What about Treva Williams?"

"Looks like she's okay. They found her in the back, unconscious but alive. The driver wasn't so lucky."

"The EMT tech? Karp?"

"Yeah, that's the name. Dead. From a broken neck."

"What about Vickers, the security guard?" Sinclair's face had hardened to stone. "Is *he* alive?"

Biegler looked miserable. "That's just it, we don't know. He wasn't in the ambulance. Or anywhere nearby at the scene. He's gone, sir."

Chapter Twelve

Leland Sinclair stood in the doorway, eyes closed, slowly massaging his temples. Fletcher came up behind him, dark features pinched with worry.

Biegler, at a loss, plunged ahead.

"Highway Patrol filed the accident report less than fifteen minutes ago," he said. "So at least we're out in front of the media on this."

"For now," Fletcher said flatly.

"God knows, that won't last." Sinclair opened his eyes, pulled himself back to the business at hand. "Don't worry, Lieutenant. I don't make a habit of killing the messenger. What steps are we taking to find Vickers?"

As if in answer, Harry Polk's heavy tread could be heard as he lumbered up the stairs behind us. Florid-faced, his breathing labored, he kept his grip on the banister when he'd reached the top. Eyes on Biegler.

"Just got word from the crash scene, Lieutenant. They put the Williams girl in a second ambulance and took her to Pittsburgh Memorial. Karp's in a coroner's wagon, on his way to Doc Bergmann at the morgue…"

Sinclair let out a breath. "Our distinguished M.E.'s having a busy day."

Another set of footsteps drew our attention as Eleanor Lowrey trotted briskly up the stairs. In marked contrast to Polk, she was barely breathing hard.

She handed a single sheet of paper to Biegler. "Here's the latest from CSU. Prints confirmed the identities of the deceased bank employees. Matches the descriptions and prints from the bank's personnel files. Tina Unswari, Phyllis Hopper, Robert Marks."

"Congratulations, Detective," Biegler said coolly, giving her back the paper. "You got the Golden Ticket, so you get to notify the next of kin."

Though I could tell she'd pretty much expected this, she still couldn't hide her reluctance. She soberly folded the paper and put it in her jeans pocket.

Sinclair spoke. "What about the dead bank robber? Has he been ID'd yet?"

Lowrey shook her head. "Still running his prints through the database."

Fletcher tapped Sinclair's arm. "Lee, we don't want to be late. And you know North Side traffic at this hour."

"Yes, of course." Sinclair flashed a tight smile to the rest of us. "If you'll excuse me…"

He paused at the top of the stairs.

"Remember, everyone. Conference call in two hours. If nothing else, it'll give me an excuse to get out of the Masonic Hall before they start serving the rubber chicken. Let's go, Brian."

With his campaign manager right behind, Sinclair went quickly down the stairs. I glanced over the banister as he and Fletcher disappeared into the main room, where a shift in the murmur of voices signaled his team's excited awareness of the candidate's appearance.

It's good to be king, I thought.

With the district attorney gone, Biegler's tone grew more officious. "Now, Harry, what about finding Vickers?"

"Uniforms on-scene are just starting the search. You got some woods, back lots. Plus residential. We figure Vickers survived the crash, but was dazed and wandered away from the scene. He's probably passed out behind some trash dumpster, bleeding to death."

Lowrey groaned. "This just gets better and better."

I got between Polk and his boss. "Look, I hate to interrupt all this cool cop stuff, but I've got to get down to the hospital. I want to see Treva Williams."

"Like hell," Biegler said.

"Listen, Lieutenant. If she's gonna talk about what happened, she'll talk to me. Besides, I'm a civilian therapist and she's under my clinical care. Technically, I don't even need to ask your permission." I showed him some teeth. "But I was trying to show my props to the chain of command. Since I'm on the payroll."

"A big mistake, if you want my opinion."

"Never have, Lieutenant. Probably never will."

His eyes darkened with malice. Finally, letting out an aggrieved sigh, he waved his hand.

"Sure, you want to go see her, go. It'll be good to have you out of my hair. But we're gonna need an official statement from her, anyway. Harry will go with you."

Polk snorted. "C'mon, Lieutenant. I figured I'd get over to the crash site, run the search for Vickers. Let Detective Lowrey interview the girl."

"Weren't you listening, Sergeant? She's doin' next-of-kin."

"Sir." Lowrey turned her violet eyes on him. I wasn't sure if it would have any effect. "Can't you assign the notification to another detective? For one thing, I worked with the Williams girl. Right next to Dr. Rinaldi. She trusts me. Besides, I believe she'll be more comfortable giving her statement to another woman."

Polk agreed vigorously. "I'm tellin' ya, Lieutenant. Detective Lowrey here takes a helluva statement. Especially from another broad. I mean, female."

Biegler looked from one of them to the other.

"You two think I'm an idiot? I know tag-team bullshit when I hear it. On the other hand, I happen to agree about female detectives being better at getting statements from female witnesses." He raised a warning finger at Lowrey. "Which is the *only* reason I'm letting you off the hook with the notification. Got it?"

"Yes, sir. I appreciate it, sir."

"Yeah, whatever. Now you and Rinaldi go down to the hospital and get what you can from Treva Williams."

◇◇◇

Eleanor Lowrey sat in the passenger seat of my car, nervously flipping through my cache of CDs.

"Miles Davis. Sarah Vaughn. Brubeck. Parker." She frowned. "Don't you listen to anything but jazz?"

"You don't like it?"

"It's okay, but I'm more of an R&B girl myself. Grew up in the Hill listening to nothing but Motown."

I took this in. "The Hill" was the Hill District, a poor, predominately black area of urban Pittsburgh. I realized then that I'd never heard her mention her background. Nor much of anything else about herself.

"Hey, you've got Diana Krall here." She held up the elegant CD cover. "She's not bad for a white chick."

"My sentiments exactly."

We were driving through heavy traffic to Pittsburgh Memorial, taking my car since Harry Polk was using their unmarked sedan. Between the APB on the second gunman, multiple next-of-kin notifications, and the usual procedural follow-up on a crime of this size, the police fleet of both black-and-whites and unmarkeds was stretched to the limit.

Eleanor finally settled on Coltrane and pushed the CD into the deck. Within moments, the simple, cool riffs of "Equinox" were filling the Mustang's snug interior.

I looked over as she settled back in her seat. Her fingers drummed on her knee. Whether it was the way this case was unfolding, or the fact of being a passenger in the car with a civilian, she seemed anxious about something.

She sensed my eyes on her and tilted her head.

"By the way, Harry told me one time that you're a boxer? Golden Gloves or something?"

"Used to be. A long time ago, in a galaxy far, far away."

"Cool. Me, too."

I raised my eyebrows in surprise.

She smiled. "The department has a club down at the PAL. I spar there once in a while. Keeps me sharp, and helps get the aggression out."

"Same reason I still throw combinations in my basement gym. Though it's hardly a gym. Just some free weights, a used bench. Hell, my heavy bag is older than you are."

"I doubt it. I'm no kid, and you're not so old."

"Thanks. I think."

I turned off Grant and past the on-ramp to the Fort Pitt Bridge. The sandstone towers of Pittsburgh Memorial rose into view.

"Speaking of Harry," I said, "how's he been? I mean, since his divorce?"

"You know Harry. Doesn't talk about it. But I can tell he's drinking more. Even had to let him crash with me a couple nights. He was in no shape to drive. But Luther doesn't mind."

I remembered about Luther. Her Doberman.

"Harry's lucky to have you."

"We're good partners. I've learned a lot from him."

I paused. "You know, if his drinking's getting worse, I should probably talk to him about a program."

She laughed. "Yeah, you do that, Dan. I just wanna be there when you bring it up. Oughtta be fun."

She pushed her hair up from the back of her neck with both hands. "God, it's hot. Even with the AC."

I nodded, then glanced over at her again. And got the distinct impression she wanted to say something more.

"Look," she said at last, face half-turned toward her window. "About Harry. There's something I've been meaning to ask you about…something that's worrying me…"

We'd just made the left into the hospital parking lot. I steered us to a vacant spot near the emergency entrance and parked.

"Is Harry in some kind of trouble?"

She kept her face angled toward the window. Took a long breath. Then slipped her sunglasses back on.

"Forget it, Dan. Forget I said anything."

"What do you mean?"

"Wrong time and place, that's all. Besides, I could be wrong. Misreading something. Shit, it's not like we don't have enough on our plates with this case."

Without another word, she climbed out of the car. I did the same, and looked at her across the roof of the Mustang. Getting a strange vibe from her.

"Are *you* okay, Eleanor?"

Her voice grew an edge. "Hey, I'm not your patient. So let's go see if *she's* okay."

She turned abruptly and headed toward the emergency room entrance. Conversation over.

I quickened my pace to catch up with her and we went inside together.

Chapter Thirteen

The nurse at reception directed us up to the ICU, where we were met by a plainclothes detective I didn't know named Robertson. Beer gut, thinning hair, pock-marked face. On the far side of middle-aged.

We all shook hands, and Robertson started leading us down the hall. Rows of single-patient rooms, fronted by plate glass. The sights and sounds of life-sustaining machines. Pumping. Blinking. Beeping.

"She's in a room at the end," he said. "Doc's still in there with her."

We reached Treva's room just in time to see, through the observation glass, her attending physician standing by her bed, writing in her chart. Then he hung it on the rail hook at the end of the bed and headed to the opened door, toward us.

I glanced past him to take a look at his patient. Treva was seemingly unconscious, with an IV drip running into her right arm. Under the starched white hospital covers, she seemed as small and slight as a child.

"I'm Lloyd Holloway," her doctor announced. More hand-shaking all around, except for Robertson. He just mumbled some version of good-bye and resumed his position outside Treva's door. Standing guard.

Which was Holloway's cue to lead us away from her room and into a visitor's lounge around the corner. The same one as in every hospital in the world. Small, with pea-green cushioned chairs. Fluorescent ceiling lights. Vending machines. We had the place to ourselves, but nobody sat.

Holloway was youngish, incongruously built like a wrestler, and with long yellow hair pulled back into a pony tail. Reminding me of that surly pony-tailed coroner's assistant from the crime scene. Must be the new sartorial trend in medicine.

"How is she?" Eleanor Lowrey asked.

"Well, she took a helluva blow to the head, but she'll probably be okay."

Holloway's manner was brusque, dismissive. Maybe he was having a rough night, I thought. Or maybe that was just who he was.

"Any concerns about a concussion?" I said.

"Not really, but we'll just have to wait and see."

Eleanor bit her lip. "Can we talk to her?"

"Not for a while. We have her sedated. From this point on, it's all about observation. Seeing how she responds."

His tone sharpened. "That order came from the hospital director's office. Apparently, in response to a request by the police. Easier to keep her isolated up here in the unit. Protected, I guess. Fewer rooms. Fewer visitors."

"Biegler's doing," I said to Eleanor. "Or maybe even the assistant chief's."

But she seemed distracted. Wasn't listening.

"And there's just the one detective on duty?" she asked Holloway. "Robertson?"

"Yeah. But he hasn't budged. I had to send one of the nurses' aides to get him some sandwiches. Robertson said he was hungry."

Eleanor chuckled without humor. "Yeah, like he couldn't afford to miss a meal or two."

Lloyd Holloway glanced at the wall clock over our heads. "Look, I've got a meeting on Ward B, all the way on the other side of the building. I'll be back soon to check up on the patient. So if you'll excuse me..."

He gave us a brief, professional smile and walked out of the lounge. I watched him go down the narrow hallway, stopping only once to chide some nurse who'd just come from another room. Whatever his grievance, he didn't wait around for her response. I watched her tired, worried face as he strode off. ICU is a tough gig.

When I turned back to talk to Eleanor, I saw that she'd crossed her arms and was leaning against the opened doorframe. She looked pretty beat herself.

"We're stretched too thin," she said quietly. "With the recent cut-backs, and some early retires that took the department by surprise, everybody's feeling the strain. This bank robbery thing is really pushing the envelope. Christ, if a jerk like *Robertson* is who we've got watching our star witness…"

I came closer and touched her shoulder. Her violet eyes rose up to meet mine.

"Listen, Treva's probably as safe in here as she'd be anywhere. The truth is, we're both feeling like we screwed up. At least, I know *I* am. I should've been in that ambulance with her. Maybe then…"

She frowned. "Yeah, about the ambulance. The crash. I mean, what do you think happened?"

"Karp probably lost control. I was told he drove off like a bat out of hell. Bergmann's orders were to get Vickers and Treva to the hospital ASAP. Unless there was some kind of mechanical problem…the brakes, or…"

"We'll know soon enough. They'll take the ambulance down to the impound, CSU will go over every inch of it. Soon as we get their report—"

"Fuck *their* report!" A familiar booming voice echoed down the hall. "Wait till you hear *mine*."

It was Harry Polk, sweat gleaming on his wide brow as he joined us in the lounge. His breathing was quick and labored, as though he was still winded from his climb up the stairs to Sinclair's campaign office. Or else it was the unending heat, his generally poor physical condition. Maybe just the booze. But he wasn't looking too good, that's for sure.

He tossed his notebook at his partner, who expertly caught it. Cover flipped back, it was opened at a page covered with Polk's scrawl.

"Check that out," he said. "If you can read my notes. I was drivin' and writin' at the same time."

As Eleanor quickly scanned it, Polk gave me a grim smile. "Not a banner day for law enforcement, Doc."

"What's going on? I thought you were heading over to Crawford Street. The crash site."

"I was, till I got a call from Biegler. Prints came back from our dead perp. The gunman at the bank. Only guess what?"

"He *wasn't* the perp," Eleanor said evenly. She looked up from the notebook.

"Bingo. His prints were in a database, all right," Polk explained. "But not VICAP. Not the FBI database, either. We finally found 'em because all security guards at private firms are fingerprinted."

I stared, as comprehension dawned.

"That's right, boys and girls," Polk said. "The dead perp *isn't* the perp. He wasn't the gunman who tried to rob the bank. He's George Vickers, the security guard."

"Jesus." Eleanor's voice dropped to a whisper. "That means we just let the real guy get away."

Polk laughed. "Get away? Hell, we escorted him from the crime scene in a city vehicle."

Chapter Fourteen

Harry Polk, unable to hide the disgust in his voice, collapsed into one of the cushioned chairs.

"Shit, I'm gettin' too old for this job."

Eleanor and I each took seats facing his.

"I think I can guess what happened," I said, though neither of them seemed interested at the moment. "Remember, Treva knew what George Vickers looked like. She saw the security guard every day at the bank. So on the drive to the hospital, Treva comes to and sees that there's another guy in the ambulance with her. Wounded, bandaged up. And wearing Vickers' uniform. She takes one look at the guy and knows something's wrong. Maybe she screamed, or said something to Karp, who was at the wheel."

Eleanor found her voice. "That must've been how it went down. The perp had no choice but to knock her out. Then, using his good arm, he grabs Karp around the neck from behind. Ambulance goes out of control, off the road and into a tree. Whether he meant to kill him or not, our guy realizes Karp is dead. So he takes off…"

"Maybe he planned to run as soon as he'd been treated at the hospital," I said. "Even though he'd switched clothes with Vickers, he had to know he'd only be able to pull off the stunt for a short while. So he probably hoped to get patched up before making his escape. At least he'd been willing to take that chance."

Eleanor said, "So now he's on the loose, somewhere in the vicinity of Crawford Street."

"But he can't get far. Not with that bullet wound I saw. Bergmann said it himself—that bandage was makeshift at best. If he doesn't get serious medical attention soon, he *will* bleed to death."

Polk finally managed to rouse himself, his police instincts overcoming his disheartened lethargy.

"I bet he's tryin' to get to his partner, the chicken-shit who ran outta the bank when the alarm went off."

Eleanor's look was doubtful. "That only makes sense if he and the partner had a place in town, or a predetermined rendezvous point somewhere. In case they got separated. Typical for a bank job with multiple perps."

"If *I* were our guy," I said, "I'd try to find the nearest hospital or urgent care facility."

"I hope he *does*," Polk said. "Since we got calls in to all the possibles in a ten-mile radius. Hospitals, clinics, doctors' offices. Whatever. Which a guy this smart would figure out, by the way."

"Maybe," I agreed. "But it's a risk he'd have to take. Unless he wants to end up losing that arm, if not his life. I'm telling you, he doesn't have much time. He's got to get his injury attended to."

"Well, that's something," Eleanor said. "At least that limits his movements." She paused thoughtfully. "Speaking of his partner, where are we with finding the second guy?"

"Nowhere." Polk rubbed his neck. "Canvas turned up shit. He could be anywhere. Even outta town by now."

We all fell silent for a long moment. Though as far as I was concerned, Polk's news had merely prompted more questions than answers.

"But how did he make the switch?" I said at last. "I mean, the killer. What exactly happened in the bank?"

Polk stirred. "I've been wonderin' the same thing. I spent the whole time drivin' over here thinkin' it over. 'Course, we'll know more when all the forensics come back. Not just the autopsies. Blood splatter patterns, locations of the spent shells. The whole story. Hell, these lab geeks are so good now, they can tell the order of who got shot when, and from what angle. Everything."

He climbed to his feet. "But ya want my guess? For whatever reasons, our guy starts shootin' hostages. Maybe he just freaked out, or panicked 'cause his partner split on him. Who knows? Anyway, he pops the two tellers and the assistant manager. Single shots, execution-style. Which is when *we* start mobilizin'. Plus the SWAT sniper across the street, shooting through the bank's windows. The prick knows he's fucked. Then he gets a brainstorm."

"Vickers, the security guard," Eleanor said evenly. "The one hostage left alive."

"Right. We're still moving into position outside the bank, so the guy figures he's got maybe a minute. He takes off his mask, makes Vickers change clothes with him, then puts the mask on Vickers and shoots him in the head. At close range, a .357's gonna do the same kinda damage as a long-range hollow point. So it'll look like Vickers is the perp, shot by the SWAT sniper." Polk gave a dry whistle. "Our guy's got brass balls, I'll give him that."

"But you think the sniper *did* actually get a piece of him?" I asked.

"Probably. Unless he shot himself in the arm, which I kinda doubt. Not at such close range. Not with a .357 Magnum. If he'd put the gun barrel against his own arm and fired, he would've shot the whole damned thing off. Thing is, I don't know whether the sniper got him before or after he killed Vickers. Either way, by the time we get in there, all we find are three dead hostages, what looks like the bank robber dead on the floor, and a wounded security guard."

"In a way," I said, "getting shot by the sniper helped our guy out. Added credibility to his story."

Eleanor clasped her hands under her chin. "And he was smart enough to leave the .357 behind. So we could find it next to Vickers' outstretched hand."

She looked up at her partner. "Too much to hope that they found any prints on the gun?"

"Wiped clean." Polk shook a cigarette out of a packet of Camel unfiltereds.

Eleanor managed a short laugh. "Jesus, Harry, you can't light up in here."

"Who said anything about lighting up?" He put the unlit cigarette between his lips. It bobbed energetically as he spoke. "I just need the oral fix."

The sergeant and I exchanged looks.

"See, I'm even pickin' up your lingo now, Doc." He gave me a doleful smile. "I'm beginnin' to think you're a bad influence on me."

But my mind was elsewhere. I'd just realized why the security guard's uniform had looked so tight on the killer. I'd thought it was vanity on Vickers' part. Actually, the killer was a bigger man than Vickers, so that when they changed clothes, the smaller-sized uniform would appear tight-fitting, especially across the chest.

Polk took his unlit cigarette from his mouth and used it as a pointer. "I'm assumin' you two ain't had time to talk to the Williams woman yet?"

Eleanor answered. "No. She's still sedated. I guess we'll come back in a couple hours."

"Before or after our conference call with Sinclair?"

"Damn, I forgot about that."

I hadn't. And this latest news wasn't going to make the District Attorney—*and* candidate for governor—very happy. Letting the criminal responsible for the deaths of four innocent people slip past the police dressed as a security guard? Who then kills an EMT driver, assaults the lone surviving bank employee, and escapes into a residential area? And was still at large?

No question, today's events would lead the local news. Maybe even make the networks, CNN, Fox. Not to mention the Internet. All the crime buffs' websites, every law-and-order fanatic's personal blog. The whole viral circus.

Polk put his unlit Camel in his breast pocket and squinted at Eleanor.

"Okay. You know Biegler will want a statement from Treva Williams. So if you gotta wait for it, wait for it. I'll get back to the precinct so at least one of us is on the phone when Sinclair calls." A wry smile. "But don't worry, I'll take notes."

"Thanks, Harry," Eleanor said. "I guess you'll need this." She tossed his notebook back to him.

He absently flipped it closed, then shoved it in his back pocket. Then he looked at me.

"Listen, since you got a couple hours to kill, maybe you could feed my partner. She don't eat regular, she gets cranky as hell."

Eleanor flushed. "Dammit, Harry…"

Polk just laughed. Then he gave each of us a good-bye nod and shuffled away. As we watched him go, I turned to Eleanor.

"You know, that wasn't a bad idea. I'm pretty hungry myself. And I know just the place."

◇◇◇

As we drove down toward Second Avenue and the river, traffic grew even thicker. Office workers heading for home, clogging the Point and the on-ramps to the bridges. Trucks coming out of the produce yards and warehouses, crossing town to get to the turnpike. Buses chugging along unused streetcar routes, before the long parkway journey to the suburbs.

The work day ending. Though the sun was still high, and the heat unbroken. I had the Mustang's air conditioning on full, its steady hum warring with Ornette Coleman's moody tenor sax from the CD speakers.

Eleanor Lowrey sat in silence next to me, apparently lost in thought. As Polk had said, it hadn't exactly been a banner day for law enforcement. And though one of the pair of violent suspects was seriously wounded, they were both still in the wind.

As I turned south toward the Monongahela River, my gaze was caught by a huge campaign billboard towering over the intersection. Leland Sinclair's cool, smiling face suddenly loomed over me. Beneath it was his now familiar slogan: "Smart. Strong. And on your side."

Jesus. There was something surrealistic about seeing the face of a man you'd been talking to just an hour before, now filling most of a twenty-by-forty-foot billboard. Casting a shadow half the size of a football field on the side of the apartment building opposite.

Then again, I thought, why shouldn't it seem strange? Unreal? The whole series of events of this day felt that way to me. The botched robbery, the deadly gun-battle, the ambulance crash. The more I reflected on it, the more everything just seemed... *off...*somehow.

It reminded me of the feeling I'd sometimes have in session with a patient, when my every instinct told me that I was missing something. Some important detail in the patient's story, a crucial secret hiding behind some gesture or turn of phrase. Behind some tell-tale sign.

As Eleanor Lowrey and I drove without speaking through the late afternoon's relentless heat, I realized I was having that same feeling now. That I was missing something. Something important.

But what?

Chapter Fifteen

Noah Frye was having a good day.

When Eleanor and I walked into Noah's Ark, a floating saloon moored at a bank below Second Avenue, we found him chatting amiably with the lone early drinker at the bar. Built like a bear, and with a similar loose-limbed ease with his size, Noah busily wiped the counter top with a damp cloth while sharing his tipsy customer's complaints about the Pirates' ongoing woes.

As Eleanor and I found stools at the far end of the bar, I gave Noah my customary half-friend, half-clinical appraisal. No involuntary twitches or wild-eyed, suspicious glares. No requests to be taken outside and crucified. No references to voices from the Unholy Realm.

Which meant that he was regularly taking his antipsychotic meds. Or, at least, that his girlfriend Charlene—who was waiting on customers at the dining tables while Noah worked the bar— was making sure he was taking them. Big-haired, big-waisted, and a paragon of common sense, Charlene was more than just what the doctor ordered when it came to Noah; she was exactly what a paranoid schizophrenic needed.

Eleanor nudged me as she swept the funky riverfront bar with her eyes. I could sense she was having a hard time reconciling its polished brass fixtures and rack of glasses poised high over the beveled counter top with the black tar paper hanging raggedly from the ceiling. Not to mention the acrid smell of oil-soaked water.

"What the hell *is* this place?" she said.

"Just what it looks like. A converted coal barge."

"That explains the port-holes."

"And the fishy aroma wafting in from the Monongahela. Noah wanted the place to still look as much like a barge as possible. What he calls its nautical motif."

I explained that I'd met Noah years before, when he was a patient at a private psychiatric clinic called Ten Oaks and I had just come on as a clinical intern. Sometime later, after being involuntarily released when his insurance ran out, Noah had to take to the streets. Though he was a gifted musician, he drifted between odd jobs and bouts of delusional terror until I happened to come upon him early one morning. Digging in a trash dumpster.

"My God. What happened?"

"The short version? A bunch of us from the clinic took him under our wing. One of the staff shrinks, Nancy Mendors, took charge of prescribing his meds. We even found him a job at this newly converted bar, whose owner took such a liking to Noah that he named the place after him. Now he and Charlene run the place together."

I pointed out the large-framed ex-hippie moving adroitly between the tightly-spaced tables. At the same moment, Charlene caught my eye and waved cheerfully, before disappearing behind the kitchen's double-hinged doors.

"That's Charlene. Trust me, she's done more good for Noah than a herd of shrinks."

Just then, a sharp, discordant chord sounded from the upright piano in the far corner. I swiveled in my seat in time to spot a fat calico cat leap from the keyboard and disappear behind a well-used trap drum set. An unplugged Fender bass guitar leaned against a grungy floor amp.

"Dammit, Thelonius!" It was Noah, hustling down the length of the bar in our direction. "Stay away from my piano! I'm gonna—"

When he reached where Eleanor and I sat, Noah wadded his cleaning cloth into a ball and threw it in the direction of the instruments. It opened in mid-flight and fluttered to the floor in front of the snare drum.

"You have a cat?" I said.

Noah made a big show of seeming aggravated.

"Not for long," he said, wiping his hands on his jeans. "The fat bastard just shows up one day and figures he'd sponge off me for a while. I keep tellin' Charlene, either Thelonius starts earnin' his keep around here or I'm throwin' him overboard."

"Like you'd really do that."

"I mean it. Yesterday I'm bringin' in crates of fryin' potatoes, sweatin' my balls off, and where is he? Plopped down behind the cash register, sleepin' off a nap. Worthless, that feline. If he wasn't so goddam cute—"

Noah stopped abruptly and smiled at Eleanor, as though just noticing her for the first time. Which was entirely possible.

"Hey, Danny, where're your manners? Who's this beautiful lady?"

"I was waiting for you to catch your breath so I could make introductions. This is Detective Eleanor Lowrey. Eleanor, Noah Frye. Part-time piano player and full-time saloon-keeper."

Noah bowed slightly and extended his beefy hand for Eleanor's. Something about his open, unassuming expression brought a rare warmth to her face. At least, it had been pretty rare today.

"Happy to meet you, Noah. And call me Eleanor."

Noah scratched his thatch of unruly hair. "Uh, this ain't a bust or nothin', right, Eleanor? 'Cause our liquor license is up to date and the Health Department just gave the kitchen an A-minus. Though, truth be told, I'm still bitter about the 'minus.' Which I also blame on Thelonius. Since I have to do most of the rodent-catchin' around here, too."

I indicated the instruments standing in the shallow corner behind us. "You got a trio playing here now?"

Noah bobbed his head. "Yeah, me and two wing-nuts from Philly. Brothers or cousins or some shit. Total coke-heads but with great chops. We call ourselves Flat Affect."

"Love the name."

"I mean it, man, we kick serious syncopated ass. I'm thinkin' o' makin' a demo."

We exchanged a few more pleasantries before getting down to business and ordering some burgers and beers. After which, Eleanor excused herself and headed for the rest rooms. Noah went back along the bar to disappear into the kitchen, presumably to give Charlene the food order, and then returned to draw us our drafts—one Iron City, one Rolling Rock—from a couple of huge kegs.

After bringing two large schooners over, Noah leaned forward and propped his crossed arms on the bar. Gave me a frank look.

"Fine-lookin' woman, that Eleanor. Good bones. I assume you're tappin' that on a regular basis."

I sipped my beer. "We're just friends, Noah. Hell, not even that. Colleagues, I guess."

"Yeah, right." Then, suddenly, his face clouded. "Hey, you ain't gettin' involved in some crazy-ass case again, are you? Didn't you get enough o' that shit last year?"

"I'm just helping them out."

Noah ducked his head down, framed by the cross formed by his huge forearms. I heard his low chuckle.

"I *mean* it, Noah," I said. "It's not like before."

"Whatever you say, man. You wanna be a big hero, impress the chicks, that's your look-out. Me, I'm happy stayin' this side of crazy and bumpin' uglies with my sweetie Charlene."

I picked up on something in his manner that made me put down my beer. I'd known Noah for almost ten years, and was fairly confident I could read his shifting moods.

"You seem pretty upbeat today," I said carefully. "No complaints about politics or the state of pop music. What's the story?"

Noah smiled wanly. "I'm practicin' gratitude, man. *Tryin'* to, anyway. 'Cause, despite everything, I'm still alive and kickin'. Still above ground."

"And somebody you know isn't?"

He sighed heavily. "Someone we *both* know, Danny. You remember Andy the Android? From the clinic?"

"Sure."

How could I forget? I'd gotten to know Andy when I first began working at Ten Oaks, soon after I'd met Noah. Andrew Parker was in his late teens at the time. Called "Andy the Android" by all the other patients, Andrew was a deeply delusional boy who believed he wasn't human. That he was actually a machine. Like Pinocchio, his biggest and only dream was to become a real person.

"What happened to him?" I asked. "Wasn't he still at Ten Oaks?"

"Oh, yeah. A lifer, that guy. Then last week, on his thirtieth birthday, he celebrated by hanging himself. They found his dead ass in the tool shed behind the rec yard. He used a bicycle chain."

"But that shed is always locked."

Noah shrugged. "Guy wants to do somethin' bad enough, he finds a way. Poor son of a bitch. I always liked him."

"How did you hear?"

"Dr. Nancy told me yesterday. She came by with my monthly head supplies and dropped the bomb."

I nodded. Though I hadn't seen her in some time, I'd heard that Dr. Nancy Mendors, the psychiatrist who'd been providing Noah his meds since I'd found him on the streets, had recently been promoted to Clinic Director at Ten Oaks.

Made sense. She was one of the city's most respected clinicians and certainly deserved the job. She and I also shared a long—and somewhat complicated—friendship. Of whose intimate details Noah was, like most people we knew, thankfully unaware.

"Dr. Nancy told me that Andy's funeral is tomorrow," Noah was saying. He toyed with the lapel of his multi-stained workshirt. "I haven't decided whether or not I'm goin'. Funerals give me the willies."

"Well, at least think it over," I said, finishing my beer. "I'm certainly going, now that I know. I liked Andy, too. A lot."

I looked down at my empty glass. Surprised at the level of quiet grief I felt. It wasn't that Andy and I had been especially close. He wasn't even a patient I'd worked with regularly back in those early days. But still…

I silently chided myself. Why did my reaction surprise me so much? Wasn't every loss, every death, some kind of marker? Some statement of finality?

Especially those of people like Andy. So haunted, tormented. Lost. For a therapist, the Andy's of this world are a daily reminder of how fundamentally fragile, how inevitably unknowable every human being is. No matter how many degrees or clinical licenses you have…

My reverie was broken by Noah, who tapped me sharply on the shoulder. When I looked up, he gave me a wink.

"Head's up, man, the cops. Flush your stash."

It was Eleanor Lowrey, coming back from the rest room.

Noah chuckled at his own joke and headed back down the bar, where his sole other customer was impatiently rapping the counter with his shot glass.

I pulled Eleanor's stool from the bar for her.

"An A-minus, eh?" She settled in her seat. "Health inspector must've skipped the bathrooms."

I watched her sip her beer. Tried on a smile.

"Is this okay, you having a drink on duty? Unless Harry's right, and I'm a bad influence on *you*, too."

She gave me a sidelong look. "He'd also say, 'this ain't a drink, it's beer.' Just a lube job for a cop."

As if for emphasis, Eleanor took a long pull from the schooner, then set it down carefully on the bar. Ran her forefinger around the thick, foamy rim.

"Helluva day, eh?" she said softly. "And this whole mess has just gotten started. God knows where it's all gonna lead. If we don't find those two guys soon…"

"Cops just need a break," I said. Averting my eyes. Readying myself for what I had to do. To say.

"Yeah. And *I* need a long, cool bath."

She took a square of napkin from the counter, dabbed at her forehead. I was sweating, too. Damn humid in here.

We sat for a long moment without talking, wrapped in the sounds of glasses tinkling, the murmur of voices coming from the dining tables, and the ambient presence of the river just beyond the walls.

Finally, she turned to me, her gaze steady. Searching my face.

"What about you, Dan? After everything that's gone down today...What do *you* need? Or don't therapists like you need anything?"

"You'd be surprised. We need the same things everybody else does. Maybe even more." I paused. "But, since you asked, there *is* one thing I need now..."

A bit taken aback, she managed a smile.

"What's that?"

I took a breath.

"I need you to stop lying to me about Treva Williams."

Chapter Sixteen

The bell rang. Start of the fourth round.

I didn't want to leave my corner. My legs felt rubbery, unreliable. They wanted to go home.

I blinked back salt water, sweat pouring from my forehead into my reddened eyes.

I brought my head up, as though underwater and trying to break the surface. Drowning in a sea of noise. It was deafening, the bounce-back acoustics from the concrete floor, particle-board ceiling and pea-green mortar walls. Of a low-rent gym in a low-rent part of Wilkes-Barre, Pennsylvania.

There were people on all sides of the ring on folding metal chairs. Pot-bellied men waving short black cigars. Middle-aged women with lacquered clouds of hair that shone white in the harsh fluorescent overheads. Sharpies and gamblers standing in clusters in the far corners, heads down, not even watching the fight. Just counting out bills into eager hands. Laughing. Arguing.

It was sometime before ten PM. Amateur night. And I was getting my ass kicked by a red-haired Irish kid with acne scars and arms like bridge cables. I was seventeen.

I glanced down at my father, standing outside the ring at my corner. Eyes glowing like angry coals in the drifting cigarette smoke. Broad, mottled drinker's face. Spider-web veins. His own huge fists clenched on the canvas, on either side of the corner post.

I nodded once in his direction, patted my gloves together with a wet slap, and pushed off from my corner.

The crowd cheered lustily as the kid and I traded blows, neither of us with an ounce of style or precision. Just two stupid kids, flailing away. At one point, I saw a patch of blood erupt over his left eye.

I felt a surge of adrenaline. Confidence. And waded in.

Nothing blurs your vision like hope. He connected with a quick combination, followed by an uppercut that felt like it came from the bowels of the earth. And suddenly I was sitting on my ass. The taste of blood in my mouth.

The fans were on their feet, screaming and cursing and shouting. The middle-aged ladies were jumping up and down, clapping their hands.

I heard my father's harsh bellow—half encouragement, half contempt—as I got shakily to my feet. Then the Irish kid lunged again and I wrapped him up in my arms. Danced into the ropes. I felt the sharp whisk of fibers slice across my back. Rope burns. Not my first.

Just as the ref came in to break us up, the bell rang. The round was over.

And then I was stumbling back to my corner, back to the opaque stare of my disappointed father. I also saw that he was raising his left hand, the old wedding band still on it. The ring he'd refused to wear when he was married to my mother. Not until she'd died, when I was three.

He'd worn it ever since. Now welded to him like his own guilt. A small gold handcuff. A relic of the dead saint he thought her to be.

Most of the crowd was still on its feet, though the tenor of their voices had changed. Angry. Demanding.

My father was calling out to me, too. Voice thick, weary. Defeated. That upraised hand pushing against empty air, motioning me back toward the center of the ring.

But why? I staggered out, confused. My eyes half-shut, caked with sweat and blood.

Then the ref was holding both our gloved hands, me and the Irish kid's, and announcing that the fight was over. We were both minors, for Christ's sake, he pointed out. And I was pretty beaten up. The crowd booed. The ref raised the Irish kid's hand in the air.

The fans were still shouting and booing as I made my way back to my corner. I sagged against the turnbuckle. Pushed out my mouth-guard with my swollen tongue. Wiped away blood and spit with the back of my hand.

"Well, at least you went back in," my father said flatly. "At least you stood up and took it."

He lifted a sponge soaked with water and something brownish-red that stung like battery acid and swabbed my face. I blinked hard against the combination of sweat, blood and whatever the hell was mixed in that water bucket. Until I finally found some words and offered them up to my old man.

"Sorry, Dad. I guess he was too good."

His look at me was pitiless.

"No, he wasn't. He just wanted it more than you did."

Then he threw the sponge back into the bucket and turned and headed to the locker room. I climbed down out of the ring and followed him.

Neither of us said another word on the whole drive back home.

◇◇◇

I thought of that night so long ago in Wilkes-Barre as I sat now with Eleanor Lowrey in Noah's bar. My father's words to me after the ref's decision. Maybe the only words of encouragement he ever spoke:

"At least you went back in. At least you stood up and took it."

It was how I felt now, as I watched Eleanor's face change. As she reacted to my accusation that she'd lied to me about Treva Williams. After—there's no other way to describe it—I'd waded in.

At first, her eyes had burned with anger, and a kind of indignation. Then, almost as quickly, the fire had burned out. "When have I lied to you about her?"

I shook my head. More customers had come in, and the bar was filling with the layered sounds of multiple voices. Familiar greetings. Relieved end-of-work-day laughter. At the far end of the counter, Noah had clicked on the flat-screen TV with his remote. CNN. The usual talking heads, arguing about the upcoming elections.

"Not here." I touched Eleanor's wrist on the bar. "Finish your food and let's go for a walk."

She forced a short laugh. "And what makes you think I want to do that? Maybe I just want to sit here and eat my overcooked burger. Maybe I want to order another beer and soak up the atmosphere."

"Well, I guess you could do that. But then I think you'll still want to go for a walk with me. And talk."

She turned on her stool, fists at her sides.

"How about I snap some cuffs on you instead and haul your ass to the station?"

"On what charge, Detective?"

"I'll think of something."

"I bet you will. You're pretty good at thinking on your feet. You've been doing it all day, since the bank got hit. Since you called me at my office to ask for my help."

Her violet eyes narrowed, stayed guarded. But a rueful note fluted her voice.

"Ya know, I liked you better five minutes ago. When I was 'Eleanor,' not 'Detective.'"

I shrugged. "That goes both ways. I liked you better when I didn't know you were holding out on me about Treva."

We stared at each other for a long, awkward moment.

Finally, I broke the impasse.

"You've trusted me with her so far, Eleanor. To look after her. Protect her. Why stop trusting me now?"

She gave me a frank, appraising look. And not just with a cop's interest. Or curiosity. Or doubt. She was literally, at that moment, coming to a decision about me.

"Okay," she said at last. And slid off her stool.

Chapter Seventeen

"What made you suspicious?"

She had her hands jammed in the pockets of her snug jeans as we walked along the riverbank on Second Avenue. Late afternoon shadows had crawled down from the hills on the far side of the river, a chiaroscuro backdrop to the low buildings still glazed by the summer sun.

"I wasn't suspicious," I said. "More like confused. Or curious."

"You'll have to explain the difference to me."

Eleanor had put her sunglasses back on once we'd left Noah's Ark and started walking south on foot. But it wasn't to protect her eyes from the sun. It was to hide what was in them from me.

The gravel shifted and crunched beneath our feet as we skirted the riverbank. Railway timbers embedded length-wise to shore up the embankment were black with pitch and age. Radiating the day's heat like great fire-charred logs.

There were no passersby down here. It was still too hot out for the homeless and train hoppers, and not yet dark enough for the panhandlers and drug dealers. Eleanor and I had this sun-baked, dusk-tinged world to ourselves.

"Look, I'm not accusing you of anything," I said. "But if I'm going to be of any real use, to you *or* Treva, I need to know the truth."

She said nothing, just kept her face pointed straight ahead as we walked. Not tilted down at the uneven earth, or even averted from my own gaze. Just straight ahead, her profile a smooth dark cameo backlit by the setting sun. Her beautiful lips pressed tightly together.

I took the plunge.

"Okay, I wondered if something was up from the first moment you contacted me. I knew that Biegler would've vetoed calling me in. And that Harry would give you all kinds of grief. Yet you called me anyway. Even though, as you yourself mentioned, there was already a departmental psychologist on scene."

Still she said nothing.

"Then, when I was working with Treva, I noticed that your interest in her emotional state was more than professional. You seemed genuinely worried about her. Later, at the bank, after I told you I had to leave to accompany Treva to the hospital, I saw you make a cell phone call. Heard you repeat a phone number you'd been given. I recognized the number. Pittsburgh Memorial. And what do I find when we get down there? That somebody from the department had ordered Treva kept in ICU, for her own protection. Fewer visitors. Easier to guard."

I let this sink in, though it was hard to gauge her reaction. I was beginning to regret having even ventured here with her. In a real way it was none of my business.

I went on anyway. "Not to mention your reaction to the detective assigned to her. Robertson. So maybe getting her stashed in the ICU was some sort of extra protection. Why?

"Which got me wondering: if you *had* been the one who'd had her put there, maybe you'd also asked that a detective be assigned to guard her. Though that made no sense either. By your own admission, the department's stretched too thin. The manhunt for the gunmen is too important, politically and otherwise, to waste a detective on that assignment. As far as anyone knows, Treva's in no physical danger. Not at the moment. Not since she'd been released from the bank. So any regular uniform could stand guard outside her room."

By this time, we'd come to an old city bench that had been placed facing the water. Wood slats for seats, curved iron legs embedded in circular concrete pockets buried in the hard earth. Civic improvement, circa 1900.

Without a word, or even a confirming nod to each other, we sat at the same time on the bench.

I waited a moment, then turned to her.

"Treva's not in some kind of danger, is she?" I asked. "I mean, not anymore. Right?"

Eleanor Lowrey gave a long sigh, then lowered her head as though its weight had finally become too much. Her chin rested on her chest.

"No." Her voice was a hush. "Not that I know of. I just… well, I wanted her sequestered in ICU. Under guard. So that when she woke up…I mean, if I happened not to be there, she'd know I'd been thinking about her. Making sure she was safe. That she'd see another detective, like me, watching over her."

She let a smile tug at her lips.

"Well, maybe not *exactly* like me."

"Tell me. I don't think Robertson would inspire much confidence in anyone."

I saw the warmth return to her violet eyes.

"Why *did* you call me, Eleanor?"

"For the same reason I told you, Dan. Because you're good. Better than the idiot shrink they had on scene. I've worked with him a few times, and believe me, calling him an idiot is an insult to *actual* idiots." She paused. "I called you because I figured I could trust you with Treva."

I waited. I'd talked enough—too much, probably—and now she needed to tell me about it in her own way. In her own time.

She took a breath. "When we found out the gunmen had released a hostage, Biegler sent me over to where the EMT guys were working on her. At first, with her head down, all wrapped up in that blanket, I almost didn't recognize her. Then, when our eyes met…I mean, Treva was definitely out of it. In shock or whatever, like you said. But she knew who I was. She didn't say a thing, but she knew. And I…well, all I said to her was that everything would be all right. That I was going to call someone who might be able to help her."

A sharp bleat of a klaxon drew my eyes to the river, and the rust-stained pilot boat skimming along its surface. A squirrel's tail of dark water plumed behind.

When I turned back to Eleanor, she was taking off the sunglasses. Folding them with a one-handed flip of her wrist and hanging them again from the deep V in her t-shirt. Then she gave me a frank look.

"I assume what I'm about to tell you is confidential?"

"I assume you'd know better than to ask. Unless you're planning to kill someone in the near future."

A brief smile. "God knows, I have a list. But no immediate plans, no...So you can rest easy."

She looked away, and I watched her watching the pilot boat disappear under the South Tenth Street Bridge.

"I met Treva in college," she began at last. "Up at Penn State, junior year. All I'd ever dated up till then were guys. Big dumb jocks I could talk rings around. So when I found myself attracted to her...I mean, what the hell? Some skinny little white girl? Who wrote bad poetry and was devastated when she didn't make the cheer squad?"

"Must've been a confusing time for you."

"Spare me the therapeutic talk, will ya, Dan? It wasn't confusing, it was *great*. Treva and I were—well, I'd never been into someone so much in my life. And I figured she felt the same. Six weeks after we first hooked up, we moved into a shitty apartment off-campus. But it felt like heaven to me. We started skipping classes, just staying in together, days on end. Making love like we invented it. Listening to music and reading to each other and talking about living overseas someday. Some Third World country. Away from everybody and everything."

Her eyes caught mine.

"Yeah, I know. Typical college romance. That kind of stupid love you only feel when you're young but think you're older.

When you don't have a goddam clue how the world works. How things really are."

I nodded carefully. "What happened?"

Her face was unreadable.

"It ended. Treva left me. For a man."

I followed her gaze back out to the river, its slow-moving current pock-marked by hundreds of troughs and shallow peaks. The last remaining sunlight danced across its surface in cascades of diamond-like glitters.

"I'm sorry, Eleanor."

"Hell, it was all a long time ago. I've had lots of shitty relationships since then."

A thin half-smile. "With men *and* women. Turns out, I'm not choosey. As long as they're good in bed and will end up treating me like dirt, I'll jump in with both feet. At least I used to. Now…"

"What about now?"

"Now my roommate is a Dobie named Luther. It works for me. I get all the testosterone, none of the bullshit."

I had to ask.

"But why so secretive? I mean, about your prior relationship with Treva? Even if you told Harry and Biegler, the worst that'd happen—"

"—Is that I'd be put on a desk for the rest of the investigation. Conflict of interest. Too personally involved with a prime witness to a multiple homicide and armed robbery." She frowned. "Not to mention the endless shit I'd get from the squad. The other guys. Not the most enlightened group on earth. I mean, most of 'em think female officers are just a bunch of dykes, anyway. Even after all that sensitivity training…"

Again, that thin half-smile. I was starting to see how her defenses worked. The cost of her cool self-assurance on the job, in what was still pretty much a man's world.

I chose my words carefully. "Maybe putting you on a desk isn't such a bad idea. Given how rattled you were by seeing her again after all these years."

She stared at me. "Ya know, for a head-shrinker, you can be goddam clueless sometimes."

"So I've been told."

"I mean, okay, so I still care about her..." She stiffened. "You don't stop loving the one love of your life. Ever. No matter how it ended. At least, *I* don't."

"Is that what Treva is? Was? The love of your life?"

"Did I say that?" A dark laugh that held no mirth. "Let's get real, Dan. I'm a cop. I bench-press two-fifty. I can take down an armed meth freak with one hand and make him cry for his momma. I mean, Christ, I'm Harry Polk with tits. Do hard-asses like me go around bawlin' about the love of their life?"

"So what exactly are you doing right now?"

She smiled then. A real one, this time.

"Bawlin' about the love of my life. What's it look like, mister?"

I took a chance and leaned in toward her. Gently touched her shoulder.

"You know, you've never struck me as a hard-ass, Eleanor. Dedicated, yeah. A solid cop. But you're no Harry Polk. I mean, hell, I *like* Harry. As much as he'll let me, I guess. But you're something very different. You know it. And so does he."

She looked as though she were going to argue the point, but then paused. Squeezed the tears at the edge of her eyes with her thumbs.

"So what now, Doc?"

"Up to you. You want to mention your past relationship with Treva Williams to your superiors, go ahead. If not, that's fine by me."

She heard the hesitation in my voice.

"But...?" she prompted.

"Look, the last thing in the world I'd ever do is tell you how to do your job. But I do think you need to ask yourself if you can still be effective on this case. If your feelings for Treva will get in the way."

"They won't."

"But soon we'll be going back to the hospital to interview her."

"So?"

"So you'll be asking her to relive—*again*—the terrors she experienced during the robbery. Not to mention what she went through in the ambulance. Waking up to find some guy she didn't know wearing Vickers' security guard uniform. Getting assaulted. Surviving a deadly crash. Frankly, I'm pretty concerned about her state of mind right about now. Worried about whether *I'll* know how best to deal with it. I can't even imagine how you'll feel."

She nodded slowly, thoughtfully.

"I get what you're saying. And maybe you're right. But maybe my being at her side when we talk to her will calm her. Make her feel protected by someone who really knows her. Who once cared about her. And still does."

She got wearily to her feet. "Look, I know I'm tryin' to make the case for myself…but I really think she'll be more helpful to us if I'm there. That we'll get more out of her. Stuff we can use to get these pricks."

I stood up, too. Rolled the stiffness out of my neck and shoulders. Felt the damp sweat on my shirt collar.

"Like I said, your call."

As we turned and headed back along the river's edge toward Noah's Ark, she put her hands once more in her jeans pockets. Then, abruptly, she took her right hand out and touched my forearm. Let it linger there as we walked.

I didn't say anything. Didn't know what to say. What signal she was sending.

"Thanks," she said at last.

"For what?"

"Being a pal. Listening. Keeping secrets."

"Hell, you just laid out my job description. Comes with the license."

"You know what I mean. Just promise me something, okay?"

"Sure."

"If, in your opinion, my feelings about Treva *are* getting in the way of the investigation, you'll give me a heads-up. Let me know."

"You can count on it."

She grinned. "I figured I could."

Thirty seconds later, her grin had faded.

Because her cell had rung. She'd answered, listened intently and then clicked off. Stood frozen. Shut her eyes for a long moment, breathing slow and hard.

When she turned back to me, her look was a mix of incomprehension and anger.

"That was Robertson at the hospital. He said Treva's doctor just informed him that she's awake and alert. And that she's able to answer questions."

"That's good. We're only ten minutes from where I'm parked."

"Not so good. For me. Treva told the doc she'll only talk to you. And that if there has to be a cop in the room, that's okay, too. As long as it's not me."

I just stared at her. Watched the light in her eyes go dim and fade.

"Treva said she doesn't want to talk to me. That she won't tell us anything if I'm there. That she never wants to see me again."

Chapter Eighteen

We drove in my Mustang back to police headquarters in a thickening dusk that still held most of the day's heat. Though the silence in my car was even thicker.

Eleanor had said only that since she couldn't take part in Treva's questioning, she might as well join Harry for the scheduled conference call with DA Sinclair. Then she'd settled back against the unforgiving bucket seats and closed her eyes. On me. On the traffic. On the world.

We hit gridlock as we neared the Liberty Bridge on-ramp. I turned on the all-news station, only to catch the last few seconds of a new campaign ad by Councilman John Garrity.

"I know how things work up in the state capitol. How to get things done. My opponent only knows how to preside over a rising crime rate and a disorganized police department. Do we really want an amateur negotiating tax codes with new businesses? With potential employers—and the jobs they bring—that this state sorely needs?"

Then Garrity's own version of stirring music, while a polished announcer intoned: "John Garrity. Experience we can count on."

"Sorry," I said to Eleanor, clicking it off before Garrity's thin voice could return, proclaiming that he approved this message.

She spoke her first words in ten minutes.

"Fuck Garrity. We're not disorganized. We're underfunded. Undermanned."

"So Sinclair has your vote?"

She didn't turn her head. "Another ambitious prick. Just a lot smarter, I guess. Some choice, eh?"

I didn't reply. My own view was that Garrity was mistaken in mocking Sinclair's lack of political experience. For one thing, voters this election season thought that having political veterans in office was the reason the state was in such trouble in the first place.

Moreover, Leland Sinclair was as canny a political animal as I'd ever seen. He'd sure as hell run the DA's office all these years with at least one eye on the prevailing winds of public sentiment. Every high-profile case he and his team prosecuted just another stepping stone on the road to higher office.

On the other hand, Garrity's much-vaunted political experience was local, as a city councilman. And before that, as a successful CEO of an interstate trucking firm. Though not as telegenic as Sinclair—John Garrity was short, overweight, and double-chinned—he nonetheless appeared the embodiment of business savvy and cool-headedness. In fact, what he mostly possessed was lots of private money and family connections.

Now, after months of hard-fought campaigning, he and Sinclair were still neck-and-neck in the polls. Which either said something about them, the voters, or the state of American politics. I just didn't know which.

◇◇◇

In another minute or two, the traffic eased and we were moving once more, now in sight of the precinct.

I didn't look for another radio station, or slip in a CD. Apparently, Eleanor appreciated the silence. She turned once to give me a sad smile, then swiveled back to stare out the window. Thinking, no doubt, about Treva.

Suddenly, Eleanor's cell rang again. I listened as she murmured a few times, nodding as though whomever was on the other end of the call could see. Then a short, wry chuckle, then more nodding. Then she clicked off.

"Feel like sharing?" I said.

"That was Harry. CSU was able to lift some prints from inside the ambulance. We finally got an ID on our guy. He got sloppy and left two clear prints on the inside driver's side door handle."

I considered this. "After the crash, he must've crawled over the driver's body and gone out that door. Which probably means the impact pushed in the passenger side in the front. He couldn't get out that way."

"Yeah. Harry said CSU came up with the same theory. Must've been one helluva big tree that ambulance hit. Crushed the whole right side in like tin foil."

"So, who's our guy?"

"You're gonna love this. Back at the bank, he told Harry the truth. He *is* an ex-cop. Chicago PD. Then he worked for Blackwater in Iraq. Private security for what passes for government officials over there."

"Worked? Past tense?"

"Blackwater threw him out. Psych problems. Excessive force. Insubordination."

"He was too much for *them*?"

"Told you you were gonna love it."

"What's this model citizen's name?"

"Roarke, Wheeler H. We got his date of birth and last known residence—Terre Haute, Indiana. Biegler has the local cops there checking it out, but odds are Roarke's not heading back home anytime soon." She rubbed her eyes. "They said it'd take at least twenty-four hours for a full work-up on Roarke. And that's only if Blackwater and Chicago PD cooperate. Which isn't likely. He's not a guy either one of 'em wants to brag about, if you know what I mean."

"Any news about his whereabouts?"

She shook her head. "Harry's just leaving the crash scene now. Gonna meet me and Biegler for Sinclair's call. But he said we still have teams searching the area around Crawford Street. Plus the ongoing alerts at area hospitals, doctors' offices. Harry even reached out to some fancy private diet clinic nearby."

"Smart move. They might have a nurse on hand. Maybe even a physician. In case Roarke figures he could get some medical help that way. He's got to be getting desperate."

"Desperate and lethal. Bad combo."

◇◇◇

I dropped Eleanor Lowrey at the precinct and turned around in the parking lot. Then I angled myself again into slow-moving traffic heading back to Pittsburgh Memorial.

I tightened my grip on the wheel as the traffic light five cars ahead turned from green to yellow. The guy in the Chevy truck in front of me sped up to beat the red, then abruptly changed his mind. Lurched to a sudden stop, forcing me to stomp on the brakes.

I was still cursing this Nascar reject under my breath when my cell rang. It was Noah.

"Not for nothin', man, but you left the bar without sayin' good-bye. We schizos got feelin's, too, ya know."

"Sorry, Noah. Kind of a spur-of-the-moment thing."

"No sweat. I know a thing or two about Happy Hour booty calls myself."

"You're way off base, man. Eleanor's—"

"I know, just a friend. Whatever. But it must be nice, her havin' her own regulation handcuffs and everything."

"It's good to know you can still entertain yourself, Noah."

"It's a gift. All those nights in lock-ups and padded cells really paid off. You oughtta see my card tricks."

"Is there some real reason you called, other than to bust my balls?"

"Well, usually, that's reason enough. But I got actual intel. Seein' how bummed out you were about Andy the Android finally deactivating himself, I called around and found out where the funeral is tomorrow."

"Really? Thanks, Noah."

"*No problemo.* There's a private thing at Bernstein's Funeral Home—just family—then they're buryin' the poor bastard at Rosewood Cemetery. You know it?"

"Been there a few times." It was where my father and mother were both buried. "What time?"

"Looks like they start diggin' at noon. Oughtta be nice and hot by then. Perfect for wearin' black. You mourners are gonna sweat buckets."

"I take it you're not going?"

"I can't, Danny. You know. That thing I said, about the willies. But I...I mean, a guy can mourn in private, right? By himself? In his own head?"

"People do it all the time, Noah. Don't worry about it. I know how you felt about Andy. More importantly, *he* knew."

"Yeah? Then why the fuck did he do it? Eh, man?"

I was surprised at the spike of anguish in his voice.

Then I took a guess.

"You're *not* Andy, Noah."

"No, I'm just a different kind o' crazy. But we're in the same fraternity, bro. Delta Sigma Psycho."

I paused, gathering my thoughts. So that's why Andy's death had spooked him so much.

And, in a sense, Noah was right. He and Andy *were* part of a select group. A special fraternity of people who'd attempted suicide.

Only Andy had pulled it off.

"Maybe we should get together and talk," I said at last.

But Noah had already clicked off.

Chapter Nineteen

Finally, night. Crowding out the last faint rays of a stubborn summer sun. Though a stale heat still lingered, fringed the air. Made the darkness heavy, oppressive.

I pulled into the parking lot at Pittsburgh Memorial, under the glowing UPMC sign. Only a few cars dotted the line of spaces, their roofs shining like new coins off the glare of the parking lot light posts.

I went into the hospital through a side entrance, by-passing the main reception area, and took the elevator up to the ICU—

Where, to my surprise, the doors opened onto a deserted corridor. Silent. Empty.

I paused a moment, then stepped out of the elevator. Heard the doors close with a whispered rumble behind me.

The corridor wasn't just deserted. It was dark. Long shadows painted the dull walls, making gray the familiar hospital white.

I looked up, saw that the overhead fluorescents were out. Tubes of flat black that ran the length of the high ceiling, disappearing at the end of the hall.

I took another step and glanced toward the nurse's station. It was empty. The wheeled chair behind the semi-circular desk was pushed back against the corner, as though shoved there.

As though somebody had bolted out of it in a hurry.

I swallowed, mouth suddenly dry as dust. Felt my heart revving up in my chest.

Something was definitely wrong.

Steeling myself, I started down the corridor toward the last room. Treva's room.

The first two rooms I passed were empty. Silent. Unlike earlier today. No sounds of machinery pumping. No beeps, blinking lights, pneumatic wheezes.

And no patients. Again, unlike earlier today. I remembered that there'd been one in each of these rooms. Now the rooms were dim as caves, lit only by a rising moon's faint glow through the windows slats. The beds were stripped. Sheets gone.

I'd been around ICUs enough to know what that meant. Or what it usually meant. The patients had died.

But where was the night nurse? More importantly, where was Treva's guard, Detective Robertson?

That thought made me swivel where I stood. Nerves wound tight, vibrating. Fight or flight.

Nothing. And no one.

Then I looked again toward the end of the long, shadowed corridor. Saw for the first time a soft, pale light that bloomed faintly up ahead, coming from the last room. Somehow more ominous for being the sole illumination in the darkness of the silent ICU.

I squinted in concentration as I drew closer to that light emanating from Treva's room. Gripped by a sudden, visceral sense of foreboding. Of dread.

The light grew brighter. A few feet more and—

Something caught my foot. Big, soft, heavy. I stumbled, clawing the air. Righting myself at last by grabbing the doorframe at the threshold to the room.

I peered down in the darkness. A body lay on the floor at my feet. A large-bellied man, jacket thrown open.

I got to my haunches, made out his features in the light from Treva's room.

Robertson.

Quickly, I checked his vitals. He was unconscious, but alive. A smear of blood tattooed the vinyl flooring beneath his head.

I spread his jacket, checked for more blood. Other wounds. Nothing.

I knew I had to get him help, but not before checking on Treva. I got to my feet again and bolted into her room. The light I'd seen had come from two small table lamps, one on each side of her bed. The overheads were out.

The shaded lamps made the room seem incongruously cozy. Safe. The pillows were pushed up against the headboard, as though perhaps she'd decided to read by lamp-light. Had in fact asked that the overheads be turned off.

Cozy. Safe. The IV drip was unhooked and coiled. Hospital slippers positioned side-by-side under the bed. Nothing seemed out of the ordinary.

Except that Treva was gone.

A trail of blood, a series of irregularly-spaced black-red droplets, shone wetly on the white floor.

Like a trail of scarlet bread crumbs in a nightmarish fairy tale, they led me away from the bed.

Out of the room.

Into the corridor behind me.

Toward a service door at the far end.

Disappearing under that door…

Without a thought, I pulled it open and half-ran, half-fell down the right-angled service stairs. The stairway was as brightly-lit as the ICU corridor had been dark, and the drops of blood glowed absurdly red against the worn paint-flecked concrete steps.

Three floors down, and the blood trail went right, under another door. I pushed it open.

Another, smaller hallway. Violently bright from the overheads. But just as empty as the corridor above.

A series of double-doors lined the wall to my left.

But the only doors that got my attention were the ones that stood open, a dozen feet or so down the hall.

I slowed my steps. Came up carefully to the opening. Took a breath. Steadied myself. For some reason—perhaps in answer to an old impulse—I clenched my fists.

And stepped inside.

It was an operating room. White-sheeted surgical bed in the center. Trays of instruments on wheeled carts. A canopy of goose-necked lamps positioned for maximum visibility, beneath the familiar ceiling fluorescents.

The room held two people, both staring at me, wide-eyed. Faces drained of color. Pinched with fear.

Lloyd Holloway. The young doctor I'd met up in the ICU. Standing at the surgical bed, hands at his sides. Linebacker's body ramrod straight, strained from tension, held upright by extreme force of will.

And Treva Williams. Sitting on the floor, knees up, her back against a far corner. Shivering in her flimsy hospital gown. Hands behind her back, obviously bound. Bare feet also bound, at the ankle.

I registered them both in what seemed only a second.

Then I saw Treva's mouth open, forming an "O," and her eyes widening, looking at me with sudden horror.

No, not *at* me. *Past* me…

I felt a searing pain at the back of my head, and looked up at the blinding overhead lights as they began to whirl like a vortex of spinning stars.

And then I saw nothing at all.

Chapter Twenty

Consciousness came back to me in a kind of roaring rush. Eyelids squeezed shut, I felt rather than saw the intensity of the OR's relentless light. Which only made the sharp throb of pain at the back of my head more insistent. Relentless.

My whole body felt stiff. Muscles aching. Then, threaded through the muffled pounding in my skull, a new sound. Voices. The soft hush of practiced movement. The clicking of metal.

When I finally risked opening my eyes, I was sitting next to Treva Williams. My own knees drawn up, feet bound at the ankles with surgical tape. Hands bound behind my back.

"Welcome to the war, buddy." A gruff, ironic voice. Vaguely familiar. I looked up.

It was Wheeler Roarke. Ex-Chicago PD. Ex-Blackwater. The man I'd once known as George Vickers.

He sat on the surgical table, the security guard's shirt thrown across it beside him. Roarke's thick chest was naked, streaked with sweat and grime. His injured left arm hung limp at his side. Caked with blood. Wound exposed. Layers of skin held by tiny clamps.

His other arm was bent at a right angle, elbow on his lap. In that hand was a gun. Thick, ugly. A revolver that I'd seen before. In George Vickers' belt holster.

It wasn't pointed at me. Nor at Treva.

It was pointed directly at Dr. Holloway, who stood at Roarke's bedside. Gloved hands deep in the gunman's wound. Face a grim mask of determination and fear. He worked feverishly, suturing through rivulets of blood trickling between his fingers.

Roarke had the gun pressed hard against the doctor's ribs. Forehead sheathed with sweat, he kept his hard eyes riveted on Holloway's every move.

Suddenly I felt Treva shifting beside me.

"Are you all right?" Voice trembling. Barely audible. The first words she'd spoken since I got here.

"I've been better."

Wincing in pain, Roarke risked a glance over at me.

"Sorry I hadda knock you out. Price o' showin' up uninvited."

He smiled at the gun in his hand. Still welded to Holloway's side.

"Just your standard .38 S&W. Nothin' like the butt-end of a .357 Magnum. But still, it makes a statement. Though you got a harder head than that loser upstairs."

"You sneak up behind *him*, too, Roarke?" My voice sounding like it belonged to someone else. Someone weak and far away.

He aimed that dark smile in my direction.

"So you guys know my name?"

I nodded. Big mistake. Pain splintered up from the base of my skull.

"Yeah, 'cause you screwed up and left some prints at the crash site. Just like you were lame enough to drip blood all the way here from the ICU."

Roarke choked out a laugh. "Lotta lip ya got there, pal. And big clankin' balls, given your current situation."

"Please," Treva whispered. Urgent, imploring. "Please don't make him angry."

Roarke laughed again. And grimaced from the pain.

"Fuck, girlie, it's *way* too late for that. Besides, Rinaldi here has a point." He raised the gun and scratched his chin with the barrel. "I mean, no question, none o' this is textbook. But sometimes you gotta improvise."

"Like in the ambulance," I said.

"Right. Soon as our girl here wakes up and sees me wearin' Vickers' uniform, she freaks. I got no choice but to put her to sleep and make a play for the driver."

"But the really smart thing was coming here anyway. You knew the cops'd be checking every medical facility in the area. The last thing they'd expect—"

"—Was for me to make straight for here. Where the ambulance was headin' anyway. Lucky for me, I got a little help from a truck I flagged down. You'll find the driver in a drainage ditch somewhere off McKnight Road."

"Still breathing?"

"Couldn't say. Seemed like it at the time. But things were happenin' kinda fast, ya know?"

I flexed and relaxed my shoulders a couple times, to get some feeling back in my arms. Tried shifting my wrists where they were bound behind me. I got nowhere.

He noticed my efforts. Shook his head.

"Now you're just bein' stupid. Chill-lax, okay? Long as the Doc here fixes me up and you two don't get cute, everybody gets outta this alive."

Roarke dug his gun deeper into Holloway's ribs.

"Speakin' of which, Doc, you wanna wrap things up here? That local you gave me is startin' to wear off."

Holloway's voice was a croak. "I told you, that wouldn't be enough to—"

"Shut up and keep workin'. My guess is, we're gonna have some unwanted company real soon."

"I just need a few more minutes. I—"

Suddenly Treva cried out and looked up. I followed her gaze to where a wide observation window looked down into the OR from a small tiered room above.

Roarke did the same.

"Fuck." He let out a weary sigh. "I get so goddam tired o' bein' right all the time."

It was Biegler, Polk, and Lowrey. Plus a few other plainclothes officers I didn't recognize. All arrayed on the other side of the window, peering down at us.

But no Robertson. He'd probably been found, and was receiving medical attention. Maybe he'd even been able to tell them what had happened. Or else the cops had just done what I did. Followed the blood.

That's when I heard it. What sounded like muffled footsteps on the other side of the OR doors. Tentative, trying for stealth. And not succeeding.

I could tell Roarke had heard it, too.

I found my voice.

"That's it, Roarke. You got cops right outside the door. You're toast."

"Shut the hell up!" His eyes became angry slits. Aimed them at Holloway. "What did I say about kickin' it in gear, Doc? Huh?"

Holloway nodded as though in a trance. Hands shaking, frantically bandaging Roarke's arm.

I heard the crackle of an intercom speaker. Looked up again to see Lt. Biegler speaking into a wall mike next to the window on their side of the observation bay.

"Give it up, Roarke. Don't make things worse for yourself."

Roarke frowned at me. "Who is this ass-wipe? I mean, who the fuck says shit like that anymore?"

"He does. Lt. Biegler. You wouldn't like him."

Roarke shook his head in disbelief. Yelled up at the window.

"You pricks gotta be *kiddin'* me! You got a goddam hostage situation here. Not the first one today, in case you forgot. *I'm* callin' the shots, not you!"

"Don't screw with me, Roarke!" Biegler's aggressive tone sounded strained, false. "There's no way out of this for you. We have teams at every exit. I got people right outside your door."

"No shit? If even *one* of 'em tries bustin' in, you're lookin' at three dead bodies here."

He swung his gun hand around, aimed in our direction.

"Startin' with the girl. In and out, right between the eyes. They'll be moppin' up blood splatter for a week. Then I do the shrink. I'm thinkin' gut shot, just 'cause he pisses me off. Hurts like a motherfucker and it'll take him forever to bleed out."

He turned back, this time pointing the gun directly at Holloway's head.

"Then the doc here. Back o' the head shot. So he can forget all about donatin' his brain to science." His eyes squinted up at the glass. "You mooks *feelin'* me?"

Silence from the wall speaker.

Looking up at the window, I saw Biegler confer with Polk, who nodded once and ran off. Eleanor Lowrey, face constricted in anguish, leaned forward, open hands splayed against the glass. Eyes riveted on Treva and me.

"Hey!" Roarke shouted again. "Up there! Do I strike you as a patient man? Get your people away from the door or else start rollin' out the body bags."

As if in answer, there was the sound of hurried movement on the other side of the doors. Footsteps receding, leaving only an eerie silence.

Which was quickly shattered when Roarke turned and fired at the room's wall speaker. It exploded in a loud, glittering shower of metal shards and bits of wire. Beside me, Treva jumped as though hit with a thousand volts.

Roarke swiveled his head to stare at Holloway's white, watery eyes. Pointed the gun once more at his head.

"Circus is leavin' town, kid."

Holloway stammered out a response. "We're…that's it. There's been some radial nerve damage. I did the best I could, but…but I'm afraid some range of motion is affected. Dexterity. Grip strength."

"I ain't lookin' to go bowlin', Doc. Long as the arm's saved, I'll get me some rehab later. Shit, I took worse hits in Iraq."

I spoke up. "The cops'll never let you leave here."

Roarke's look at me was flat. As though his hours of pain had cauterized his feelings. Left him blank, empty.

"I ain't done too bad so far. After I got here, I hid out in one of the morgue rooms downstairs—nobody minded. Just the poor bastard workin' there, and he wasn't much trouble. Neither was that lame excuse for a detective up in the ICU. Department oughtta pension his ass out, you want my opinion. That limp-dick motherfucker wouldn'ta lasted a week in my old squad."

I risked needling him. Giving the cops a chance to re-group. Come up with a move.

"Speaking of limp-dicks," I said, "where's your partner? The other guy in the bank."

Roarke's face reddened. "*Fuck* him."

He slipped off the surgical table, stood and worked his way back into the torn security guard shirt. Moved his wounded arm gingerly from the shoulder. I couldn't tell if the limited range of motion was due to the pain or the tight constriction of the heavy bandages.

Roarke flexed his fingers, wincing.

Holloway gasped. "I told you, there might be—"

"No worries, Doc." Roarke gave him a sidelong look. "What do I owe ya?"

Holloway blinked in confusion, which only made Roarke smile. Before he swung and raked the barrel of his gun across the doctor's wide jaw.

Holloway, without a sound, collapsed to the floor.

Roarke looked down at his inert form. "Hope that covers it."

I heard Treva's breath coming in shallow gasps beside me. I turned, saw her eyes rolling up. She was seconds away from passing out.

Meanwhile, Roarke scooped up a scalpel in his left hand. Carefully closed his fingers around the handle. Held it menacingly, sharp tip pointed up. He thrust at the air. Once, twice.

"Could be worse," he said to me. Oddly personal. As though I'd been concerned about his condition.

"Like I give a shit." I kept my voice hard, to cover my mounting anxiety about that scalpel. "Think this is some kinda bonding moment for us?"

He laughed, almost appreciatively.

"Not you and me, Rinaldi. Little Treva here."

With that, he moved to where Treva cowered in the corner. Bent and slid the scalpel's blade under the tape binding her ankles. One quick slice and her feet were free.

"C'mon, girlie. You and me are gonna tango right outta here. Like *Dancin' with the Stars*."

Treva's head fell forward, as though her neck muscles had gone slack. Ignoring this, Roarke pulled her roughly to her feet. Which promptly gave out beneath her.

I struggled against my bonds. "Roarke, no—!"

Now Roarke was awkwardly keeping her upright, leaning her against his bandaged arm.

"*Dammit*, girlie—" His tone had lost its mocking self-assurance. Was all malice now.

With his good arm, he pointed the gun at her temple.

"Roarke!" My shout drew his look. "For Christ's sake, she's no good as a hostage. She can't even walk. You wanna try to drag her outta here past a dozen cops?"

This made Roarke shift position, arm still hugging the limp girl, and train his gaze back up at the observation window. I looked, too, and saw that Polk had returned. He and Biegler were conferring, gesturing angrily at each other. While Lowrey was saying something into her two-way.

"Every second you delay, it's gonna be harder to make it out," I said to Roarke's profile. His jaw working as he stared up at the cops above him.

"Take *me*, Roarke." I shifted again, using the wall corner to help me lever my way to a half-standing position. My legs, bound at the ankles, turned awkwardly beneath me.

Roarke took only another moment to decide. Then he simply let go of Treva, who slumped to the floor, hospital gown settling with a flutter over her thin arms and legs.

In two quick steps Roarke was next to me. Bending to cut the tape binding my ankles. Leaving my hands still bound behind my back.

Then he straightened, dropping the scalpel to the floor. Glancing reflexively at his hand. Stiffly curled fingers. I could tell that holding the scalpel had been difficult. More painful than he'd hoped.

Face bathed in grimy sweat, he motioned with his head for me to get all the way to my feet. As I did, I felt momentarily dizzy. Aware again of the throbbing at the back of my head, where Roarke had struck me. Standing, the pain was even worse.

"Looks like it's you an' me, Rinaldi." He indicated for me to turn around. "Last dance."

The nose of the gun dug into my spine.

My heart was thumping so loud I was sure he could hear it. Adrenaline surged through me. Blocked, thwarted.

Nowhere to run, no way to fight.

My mind raced, as panic rose to the surface. Thoughts of my own death. Images from the bank, those bodies on the floor. Swimming in their own blood.

Roarke made some harsh sound in his throat. As though readying himself, too. For whatever lay ahead.

Pushing me before him, we made our way to the doors.

Chapter Twenty-one

The corridor just beyond those doors was as empty as before. And as eerily silent.

Roarke gave me another nudge in the back with his gun and we headed in the opposite direction from the way I'd first come. Past another operating room, its double doors sealed. Then past another.

At the end of the corridor was a metal-sheathed, green-tinted, double-sized elevator. Our destination.

Our footsteps echoed off the worn linoleum and bounced back at us from the windowless walls. I turned my head left and right. As I could feel Roarke doing, behind me.

For different reasons, we were both on the lookout for the police. For some sign of a trap.

"They're sure being good little boys and girls," he muttered dryly into the back of my neck.

I tried to sound more confident than I was.

"You know they've got eyes on you, Roarke. Watching from somewhere."

He grunted. "Let's find out."

With that, he shoved me with the gun. Hard. I stumbled forward, tripped. Without my hands free to help correct my balance, I fell to my knees.

Gasping, I craned my neck around to glare at him.

"What the hell—?!"

But Roarke was staring past me, at the huge silent elevator. The revolver was trained at my head.

"Whoever the fuck's in that elevator, you got three seconds to make an appearance. Or I blow Rinaldi away."

I swiveled back again, eyes front, still on my knees. Gaze riveted on those wide green doors. Nothing happened. They didn't budge.

"Okay, assholes, I'll just start countin'." Roarke took two long steps and I felt the cold, hard muzzle of the gun at the back of my head.

I froze. Breath held in a tight knot in my chest.

"One...two..."

Still, the elevator doors remained closed. Silent.

I was going to die.

Suddenly, one of the operating room doors to our left opened. I heard the swish of the rubber sealant at the bottom of the door as it brushed against linoleum.

I turned, feeling the gun moving along the base of my skull as I did so. But I had to see.

It was Polk. Plus two uniforms in flak jackets. Both tall, male, young. All three with guns pointing impotently at the floor.

I heard Roarke's hoarse laugh.

"Well, shit. I called the play right, but had the wrong fuckin' door."

I felt the pressure of the gun ease off my neck.

As I got unsteadily to my feet, I saw that Roarke had returned to pointing the revolver at my ribs. Though his eyes were glued to Polk's own.

"Stupid move," Roarke said. "Riskin' Rinaldi's life."

One of the uniforms grumbled. "It was worth a shot."

Roarke smiled. "Strange choice of words. But what the hell, it ain't *your* life on the line. Or is it?"

As Roarke turned and shot the cop right in the throat.

Chapter Twenty-two

Everything happened at once.

The cop fell backwards, blood gushing from his throat. Gagging, sputtering. Polk and the other cop, momentarily stunned, took a full second to register what had just happened. And then they were crouching beside the downed man, yelling for help, cupping their hands over his throat to staunch the dark burble of blood.

Stunned myself, I was barely aware that Roarke had grabbed my elbow and was racing us down the corridor toward the elevator.

Other cops poured into the corridor at the far end, through the access door. Roarke hit the elevator button. The car must have been stopped at our floor already, since the doors opened immediately. Roarke's luck was holding.

He shoved me inside, shouldered in beside me, and pushed the interior button. The doors started to close.

Moments before they came together, I caught sight of Biegler and Lowrey, both with guns raised, joining the other cops coming through the access door.

I saw Eleanor's face come up, her eyes meeting mine from her end of the corridor. Then the doors closed, and she disappeared from sight.

It was just Roarke and me.

He said nothing, keeping the gun in my ribs for the full sixty seconds it took for the elevator car to settle with a shudder on a lower floor. I glanced at the button he'd pushed. Basement level.

The doors opened and we stepped out into a cavernous, concrete-walled maintenance area. Hulking machinery. Beds stacked atop each other. Surgical carts with damaged wheels. Shelves of bottles, tubes. Linen supplies.

"Move." Roarke snarled.

He prodded me again with the gun, and we started walking. Fast. Footsteps echoing. A hollow, staccato sound. In less than a minute we were across the broad expanse of the room and going through the rear exit.

Roarke was smart enough to keep me in front of him as we stepped out into the deserted parking lot. Just in case any cops with visions of commendations dancing in their heads were waiting outside.

The night was black, and still heavy with the residue of the day's heat. Maybe a hundred cars were parked in the huge, open-air lot. Soft spheres of light shone under the evenly spaced lamp poles.

Again, we mirrored each other in glancing quickly about us as we walked. Both looking for telltale movement in the shadows. Some sign of a police presence.

Roarke headed us toward a far corner, where two cars—featureless sedans in the dim light—were parked a couple spaces apart. No other vehicles around.

By now, my hands and arms had gone numb from being constrained so long against my back. I didn't even feel Roarke's grip as he steered us toward one of the sedans.

He'd just brought us to the driver's side door when a sudden burst of light split the darkness to our left. Then another stream of light spilled into the night from our other side.

Headlights from a half-dozen parked cars, arrayed on either side of us, glowed like angry suns against the blackness. Roarke and I were illuminated as if on stage, pinned where we stood by the cold bright light.

Roarke squinted at me. Eyes dark points in the glare of the lights.

"Maybe you ain't as valuable as you think, Rinaldi. They keep doin' their best to get you whacked."

Before I could react, Roarke shoved me hard with his shoulder and I went stumbling backwards. I stayed on my feet this time, but could only watch helplessly as he got in behind the wheel of the sedan and started it up.

I stared in disbelief. Door unlocked. Key in the ignition. Whoever owned the car was a complete fool.

Suddenly, I heard the sound of running feet, and a rising crescendo of voices as Roarke put the car in gear.

I hit the pavement, scrambling as well as I could manage with my hands bound behind me toward a large cement planter in a near corner. Ducked my head down low.

In case bullets started flying.

Which they did.

Roarke peeled out of the parking space and headed in a straight, unheeding diagonal across the pavement toward the closest exit. Steering with his bad hand, he'd let down the window on the passenger side and was firing randomly into the night. In the direction of the approaching cops.

I knew he wasn't aiming for anything. Just shooting to cover himself and keep the cops honest. And wary. And backed up far enough not to block his exit.

I raised my head, risked a look. Saw the sedan's tail end bouncing on the concrete as Roarke drove hard and fast through the exit, then made a sharp turn onto the street.

Almost immediately, two patrol cars, positioned on the other side of the intersection, roared into gear and came barreling down the street in pursuit. Lights flashing, sirens wailing.

Roarke made another turn, wheels squealing in protest, and gunned the engine. The cops stayed right with him. And then all three cars were swallowed up by the night-shrouded city. Gone from view. The sirens' wail grew faint, and then faded away.

Meanwhile, more cops had poured out of their parked cars, blurred figures backlit by blazing headlights. Running. Heading my way. All talking and shouting at once. Some at me, some into their two-ways. Getting instructions. Giving Roarke's probable heading.

I rolled up to a sitting position as a female cop in Kevlar knelt beside me. With a conspiratorial smile, she took a pearl-handled Swiss Army knife from her pocket and cut my hands free.

"Against department regs," she whispered, pocketing the knife again. Then a wink.

When I gratefully pulled my arms around to their normal positions at my side, they just hung there, burning. Pretty much useless for the moment. I didn't care.

My head was another story. The throbbing hadn't slackened, and I carefully reached up to touch where I'd been hit. Felt the pulp of soft, raised skin. The moisture on my fingers was my own slow-welling blood.

Great, I thought. Maybe a concussion. Or worse.

The female cop stood up then, to allow room for Biegler and Lowrey to squat on either side of me. Eleanor's face reflected real concern. Biegler, as usual, just looked unhappy.

He watched me fingering the back of my head.

"What happened?" he said.

"I got clobbered with a gun-butt."

Eleanor leaned in. "How does it feel?"

"Like I got clobbered with a gun-butt."

She gave me a wry smile.

"You can't stay out of trouble, can you, Rinaldi? Any idea why?"

"Just lucky, I guess."

I roused myself, sat up straighter. Unless it was my imagination—or just wishful thinking—it seemed like my head was starting to clear a bit.

"What about Treva? How is she?"

"Fine. They're seeing to her now. Dr. Holloway's okay, too. Just shaken up. He's got a jaw like a hunk of marble, apparently."

"What about that cop Roarke shot? Did he make it?"

"Yes, thank God. He's in emergency surgery, but all his vital signs are good. The docs say he'll probably need some vocal rehab, and maybe more surgery down the line, but considering…"

"I guess if you're gonna get shot, a hospital's the best place for it. And Detective Robertson?"

"Concussion, but otherwise fine. Though talk about irony. He's in one of the empty beds in ICU. Not two steps from where he was found on the floor."

I peered up at her. "What the hell happened up there, anyway? The lights were all out. Nobody around."

"That's what we're gonna find out."

Finally, with her hand under my elbow, I got to my feet. The cluster of cops around me had begun to disperse, Biegler barking orders to them in two's and three's. The usual protocols in the aftermath of a crisis situation. Secure the perimeter. Check everywhere for any wounded, missing, hiding. Start crafting a timeline for what happened, and when.

And, most importantly, begin building a case for which poor bastard to blame for the fuck-up.

Not my department, I thought sullenly, as I started to walk back toward the hospital. Without saying a word, Eleanor came along beside me. I gave her a quizzical look.

"Just to make sure you get your head examined." She was smiling. "If you know what I mean."

"Funny. You're a funny person."

We were about a dozen feet away from the entrance when I heard Lt. Biegler explode in anger. I looked back to see him screaming curses to the few remaining uniforms. Waving his arms. Literally ranting.

"What's going on?" I asked Eleanor.

"I think he just realized something. I noticed it myself a minute ago, but kept my mouth shut."

"Realized what?"

"The car Roarke escaped in. It's Biegler's."

Chapter Twenty-three

Within an hour, I'd learned two more things:

First, a harried ER doc checked me out and determined that, except for a nasty headache, I'd probably be none the worse for wear. Turns out I *did* have a harder head than Detective Robertson.

"No surprise there," Eleanor had said, as the doctor applied a bandage to the back of my skull.

The second piece of news wasn't as good: Wheeler Roarke had escaped. By the time police choppers had been called in to help, he'd led the pursuing squad cars through a maze of streets on the North Side. And then into a sprawling construction site, where he abandoned the stolen car and disappeared. The cops searched the site from the air and on the ground, but Roarke had vanished. Again.

But how? One possible answer emerged when the police found the trucker that Roarke had flagged down after the ambulance crash. Right where Roarke said he'd be, in a ditch off Crawford Street. And, thankfully, still alive.

He was also alert enough to tell the cops that in addition to the truck, Roarke had taken his cell phone.

Maybe, the cops figured, Roarke had called someone early on in the pursuit. His partner from the bank, probably. Who could have driven to the construction site and been waiting there to pick him up.

The stolen truck itself had also been found, parked in an alley behind the hospital. Where Roarke had left it. Near the loading area, ground floor. Same level as the morgue. Where he told me he'd hidden.

I got all this from Harry Polk, who'd joined Eleanor Lowrey and me as we left the ER.

He spoke in short, mumbled bursts. Tie unknotted and dangling, shoulders slumped under his worn suit jacket, Harry looked wrung out. Spent. More from frustration than exhaustion, I guessed.

"Can't believe that fucker slipped the net again."

Polk squinted in the glare of the unforgiving overheads as we waited at an elevator. We were heading up to the main patient floors to talk with Lloyd Holloway.

"If he *did* use the trucker's cell to call somebody," Eleanor said carefully, "we could get the records from the phone company. I mean, assuming it was his partner—"

"Biegler's got the techs following up on that already. But I'm bettin' the partner was smart enough to use a throw-away cell. Untraceable."

Eleanor took this in without comment. Then: "What about that conference call with Sinclair?"

"Change of plans. After this newest screw-up, the DA just wanted Biegler and the Chief on the line."

"I'm not surprised," I said. "Now it's more about controlling the message than anything else. Figuring out how to spin it for the media."

Polk snorted. "Ya got that right. No sense havin' us grunts puttin' in our two cents. Messin' things up by actually tryin' to run an investigation."

"That reminds me," Eleanor said. "Did we ever send anybody over to talk to James Franconi, the bank manager? Guy who was home all day with a cold."

"Yeah, I almost forgot. Couple detectives from the one-three questioned Franconi earlier tonight. At his home. Better them than me. They said the guy was laid up with a bad cold. Probably still contagious. Who needs that, right? I mean, summer colds are the worst."

Eleanor smiled. "Franconi give them anything? Other than his germs?"

"Just that he was sick in bed all day. Wife can verify that. Also, that he wasn't worried when he heard about the robbery attempt."

"Why not?" I asked.

"Turns out, the bank vault's on a timer. Roarke and his buddy woulda needed a fuckin' bomb to open that thing. So Franconi wasn't surprised when our guys told him no money had been taken."

Eleanor said, "Any way around the timer?"

"Just one," Polk said. "The assistant manager. Bobby Marks. He had the over-ride codes."

"Maybe Roarke knew that. Or at least suspected it. Maybe he planned to force Marks to open the vault."

"That's what the one-three thinks, too. Then things go belly-up. The only guy who could open the vault gets shot. Roarke panics and starts shootin' the other people."

I considered this. "Not the brightest move, was it? Shooting Marks. No wonder a guy as smart as Roarke went off the rails."

"I still think we oughtta take another run at Franconi," said Eleanor. "He'd know the override codes, too. So it could still be an inside job."

"What do you mean?"

"Maybe he and Roarke cooked it up together. He gives the codes to Roarke, stays home sick with his wife to alibi himself. But then things blow up in the bank. The alarm goes off, Roarke's partner runs away. Roarke freaks and starts killing hostages. Which triggers our guys goin' in. SWAT. Everybody. No time to get the vault open and grab the cash. The whole plan falls apart."

"Not bad," I said, as the elevator doors slid open and we stepped inside.

Polk stifled a yawn. "One thing's for sure. It's worth takin' another look at Franconi."

Then he winked at his partner. "*You* oughtta go talk to him tomorrow morning. Those douche-bags in the one-three couldn't get a confession out of a nun on her death-bed."

Eleanor's eyebrows rose. "You're not coming, too?"

"Can't. Got some bullshit personal thing." He gave a short cough. "Cover for me with Biegler, okay?"

"Uh, sure."

Polk muttered his thanks. Then, hands in his pockets, he studied something interesting on the elevator floor.

As we rode the rest of the way up in silence.

Chapter Twenty-four

"Where the hell's that nurse with my Percodan?"

It was Dr. Lloyd Holloway, sitting up in one of the two beds in a semiprivate room on Ward B. Arms folded, he studiously ignored his three unwanted visitors as he scanned the corridor outside.

Holloway was in a fresh pair of hospital scrubs and sported a wide bandage on the left side of his jaw. As well as a lot of attitude.

"I mean, how long can it—"

He squeezed his eyes shut.

I could tell it was difficult for him to talk. The bruise peeking out from the sides of his bandage looked particularly nasty. His jaw must've hurt like hell.

"She said she'd be right back," Eleanor reminded him. "As soon as your attending physician gives the okay."

Lowrey sat next to Holloway's bed on one of the straight-backed visitor's chairs. Polk occupied the other one, which he'd maneuvered into a corner. I sat on Holloway's opposite side, in the room's other bed.

Rousing himself, the young physician scowled at Eleanor. "My attending? You mean, Dr. Chen? Hell, up till last week she was a goddam *intern*."

"Staff's stretched pretty thin, Doctor." I smiled. "Lots of activity tonight. You know that better than anyone. Low-risk patients like you and me aren't a top priority."

He didn't appreciate my attempt at solidarity. He sighed dramatically, then sat back against his pillow. I had to admit, Holloway didn't look good. Skin pale, almost translucent. Slight anxiety tic under his left eye. He was physically and emotionally exhausted. It was evident—at least to me—that his ordeal with Roarke had taken a huge toll.

I also speculated that, given his solid, muscular build and relative youth, his friends and colleagues would probably under-estimate its traumatic effects. They'd assume that Holloway would have little trouble coping, and "moving on." In fact, all too soon, they'd insist upon it.

Under different circumstances, I thought, I'd probably offer him my card. Which I suspected he'd refuse.

Polk stirred unhappily in his chair.

"Much as I'm enjoyin' this get-together, I'd like to get some kind of statement from the doc here. *Before* he tranks out on meds and starts forgettin' those pesky little details that make doin' our jobs even half-way possible. If nobody minds."

He raised an eyebrow at Lowrey, who nodded and leaned in closer to Holloway. Gave him a brief but warm smile.

I'd asked that the overheads be shut off, to spare both Hol-loway and myself the inevitable headaches our injuries often created. So the room was lit only by small table lamps on either side of the bed. A similar tableau to that which I'd come upon in Treva's room in the ICU.

The overall effect was of an intimate, unofficial meeting. Less an interview than a conversation. Which was also something I'd hoped to accomplish, though I hadn't mentioned this notion to Polk and Lowrey.

My reading of Holloway was that a strictly by-the-book, authoritative approach would meet with greater resistance from the young doctor. I guessed that he prided himself on his inde-pendence. On being a maverick. After all, he didn't wear that pony tail for nothing.

"I know you're in a lot of pain, Dr. Holloway," Eleanor began, her voice soothing. "But we really need to hear your version of events. Get a sense of this guy's moves. The sooner the better, if we're gonna catch him."

Smart approach, I thought. *We* need *you*, she was saying. As a prime eyewitness to what happened, *you're* the authority figure, not us.

"Yeah, okay." Holloway sniffed. "Probably be good to lay it all out now, while it's still fresh in my mind. While I can still feel that bastard's gun in my ribs."

He sat up again, hands gripping the bed rails as though to launch himself into his story.

"I shoulda known something weird was going to happen. I mean, I could *feel* it. ICU was too quiet."

"Is that because the two other patients had been removed from their rooms?" I asked.

"Yeah. One had died, and the other was upgraded to stable and taken to the regular patient wing. She's just down the hall from us, matter of fact. So like I said, it was suddenly pretty quiet up there. Just the night nurse, at her station at the other end of the corridor. And me with Treva Williams, in her room. I'd just gotten there to check up on her. Update her chart."

Eleanor cut in. "Where was Detective Robertson?"

"Where he usually was, standing outside the door. Treva was awake and responsive, so I informed Robertson that it was okay if you guys wanted to talk to her."

"Right. That's when Robertson called me. But he also said Ms. Williams insisted that I not be present for the questioning."

Holloway shrugged. "Hey, I just told Robertson what Treva said to me. She was adamant about it."

I glanced over at Eleanor. Saw the pain in her eyes. I quickly spoke up.

"What happened next?"

Holloway turned to me. "Right after that, the night nurse went to take her break. Then Robertson pokes his head into the room and says 'Why don't I give you two some privacy?' and goes down to the nurse's station."

Polk clucked his tongue. "To sit in her chair. Take a load off."

Holloway gave a half-smile, the most he could manage under the bandage. "Hell, it was fine with me. Guy's a big waste of space, in my opinion. Treva and I were both laughing about it. 'cause you could hear Robertson snoring all the way down the hall."

"That's when Roarke saw his chance," I said. "He must have come up from where he'd hidden downstairs, in the morgue. Then he waits behind the access door."

"That's the way we see it, too." Polk leaned forward. "Especially since there's an electrical panel right inside that door. Controls the juice for the whole floor. He musta praised Jesus when he saw it there. Givin' him an added edge." He laughed. "Guy's not just smart. He's lucky."

"Whatever," Holloway said flatly. "Anyway, all of a sudden the lights go out. Treva becomes upset, so I try to calm her. I also call out to Robertson. Tell him to get a hold of maintenance. We've got a short or something. Next thing I know, I see a guy standing in the doorway to the room. Can't make him out in the darkness, but I could tell he was big. Treva sees him, too, and starts screaming."

Holloway paused, drew a hand tentatively up to touch his jaw. All the talking was probably taking its toll.

"So Robertson comes running down the hall. But by then, the big guy is out of sight. Robertson appears in the doorway, peering in at Treva and me. Then suddenly the big guy steps in and hits him from behind. Robertson drops like a stone. And I knew right then I was fucked."

I looked past Holloway at Polk and Lowrey. "Roarke needed two things: a doctor to tend to his wound, and a hostage to force him to do it. Just in case the doc was resistant."

Holloway gave a short, bitter laugh. "He didn't need to worry. He had me at 'Hello…I've got a gun.'"

His laugh turned into a spasmodic cough. Eleanor reached and touched his shoulder. He waved her away.

"Let me finish the damn story. Since apparently I'm not getting juiced with happy pills any time soon."

Eleanor rose. "I'll go check up on that, okay?" Then she left the room.

Holloway took a long breath. "Now where was I? Oh, yeah. After taking care of Robertson, Roarke comes over to Treva's bed. He's bleeding all over the floor from his wound. Treva sees this and goes white. Like she's about to faint. Roarke doesn't care, just puts his gun to her head. Then he turns to me, says he'll kill her unless I go with them to an empty OR and fix him up. Believe me, I wasn't going to argue. So off we go, through the access door and down to the OR bay."

"Was Treva conscious?" I asked.

"Just barely. Roarke has to drag her by the arm, keeping her upright, with one eye on me the whole time."

He paused, swallowed. "Once we're in the OR, he ties Treva up and plants her in a corner. Then he gets up on the surgical table, and I help him off with his shirt. His arm's a goddam mess. I tell him he'll need a general anesthetic, but he says no, just a local. He needs to be awake to watch me. So I give him a shot and go to work."

Holloway narrowed his eyes at me. "Not long after that, you joined the party."

"I assume he heard me coming down the hall."

"Yeah. Soon as does, he gets off the table. Says, 'Not a word or everybody dies.' Then he hobbles over to the door, waits just inside for you to come in. Then he takes a divot out of the back of your head."

"I remember. I was there."

Holloway smiled coolly. "After that, he ties you up, climbs up on the table again and I go back to work. Just your average meatball surgery, with a loaded gun in my ribs. Under the circumstances, I think I did a pretty good job on that arm."

"That's swell," Polk grumbled. "Maybe they'll give you a raise."

"I don't want a raise. I just want my meds, and a couple sick days. I need a break from this place."

As if on cue, Eleanor entered with a young Asian woman. Slim, with wire-rim glasses. Dr. Chen, I presumed.

Holloway screwed his face up at her.

"What do you have for me, Harriet?"

"Percodan. As requested." She stepped over to his bedside and handed him a paper cup. Rattled the pills inside. "Though I'm starting to feel like a drug dealer."

He gave her a smug grin. "You work in a hospital, Harriet. Get used to it."

Holloway threw back the pills and reached for a water glass on the bedside table. Sank back against his pillow with a satisfied smile.

Polk gave me a caustic look, which I returned with a shrug. Then Eleanor turned to Dr. Chen.

"What about Treva Williams? May we talk to her?"

"Not till tomorrow afternoon, at the earliest. She's been sedated. Shows symptoms of shock. Disorientation. We'll need that long to be able to assess her properly."

I stepped forward. "I'd like to be here when you do." I offered my hand. "Dr. Daniel Rinaldi."

"Yes, Doctor. She was barely coherent, but she did ask about you. And said that she wanted to talk to you."

Polk noisily cleared his throat. "Not without a cop in the room. In case she has something important to tell us."

Dr. Chen folded her arms across her hospital greens.

"As long as it's not before two or three PM."

Eleanor looked at her watch. "It's past one AM now."

"After what she's been through," I said, "I guess Treva's entitled to twenty-four hours of peace and quiet."

"Fine with me." Polk hauled himself out of his chair and poked me in the chest with a stubby forefinger. "I'll meet you here at three tomorrow, okay?"

"Three PM. Got it."

But I wasn't thinking about Treva just then.

With Polk's face so close to mine, I got a good look at the rheumy film in his eyes. Smelled the alcohol on his breath. On his clothes. And remembered how worried Eleanor had been earlier tonight. About Harry.

It wasn't just that Harry seemed to be off his game. Something else was going on.

Like his partner, Harry Polk was harboring a secret. But unlike Eleanor's, I didn't know what it was.

As he shuffled out of the room, I wondered if I'd ever find out.

Chapter Twenty-five

It was nearing two AM as I drove the Mustang up the hill toward Mt. Washington and home. Ornette Coleman's lulling sax pillowed my ears, drew my mind away from its turbulent thoughts. The chaos of that long, long day.

The night had cooled, gleaming black and cloudless, and I had the windows open. Grateful for air that didn't feel superheated, thick, torpid.

I wasn't alone. The few other cars I saw had their windows open, too. As did the modest homes I passed when I turned onto Grandview. My street. I could see a few folks sitting by those open windows. Reading. Watching TV. Holding a cold glass up to their foreheads. In the heat of a Pittsburgh summer, it wasn't surprising that most people became temporarily nocturnal.

I'd just pulled into my driveway when my cell rang. I checked the display. Angie Villanova. At this hour?

"Hey, Angie. You know what time it is?"

"Tell me about it." Her throaty laugh pinged off the cell's thin speaker. "Sonny's havin' a fit, lyin' here next to me tryin' to sleep. Fuck him. This is business."

"Police business?"

"Is there any other kind? I'm the Community Liaison Officer, right? So this is me liasoning, if that's a word. Anyway, we need you to clear your schedule for the rest of the week. Reschedule your patients."

"Why?"

"'Cause you're a police consultant, which means you draw a salary from the city. Which means we get to make requests like this once in a while."

"But you still haven't told me why."

"Treva Williams, for one thing. The detectives workin' the case say she's formed a real bond with you. Trusts you. As the sole surviving hostage, we need her help. So we need *your* help to keep her from freakin' out on us."

"This is coming from Biegler?"

"Don't think so small, Danny boy. Sinclair himself called me. And told me the mayor called *him*. Remember, you're still considered a real PR asset to the department. Though I've always thought you were over-rated."

Again, that throaty laugh came through the phone.

"Love you, too, Angie. Truth is, I was thinking along those same lines myself. About cancelling my next few days. I've got a funeral to go to, as well as another session scheduled with Treva and the cops. Plus anything else the department may need from me."

"Then we're all on the same page. Thank God for small favors. So. Now that we've conducted our official business, how 'bout some *un*official gossip?"

"Do I even want to hear this?"

"I'm bettin' you do. You know that sedan Roarke stole from the hospital parking lot?"

"The one he ditched at the construction site. I heard it's Biegler's unmarked."

"That's right. So they bring it back to impound and CSU's all over it. Meanwhile, Biegler's spittin' nails, he's so mad. He'd just had the motor pool detail it for him. Like new, they made it. Now it's all banged up, windows smashed, whatever. The only good news is that it was cleaned so recently, all the prints are brand new."

"Roarke's, I assume. And Biegler's. Right?"

"Now here's where it gets interesting. There's one other set of prints. Perfect match for ones we already got in the system. Guess whose?"

"Biegler's wife?"

"He wishes. Prints belong to a hooker named LaWanda Collins. Real street veteran. They call her the Golden Tongue. Very cop-friendly, if ya know what I mean."

"Jesus. Are you telling me that Biegler was stupid enough to pick up a hooker in his unmarked?"

"Yeah, probably to take her for a soda. One can only speculate. Maybe he figured she'd be impressed by what a nice clean car he drives."

I looked out at the night through my windshield. The story almost made me feel sorry for Stu Biegler. It was embarrassing enough that a police lieutenant would leave his car unlocked and the keys in the ignition. Now this?

"How's Biegler dealing with it?"

"How do you think? Word is, he's trying to bury it. Lose the CSU report. Wouldn't surprise me if he tried to bribe the techs."

"Well, he's screwed if gets back to the chief."

"Not as screwed as he'll be if it gets back to his wife."

◇◇◇

I got out of the car and unlocked the front door of my small, split-level house overlooking the Point. The timer had turned on the living room lamps, so I walked in and out of the shadowed spaces in between and entered the bedroom.

Then the bathroom. Then, after a long, hot shower, I changed into shorts and a Pitt t-shirt and went back to the living room.

I poured myself a Jack Daniels, neat, and pulled up a chair at the roll top desk. Looked sleepily at the blinking light on the land-line answering machine. And didn't move a muscle.

It wouldn't be a patient. They only had my office number. Some worried friends or colleagues, maybe? Because I knew enough from my experiences last year that a case of this size would be all over the news. And that I'd be mentioned. A lot.

Because somehow, without seeking it, I'd once again gotten involved in a major police investigation.

I took a sip of my drink, recalling something that Harry Polk had said. That my only job was to head-shrink the crime victims sent to me by the department. And that's all I'd been doing this past year, ever since the Wingfield case. Seeing patients. Helping them cope with whatever horrors they'd endured. Dutifully filing follow-up reports to Angie Villanova. And staying out of trouble myself.

Until now.

I downed my drink, got up and poured another, then came back and sat down. Pushed the button on the answering machine.

The first message was from Noah Frye. In his typical roundabout, fragmented way, he apologized for hanging up on me earlier. The bar had gotten busy, Charlene was busting his balls, etc.

Bullshit, I thought. We'd been talking about Andy the Android. His suicide. And Noah had grown increasingly upset about it. Understandably, given Noah's own history. I just hoped that what happened to Andy didn't derail the progress Noah had been making lately.

I rubbed my eyes, and made a mental note to confirm with Charlene that Noah stayed committed to taking his meds. Then, swallowing the rest of my drink, I listened to the second message.

The caller was Brian Fletcher. Though it took me a moment to place the name. Leland Sinclair's campaign manager. The slick guy with the gold cufflinks I'd met in Sinclair's downtown office.

Christ, I thought. Seemed like a year ago, yet it was only fourteen hours.

I hit replay and listened more closely this time. Fletcher was reminding me about the big fundraiser at the Burgoyne Plaza tomorrow night. Or, to be accurate, since it was three in the morning, later tonight.

"Lee will expect you there at seven. Black tie. No attitude. Okay, buddy?"

I looked down at the answering machine. "Gotcha," I said aloud. "Buddy."

By now, I could barely keep my eyes open, so I went into the kitchen, put the glass in the sink and the Jack Daniels in the liquor cabinet and went to bed.

Before I let myself crash, however, I used the TV remote to find the local CNN affiliate. As I expected, the manhunt for Roarke was the lead story. The assistant chief, face pinched and haggard, spoke to a row of microphones, detailing the extent and breadth of the search. Including putting security personnel on special alert at the airport, train stations and the central bus terminal. And how this was all being coordinated in conjunction with the FBI.

Next up was a short piece on the young cop Roarke had shot in the throat during his escape. Thankfully, his surgery had been successful, and his doctors soon upgraded his status from critical to stable. "He's expected to make a full recovery," said the reporter on-scene.

From here, the story switched to short bios of the three dead bank employees, as well as an exclusive interview with security guard George Vickers' grief-stricken widow. To help viewers better relate to what she was going through, the camera helpfully zoomed in on her blanched, tear-streaked face.

Fuck this, I thought, and was about to click it off when I saw a video replay from First Allegheny's home office in Harrisburg. The CEO stood uncomfortably in the lobby of their corporate headquarters, the bank's logo bannered over his left shoulder. He read a prepared statement expressing his outrage over the attempted robbery, and offering his sincere condolences to the families of the victims.

Finally, the story's cycle ended with statements from both Sinclair's office and that of City Councilman John Garrity. As suggested this afternoon in Sinclair's office, the DA's media flacks delivered an earnest spiel about how the brave actions of the Pittsburgh police routed the gunmen and prevented further violence.

I shut off the TV before seeing Garrity's response to the day's events. Having heard him speak a few times before, I knew the short, heavy-set politician would say something either pious or stupid. Probably both. Then he'd end with some veiled comments about Sinclair's failings as the city's district attorney.

Seeing the news made me think of something, though, and I reached for the phone on the bedside table. And called Nancy Mendors.

I figured she'd be up, since I knew she was an insomniac. I had to assume she'd been watching the news, or at least had heard about the day's events, and I didn't want her to worry about me.

To my surprise, Nancy didn't answer. Instead, I got her machine.

"Nancy, it's Danny. Sorry to be calling so late, but I figured you'd heard about the bank thing and my involvement in the whole mess. I just didn't want you to worry. I'm fine. The media's got half the story wrong anyway, which is why it's a good idea not to believe everything you see on the news."

I paused, thinking she might have been in another room. The bathroom or somewhere. But she didn't pick up.

"Okay, well, that's it, I guess. I'll see you tomorrow at Andy Parker's burial service. Bye."

I was about to hang up when I had another thought.

"One more thing, Nancy. Could you email me Andy's records from the clinic as soon as you get this? I'd really appreciate it. Thanks. Good-night."

Then I hung up. Lay back against the bed pillows, staring up at the ceiling. The play of the city's lights arrayed there, coming from the window.

I found myself wondering why I'd asked to see Andy's medical records. It was just an impulse, but I'd long ago decided that I rarely went wrong following one. Even if I didn't know why I was doing so, or where it would lead.

Plus, something that Noah had said earlier today on the phone kept nagging at the back of my mind. About Andy's suicide. Probably meant nothing. But still…

As I felt myself drifting off, I replayed those horrific images from inside the bank. The bodies sprawled on the cold marble. The dark blood, pooling beneath them.

Until, not surprisingly, I fell into a restless, dream-troubled sleep.

Chapter Twenty-six

Rosemont Cemetery, in suburban Edgewood, was a rolling sprawl of low hills carpeted in thick grass leached of its greenish hue by days of punishing sun. Even the shade thrown by the occasional small grove of oak and maple trees did little to offset the sense of parched, acrid stillness that enveloped the place.

It was nearing noon, and—as Noah had predicted—I was roasting in my one dark suit I kept for such occasions. I parked in the graveled lot, sunlight flaring off the windshields of adjacent cars like mini-novas. As I made my way to the ancient wrought-iron entrance gate, I remembered the last time I'd been here.

Too long ago, I realized bitterly. My annual visit to my parents' parallel graves on their anniversary. A promise I'd made to my old man right before his inevitable death from liver failure. Echoing a promise he'd made to my mother right before she herself had died.

I wondered, as I headed toward the small cluster of mourners on the knoll up ahead, if there'd be anyone around at the end of *my* life. Someone from whom I could extract, through guilt or guile, a similar promise.

By the time I'd reached the burial site, the cemetery chaplain had already begun the service. About a dozen people stood looking down at the coffin, its sleek black lines glazed by sunlight. From where I stood, just across from the array of mourners, I could sense their palpable discomfort in the blazing heat.

Almost feel the sweat beading their foreheads, streaking their dark jackets.

I only recognized a few of them. A couple staff clinicians from Ten Oaks, eyes hidden behind dark glasses. Plus some long-term patients who'd been residents at the clinic since before I even interned there. They stood huddled together, awkward and dismayed, as though there'd be strength in numbers against these troubling rituals of an alien world.

Closer to the grave itself were a couple I took to be Andy's parents. Though they were obviously estranged. Separate. Both expensively, tastefully dressed. Both with heads turned toward the chaplain. The polite attentiveness of the disinterested. My guess was that, in their minds, their son had been lost to them a long time ago.

Then a woman's plaintive sobs, audible above the pious drone of the chaplain, drew my attention. She was young, barely twenty, pale and thin. One of the group of mourners from Ten Oaks. Though she stood apart from them, alongside an equally young man with close-cropped brown hair. He was attempting to comfort her, putting his arm around her waist. But she shoved him away, her eyes flinty with anger and disgust. Boring into his, until he had to turn away.

Which brought him into eye contact with me. For a long moment, we just stared across the open grave at each other. Then he adjusted the sleeves of his ill-fitting suit jacket and walked stiffly back to join the rest of the mourners.

As the chaplain finished his prayers, we all bowed our heads and watched through hooded eyes as two burly cemetery workers began shoveling dirt over the coffin. Consigning Andrew Parker once more to the unforgiving earth.

It was then that I saw Nancy Mendors, her slim form having been hidden behind that of the stout chaplain. I hadn't seen her in some time, yet she didn't seem to have changed. The same frank, solemn eyes. Pretty oval face framed by rich dark hair. Though she was a year or two older than me, her body was still slender, compact.

She noticed me then, too, and we exchanged brief, sad smiles. And not just because of our shared grief about Andy's death.

It was more or less the way we always greeted each other, no matter how much time had gone by.

And probably always would.

◇◇◇

Earlier this morning, after getting dressed and phoning my patients to reschedule the week's appointments, I'd checked my email to see if Nancy had forwarded Andy Parker's medical records. She had. At four AM.

While I printed them out, I poured a second cup of black coffee and checked the TV news for updates about the robbery investigation. Nothing new there. More details about the slain bank employees and their families. Including footage of a makeshift memorial someone had placed in front of the bank. Photos of the victims, in and among an array of flowers. Hand-made placards displaying words of sympathy, condolence. Verses from the Bible.

There was also a second interview with George Vickers' widow. I noted that she'd had a bit of a makeover since the first one. Hair done up, more stylish glasses. And she had a grim-faced man in a three-piece-suit standing next to her. "A family friend," according to the news reporter, "as well as an attorney representing Mrs. Vickers."

So it begins, I thought. The media-stoked bonfire of grief and outrage. The finger-pointing. The civil suits. The on-screen parade of lawyers and pundits.

I clicked to another local channel, whose coverage focused more on the search for the two bank robbers. I caught the tail end of the anchorman's report, which seemed merely to reflect the official party line.

As with most newscasts when there isn't much new information to impart, the report emphasized those few facts available. These being limited to biographical details about one of the gunmen, Wheeler Roarke, whose past links to both law enforcement and private security in the Middle East formed the bulk of the report. Moreover, by now photos of Roarke (including, unfortunately, one showing him in his Chicago PD uniform) were all over the Internet, which the program displayed in continuous rotation behind the anchorman as he spoke.

I finished my coffee, shut off the TV and retrieved the printed copies of Andy's records. I took them with me into the kitchen, now suffused with light through the broad bay window, and stood reading by the sink.

According to his file, Andrew Parker had been a patient at Ten Oaks since his teens. The child of wealthy, divorced parents who'd been more than happy to unload him on someone else, Andy had been immediately diagnosed as a paranoid schizophrenic and assigned to various staff therapists and case managers over the ensuing years.

As I already knew, his primary delusion was his conviction that he wasn't human. That he was an android, a mechanical man like out of a sci-fi movie. As a result, he often had to be fed intravenously, against his will, since, as he claimed, "machines don't need to eat."

He'd been placed on a variety of psychotropic meds over the years, with varying degrees of success. Sometimes he'd go for months at a time in which the delusion receded, and, though depressed and uncommunicative, he seemed less tormented.

But these periods were few and far between. Plus he was reporting more intense physical discomfort. He complained frequently that his CPS—whatever that was—hurt. Whenever his case manager expressed confusion as to what these initials referred to, Andy would fly into a kind of controlled rage. Arms and legs moving stiffly, robotically. Hurling himself around the office.

Of more concern were the increasing number of suicide attempts, especially in this past year. Self-inflicted puncture wounds to his neck, abdomen. Often using tools from the shed at the rear end of the rec yard. The same building in which he'd hanged himself last week.

I put aside the sheaf of papers with a heavy sigh. Though his particular set of symptoms were unusual, the pattern of behavior was achingly familiar for a patient like Andy. The occasional respite from delusion. The promising initial results of a new medication cocktail giving way to lowered expectations. The slow but undeterred deterioration. The increasing number of suicide attempts, leading up to some significant marker—in this case, Andy's thirtieth birthday.

All numbingly familiar. Another sober statistic to add to the reams of data compiled by every psychiatric facility in every city in the world.

I bent at the sink then, hands gripping the counter. Looked out at the obscenely bright, sunlit day. Rolled my shoulders against the tight knots lodged there like marbles under the skin.

I felt somehow jangly and dispirited at the same time. I needed to do something physical. Go for a run. Hit the well-worn heavy bag that hung from a hook in my basement gym. Punch…something.

Instead, I straightened my tie in the reflection from the refrigerator door, went out to my car, and drove down the hill to watch them bury Andy the Android.

Chapter Twenty-seven

When Nancy and I finally hugged, I noticed one thing about her that had changed. Her perfume. It was something slightly more exotic. I don't know anything about scents, but it seemed tinged with some kind of spice. All I knew for sure was that she smelled different from how she used to when I held her close.

We were standing just beyond the ring of mourners, a few of whom were talking in hushed tones, or exchanging commiserating comments with the chaplain. Again, though part of the group from the clinic, the pale young woman and the brown-haired man were standing apart. Arguing in fierce, barely contained whispers.

Finally, the young woman pushed herself away from the man and ran over to speak to one of the Ten Oaks clinicians who'd attended the ceremony.

Nancy, her hand still on my shoulder, had noticed me watching the couple and followed my eyes. I turned back to look at her.

"You know those two lovebirds?"

"Her name's Victoria Tolan. Been a patient at Ten Oaks for a couple years. He's a newbie named Stan Willis."

"What's their story?"

"Beats me. I didn't even know they knew each other. I mean, that well. Though Ten Oaks is a pretty tight-knit community. Everybody knows everybody else."

"I know. I remember."

She smiled warmly. "It's good to see you, Dan. It's been too long."

"Since that whole Wingfield thing, I guess."

I took her arm and we started walking across the grass toward the parking lot.

Nancy Mendors and I had met when I was an intern at Ten Oaks. Then, years later, and only a few months after my wife's murder, Nancy went through a bitter divorce. Both of us still reeling, we fell into a brief, passionate affair. Using clinging, desperate sex as a salve against loss and regret.

When it ended as abruptly as it had begun, we managed to remain good friends. Even though we saw each other infrequently, our worlds rarely intersecting. Nancy had stayed on staff at Ten Oaks, while I'd gone into private practice. Yet, for some reason, the bond we'd formed during that period of shared pain and mutual solace still sustained us.

It also allowed for a bracing honesty.

"You know," I said as we neared the parking lot, "I feel like a jerk for not calling you when I heard the news. About your being made clinical director at Ten Oaks."

"You *should* feel like a jerk." Though her voice was smiling. "Are you too famous now to get together with old friends?"

I ducked my head. Pulled her closer to me. "Truth is, all I've done since the Wingfield case is concentrate on work. Try to recuperate—mentally *and* physically—from what happened."

"Then what are you doing mixed up in this bank thing?"

"God only knows. I don't even know if I can be of any help, but the cops've pulled rank on me. Put me on call for the week."

Nancy gave an involuntary shiver. "I saw that guy Roarke's picture on TV. Those shark eyes. God, I hope they catch him soon."

"Me, too. My head still hurts from where he slugged me."

She stopped, fists clenched on her hips.

"See, that's my point, Danny. You're a therapist, for Christ's sake. Not a cop. What the hell were you doing, mixing it up with some bank robber? Didn't you get your fill of stupid danger last year?"

"Funny, Noah scolded me about the same thing. Are you two talking behind my back?"

"I would if I thought it would do any good. But…"

She sighed, brought her hands up to grasp mine. Clutched them to my chest. "Please, Danny. Just be careful. For once in your life, stay on the goddam sidelines."

"Now that *is* funny, coming from the clinical director of a prominent psych hospital. Hell, you're on the front lines every day, fighting the good fight."

She laughed. "Right. If you consider wading through oceans of paperwork and haggling with insurance companies the front lines…"

"Believe me, I do. Give me a stone killer with a loaded gun anytime."

By then, we'd reached the edge of the parking lot. To our left, the two Ten Oaks clinicians were leading a crooked line of patients to a small yellow bus idling at the curb. Waiting to take them back to the clinic.

Nancy nodded in their direction.

"I'm glad we were able to organize this for Andy. Especially given how long he'd been at Ten Oaks. Still, only a few patients were that close to him, as you can imagine. He didn't welcome it. Particularly given his difficulty in reading social cues."

"Was he bothered by that?"

Her look was rueful. "Why would he be? Since when do machines pick up on social cues?"

I nodded. Andy's delusion—as was true with many schizophrenics—had served a multitude of functions. Protective. Isolating. And, of course, providing him an explicit explanation for his alienation, his intense feelings of estrangement. To patients like Andy, their delusions were often the only thing that made sense in a senseless world.

One of the staff therapists was waving now in our direction, as he shepherded the last two patients onto the bus. I wasn't surprised to see that it was the couple I'd noticed arguing at the grave. Victoria Tolan and Stan Willis.

As the therapist climbed aboard the bus behind them, Nancy turned to me.

"I probably should head back, too, Danny. Walk me to my car?"

The patient bus roared to life and headed toward the exit. Nancy and I involuntarily stepped back as a plume of exhaust trailed from the bus and hung, suspended like a low-lying cloud, in the still air.

Her car was parked not far from mine. We reached it in another minute, during which neither of us spoke.

As she rummaged in her purse for her car keys, I leaned against the hood, arms folded.

"Can I ask you a couple questions about Andy? I'm curious about a few things I read in his file."

"Only a few?"

"Good point. Well, for one thing, he complained to his case manager about his CPS, whatever the hell that is. Says it hurt a lot."

Nancy chuckled. "Yeah, that one stumped us for a while. CPS stands for Cranial Processing Software. His android brain. All it meant was that he had a headache."

I took this in. "What about his earlier suicide attempts? Didn't that indicate a need to change his meds?"

"Of course. Which we did, frequently. Plus we monitored him more strictly. Or as much as possible. You know what it's like managing that many patients."

"But according to his files, he seemed to be getting worse."

Nancy opened the driver's side door and stood up inside it. Intentionally or not, keeping it between me and her. A barrier.

"I know. From personal experience." She paused. "I found him once. After one of his last suicide attempts. In the pantry off the kitchen. He'd stolen a screwdriver from the work shed and stabbed himself in the abdomen."

"Poor bastard."

She bit her lip. "He almost succeeded that time. Given the blood loss. Internal injuries."

We both grew quiet. Nancy still standing behind the opened door. Me still leaning against the hood.

Something hung, unsaid, in the air. Like that exhaust cloud from the bus.

"Look," I said at last, "I know you have to go. We can discuss Andy some other—"

"Dan, there's something I have to tell you."

Her voice was uncustomarily sharp. Clipped. As though she'd had to screw up her courage to get the words out. Hands clutching the door frame, as if for support.

"What is it?"

She swallowed. Her eyes were moist.

"I…I've met someone. A pediatric surgeon. Over at Children's Hospital." A careful pause. "That's why I wasn't home when you called last night. I was with Warren."

I nodded. Which was all I could think to do.

Nancy took another breath.

"Warren and I…well, I wanted you to know. To find out from me first. We're engaged."

Chapter Twenty-eight

After I'd watched Nancy pull out of the parking lot, I retraced my steps back into the cemetery and sought out my parents' graves. Standing alone on a treeless patch of yellowed grass, I looked down at the small, plain headstones. Feeling the familiar mix of loss and regret. For the mother I barely knew, the father I knew only too well.

At least the part of him I got to see: the anger, the bitterness. The disappointment with the way his life had turned out. Including, I suspected, the way *I'd* turned out. Too much like him, in some ways, and at the same time so different as to seem like an alien.

No epiphany visited me as I stood there, head bowed, the sun beating down like a shower of white heat. Until I didn't want to stand there any longer and went back to where my car was parked. The only one left in the graveled lot. I got in and steered my way to the exit. In minutes, I was on the parkway heading into town.

Replaying in my head my conversation with Nancy.

I had to admit, her news had come as a shock. Of course, I'd made all the appropriate noises after she told me. Congratulated her. Wished her the best.

Which was how I truly felt.

Yet, as I hugged her good-bye, and kissed her neck, the scent of that unfamiliar perfume stung me. To my shame, I felt envious. The new perfume signifying to me that her life had changed. That *she'd* changed. Moved on.

And I had not.

But did I even want to? After our romantic relationship ended, had I ever wanted more from Nancy than just friendship? No matter how close, how intimate. Had she?

I pulled into the parking lot at Pittsburgh Memorial and cut the engine. Sat staring out the windshield at the bright, cloudless day.

It didn't matter now. Nancy had found someone who made her happy, and as her friend I was sincerely glad for her.

Just as it was my duty—as her friend—to let her go.

◇◇◇

"How much have you had to drink?" I asked Harry Polk as we rode up in the elevator to Ward B.

He frowned, as though he hadn't heard right. "When?"

"Just now. At lunch."

"What are you, my mother?"

"Don't bullshit me, Harry. I'm starting to worry about you."

He pursed his lips. "Is that a fact? Well, don't put yourself out. And don't play therapist with me. You know what I think o' that stuff. Voodoo horseshit for wing-nuts and losers."

I reached across and hit the elevator's stop button. The car rumbled to a halt.

"Indulge me," I said.

Now he was fuming. Stood shifting his weight from one foot to the other.

"You been talkin' to Lowrey, ain'tcha?"

"I don't need to talk to her. Or anyone. I have eyes, Harry. And a nose. I can smell it on your breath. Hell, even your clothes reek."

A dark grin. "That's why God invented breath mints. *And* after-shave."

"Well, He didn't invent enough of it. You think Biegler doesn't know what's going on?"

"From what I hear, he's got enough to deal with without worryin' about me. Nice piece o' ass, that LaWanda. Real cop-friendly." A sidelong look. "So I've heard."

"Me, too. But I'm serious, Harry. You know that the whole 'tough, hard-drinking cop' thing is just Hollywood nonsense. Guys like that don't stay detectives for long. Guys like that get transferred. Or suspended and sent to the department shrink. Or just kicked off the force."

"Is that so? How do you know?" Polk stepped forward, eyes narrowing. "Unless you're just goin' down Memory Lane, thinkin' about your old man. Kind of a legend around here, that mook. Put it away pretty good, on duty and off. Till his liver couldn't take it no more."

I felt the anger build in my chest. Forced myself to breathe evenly. Slowly.

"What?" Polk's voice held a challenge. "You gonna take a swing at me? A cop? I don't think you'll like county lock-up, Danny boy. I hear the wine list sucks."

We stood eyeball-to-eyeball in the cramped, unmoving elevator car. I felt the tension climbing up my arms, gathering in my throat.

I knew at that moment that one of us had to take a step back. I also saw that Polk wasn't going to budge.

He was the law. He didn't have to.

Finally, I let out a long breath and back-stepped into the near corner. Extended my hand until I could reach the stop button and release it. With a shudder, the car lurched into motion again.

When the elevator doors opened on Ward B, Harry Polk adjusted his tie and squinted at me.

"Glad we had this little chat," he said. "But let's not make it a habit."

"Listen, Harry…"

"No, *you* listen. Maybe we're friends, maybe we ain't. But keep your goddam nose outta my business, okay?"

Then, voice thick and hard: "And tell Lowrey that goes for her, too."

◇◇◇

They'd moved Treva to a private room at the end of the hall. As Polk and I entered, the seasoned, sturdily-built duty nurse turned from adjusting the window blinds and smiled. The afternoon sun threw soft, diffused light against the opposite wall.

The nurse nodded at Treva, who lay against her bed pillows, eyes half-lidded. But awake. With no IV drip, no monitors.

"They've given permission for you gentlemen to talk to her," the nurse said. "But not for too long. Okay?"

Treva opened her eyes. "It's okay, Ruth. I'm fine."

"And where did you get your medical degree, dear?"

The nurse waved her hand at Treva, gave Polk and me a serious look, and brushed past us out the door.

I went over to Treva's bedside and smiled down at her.

"I wouldn't mess with Ruth if I were you." I pulled a chair from the near corner and sat.

Treva took her hand from under the bed covers and put it gently on mine.

"It's nice to see you again, Dr. Rinaldi."

"You can call me Dan."

Polk came closer then, too, standing stiffly at the end of her bed.

"And you can call me Sergeant Polk, Ms. Williams." He pulled a notebook from his back pocket. "I know we have to keep this short, but we do need a statement from you. About what happened in the bank."

"I know." Treva wet her lips. "I also know everyone's been very patient with me."

"Not at all," I said. "After what you've been through, if you still want a little more time to rest…"

Polk angrily cleared his throat, a sound like a truck backfiring.

Treva gave him a wry look. "I'm happy to tell you what I can."

"Good." Casting a warning glance at me. "Now, how 'bout you start at the beginning, Ms. Williams. At the bank. When the first masked man entered…"

I just sat back and listened as Treva repeated the story she'd told me on the curb outside the bank. This time, there was no hesitation. No confusion. Though her voice quavered at certain points. Or grew so quiet you could barely hear it.

What was more surprising was Polk's reaction. Rather than encouraging his witness to take her time, letting her story unspool in as much detail as possible, he kept interrupting her. He seemed impatient, irritated. More than once he tapped his pen briskly on his pad.

If Treva was upset by this, or even noticed it at all, she didn't show it. Instead, what I saw on her face was a rising grief, the slow-welling sorrow of remembrance.

And I knew why. As she gave her statement, it was clear that she'd relinquished the comforting fantasy that what happened in the bank had been a dream. Enough time had gone by that her conscious mind had grasped and accepted the reality of what had occurred.

Which was why, as she finished her narrative, the emotional strain of the experience was plainly evident. Her face had paled. Eyes pinched, almost to a squint. Fingers twitching anxiously on the sheets.

"Then…well, the last thing I remember is the tall man looking out the window. Real upset."

"Probably when he saw SWAT taking up positions outside the bank," Polk said.

"I guess. All of a sudden he called out to the police that he was letting one hostage leave. Just one." Treva paused. "Then he pointed his gun at me and said, 'You're it, girlie.' And pushed me out the front door. Suddenly, all these policemen surrounded me, grabbing my arms. Pulling me away from the bank…"

Another, longer pause. "Then I sort of…went blank. And that's all I can remember. Until…" She looked at me. "Until I was sitting on the curb with you."

"You did fine, Treva," I said.

"Yeah." Polk pocketed his notebook. Glanced at his watch. "Real good. Thanks, Ms. Williams."

Treva pushed herself up to a sitting position. "I guess you want to ask me about last night, too? When that man took me and Dr. Holloway down to fix his arm."

"Hold on," I said. "That's enough for now. There'll be plenty of time later to—"

"But I'm feeling better. Honest. And I want to be helpful…"

"You've been *very* helpful," Polk said quickly. "But Doc Rinaldi is right. You oughtta rest up. Besides, we got Holloway's statement about what happened. We can talk to you about it later. In case we need to fill in any gaps."

I could tell Polk was getting more and more anxious to leave. Not that he was being exactly subtle about it.

"Ready to roll, Doc?"

As I started to rise from my chair, Treva clutched my arm through the bed rails.

"Would it be okay if you stayed a few minutes?" Eyes searching my face. "Just to talk?"

I turned to Polk. "You need me for anything else?"

He shrugged. "I didn't need ya for *this*. But, sure…far as I'm concerned, you're off the departmental clock."

Then, with a quick nod at Treva, he strode out of the room. Footsteps clicking purposefully on the well-scuffed linoleum as he went down the hall.

Some instinct made me step to the door and look out. Polk had just pushed the elevator button, and was pacing impatiently back and forth in front of the closed doors. Stopping only to jab the elevator button again.

I turned back into the room. My first impression about Polk had been mistaken. He wasn't deteriorating from booze, or poor health, or lack of sleep. Nor some deep distress.

He was gripped by urgency. Impatience.

Harry Polk was a man on a mission.

Chapter Twenty-nine

"Ellie's told you about us, hasn't she?"

Treva's gaze at me was frank, unwavering. She was sitting up now, hands kneading on her lap. Yet she seemed calmer, more assured. Less fragile.

I was back in my chair at her bedside.

"How do you know what Eleanor's told me?"

"It wasn't hard to guess. She told me she was calling someone who could help. Someone she trusted. So I figured she'd end up telling you."

"Is that okay? I mean, that I know about your prior relationship?"

She smiled. "Now you sound like this shrink I had once. Guy was totally full of shit."

"Then I'll try not to sound like him."

Treva leaned back, gazed at me warily. As though, perhaps for the first time, sizing me up.

"I'm…well, I guess I'm not real good at trusting men. Not used to the idea, anyway."

I said nothing. Waited.

She closed her eyes then, took a long breath. When she opened them again, her look was as clear and focused as I'd ever seen in her.

"I guess you're surprised that I didn't want Ellie to be here. That I didn't want to see her."

"I *was* surprised, yes. Why was that?"

"Because I feel too guilty. Because of what I did."

"You mean, when you left her? All those years ago?"

She nodded. "She really loved me. And I left her for some guy who turned out to be a real bastard. Who cheated on me... beat me..."

"He beat you?"

"I thought he was exciting. Dangerous. You know, in that sexy, bad-boy way. I wanted someone different, someone who'd rock my world. Well, he sure did. Rocked the hell out of it. And I had the broken heart—*and* broken bones—to prove it."

Her slender shoulders lifted. A weary shrug.

"Karmic payback, I guess. For what I did to Ellie. Do you believe in things like that, Dr. Rinaldi?"

"I'm afraid that question's above my pay grade. And, please— call me Dan."

She shook her head.

"No, it feels better calling you 'doctor.'"

"Then, of course. Whatever's most comfortable."

Treva looked past me, toward the sunlight serrated by the window blinds.

"I've had a lot of stupid relationships since then. Done a lot of stupid things. Bounced around. Lost. And then...see, this job at the bank is the first good job I've ever had. I'm only a junior associate, but Mr. Franconi—he's the manager—Mr. Franconi said I showed real promise. That I had a flair." A rueful smile. "First time anybody's ever told me something like *that*."

I leaned forward, but kept silent. Watched conflicting emotions flicker across her face.

"Then there was this other thing that happened. A man. A good man, who loved me. And I loved him."

I spoke carefully. "Bobby Marks."

Her chin lowered, and she began to cry. Silent tears, that welled up at the corners of her eyes.

"I...Bobby and I had been seeing each other for months. We'd even begun talking about moving in together. Maybe marriage.

But Bobby wanted to be cautious about things. He said Mr. Franconi frowned on office romances. That if they went wrong, it was bad for office morale."

"It must have been difficult," I said. "Keeping it a secret."

"It was. Especially because I was so happy...I mean, I hadn't felt like that since...Well, since Ellie and I were together."

She gave me a sharp look. "And you don't believe in karma? I finally find someone, and then this...*thing*...happens. Poor Bobby. He was so sweet. So..."

I let her sit with her pain, her sorrow, for a few minutes. Then I risked touching her shoulder.

"I'm so sorry, Treva."

More than she knew, I could relate to what she was feeling. The unbearable grief. Trying to come to terms with the inexplicable randomness of violence. How—in a matter of moments—it can tear your life apart.

Her sobs grew more intense, wracked her whole body. At first, I was alarmed. Concerned that she might be convulsing. I was about to call out for the nurse. What the hell was her name—?

Then, just as quickly, Treva's tremors subsided. But her breathing turned to shallow gasps.

She finally looked up, her eyes wide, ghostly white. They held not grief, but fear. A kind of terror.

"Please, Dr. Rinaldi..."

Suddenly, her hands—both hands—were gripping mine. Clutching as though clinging for life.

"Treva, what is it?"

"*Please*..." She was distraught. Terrified. "Please promise you'll take care of me."

"Of course, I..."

"No, *promise* me! You promised you'd ride in the ambulance with me, and you *didn't*."

Her fingers tightened their grip. Went white. I felt the strength of her panic.

"*Please!*" Her words thick with anguish.

"Treva, I..."

I hesitated only a moment. Unsure exactly what she was talking about. What was going on inside her.

Until, at a loss, I nodded. "I promise."

Chapter Thirty

"Stand still, will ya?" Noah said. "You're breakin' my concentration."

We were standing together in the riverfront bar's small kitchen, and Noah Frye was helping me with my tux. To be exact, he was fixing the knot on my tie.

"Hurry it up, Noah. Traffic's gonna be murder."

Ignoring me, Noah unhurriedly tugged on one end of the tie's bow, then the other. Making them even.

"I don't mean to go all OCD on your ass, man, but if a thing's worth doin', it's worth doin' right. Right?"

Which was Thelonius' cue to meow his agreement. The cat was perched atop the refrigerator, peering down with detached curiosity. A Zen monk with fur.

"Dammit, Noah—"

"There!" He stepped back, hands outstretched as though a magician who's pulled off a miracle. "Given what I had to work with, you're not half-bad lookin' in that tux."

"Half-bad is good enough for me. It's a rental. Now let me go, okay? I should've been at the Burgoyne Plaza a half hour ago."

"So you'll be fashionably late. As Miss Manners says, 'Fuck 'em if they can't take a joke.'"

Just then, Charlene came through the doors from the bar area. Gave me a broad, leering grin.

"Hey, Danny. You look good enough to put on top of a wedding cake."

"Thanks. But I just came by to talk to Noah for a few minutes."

Her mood changed quickly. "About that Andy kid, I hope. Noah's been mopin' around all day about it."

"I don't mope." Noah folded his arms over his broad chest. "I reflect. I ponder."

"Whatever." Charlene came over to me, gave me a kiss on the cheek, and headed back out to the bar. Calling over her shoulder to Noah: "I'll just be out here, reflecting and pondering about why I put up with you."

After she'd gone, he turned to me: "Chick's crazy about me. It's kinda touching, eh? The way she keeps her true feelings bottled up."

"She's right about one thing, Noah." I smoothed the sleeves of the tux jacket. Damn thing felt tight across the shoulders. Not that I cared. "You're upset about Andy's suicide. Perfectly understandable, of course, but…"

Noah waved me away. Turned and started stacking dirty dishes in the dishwasher.

"You *know* you need to talk about it," I said. "If not with me, with Charlene. Or maybe Nancy Mendors."

"No, I don't need to talk about it." Keeping his back to me. "I need to stop thinkin' about it."

"Why?"

"Because it don't make any sense."

He straightened, rubbing his hands on his jeans. But still not looking at me.

"I heard from some bros o' mine over at Ten Oaks that Andy been actin' worse and worse these last couple weeks. I mean, it looked for a time like his new meds were workin'. He wasn't acting so fucked up. Talkin' that android shit. Then all of a sudden, he starts up again. About not bein' human and everything."

I took a guess.

"Are you worried that your own medications will stop working? That things…that they might get bad again…?"

Without turning, his head bobbed slowly. As though he were ashamed. Revealed. This big, shaggy bear of a man, standing in a too-small kitchen. In a converted coal barge moored by the river.

As I was reminded again of the effort it took for him to hold things together. Meds or no meds. To keep walking his own, hazardous path. In Noah's words, keeping this side of crazy.

"You're not Andy Parker," I said at last. "What happened to him isn't going to happen to you."

Finally, he turned back around. Faced me.

"It almost did. Remember?"

"I'll never forget it. But we—you and me, Charlene, all of us—we just have to stay vigilant. Keep our eye on the prize."

A doubtful look. "And what would *that* be?"

I reached over and gripped his shoulders. Met his skeptical gaze. "*You*, Noah. Alive and kicking and annoying the hell out of everybody. The prize would be you."

◇◇◇

Just a few hours before, I'd left Treva Williams at the hospital and headed home to change for Sinclair's political bash tonight. Which was when I remembered that the affair was formal.

Cursing under my breath, I made a U-turn onto Fifth and crawled along the row of storefronts, looking for a tux place. To my surprise, I spotted one pretty quickly, and even found a parking space less than two blocks away.

It took about thirty minutes to try on a traditional tuxedo, half of which were spent listening to the tailor fuss and fret about inseams, sleeve length, and creases.

Though I didn't hear a word of it. I was thinking about Treva, and what had happened in her hospital room.

At first thought, her panic made perfect sense. It was a classic symptom among victims of violence: the expectation of some future horror. A kind of hyper-vigilance about the potential dangers that lay ahead.

Particularly in her case. Not only had she been held hostage in an armed hold-up, she'd suffered the trauma of witnessing the cold-blooded murder of the man she loved.

Then, that same night, Roarke had taken her at gunpoint from the apparent safety of her hospital room. Bound her with duct tape. She was trapped by the same armed madman who would most likely kill her as soon as his wounds had been attended to.

If a person as seemingly sturdy and psychologically well-armored as Lloyd Holloway was shaken to the core by that experience, I couldn't even imagine what it had done to Treva. Someone whose psyche was decidedly more fragile.

It was now my job to find out.

Chapter Thirty-one

The lobby of the Burgoyne Plaza had the grandeur of a French chateau, complete with *belle époque* furnishings whose hand-carved lines gleamed beneath the massive crystal chandelier. According to the Pittsburgh Chamber of Commerce, the newly-built hotel was the crown jewel of the city's Renaissance. The perfect accommodation for visiting presidents, dignitaries, and corporate giants.

So, naturally, I fit right in.

Though I must admit, as I walked up the enormous winding stairway to the mezzanine, I've always felt like an imposter wearing a tuxedo.

Now, as I heard the hushed pad of my footsteps on the carpeted stairs, I realized there was another reason for my discomfort. The last time I'd been here was in connection with the Wingfield case, a year ago, and it hadn't been a congenial visit. The memory of that time flooded over me as I stood on the top step, looking at my reflection in the floor-to-ceiling mirror facing the staircase.

I shook it off and walked over to the reception desk guarding the open double doors that led to the convention room, the site of Sinclair's campaign dinner. There I fell in line with other formally dressed men and women, all waiting impatiently—and importantly—for their names to be found on the exclusive guest list.

The young guy in an Armani suit manning the desk was *GQ*-handsome, his smile somehow both gracious and insincere as he drew a line through each VIP's name. After which, we were ushered into the huge, opulent room by an equally young, beautiful hostess in a dress so tight and heels so high she could barely move.

"On behalf of District Attorney Sinclair," she said to each of us in turn, "thank you for lending your valuable support to his campaign."

I guess the thinking was having a hottie like this welcome you to the affair took the sting out of the thousand bucks it cost you for the privilege. Though given the disapproving look the girl was getting from some of the older, jewel-bedecked women, it may have been a mistake.

There must have been over two hundred people inside the sparkling hall. Lining up at the appetizer buffet, standing in groups of two's and three's, getting drinks from the bar. Only a few had already taken their seats at one of the many elegant dining tables that took up most of the floor space. As though displaced and abandoned, they looked awkwardly around the room for a familiar face. Sipped absently from their water glasses. Poked the salads that had already been placed at every table setting.

I also noticed, as I made my way through the throng, about a dozen thick-shouldered guys strategically placed at various points along the walls. Tuxedos stretched tight against their crossed arms. All wearing the same stolid, watchful expressions. As well as the same earpieces.

Security. Even at an event like this, Sinclair and his people were taking no chances. The campaign had been a particularly bitter, divisive one from the start, and the volley of attacks and counter-attacks had only increased in recent weeks. Not to mention the usual barrage of crank calls, Internet ravings, and anonymous threats. Though, given the monied, invitation-only nature of the crowd, this kind of obvious security presence seemed like overkill.

The noise level in the place was off the charts. Not only as a result of the cacophony of small talk, forced laughter, and repeated introductions, but also due to the jazz trio playing in a far corner. Badly. Amps turned up full, these guys were doing more damage to Charlie Parker's rep than all his drug busts combined.

Which sent me scurrying to the other side of the room, dodging waiters, clusters of Chamber of Commerce types, and low-level civil servants grateful for the free booze.

I finally managed to find an empty corner, near the swinging service door to the kitchen. Taking a breath, I surveyed the assembled group. Eventually I began putting names to some of the faces. State politicians. Media big-wigs. A few corporate CEO's I recognized from news stories and magazine articles.

The people who ran the city.

As opposed to the waiters and hotel staff. Truck drivers and school teachers. Cops like Polk and Lowrey. Even docs like Holloway and Nancy and me.

The people who made the city run.

Events like this one always reminded me of that invisible, yet uncrossable divide. It also made me wonder why I'd accepted Sinclair's invitation in the first place.

Turns out, I wasn't the only one wondering that.

"Danny!" The familiar voice made me turn. "What the hell are *you* doing here?"

It was Sam Weiss, an old acquaintance and feature writer for the *Pittsburgh Post-Gazette*. Though he was best known for his top-selling book about Troy David Dowd, the Handyman. Which only fueled the interest in his upcoming one about the Wingfield investigation.

Although my own age and the married father of two, Sam always looked to me like some harried grad student. Even tonight, in his tux, he had the tousled-hair look of having just leapt from a shower into a cab, after which he'd bounded headlong up the steps to the convention room. His smile was as crooked and knowing as I remembered, too.

"I might ask *you* the same question," I said, as we shook hands. "Shouldn't you be home, bent over a keyboard, writing your next best-seller?"

"I wish. But I still have my gig at the paper. At least until the next round of lay-offs. And with two kids in private school, I can't give up my day job. Not yet, anyway."

He took a sip from his wine glass. "Meanwhile, what's *your* excuse? You never struck me as a big Sinclair fan."

"I'm not. He asked me to come. Figures it'll help."

"Price o' fame, Danny. Speaking of which, I see you've managed to get your name all over the news again today."

"What can I say? It's a gift. I just wish I could return it for a refund."

"Forget it, man. If you're gonna get held hostage by a homicidal bank robber, you're gonna pique the public's interest. Looks like you're still in one piece, though."

"More or less. I'll feel even better when the cops track down Wheeler Roarke."

"Dream on. My source in the department says the cops figure Roarke is long gone. Him *and* his partner in crime. Out of state by now. Maybe even out of the country."

Sam and I watched the humming crowd disperse, finding their assigned seats at the dining tables. A few hold-outs lingered at the bar, ordering another round. Fortification for the upcoming speeches.

I felt Sam's hand on my arm. "Look, any chance I could get an exclusive interview? About what happened in that OR with Roarke?"

"I'll have my people call your people."

"Come on, man. At least give me something about the survivor from the bank robbery. Treva Williams. Christ, what a day *she* had. First in the bank, then again at the hospital. Talk about trauma, right? She gonna be okay?"

I turned, irritation threading my voice.

"Are you kidding me, Sam? I'm not going to talk about her. Besides, how do you know who she is? I thought the cops were withholding her name from the media. At least for a day or two."

"Believe me, they tried. But it's a new world, Danny. We've got the Internet. More important, we've got guys who know how to *hack* the Internet. Most news outfits had the names of all the bank's employees an hour after the hold-up went down. Not just the ones who got killed. The lone hostage Roarke released, too. Treva Williams. She's in the First Allegheny database."

"So when they released the names of the three dead employees…"

He nodded. "Process of elimination. Treva was the only one left. Is she still in the hospital?"

"I think so. Though they're talking about letting her go home tomorrow morning. There's nothing physically wrong with her, and I guess they need the bed."

Sam pulled on his lower lip. "You gonna keep helping her, Dan? Like you did my sister?"

Sam's beloved younger sister had been the victim of a vicious rape and assault some years back. To this day, he believes my work with her saved her sanity. More credit than I deserve, I think. But I also know I'm unlikely to ever convince him of that.

"Treva and I went through a horrific experience together," I said carefully. "I think that connection gives us something to work with. If she wants to. Just as many trauma victims choose to try to block it out. Put the whole thing behind them. It rarely works. But it's really up to her. At this point, I don't know what's going to happen."

He gave a reflexive nod, but I got the feeling he didn't believe me. He'd guessed I was already too invested in Treva, in her psychological welfare. Sam was too good at his job to buy anyone's party line—even mine.

◇◇◇

As people continued to take their seats, the raised dais at the back of the room became more visible. A broad banner stretched along the wall above and behind it proclaimed, "Sinclair for

Governor." With his usual slogan emblazoned beneath: "Smart. Strong. And on your side."

Peering over the sea of expensive hair-dos and Botoxed faces, I caught sight of the man himself. Sitting in the middle of a long table on the dais. What I took to be his wife and children sat at his right. To his left were the chief of police, some city council-woman whose name escaped me, and the mayor.

Though too far away to hear above the din of the crowd, they all seemed to be chatting breezily. Meanwhile, photographers and videographers moved stealthily on the floor in front of the tableau, capturing the moment.

"Ever meet *Mrs.* Sinclair?" Sam drained his wine glass and put it on an empty tray stand in the corner. "Classic politician's wife. Thin, blond, and bland. Lives on diet pills and Prozac, according to press gossip. Last time she had an opinion about anything, Bush One was president."

I gave him a sidelong look. "Does she know…?"

"About Sinclair's affairs? Hell, Danny, if she doesn't, she's the only one. It's always possible, of course. I heard that during the Monica Lewinsky thing, Jay Leno did a joke in his monologue about Bill Clinton and the cigar. Brought the house down. The only one who didn't get the reference was Hillary." He shook his head. "From what I hear, to this day she's never read the Ken Starr report."

I thought about this.

"Think these rumors about Sinclair will hurt him?"

"Probably not. He was always discreet. Usually chased some tail who had more to lose than he did. Paralegals. Assistant DA's looking to move up the ladder."

Of course, I knew—from personal experience—a lot more about the kind of woman Sinclair slept with than Sam could ever suspect. Or would ever find out.

"Then what's your angle on the Sinclair campaign?" I leaned back against the corner. "I know you have one, or else you wouldn't be here. Any staff guy from the paper could cover this fund-raiser."

He laughed. "The first and best angle there is when it comes to a politician: the money. Where's the campaign getting it? Who's behind the PAC supplying it?"

He raised his chin, indicating the whole room.

"Which of these rich, connected bastards is buying Sinclair's loyalty? His support on some upcoming crucial policy initiative? His going soft on corporate taxes, or environmental regs?"

I shrugged. "I don't know, Sam. Sinclair's a pretty tough guy. Confident to the point of arrogance. I don't see him taking orders from some shady big-money people."

"Then he won't make it up the mountain, Danny. Not all the way, which is what I think he wants. *Nobody* does without making some kinda deal with the devil."

Something in Sam's voice caught my attention.

"Are you just poking around," I said, "or do you have something?"

He smiled darkly. "I have something, all right. More than a tip, less than a fact. But my gut says it's worth looking into."

"Meaning what?"

"Meaning," he said deliberately, "I think your pal Leland Sinclair is dirty."

Chapter Thirty-two

Apparently continuing with their Charlie Parker theme, the trio in the corner had begun an assault on Zawinul's "Birdland." With the volume turned up even higher.

"Jesus." Sam held his ears. "Catch you later, okay?"

Before I could stop him, he strode off, waving at some guy with a video cam on his shoulder. I started in another direction, toward a cluster of half-empty tables. I figured one of these had a place setting with my name on it. With luck, not at a table too close to the dais.

Though what occupied my mind was Sam's assertion about Leland Sinclair. Not that I knew the DA that well, or even liked him. Sure, there was no question he could be a real prick, and ravenously ambitious to boot. But corrupt? On somebody's pad? Somehow I couldn't see it.

Even with more than half the crowd seated, it was still a game of dodge-and-weave getting across the room. Until, up ahead, I saw another familiar face. Broad, robust. It was Harvey Blalock, president of the Pittsburgh Black Attorneys organization. Another blast from the past.

He was talking animatedly with a woman whose smooth, ebony back was toward me. Her tight-fitting dress displayed strong, shapely curves, accentuated by stiletto heels.

As I approached the pair, I noted how strikingly poised she seemed. The confident tilt of her hips. The languid way she held her wine glass suspended between her fingers.

Fingers whose nails, I realized, were painted a burnt red. It was Eleanor Lowrey.

She turned as Harvey raised his eyebrows in greeting. The big attorney and I shook hands. He had the grip of a velvet-lined vice.

"Dan Rinaldi." Blalock beamed. "I saw you on the tube today and I had the same thought I always do: Does that white man owe me money?"

He laughed heartily, then turned to Eleanor.

"Eleanor, this is—"

"Oh, I know this guy." Her appraising look at me was knowing, but warm. "Though I've never seen him dressed up before."

"Likewise." I gave her a careful perusal right back. Or maybe I just stared. She was...stunning. The sleek, sleeveless dress accentuated her well-toned arms, while its plunging neckline did the same for her full breasts.

Eleanor gave me a wry smile. "It's a special occasion, Danny. So I thought I'd work the cleavage."

"Really? I hadn't noticed."

Which only made Harvey Blalock laugh again.

"You two carry on without me, okay?" He raised his empty shot glass. "I need a refill if I'm gonna make it through the District Attorney's stump speech."

After he'd gone, I turned back to Eleanor.

"I didn't know you were coming to this thing."

"Neither did I. Till the last minute, when Sinclair's guy called. What's his name? Fletcher. He practically begged me to show up. I think they wanted some more black faces." She glanced around the room. "We're kinda at a premium around here."

"Well, I'm glad you're here. Makes putting on a tux worth it." I grinned. "Almost."

She aimed her violet eyes at me over the rim of her glass. "Please, Danny, don't even try. I saw you checking me out yesterday. When we were working together."

"Was it that obvious?"

"Look, it's okay. Luther and I have an open relationship. I don't mess with *his* bitches, and he doesn't—"

I raised my hand, palm up. "I get it."

Again, her wry smile. I admit, I was somewhat taken aback by the whole conversation. Where the hell was this going? If it was going anywhere.

I changed tacks. "How do you know Harvey Blalock?"

"He represented a cousin of mine, a surgeon, in some bullshit malpractice suit."

"Same thing with me. Malpractice suit. Also bullshit. Luckily, it went away before I racked up a fortune in lawyer's fees."

"My cousin wasn't so lucky. The case went to trial. Harvey got him acquitted, but it cost a ton. The family joke is that Harvey's boat oughtta be named after us."

"He has a boat?"

"Who doesn't?" Her smile was a tease. "Hey, maybe we can get him to take us out for a river cruise sometime. I hear they can be very romantic."

"Never had the pleasure."

"I mean, if you *go* for that kind of thing. Hard-asses like you and me…well, I don't know. Probably not."

She lowered her eyes then, stared at her wine glass.

I got the sense she felt she'd over-stepped. Said too much.

I also recalled her grief when recounting how her relationship with Treva had ended. Hard-ass? Not always. Not either one of us, really. Maybe that was something that tugged us in the same direction. That, even now, seemed to be drawing us closer.

Unless, on her end, it was merely the stress of the past two days. The frustration of the investigation. The multiple—and very public—murders, with the accompanying political pressure. And with the culprits long gone.

Because suddenly her eyes came up, clear and focused.

Whatever invitation I'd seen in them, whatever hint of intimacy, was now hidden. Put away.

"I *did* want to ask you something," she said. "About Treva. When you and Polk saw her today. How was she?"

"Pretty much as I expected. The reality of what's happened to her has sunk in. She's certainly still frightened. Terrified, I'd say."

"Of what? It's all over now."

"Try telling *her* that. Or any victim of violent assault. For some survivors, it's never over."

"So what do you think? Is she gonna be okay?"

"Hard to say. I'll know more when I get to do some work with her. *If* I do." I paused. "I hear they're sending her home tomorrow."

"Yes. The hospital says she's insisting on it. She says she doesn't feel safe there. I can't say I blame her."

"I assume you've offered her police protection."

Eleanor looked puzzled. "For what? You mean, to keep the press from hounding her? Sleeping outside her front door? Taking pictures through her windows?"

"That's as good a reason as any. Don't you agree?"

"Doesn't matter whether I agree or not. No way we can spare the manpower. Not in the middle of a full-scale investigation. Plus all the resources devoted to locating the two bank robbers."

I mulled this over. I saw her point. There was no apparent threat to Treva's safety. Still—

"What about Victims' Services, at least…"

"Give us some credit, eh, Danny? We have their people set up for home visits a couple times a day. To make sure she's eating, resting. Or in case she needs someone to talk to. Though Treva isn't too happy about it."

"Really? Why not?"

Eleanor took a breath. "I heard from Biegler that she said if she needs anything, she'll get it from you. She says you're the only one she trusts."

She threw back her drink, drained it. "So do us all a favor, okay? Keep your cell phone on."

I could tell from the coolness in her voice that Treva's last comment—though merely a repeat of what she'd said before—had still stung. And that, as if in answer to it, Eleanor had suddenly put up a wall between us.

And while I wasn't exactly surprised, it didn't feel good, either.

◇◇◇

"Detective Lowrey!"

Eleanor and I both turned to find Brian Fletcher— taller than I remembered in his stylish, tailored tuxedo— striding across the polished floor in our direction. Professional smile widening beneath his trim mustache.

Stepping between us, he took Eleanor's hand in both of his. "So glad you could make it, Detective. You look amazing."

Eleanor regarded him warily. "Thanks, Mr. Fletcher."

"Everybody calls me Brian." He turned to me. "Happy to see *you* here, too, Dr. Rinaldi. I wasn't sure you'd get on-board for this."

"Me, neither. But then I've always been a sucker for free hors d'oeuvres."

"Hey, this is a political fund-raiser, okay? So easy on the irony. It makes potential donors nervous."

"Maybe they should be. Considering how the last couple days have played out. For Sinclair, I mean."

Fletcher tilted his head. "You cut right to the chase, don't you? Well, I'm going to break a cardinal rule among campaign managers and tell you the truth: it's not helping us. It's tough running as a big-dick law-and-order man when armed robbers are making fools out of the cops."

Eleanor folded her arms. "I don't think that's fair, Mr. Fletcher. In fact, I think it's bullshit. There's no way the department can—"

Fletcher chuckled. "Whoa, wait a minute. I'm getting double-teamed here. I only came over to say hello. Pump the flesh. Know what I mean? Just your friendly neighborhood political hack."

"Somehow I doubt that," I said.

He cupped his hand on my shoulder. "I'll take that as a compliment. Meanwhile, I want to invite you both to come as my personal guests to the debate Saturday night. It's going to be on-campus at Pitt. Hillman Library. And aired live throughout the state."

"So you and Garrity's handlers finally agreed on the ground rules?"

He nodded vigorously. "Closed the deal an hour ago. Had to bargain away Lee's left nut—sorry, Detective—but John Garrity's such a coward we had no choice. Though it sure ain't pretty. Two minute time limits. No rebuttals. Rules so restrictive you can barely call it a debate."

Eleanor said, "Then why do it?"

"Because the public expects it. They rarely *watch* it, you understand. But they like to know the candidates are doing it. Duking it out. *Mano a mano.*" He shrugged. "Hey, we're a helluva long way from Lincoln-Douglas, but it's great political theater."

"I'll bring the popcorn," I said.

He eyed me ruefully. "What did I say a minute ago about irony? Do I have to send you a memo?"

Then, abruptly, he laughed. A bit too loud.

"Hey, this is fun, but I've actually got a job to do. Danny, Lee wants to do the photo-op with you, him, and the mayor before dinner starts. Probably so His Honor doesn't have soup stains on his shirt for the picture."

"I take it the mayor's already sampled the punch?"

Fletcher ignored this. "I'll come back and get you in five minutes or so. I figure we'll line you guys up on the floor in front of the dais. The Mayor wants the photo shot up from a low angle to make him look taller. Fine with me—that way, it'll get the banner in there, too."

He started to walk off, then turned back to Eleanor.

"Sorry, Detective, I almost forgot. Lee and Lt. Biegler want to see you right away. Lee wants an update on the bank case. From the troops on the ground."

Eleanor frowned. "Why me?"

"Apparently, Biegler tried to get hold of Sgt. Polk but can't find him. So you're the next batter up."

He pointed a manicured finger at me. "Five minutes, okay, Doc? Big smile, no irony. *Capice?*"

He swiveled on his heel and hurried away before I could say anything. Given the response that had come to mind, it was probably just as well.

When I turned back to Eleanor, I saw that she was looking toward the front of the hall. Following her gaze, I spotted Sinclair standing behind his chair on the dais.

Talking with Biegler, who seemed almost painfully out of place in his ordinary jacket and tie. The uninvited interruption. Moreover, from the strained looks on their faces, and the lieutenant's desultory gestures, I could tell it wasn't a pleasant conversation.

"Jesus, Harry," Eleanor said aloud.

I touched her elbow. "C'mon, Eleanor. Tell me what's going on with Polk."

"That's just it, Danny. I don't know. He's been missing roll calls. Disappears from the precinct for hours, and nobody knows where he is. I've had to cover for him a dozen times." She shook her head. "If he doesn't get his shit together, he's gonna be out on his ass. Biegler's ready to drop a rock on him already, I can tell. God knows, he's been looking for an excuse for years."

Suddenly I understood her behavior in the hospital parking lot the day before. When she'd first brought up her concerns about Harry, and then brusquely cut the conversation short. She'd felt disloyal for talking about him behind his back. For seeming to narc on her own partner.

Yet she was worried. Both for his career, and for him personally. I could see the bind she was in.

"Look, Eleanor. I tried to broach the subject with Harry myself and got told to back off. I don't know what he's doing, or gotten himself mixed up in, but we can't beat it out of him."

She clenched her fists. "Don't tempt me."

Then, with a rueful smile, she turned and—to my surprise— kissed me on the cheek.

"Thanks, Danny. For giving a damn. About Harry."

She took her thumb and rubbed her lipstick off my face. "And about me."

I watched as she threaded her way through the maze of tables to the front of the hall and the dais, where an impatient Sinclair and Biegler waited.

I reached up to touch the still-warm imprint of her lips on my cheek.

Chapter Thirty-two

I glanced at my watch.

"Five minutes," Brian Fletcher had said. That was ten minutes ago.

From where I stood, I could see Sinclair, Biegler, and Eleanor still huddled at the table, deep in conversation. Fletcher himself was pacing on the floor in front of the dais, talking with a couple desultory press photographers whose cameras hung heavily from their shoulders.

By now, practically all the guests had found seats at the tables. So I figured I had no choice but to join them.

When I finally spotted the little placard with my name on it, at a crowded table near the front, I discovered I'd been seated next to Sam Weiss. He was talking to a stocky man sitting uncomfortably in a tux on his other side. Grim-faced, middle-aged, with a receding hairline he tried to hide with a dubious comb-over.

Before I could pull out my chair and sit down, Sam was already making introductions.

"Danny! We were just talking about you." He gestured to the other man. "Dr. Daniel Rinaldi, this is Dave Parnelli. Assistant District Attorney."

Parnelli and I shook hands.

"Your name sounds familiar," I said.

"It should." His manner was brisk, his accent sharp. I was thinking Brooklyn or Queens. "I'm handling the Mary Lewicki car-jacking. At least, I *was*, till I realized she'd crap out on us on the stand. So I made the usual deal with the scumbag in question and moved on. That's life in the big city. Or at least a medium-sized one."

"Yes, I remember Angie Villanova mentioning you."

"She mentioned *you*, too. When she said she was going to refer Mary to you for counseling. Which surprised the fuck outta me, since I didn't know we were running a social work agency."

Sam grinned. "Dave's from New York, Danny."

As if that explained the attitude. Which it very well might have.

Parnelli broke a bread stick in two. "All I'm sayin' is, we did things a little differently back home. But I don't want you to think I'm some kind of hard case, Dr. Rinaldi. Ask your friend Sam here. Hell, in New York, I wasn't even a prosecutor. I worked for the public defender's office."

"So what are you doing in Pittsburgh? Working for the district attorney?"

"Long story. Here's the short version: I got tired of defending gang-bangers, rapists, and child molesters. Meth addicts and crack-whore mothers. Trust me, you can only deal with so many dead babies in freezers before you start to wig out. I wigged. No apologies."

He tossed one half of the bread stick on his plate, began gnawing on the other.

"So I came to Pittsburgh to see how the other half lives. The half that gets to put the bad guys in jail and sleep easy at night."

"Makes sense." I took a long drink from my water glass. "But, again, why Pittsburgh?"

"I got a sister who moved here a couple years back. She liked it, so I figured, what the fuck? It's got rivers and bridges, too, just like the five boroughs. People are friendly. Blah-blah-blah. Just wanted a change. Don't make a big deal out of it."

Sam smirked. "Danny's a shrink, Dave. They do that."

"Psychologist," I corrected him.

"You know what I mean." Sam leaned back in his chair. "But I figured you guys oughtta meet. I told Dave all about your being a consultant for the police. So don't let his charm school manner fool you. He's suitably impressed."

"My ass." Parnelli chewed loudly.

"Always happy to meet new fans." I finished the whole goblet of water. Still a bit dry-mouthed from whatever was happening between Eleanor and me. If anything.

I was also getting anxious to get the photo op over with, so I could leave. I'd hoped to be out of here a half hour ago. I certainly didn't want to hang around for the dinner and speeches.

Plus I wanted to check back in with Treva. I wasn't satisfied with the way we had left things. I needed to know more. About what she was afraid of. What she feared might happen to her.

All the guests were seated now, and dozens of waiters were moving around the tables, bringing soup, the first course. I stared glumly at the wilting salad in front of me, nudging my fork around on the tablecloth.

Sam watched me with rising amusement. "Looks like you're joining us for the duration, Danny. Hope you brought your appetite."

I grunted. The only thing that might've kept me at that table with Sam was the opportunity to grill him about what he'd said about Sinclair being dirty. What he actually knew, or even suspected.

But there was no way we could discuss it now. Not sitting at a table full of other guests, one of whom was an ADA in Sinclair's office.

Just then, a waiter appeared as if out of nowhere and placed a wide-mouthed bowl of mushroom soup in front of me. I mumbled my thanks and looked up at Sam's smiling face.

"*Bon appétit!*" he said, enjoying himself.

As the waiter circled around to serve Parnelli, and then Sam, I heard a sudden tinkling of glass coming from the front of the room.

Leland Sinclair stood at his place at the table, tapping his water glass with a spoon. Its soft peal echoed.

"Before we start our dinner," he said, "I wonder if I could ask one of our distinguished guests, Dr. Daniel Rinaldi, to join us down here at the dais?"

I glanced up at Sam. "Saved by the bell."

With a couple hundred pairs of eyes on me, I made my way down to the front of the room. By the time I reached the dais, Sinclair, the chief of police, and the mayor had already climbed down the side steps and were waiting to greet me on the floor. Leaving Sinclair's family, Biegler, Eleanor, and the councilwoman still seated at the table.

As the four of us "distinguished guests" exchanged pleasantries, Brian Fletcher came over, beckoning to his photographers to follow him.

"Okay, gentlemen," Fletcher said to us. "Let's have you form a tight line, so we can get you all in. Maybe a shot of Lee shaking hands with the chief, as the mayor and Dr. Rinaldi look on. Then we change partners. Lee shaking hands with the mayor. Then with Dr. Rinaldi. Then—"

Sinclair chuckled smoothly. "I think we all get your drift, Brian."

Which brought a round of equally smooth chuckles from the posh crowd at the tables. *If you can't be king,* I thought, peering out at their glowing faces, *it's good to be friends of the king. Or at least believe that you are.*

At the same time, I noted that the scurrying waiters, laden with trays and soup tureens, didn't even look up. In the same room as everyone else, listening to the same self-serving jibes and remarks, yet as removed as though in a parallel universe.

Eyes down. Voices low.

Unseen. Unnoticed.

Except for one waiter. Dark-haired, wiry. Sweat-beaded brow over severe thick-framed glasses. Moving slowly around his appointed table. One very near the dais. Fumbling with the lid of a large tureen.

With eyes up. Watching us.

As Fletcher moved his candidate and the rest of us around, placing us in various collegial positions, the photographers roved back and forth in a crouch. Shooting up at us. As though we were a mobile Mt. Rushmore, posing for the ages.

The whole thing was ludicrous. Absurdly comic. And would have remained so—

Except for that waiter.

The one at the near table, who now stood ramrod straight. The closed soup tureen held perfectly still, balanced on the palm of one hand.

As he watched us. Not serving. Not even moving.

Watching.

Until I noticed him watching. And not moving.

And he noticed me doing so.

Then he was pulling the lid off the tureen. Letting it drop with a jarring crash as he reached into the bowl.

Bringing his hand up. With something in it.

Which was when I called out.

"Gun!"

Going into a crouch. Rushing him, hands outstretched—

Too late.

The gun went off.

Chapter Thirty-three

I got lucky. Everybody did.

The shooter must've panicked, seeing me lunging straight for him. His arm involuntarily went up as I connected, tackling him.

The gunshot thundered loudly as I literally felt the bullet whiz past my ear. Then the shooter was stumbling backwards, my momentum carrying us both down to the floor.

I was on top, scrabbling for the gun still in his hand. Barely aware of a rising crescendo of voices, cries, urgent shouts. And a riotous scuffle of feet.

Gasping, grunting, the shooter wrestled with me for the gun. Squirming and bucking beneath me. Hate-filled eyes boring up at me through his thick glasses.

It felt like we grappled this way forever, yet it was merely seconds. And then the first of the security guys reached us. Pinning the gunman's arm down to the floor.

And then there were three or four of them, pushing me aside to constrain both the shooter's arms and his frantically kicking legs. I rolled to the floor, panting, gulping air. The security men shouting and cursing as they immobilized the guy. One pocketed his gun.

Then a swarm of people grew around me, all talking and shouting at once. Somehow Biegler and Eleanor had vaulted down from the dais and were on the floor beside me. Still on my haunches, I swiveled my head in time to see other security personnel hustling the rest of the honored guests—Sinclair and his family, the chief, the councilwoman, and the mayor—out the near service door.

"Are you all right?" Eleanor clutched my shoulder.

"I'm fine. Anybody get hit?"

"I don't think so."

As I got to my feet, still winded, I saw Brian Fletcher standing with his hands outstretched, facing the frenzied guests. All talking, yelling at once. Stumbling out of their chairs. I could barely hear him above their cries of confusion, panic. Shouted questions from the media types heading toward us.

"Please, people!" Fletcher was shouting now, too. "Please stay back! Stay in your seats! Everything's under control!"

He turned toward where the shooter lay, strait-jacketed by a phalanx of security guys.

"You got that prick wrapped up?" Fletcher yelled.

When one of the security guys—the head man, it looked like—nodded firmly, Fletcher motioned for him to join him. He lumbered over.

"I need a couple of your men to keep everybody seated, okay? Especially the press. I want things contained."

The head of security said nothing, merely went back to his men and began giving orders in a cool, detached tone.

Then Fletcher turned again to the crowd of guests, only a few of whom had retaken their seats. His voice calm, placating. "Please, we need your co-operation. Nobody's been hurt. Please...we need you to stay in your seats. Let the police and security do their jobs."

Finally catching my breath, I looked down at the shooter. On his back on the floor, arms and legs pinned, he glared up at all of us with naked contempt.

"Did I get him?" Spitting out the words, as though acid in his mouth. "Did I get that motherfucker Sinclair?"

At this, one of the security guys cuffed him on the cheek with a huge fist. The shooter barely blinked.

"Did I kill him? Eh? Is that fucker dead?"

Biegler gestured angrily at the security detail.

"Get this piece o' shit outta here." Then he turned to Eleanor. "Go check on the mayor and the others. Make sure nobody's hurt."

She nodded and went out through that same service door. Meanwhile, the guests had more or less settled down, the majority now back in their seats. I saw a number still standing, though. Mostly press, barking into their cell phones. I also noticed that our two photographers were still in action, now snapping off candid shots of the chaotic scene. With a lot more enthusiasm than earlier.

Until Fletcher caught sight of them and ran over, shouting at them to shut off their cameras. When he came back to where we stood, his head was shaking. Incredulous.

"Fucking vultures." Rubbing his temples.

Security had the shooter up on his feet now, though he still struggled and kicked. Shouting curses. Eyes manic and gleaming behind those thick lenses.

Biegler growled at the big men holding him. "Will you get him the hell outta here?"

As they started to lead him off, a shout cut through the continuing hum of voices.

"No! Wait!"

It was Dave Parnelli, jostling through the crowd toward the dais. A security guy made a move to stop him, but Parnelli flashed his ID and was allowed through.

He gave Biegler and me a curt nod, then peered right in the shooter's glowering face.

"I know this prick. Jimmy Gordon. Felix Gordon's brother."

"Holy shit," Biegler said. "You're right."

As soon as I heard Felix Gordon's name, the pieces started to fit together. I remembered the trial.

Apparently, Fletcher didn't. "What are you talking about? Who's Felix Gordon?"

"You don't know Felix?!" Jimmy Gordon sputtered in anger. "You fuck! They *killed* him! My baby brother and you don't remember?! You fucking bastard—"

Which started another round of kicking and screaming. Before the security guy on his left hit Jimmy so hard his eyes rolled up in his head. He stayed conscious, but barely. Just enough to keep the fires of rage burning, banked and low, in his eyes.

Parnelli kept his own gaze on Jimmy's livid, contorted face. Though his voice was controlled. Matter-of-fact.

"I prosecuted Felix for a double-homicide last year. Brutal. Sadistic. *And* premeditated. After convicting the slimeball, I went to Sinclair and asked permission to seek the death penalty. Which he gave me. So did the jury. Then Felix took a shiv from a fellow inmate three months ago, so justice was speeded up."

Parnelli finally turned to Biegler and me. "I'm sure you remember big brother Jimmy here sitting every day in the court-room. Having to be restrained after the death penalty decision came down. Swearing that he'd get revenge on the DA's office. On the whole damn system."

Biegler sighed, disgusted.

"Yeah, I remember, all right—some punk from East Liberty. From a family of punks. Real bottom feeders. Burglary, home invasions. Assaults. Low-life scum."

Parnelli swiveled back to glare sharply at Jimmy, whose head lolled now. Much of the fight gone out of him.

"You figure you'd make your bones doin' the DA, eh, Jimmy? Another loser like your brother Felix. Well, it's gonna be fun prosecuting another member of the family."

"Fuck you." Jimmy Gordon wasn't raging now. His voice had fallen to a low, menacing growl. "Don't matter what you do to me. Not now. See, I ain't in this alone."

"Meaning what?" Parnelli looked unimpressed.

"Meanin', it don't matter that I didn't get Sinclair. It's all set up. He ain't gonna make it to that bullshit debate on Saturday."

His face screwed up, and a dark, scar-like grin creased its lower half.

"'Cause he ain't gonna live that long."

Chapter Thirty-four

"What the hell happened out there?"

It was the normally unflappable Leland Sinclair, pacing in one of the hotel's exclusive guest suites. Brian Fletcher and I gave him a wide berth, standing near the sleek French windows leading to the balcony. Outside, the humid night had finally darkened, a somber black backdrop to the Steel City's array of lights.

"Well, I'm no expert," I said. "But I think that guy was trying to punch your ticket."

Sinclair stopped and glared at me. Then at his beleaguered campaign manager, whose face had paled three shades down to chalk white.

"What's Dr. Rinaldi doing here?"

Fletcher tried on a smile. "C'mon, Lee. I figured since the Doc saved your life, it'd be okay…"

Sinclair took a long, exaggerated breath. Then let his gaze rest on me again.

"Yes, well…I suppose I should thank you."

I shrugged. "Right place, right time. Glad it worked out."

Sinclair chuckled then, without humor, and stepped over to me. Held out his hand. I took it.

"Sorry. It's just—" He swallowed hard. Flustered. More agitated than I'd ever seen him. The attempt on his life had not only shaken him, as it would anyone. It had also challenged his grip on events, his need for control.

"I *am* grateful, Dan," he managed to add.

"We *both* are," Fletcher chimed in.

Just then, there was a knock on the suite's gilt-edged door. Fletcher strode over, squinted through the peep-hole, and admitted Dave Parnelli and Eleanor Lowrey.

As they approached him, Sinclair took another long slow breath, combing his hair back with his fingers. Obviously welcoming the opportunity to reassert his authority. Back on familiar ground once more.

"Well?" He raised his eyebrows at his ADA.

"Everything's squared away, Lee," Parnelli said. "We got Jimmy Gordon in lockup. Screamin' for a lawyer, natch. But he's not goin' anywhere anytime soon."

"I figured that. What about the Mayor?"

"Probably home by now, nursing a drink. First thing we did after the fireworks was get him back in his limo."

"And Councilwoman Reeves?—or shouldn't I ask?"

Parnelli grimaced. "There we weren't so lucky. She grabbed some TV people outside on the street and started talking. The usual bullshit. Our culture of violence. The break-down of society. Et cetera. Film at eleven."

Sinclair sighed. "Terrific."

Eleanor spoke up. "Sir, the chief is pulling some of the squad off the bank investigation, to form a joint task force with the FBI—"

"What?"

"Standard procedure in a case like this. Agent Alcott insisted on it. Especially in light of Gordon's threats. His promise of another attempt on your life."

"She's right." Parnelli shook his head. "No way to keep the Bureau out of this. And, fuck it, why should we? They have the experience, the resources. This is your *life* we're talkin' about, Lee."

Sinclair grew irritated. "Great. Just what the public needs to see. Diverting manpower from the hunt for two ruthless killers, all to protect the DA. The guy who's supposed to be in charge of protecting *them*. Helluva way to inspire voter confidence."

"It doesn't have to play out that way, Lee," said Fletcher. "We can say that law enforcement offered to put a full-court press on the Gordon threat, but that you declined. In the name of public safety. That you aren't afraid of idle threats, and that nothing matters more than apprehending the murder suspects. Meanwhile, we let the cops and the Feds do it all back-channel."

"Okay." Sinclair sniffed. "I can live with that."

"Except it *wasn't* an idle threat," I said. "Anybody else remember the guy with the gun?"

"That's another thing." Parnelli massaged his chin. "With all that security, how the fuck did Jimmy Gordon get in here? With a goddam *gun*, for Christ's sake."

Fletcher seemed to take this personally.

"Listen, we've got the best security detail money can buy. Half these guys used to be Special Forces."

"Maybe not 'special' enough." Parnelli took a step toward the campaign manager. "I mean, dressed as a waiter? Not exactly an original approach. Besides, I assume they checked out everybody on the hotel staff working the fund-raiser tonight. So again—how did your people miss him?"

"I don't know." Fletcher looked genuinely chagrined.

Both personally and professionally. Fumbling with his tuxedo tie, undoing it. As though giving some slack to a noose tightening around his neck.

"Well, you better find out." Parnelli turned and faced Eleanor. "What *do* we know so far, Detective? If anything."

I noticed that she straightened a bit, as though to prepare herself for a similar dressing down from the ADA.

I also guessed she'd have felt a lot more confident giving her report in her street clothes. It probably wasn't fun trying to seem professional wearing a tight, low-cut dress. Especially in a roomful of men.

"CSU just dug the bullet out of the wall behind the dais," she said. "Though I picked up the shell casing myself. Standard issue. The gun's tagged and bagged, and the lab knows to red-ball it. But we got the basics. A .38, with the serial numbers filed down. You can pick one up on any street corner in town."

"And this Jimmy Gordon?" Sinclair asked.

"You remember his brother Felix," Parnelli answered before Eleanor could. "Double-dip conviction, then the death penalty. Though he didn't live long enough to get the needle."

Sinclair blew air from his cheeks. "I also remember the news stories about Jimmy in the courtroom. The things he said."

He walked briskly over to the suite's mahogany-framed wet-bar. Poured himself a Dewar's on ice. Downed half of it. Then spoke to the wall in front of him.

"A convicted man's brother threatens revenge on the DA. In open court. Until he's dragged away by the cops. Jesus, it sounds like some old movie. Hollywood bullshit."

Parnelli spoke carefully.

"Actually, Lee, if you look at the court records, it happens all the time. Family members making threats. Of course, they rarely act on them. Usually it's just shit they say in the heat of the moment. Only this time…"

He let the words hang there in the air for a long moment. Nobody else spoke, either.

Sinclair finally turned, tumbler in hand. The ice tinkled and cracked.

"It's…well, it's hard to believe." He glanced at Eleanor. "And the police are taking Gordon's threat seriously? That there might be another attempt?"

"We're taking it *very* seriously, sir." She pursed her lips. "And, frankly, I think you should, too."

Fletcher folded his arms importantly. Still stung by Parnelli's rebuke, I figured.

"I agree with Detective Lowrey," he said. "I think we should cancel the debate on Saturday night."

Sinclair shook his head vehemently. "No. It can't look like I'm afraid. That I let some thug intimidate me."

"Okay, okay. Then at least let's beef up security, from now till Saturday. Maybe even change the venue at the last minute. Hillman Library's pretty damn public…which means pretty damn accessible."

Sinclair laughed bitterly. "Maybe we should hold the debate at police headquarters. If all we're interested in is security."

"What do you mean?"

Sinclair looked down at his glass. "Brian, you know better than anyone that politics is about perception. If we move too aggressively to protect me, I look both privileged and cowardly. Neither of which garners votes from blue-collar types. The demo we need the most."

"Maybe." For the first time, Fletcher let some grit come into his voice. "But as your campaign manager *and* your friend, I say we've got to take appropriate precautions."

Parnelli regarded Eleanor. "Which includes, I assume, checking on any *other* members of the Gordon family. Known associates. Anyone who might be working with Jimmy."

She gave him a tight smile. "Already in motion, sir. In fact, it's the first thing on the task force agenda. Develop a list of possibles in terms of another attempt on Mr. Sinclair."

"Good. And keep me in the loop, okay, Detective?"

"Yes, sir."

I watched carefully as Sinclair finished his drink. The tight lines around his eyes. I could almost see his internal conflict. The battle between ambition and self-preservation. Between aspiration and common sense.

"Okay, Brian," he said at last. "I just hope to Christ we can keep the investigation under the radar. As much as possible, anyway. And I promise to give some thought to changing the debate venue. Meanwhile, I need to shoo all you people out of here. I have some calls to make."

I could guess what he meant. He had about two hundred guests to call and calm down after tonight's events. Two hundred potential contributors who'd paid a thousand bucks each for a dinner they never got to eat. Which also meant they'd missed out on the chance—motivated by Sinclair's after-dinner speech—to cough up even more.

With Fletcher in the lead, we all trooped quietly out of the room. Though, as I glanced back on my way out, I noticed Sinclair wasn't heading for the phone, but for the wet-bar. Where he again poured a good-sized Dewar's on ice.

And, again, stared at the wall.

Chapter Thirty-five

As I'd learned on my previous visit to the Burgoyne, the hotel had a private elevator for VIP guests. The same one that was carrying Fletcher, Parnelli, Eleanor, and me down to the lower parking level. The campaign manager had wanted us to avoid running into the press, or perhaps some lingering fund-raiser guests. Parnelli readily agreed.

Nobody had said much on the way down, but now, as we stepped out onto the sprawling concrete floor of the garage, Brian Fletcher took hold of my hand with both of his. As he'd done with Eleanor upstairs, in the conference hall. His signature gesture of sincerity, apparently.

"I want to thank you again, Doctor, on Lee's behalf. *And* mine. I got a helluva scare tonight."

"Me, too."

Parnelli grunted noisily. "And it isn't over. Far as I'm concerned, the clock's started ticking, and it won't stop until the debate Saturday night. You heard what Jimmy Gordon said. Lee's in danger from this moment till then."

Eleanor said, "Unless the next attempt is at the debate itself. Same kind of situation. Big crowd. Lots of distraction. Tough on security."

"That's why I want to move the venue," Fletcher said. "Though I don't think Lee will go for it. And he's probably right. He can't look like he's scared."

"C'mon, give the people some credit. Even *you* can't believe they're that easily swayed."

"Doesn't matter what *I* believe, Detective. It's what the electorate thinks. Or can be persuaded to think. If you can even *call* it thinking. I've been in this game a long time, and I never forget something Churchill said."

"Which was?" I asked.

He grinned. "'The best argument against democracy is a five-minute conversation with a registered voter.'"

Scowling, Parnelli dug a short cigar from his tux jacket's inside pocket. "Well, aren't you the clever boy? While you and the doc here exchange Bartlett's-fucking-Quotations, the police and I have work to do. Isn't that right, Detective?"

"Yes, sir."

Waving a dismissive hand, Parnelli bit down on his cigar and went off across the low-ceilinged enclosure in search of his car. Muttering to himself as he patted his pockets, obviously looking for a light. Without success.

Fletcher turned then to Eleanor and me. "I better go back upstairs and check in on Lee. *And* get our spin doctors started on drafting an official statement about tonight for the media."

"I look forward to seeing it," I said.

"Thanks." Smiling as he stepped back inside the elevator. "And don't worry, Doc. I'll make sure they spell your name right."

Before I could reply, he'd taken a Blackberry out of his pocket and begun pushing buttons. As the elevator doors closed with a muffled click.

Eleanor gave me a wry look. "I don't like him."

"Which one, Parnelli or Fletcher?"

"Do I have to choose?"

"Point taken."

She gestured toward the multiple rows of parked cars gleaming under the harsh, uneven garage lights.

"My car's over there. Somewhere."

"Don't worry, you're a detective. You'll find it."

She playfully punched my arm, then headed us toward the first line of cars.

I saw her brow furrow.

"Parnelli was right, though. Long night's work ahead of me. I just have to go home and change, and then it's back to the precinct."

It's what she didn't say that registered.

"You're worried about Harry, aren't you? Wondering if he'll be there."

"Even if he *is* there, I'll bet Biegler's tearing him a new one. He must be furious about having to tell Sinclair that he was unable to reach Harry tonight. That he couldn't provide the latest info about the bank case."

We walked in silence for a few moments, our footsteps echoing hollowly on the concrete. Then she indicated a late model Chevy sedan parked near a massive pillar.

As she searched her small purse for her keys, I found myself putting my hand on her bare shoulder. Then instantly regretted it. I'd meant it to be supportive, reassuring. Yet it seemed suddenly too familiar, too—

But Eleanor just turned her head and smiled. Put her own hand on mine.

"I like you, too, Danny." Giving my hand the slightest squeeze. Then letting her fingers linger a moment, softly stroking my knuckles.

Before she bent to unlock the driver's side door, and slipped easily behind the wheel.

And then, giving me another brief smile, she put the car in gear and pulled away.

◇◇◇

My Mustang was in another section of the lower level. I headed up the ramp to the street, took out my cell, and called Pittsburgh Memorial. And asked for Treva's room.

I knew it was after visiting hours, and that it was unlikely they'd put me through. But I wanted to at least get a report on her condition.

When the switchboard connected me to the duty nurse, I was pleased to find that it was Ruth. The same one I'd met when Polk and I had questioned Treva earlier that day.

"This is Dr. Rinaldi. I know you probably won't let me speak to Treva Williams at this hour, but I was wondering how she's doing?"

Ruth's raspy chuckle was made tinnier by the cell's speaker. "Hell, Doctor, I don't mind bending hospital rules once in a while. Especially since Treva likes you so much. She talked about you a lot."

"That's nice of you to say. So I can speak to her? I'll only take a minute or two."

"Like I said, I'd be happy to. Thing is, she ain't here. She checked herself out about an hour ago."

I let this news sink in.

"And the doctor was okay with this?"

"Sure. Treva's just tired. Physically and emotionally. The police were fine with it, too. They were here right before, with that obnoxious man from the DA's office."

"You mean Dave Parnelli?"

"That's him. Real charmer. But he signed off on Treva going home."

This threw me. Why had Parnelli bothered to visit Treva at the hospital? He could've given the okay by phone. More importantly, why hadn't he mentioned it?

"Hello?" Ruth said the word with emphasis.

I got the hint. I quickly thanked her for her time, and for the good care she'd provided Treva. Which merely brought another weary chuckle from the veteran nurse before she hung up.

I sat back against the Mustang's cool leather. I'd been told that Treva was probably going to be released, but it had happened sooner than I'd expected. Still, no reason she shouldn't have been.

As I thought this over, I absently checked my office voice mail. No urgent calls. One was from a prospectice new patient. Another was a request from a psych journal I sometimes contribute to for an article on childhood trauma.

The last message, to my surprise, was from Treva Williams. Leaving her home number, and asking that I call her. Regardless of the hour.

I punched in the number, heard the phone ring three times. Then she picked up. Her voice faint, sleepy.

"Thanks for calling, Dr. Rinaldi. I was hoping you would."

"How are you, Treva? I just heard you checked yourself out of the hospital."

"Yeah." She yawned. "The doctors said it was okay, and I wanted to go home. So that's what I did."

"You're home now?"

"In bed. I have an apartment in Monroeville. Near the Mall, on Route 22."

"I know the area. Listen, Treva…"

"Before you say anything, I just want you to know I'm fine. Really. That's why I left you a message. I knew you were worried about me, but I'm fine."

"Physically, perhaps. But earlier today, you…"

"The truth? All I want to do is burrow under these covers and sleep for a week."

"I understand. You must be exhausted. But I wonder if we could arrange to meet sometime soon. Maybe tomorrow. Or the next day."

"Okay, whatever. Those Victim Services people are coming to see me in the morning, so I'm covered. Unless I don't answer the door."

"Now, Treva…"

Her laugh was soft, almost playful. "I just want to shut out the whole world. No more cops and doctors. Except *you*, of course, Dr. Rinaldi."

Now I was getting concerned.

Like many trauma victims, she was trying to retreat from dealing with what had happened to her. Using sleep, or reasonable-sounding assurances that everything was okay. Or even an amiable, knowing denial. All to keep potential caregivers at a distance. To keep from really looking at the emotional turmoil roiling inside her.

None of which I shared with her. Instead, I merely said, "How about if I call you later tomorrow? Or in the evening."

"Okay. If you want." A pause. "Truth is, I guess I'd be disappointed if you didn't."

Wanting help, and not wanting it. Pulling back on the lifeline whenever it threatened to go slack.

"Well, the last thing I'd want to do is disappoint you, Treva."

An awkward beat of silence.

"You mean like with the ambulance?"

I admit, I was a bit taken aback. But I only paused for a moment before responding.

"Yes, Treva. Like with the ambulance."

Her next words were guarded. "But that other promise you made today…in the hospital room…you'll keep *that* promise, right?"

"Yes, I will. But I need to know more—"

"Maybe tomorrow, okay, Dr. Rinaldi? I'm so tired."

Another, heavier yawn. Insistent. "Bye."

Chapter Thirty-six

The city's silhouette glowed dully against the thick summer night as I drove aimlessly through the urban core. It was late, past midnight, but I was too wired to sleep. Too jangly from the past days' chaotic events.

I headed in the general direction of the Point, the storied juncture of the Three Rivers. Lights spilled from its slim, gleaming buildings onto the new construction site below, threading odd-angled shadows through its erector-set scaffolding. Like the crystals we used to grow as kids in science class, every year brought new facets and planes to the gentrified expanse of downtown Pittsburgh.

I turned down the volume from my dashboard speakers. Since pulling out of the garage beneath the Burgoyne Plaza, I'd been listening to Nina Simone singing about heartbreak and hope in that classic, mournful voice. But now, as though unwilling to allow myself a respite from the thoughts crowding my mind, I dutifully clicked off the CD player and tuned in the all-news radio station.

Dutiful? I thought. Or just a glutton for punishment.

As I expected, the attempt on Leland Sinclair's life led the news. I tried another station, where I heard various local pundits weighing in on the political aspects of the event. What would the polls say?

One of these commentators reported mentioning the polls to Sinclair's campaign manager, Brian Fletcher, who apparently took great offense at the question. According to Fletcher, elections weren't about polls, weren't about some media-fueled horse race. Elections were about what was best for the people of Pennsylvania.

"I mean, the guy practically took my head off," the journalist said, laughing. "On the other hand, Fletcher has been with the Sinclair campaign from its beginning. There's no question the two men have developed a deep, mutually-supportive bond. Should Lee Sinclair go on to win the governor's seat, I believe he's certain to name Brian Fletcher as his chief of staff."

Which brought another flurry of disagreement from the other commentators, some of whom felt such appointments should only be made from outside the campaign. Perhaps from the business world, or academia. Et cetera, et cetera.

After finding similar stories on other stations, I realized that the hunt for the two bank robbers was barely being covered. Other than a cursory recap of details most people already knew. It reminded me of what Sam Weiss had taught me about news cycles. How, as a result of the Internet and other technologies, they'd essentially morphed into one continuous loop. Which meant that what was now considered newsworthy had a pretty short shelf-life. Unless fresh information became available—new facts suggesting an exciting, unexpected angle—the story itself soon stopped *being* "news."

Soon weary of channel-surfing and yet still nowhere near ready to go home, I decided to drive down to the river for a nightcap at Noah's. Sometimes, it seemed to me, his particular brand of crazy was just what my conflicted, over-heated mind needed.

Suddenly my cell rang. I looked at the dash clock. Almost one AM. Who—?

It was Nancy Mendors.

"Danny, it's me. I just heard on the news about Leland Sinclair. They're saying you saved his life."

"It was kind of a group effort."

"Whatever. Not that I'm surprised. It's exactly the kind of bone-headed thing you'd do."

"If you say so. I assume there's a reason for this late-night call?"

"Depends. Where are you?"

"In my car. Heading down to Noah's."

"Great. I'll meet you there."

◇◇◇

By the time I arrived at the riverfront bar, Noah Frye and his two new best friends were finishing their last set. I saw right away that, as Noah had reported, the side-men could easily be cousins, or at least somehow related. Both tall, skinny, with tufts of unruly sand-colored hair. Both also displayed the bored, too-cool-for-this-world look of your typical jazz veteran.

I leaned back on my bar stool, Scotch in hand, and reveled in Noah's soulful touch at the keyboard. Especially on the hauntingly beautiful "Lush Life."

The trio was paying homage to one of Pittsburgh's home-grown heroes, Billy Strayhorn, who wrote that song while still in his teens. Noah told me once, not long after he'd started working at the bar, that he wanted to showcase music representing Pittsburgh's rich contribution to jazz. So he often devoted whole sets—sometimes whole evenings—to one of our famous local artists.

As the few remaining customers and I broke into applause at song's end, I reflected on how many Pittsburgh-born musicians there were to choose from. People as varied as Billy Eckstein and Erroll Garner. Harold Betters and Ahmad Jamal. Kenny Clarke, Maxine Sullivan, Art Blakey, Ray Brown. Stanley Turrentine and Mary Ann Williams. And on and on…

"How about a refill, Danny?"

Charlene's booming voice made me swivel in my seat. With Noah at the piano, she was on bartender duty. Made sense, too, since I knew from long experience that the kitchen closed at eleven.

"I'll just nurse this awhile, Charlene. I'm waiting for Nancy Mendors."

Charlene smiled sardonically and peered past my shoulder. "Waitin's over, Doc."

There was something knowing in her eyes that probably deserved further investigation, but I let it go. With her finely-tuned intuition, it wouldn't have surprised me if Charlene had long since guessed that there'd once been something between Nancy and me.

I also suspected that she'd never share this notion with Noah. No way Charlene would risk saying anything that might complicate Noah's clinical relationship with her. At the best of times, Noah Frye walked an exceedingly fine line.

I followed Charlene's gaze and spotted Nancy standing inside the door, waving in my direction.

"Are we closing up the place?" She came quickly across the floor, booted heels clicking on the hardwood. Small, trim body in what looked like new jeans and a scooped-necked silk blouse. Highlights in her dark hair. Frosted pink lipstick.

And again, as she sidled up to me, the scent of that unfamiliar new perfume.

Only her eyes, despite an over-bright sheen, displayed their usual solemnity. As always, I saw the weariness, the slight though unremitting strain, that lay deep within. The residue of a life's trials, disappointments.

Nancy gave me a quick kiss. Then, with one knee on the stool next to mine for support, leaned awkwardly across the bar to offer Charlene a hug. The two women met more or less in the middle and embraced warmly.

"Careful, Dr. Mendors," Charlene said cheerfully. "If Noah catches sight of us, he's gonna want a threesome."

Nancy laughed. "In his dreams."

Charlene straightened up again, waved her hand, and moved down the length of the bar to serve another customer. Meanwhile, Nancy took her seat on the stool next to me. Avidly eyed my drink.

"I hope that's Scotch."

Bowing slightly, I handed her my glass. She took a tentative sip. Then a larger one.

She smiled shyly up at me. "You ought to get yourself one, too."

"Now why didn't I think of that?"

As I watched her take another swallow, I had the disquieting thought that this wasn't her first drink of the evening. Nor perhaps her second. Again, uncharacteristic.

I was still thinking about it when Noah ambled over, his shirt dark with honest sweat.

"Great set, Noah," I said.

He beamed. "So I wasn't hallucinating? People were really digging it?"

"Absolutely. Unless *I* was hallucinating, too."

Noah feigned offense. "Hey, don't knock it till you've tried it."

Then, turning: "Dr. Nancy. Lookin' fine, I must say."

"Thanks. How are you doing, Noah?"

"Same old. Breathin' in, breathin' out. Not that I'm complainin'. Beats the fuck outta the alternative."

His opaque eyes betrayed a flicker of sadness, which just as quickly disappeared. Then he too-elaborately clapped his huge hands together.

"Anyway, time to go dig some cash out of the old vault. I gotta pay them other two head-cases or they'll key Charlene's car. They done it before."

"Then why still play with them?" Nancy asked.

"You shittin' me? You *heard* 'em. Petty vandalism's a small price to pay for such kick-ass chops."

I was about to ask whether Charlene shared his opinion on the subject when he turned—pretty damned gracefully for a big man—and took off. Soon to vanish behind the swinging doors to the kitchen.

"He's still upset about Andy's suicide," Nancy said.

"Easy to understand why."

She finished the rest of my drink just as Charlene sauntered back our way. I ordered two more, and she shuffled off. When I was sure she was out of earshot, I turned back to Nancy.

"Maybe you ought to adjust his meds. Just in case."

"I'll come by tomorrow and see him. Noah's too high-strung after a long night playing. Mornings are better. He's more vulnerable." A slight smile. "And, to be honest, more compliant."

"Compliant? Are we talking about the same guy? Then you really *do* have a magic touch."

Charlene returned with our drinks, then hurriedly disappeared into the back room. Probably to make sure Noah wasn't feeling too generous toward his band-mates.

Nancy and I touched glasses. Sipped our drinks.

"Funny." She looked off. "Noah's not the only one rattled by Andy's death. Given the usual housing issues at Ten Oaks, we've tried assigning his empty room to another patient. But nobody wants it. Even patients who hate their roommates and have been begging for a single. Because of the suicide, everybody thinks Andy's room is haunted. That it'll bring bad luck."

I shrugged. "No surprise there. A lot of people—and not just psychiatric patients—think suicide is catching. Like the flu."

"I know. Even the cleaning crew is reluctant to go inside. So we're leaving it the way Andy left it. For now, at least. Until we get our next new patient. Someone who didn't know Andy. Then we'll clear it out and put 'em in there."

Her words had begun to slur. Though if she noticed this, she gave no indication. Instead, she took another sip of whiskey, then swirled the amber liquid in her glass.

"There's something else," she said, tilting her head to peer up at me. "Remember those two patients from the clinic who came to Andy's funeral? The young girl, arguing with that boy?"

"Yes." I struggled to retrieve their names from the Rolodex in my mind. "Victoria Tolan, right? And Stan Willis. What about them?"

"It's just odd, because Victoria has always seemed happy with us. But now she's asked her family to find her another facility. She wants to leave Ten Oaks."

"Did she say why?"

"No, though according to clinic gossip, it's because Stan is bothering her. Whatever that means. We've spoken to him, but he denies it."

"So what are you going to do?"

A frown. "You mean, besides stepping down as clinical director?"

"Bullshit. You're the best thing to happen to Ten Oaks since the doors opened."

"Liar. But I appreciate it." She took a long breath, then downed the rest of her drink. "The thing is, we've made excellent progress with Victoria Tolan. Or, to be fair, *she* has. I know we're the right facility for her. But if I can't keep a patient like Victoria, or don't know how to get to the bottom of this thing with Stan Willis, then maybe I'm in the wrong job. Maybe I should just go back to being a case manager. Do my rounds. Prescribe their drugs. And go on home."

She paused suddenly, and blinked. Rapidly. Then, very deliberately, put her empty glass on the bar.

I touched her elbow.

"Speaking of going home," I said, "how about if I call you a cab? Better yet, I'll drive you."

Chapter Thirty-seven

"God, I'm such a lightweight."

Nancy sat forward in the passenger side of my car, holding her head in her hands. I'd opened both windows, figuring that fresh air—even though, at two AM, it still pouted with humidity—was better than the AC.

"Yeah, but in your case that's *literally* true. So don't feel bad about it."

With her head down, face curtained by her tumble of hair, I couldn't see her reaction. But I could guess.

We were driving across the Pitt campus, under the looming spire of the Cathedral of Learning, on our way to Shadyside. Nancy's apartment was in an old gabled building that had become, like much else in the city proper, newly fashionable.

"What about my car?" More like a groan than a question. "It's still parked outside the bar."

"We can figure that one out tomorrow. Right now, I just want to get you home."

Her head came up at last, and she turned to look at me with bleary-eyed indignation.

"I'm really all right, Danny. Stop acting like I've never had a drink before."

"I will if you will."

She paused a moment, then broke into warm laughter. I joined her. I could tell that the easy drive through near-empty city streets, moving through low canyons of concrete and shadow, was making us both feel better.

"Actually," she said, "the one I'm worried about is you."

I searched her face in the dim light of the car. She was suddenly serious.

"Me?"

"I just wanted to make sure you're okay about Warren and me. I mean, about the engagement."

"First of all, I'm more than okay. I'm really happy for you. Secondly, the truth is, it's none of my business. As we both know."

"Really?" Rubbing her brow. "Since when did we become so mature about things? So...I don't know...sophisticated."

I laughed. "Hardly that, Nancy. It's just...after all this time..."

She finished my sentence. "We're just friends. Right. I get that."

"Friends," I repeated, looking directly at her moist, somber eyes. "But also *more* than friends. At least, that's how it's always seemed to me."

"And to me. Of course, you're right. And I'm glad... well, I'm glad you're good with it. About Warren and me."

"I am. Truly."

She nodded slowly, as though not quite convinced. Then turned away, to look out her open window.

"I *do* want you to meet Warren. You'd like him, Danny. In fact, I was going to try to arrange something for tonight. But he had an emergency surgery, and you were at the Burgoyne, playing hero. Again."

She seemed aware of the edge in her voice even before I was, and sank lower in her seat. Arms hugging herself.

I said nothing, just drove carefully as I neared the row of apartment buildings off Walnut. The street was dark as a tunnel beneath a dense canopy of trees.

I looked over at her again, but she kept her face in profile. I knew she was upset. I also knew it wasn't just the alcohol. She'd been jangly, ill at ease, since she came into Noah's Ark. Overly vivacious, as though to mask—

What? I wondered. Was it merely her concern about my reaction to her engagement? Maybe she wanted some assurance that it wouldn't change the tenor of our friendship.

I found her building near the corner and pulled over to the curb. Turned in my seat, facing her.

"C'mon, I'll walk you up."

"No need to, Danny. Besides, I want to be by myself. Gives me time to compose the apology I'm going to email you tomorrow."

"Apology for what?"

But she merely smiled, then leaned over and kissed me lightly on the lips. Friendship kiss.

Then, without another word, she slipped out of my car and went through the front door into her building.

◇◇◇

I was heading up to Mt. Washington under a charcoal-black sky when my cell rang. It was nearly three. Wasn't anyone asleep in this town?

It was Sam Weiss.

"Hey, Danny. Glad I got you. I'm just finishing up here at the Burgoyne."

"You're still at the hotel?"

"What can I say, I'm dedicated. I wrote up the story on my laptop here in the service kitchen and emailed it to my editor. No worries, the busboy proofed it. Only one thing missing."

"What's that?"

"An exclusive interview with the lunatic who tackled Sinclair's shooter. You got a minute?"

"Forget it. I'm saving all my sound-bites for CNN. Besides, I have some questions for *you*. But not now. I gotta get some sleep."

"What kinda questions?"

"About Sinclair being dirty. I need to know what you have on him. Or *think* you have."

"Hell, I can do better than that. I'll take you to the guy tomorrow. My source. Says he has proof."

"You want me to go with you?"

"Yeah. Truth is, I could use your take on him. He's kinda squirrelly. But I think he's credible. Meet me at noon sharp, okay?"

I was surprised when he told me where.

Chapter Thirty-eight

We were in a single-engine Cessna, climbing through twenty-five hundred feet, heading east toward Harrisburg. The engine's roar was more like a rattling whine, high and insistent. The passenger seat vibrated beneath me.

Sitting next to me in the pilot's seat, so close that our shoulders touched, Sam Weiss was busily punching buttons in the on-board GPS. Humming out of key. We each wore headsets with boom mikes, which beat hell out of shouting to hear each other over the engine noise.

"You sure you've done this before?" I said.

"No, but I've read the manual. Twice."

A licensed pilot, Sam had—as promised—met me at noon at the Gold Star Aviation Training facility, a complex of low-roofed buildings and private hangars a few miles south of Pittsburgh International Airport. Though I knew he often rented planes there, either for business or to take his family on vacation, I'd never flown with him before.

The compact green-and-white two-seater he walked us to on an asphalt apron near the tarmac was easily the smallest airplane I'd ever seen.

"Only thing available on such short notice," he'd explained, as he climbed up on the near wing and then wriggled through the one narrow door. He strapped himself in and patted the leather seat next to him. "You comin' or what? It's real comfy."

I laughed and clambered up after him. Strapped in, put on the headset he offered me, sat back and waited. In less than five minutes he was barking flight info into his mike, exchanging weather and wind conditions with the tower, and revving the engine. Five minutes after that, we taxied out onto the slender ribbon of runway and lifted smoothly into the air. And another blistering mid-summer day.

With the exception of a few interesting pockets of turbulence, it had been a pretty smooth flight. So far.

Below and beyond us, a rolling patchwork of sun-blanched greens and yellows spread under a slight haze to the distant horizon. We'd left Allegheny County some twenty minutes ago, and were flying through a heat-scorched sky over rural Pennsylvania. Small towns and old farms. Brown pastures and abandoned factories. The spreading tendrils of Interstate 76 reaching delicately into furrowed valleys, sparsely-populated residential communities. River and lakeside expanses of forested tuffs and strip-mined hills.

Sam's voice crackled in my earphones. "We'll touch down at Harrisburg in less than an hour. I already rented a car."

"Where are we going?"

"Small backwoods town called Harville, thirty miles west of Harrisburg. Wants to be a dot on the map when it grows up. Nothin' but dirt, trees, and dying farms."

He turned the wheel and we dipped our left wing. I held fast to the handle grip above the door as an updraft lifted us. The whole plane shuddered.

"And your guy wants to do this in person?"

"Only way he'll talk. He also said it was now or never. Like I told you, he sounded funny."

As we banked, sunlight danced quickly across the windshield. Sudden, blinding. Then, as Sam righted us again, adjusting his course, the light shifted, fled. I heard the wind above the engine's whine for a brief moment, before it too dopplered away. As though now in our wake.

"You get a real appreciation of the weather up here," Sam was saying. "How things are always rockin' and rollin' at altitude, no matter what it feels like on the ground."

"Yeah." I swallowed hard. "Appreciation is exactly the word I was looking for."

He ignored me, and pointed through his side window, down and to the left. Clusters of houses, grain silos and farms. Huddled together as though for mutual protection in a tractless expanse of forested land, forlorn gray hills.

"Harville's down there," Sam announced. "Somewhere."

I peered down through my own window, as though if I looked hard enough I could distinguish one community from another, one farmhouse from another.

Finally, I sat back in my seat and closed my eyes. Settled in for the brief remaining flight time. And went over in my mind all that I'd learned since waking up that morning, six hours before.

◇◇◇

After a short, restless couple hours of sleep, I was groggy and listless when I pulled myself out of bed. Two cups of coffee, a sluggish morning's run up and down Grandview Avenue in the pale dawn sun, and a long, hot shower later, I felt more or less ready to start the day.

At least I was together enough to remember about the joint police-FBI press conference scheduled for seven AM. No need. Sprawled on the sofa in shorts and a Pitt t-shirt, freshly-brewed third cup of coffee in hand, I clicked on WTAE-TV just in time to hear that it had been canceled.

According to a statement released by the authorities, the "sensitive nature" of the investigation into the attempt on Leland Sinclair's life made a press conference at this early juncture inadvisable. The reporter on-scene at the Federal Building promised viewers that WTAE would keep tracking the story, and would share any breaking news as soon as it happened.

I sat forward, balanced my coffee mug on my knee. Sinclair had indeed managed to keep the task force's investigation off the media grid, at least for the time being. Not that his concerns were unjustified. For a political candidate in a tight race, such an investigation would be a distraction he couldn't afford. If nothing else, it would veer Sinclair's candidacy off-message. And would have voters thinking about the upcoming debate with Garrity for all the wrong reasons.

On the other hand, I thought, it might actually boost viewership for the event. Nothing like the possibility of sudden, unexpected violence to pique interest. Hell, it seems to work for hockey and Nascar.

I was about to click off the TV when another report followed, from a different reporter, standing in a different corridor in the Federal Building. Apparently, FBI Special Agent Neal Alcott had called an impromptu press conference of his own, to provide an update on the hunt for the two bank robbers.

The reporter then cut to a video obviously shot just minutes before. Which gave me my first look at Neal Alcott, a tall, fairly young man. Broad-shouldered in his tailored suit. Close-cropped blond hair. Voice clear and assured. Unlike many law enforcement types, he was practiced and relaxed before the array of cameras and mikes.

Though it was hardly a press conference. Reading from a prepared statement, Alcott merely announced that the manhunt for the two killers had gone nationwide. Moreover, though he didn't want to get into specifics, the Bureau felt confident that they'd identified the second gunman, Wheeler Roarke's partner in the crime.

This brought a swell of questions from the reporters on-scene, which Alcott answered only with a guarded smile and an upraised palm. Then he folded his prepared statement into two perfect halves and walked briskly out of view.

No question, the guy was good. And, I suspected, unlikely to stay local for very long. Neal Alcott would probably end up in Quantico sooner rather than later.

I threw back the rest of my coffee and rinsed the mug in the sink. I figured I'd pretty much exhausted whatever benefits caffeine was going to provide. I'd had too little sleep. My head still ached from where Roarke slugged me. And my tussle with Jimmy Gordon, though brief, had left me with sore muscles and a painful bruise in my left side.

All of which reminded me that I was no longer a young amateur boxer, but a forty-year-old with a sedentary day job and piss-poor impulse control. Or an ill-advised hero complex. Or *something.*

I smiled to myself. Good issue to take up with my own therapist. If I ever got the time to make an appointment. Which was something *else* to take up with him...

Before dressing and heading out, I checked my voice mail for messages. Again, thankfully, nothing urgent.

Then, just as I was collecting my wallet and car keys, my cell rang. Eleanor Lowrey.

"Are you still at the precinct?" I settled into one of my hard-backed kitchen chairs.

"No, at the police gym." She sounded winded, but energized. I knew the feeling. "We worked through the night, but I was too wired to go home. So I've been lifting weights. Plus some cardio. To clear my head."

"Good idea."

"Hey, we oughtta work out together sometime, Danny. *If* you can keep up."

"I'll be sure to eat my Wheaties that morning."

"Better make it two bowls." Voice light, playful. Fueled by the surge of endorphins, the mood-elevating neurochemical bonus from a solid workout.

I also heard other voices in the background. Plus the clank of weights, the rolling rumble of a treadmill.

"Let me move to where it's more private," she said quickly. I waited a full minute. The next time she spoke, what few sounds I heard over the phone were muffled. Some distance away.

"This'll have to do." Her breathing more regular, measured. "A stall in the women's locker room."

"Is this about Harry? Was he at work when you got there last night?"

"Yeah, thank God. Still, as I guessed, Biegler really chewed him out. Threatened to put him on a desk and ask for an official review."

"What happened?"

"Harry *apologized*, if you can believe it. He told the lieutenant he had some personal issues which had interfered with the job, but that they were all cleared up now."

"Did Biegler believe him?"

"Looked like it. And hell, he knows he can't afford to bench a guy with Harry's experience right now. Not with everything that's going on."

"That's for damn sure."

"But that's not the big news. We have a possible ID on the second bank robber."

"So I heard. Alcott was on the news, talking about it. But with no details."

"I'm not surprised. No reason to spook the guy."

"So who is he?"

"A known associate of Roarke's. Name is Ronny Baxter. Apparently they worked at Blackwater together. Baxter's ex-Army. Got bounced from Blackwater soon after Roarke. He's built up a sweet criminal record since leaving Iraq. All ground level stuff. Assault, B and E."

"FBI have any idea where he is?"

"Not yet. They hit his last known address a couple hours ago, but he'd cleared out. An apartment in Dayton, Ohio. So the Bureau's going nationwide with the search. Like with Roarke."

"Well, at least that's something. Progress."

"Tell me. About time we caught a break, too."

I heard another rush of new voices, much closer. Doors banging open. Laughter.

"Gotta go," Eleanor said. "Some sisters in blue are crashing the party. I better grab a shower before they use up all the soap and hot water. And you're welcome."

"For what?"

"For that image. Have a nice day, Doctor."

Chapter Thirty-nine

We were about twenty minutes out of Harrisburg, cruising through a cloudless sky. Sam had just finished radioing his position to the airport tower, receiving instructions back as to available runways. Earlier, he'd explained that, for safety and security reasons, private and corporate planes were routed to a special landing area far to the west of the big carriers.

"Gets us in and out faster, too." Sam scanned the horizon, aviator shades hanging by a cord around his neck. "Which is good, because I want to get back by seven, if possible. Sinclair's scheduled a press conference to address concerns about the attempt on his life."

I had to smile. "He got the cops and feds to cancel theirs, only to have one of his own. Probably figures he can control the message a lot better that way."

"You're right. Word is, he plans a short speech to assure voters that he won't be intimidated by the criminal element. That his tough law-and-order stand has always entailed risk. But he has every faith in law enforcement, has no concern about any further attempts, and is looking forward to the debate on Saturday."

"Smart move. He addresses it, puts it in a box, then puts the box behind him."

"*If* he can get away with it. On the other hand, maybe Jimmy Gordon takin' a shot at Sinclair did him some good. Did you see the latest polls this morning? He's pulled slightly ahead of

Garrity since it happened. And his favorables are up among blue-collar and undecided voters."

I looked at his profile. His jaw tightening.

"You really don't like him, do you, Sam? You really think he's dirty."

"I don't know, man. Hell, they're *all* dirty to some extent. Politics is a dirty business. Always has been. The stakes are too goddam high. And as long as there are lobbyists and PACS, politics will stay dirty. I mean, in the end it doesn't matter who the candidate is. What kind of person. Just depends on how much dirt you're willing to roll around in to get elected. And stay elected."

"Sinclair's a hard-ass, no question. And ambitious. But how can you be so sure he's in bed with the wrong people?"

"I'm not. But my source says he can prove it. Unless he's full of shit. That's what I have to find out."

Sam gave the wheel a slight turn, and the plane banked to the right. A square of sunlight moved across my line of sight, set the windshield ablaze for a few seconds, then moved on. As though a living thing, seeking something.

Finally, I said, "How long are you gonna be cagey about this guy, Sam? Who is this source? What's his name?"

"Sorry." He chuckled behind the mike. "Old habits and all that—never divulge the name of a source."

"Except I'm going to be looking him in the eye pretty soon, right? Probably catch his name at some point, too. *You* invited *me*, remember?"

"I know. I also figure I can count on your keeping his identity confidential. But there's something about this guy, Danny. Something…I don't know…I guess I just need a second opinion."

Sam stifled a yawn. Like me, he'd had a pretty long night, and probably as little sleep.

"His name's Henry Stubbs. A former investigator with the Federal Trade Commission. One of those guys who looks into alleged illegalities committed by law firms. Or specific lawyers in the firm."

"Never heard of him."

"No reason you should. Just another retired government drone with a pension and health problems. But I bet you've heard of McCloskey, Singer, and Ganz."

"Sounds familiar. 'Course, I could be thinking of Crosby, Stills, and Nash. I take it you're talking about a law firm."

"Not just *a* law firm. One of the biggest, and very influential. Offices in New York, DC, Chicago, Atlanta. Represents huge clients. The ones with deep pockets. Agribusiness. Pharmaceuticals. Major retail chains."

"What do they have to do with Sinclair?"

"According to Stubbs, plenty. He knows the firm inside and out. Spent a year investigating them on charges of financial malfeasance, fraud, unethical practices. A whole laundry list. Came down here from New York."

"Here?"

"Harrisburg. The home office. Turns out it's where Evan McCloskey is from. Started the business from a small office near the capitol building. Took on Singer and Ganz as full partners after the firm won that huge class action suit for Consolidated Feed and Grain."

"I remember seeing that on the news. The environmental impact claims against them were reversed. It was considered a major defeat for the green movement."

"That's because it was. The point is, McCloskey's firm really took off after that. Became the go-to guys for corporations in trouble over government regs. Or hassled by activist groups. Made McCloskey very, very rich."

I tried to recall if I'd ever seen McCloskey's picture somewhere. Online, on TV, or in a magazine. But no image sprang up in my mind. "He must keep a pretty low profile."

"All these guys do. We know the names of the firms, maybe. Know about their biggest cases. But the partners are always these faceless white guys in designer suits. In a private world of golf, company jets, and cocktails. And always smart enough to let the spotlight stay on their famous clients. You know who Donald

Trump is, right? And Warren Buffet. What they look like. But do you know what their *lawyers* look like?"

"I get it. But what does this have to do with Henry Stubbs? Or, more importantly, with Lee Sinclair?"

"I told you, Stubbs has been inside the castle. Down below, where they keep the dragons. And the bones of the poor bastards the dragons had for lunch."

"Jesus, I hate it when you get all cryptic. Does Stubbs know something he shouldn't about the firm? About Evan McCloskey?"

Sam turned enough to let me see the corners of that familiar, crooked smile.

"It's not just what he knows. It's what he heard. And can prove. When McCloskey was talking about Sinclair's campaign. And how the firm might get involved."

"Involved? What does that mean?"

"I'm looking forward to finding out. One juicy tidbit Stubbs told me already. To whet my appetite, I guess. One of the things McCloskey said about Sinclair."

"Which was?"

"That it was going to be fun to own a governor."

Chapter Forty

Twenty minutes later, we were on the ground at Harrisburg International, a satellite strip some short distance from the main terminals. Twenty minutes after that, we were standing under a merciless sun, deepening our tans against our will, at a curbside car rental stall. Waiting for the sedan Sam had ordered ahead of time.

"Don't worry, I got a Buick." Sam wiped his brow with a sleeve. "Lousy gas mileage but great AC."

The valet was just pulling the late-model Buick up to the curb when Sam's cell rang. He put down his carry-all, lifted the cell to his ear and walked a few feet away. In moments, a mask of consternation and frustration etched itself onto his face.

After getting the keys from the valet, I swung into the passenger seat and rolled down the window, letting out stale hot air. Then Sam hung up, retrieved his carry-all and trotted to the car. Motioned for me to shove over to the driver's seat, while he took mine.

"You want me to drive?"

"You better." His eyes were angry points. "Since you're the only one going."

"What are you talking about?"

He pulled his carry-all up onto his lap, started un-zipping it.

"That was my editor. He wants me to do a detailed sidebar on the Sinclair shooting. Rehashing all the Felix Gordon stuff.

The trial, the threats by his brother Jimmy. All the way up to Felix getting killed in prison."

"Oh, man."

"Tell me. He wants it to accompany the story on Sinclair's press conference tonight. Run it down the whole left side, front page." A dark smile. "Total steal from the *LA Times*, but, shit, it got them a Pulitzer, right?"

By now, he'd taken out his laptop computer, and, using the carry-all laid across his knees as a desk, was booting it up.

"Can't it wait till after we talk to Stubbs?"

Sam shook his head. "Boss wants it now. As in *right now*. Gonna take me at least two hours to write it up and email it in. Gotta drag up all the old files, previous Gordon stories. Total pain in the ass."

I peered at his laptop screen.

"So what are you doing now?"

"Bringing up all the stuff I have on Henry Stubbs. My plan was for you to read it on our drive out to Harville. Get you up to speed on the guy."

He tapped some keys, hit SEND, and closed the laptop's lid. Turned in his seat.

"Okay, here's the deal: I gotta go find a quiet room and a six-pack of Red Bull. So I just emailed everything I have to a buddy of mine, an editor at the *Harville Sentinel*, the local rag. He'll have somebody print it out for you."

I held up my hand. "Wait a minute, Sam. You want me to go see Stubbs myself?"

"No choice, Danny. Take the car, go meet the guy. Tell him you work for me. Get him talking, and try to make it stretch. Ask a lot of questions. Whatever. Soon as I get my story in, I'll rent another car and join you."

"This is crazy."

"Then it's right up your alley, isn't it?"

He'd already zippered the laptop back in its pouch in the carry-all. Then he opened the passenger side door.

"Stubbs may not go for this." Did I sound as lame as I suspected?

"He's a source, remember? Stubbs contacted *me*. No matter what, this guy wants to talk."

I saw his logic. "Then we both better get it in gear."

"Now we're talkin'. We each got our marchin' orders, right? See ya when I see ya."

◇◇◇

The girl told me the oversized letter jacket she wore belonged to her boyfriend. Good thing, too, despite the heat, since her boss always kept the office temperature cold enough to hang meat. Besides, Billy liked her wearing something of his so she'd keep him in mind.

"Like I'd forget about him or something." She reached in front of me to adjust the printer. She was cheerleader-pretty, but with grave green eyes that hinted at some rough times in the past. Her name was April. She was seventeen and interning at the paper.

It had taken only forty minutes to make the drive from the airport to Harville. After I got off the interstate, the route west took me through the same rural landscape I'd seen from the air. Which only looked more sun-blanched and isolated at ground level. More a sprawling, topographical quilt of fallow pastures and ill-tended groves. Only the hardiest of maples, oaks and sycamores showed healthy green leaves, and this primarily due to the automated sprinklers and irrigation pipes put in by the larger, still-viable farms.

In fact, as I neared Harville, what struck me most was the thickening expanse of trees. In an area left unshorn and uncultivated for farmland, perhaps because of a poor quality of soil, I drove along entire stretches of highway shouldered on either side by dense forest. For the first time since leaving Harrisburg, I found myself passing through deep shadows, offering a much-needed solace from the blazing sun.

At last, I spotted the exit sign the car rental valet had described. Sam had been right about the town of Harville: it barely qualified for the term. Isolated, a hodge-podge of small, desiccated-looking farms, it boasted only a few proper civic buildings and retail outlet stores. A forlorn minimall at either end of the main business street. A McDonald's. A convenience store. Mobil station.

It didn't take me long to find the Depression-era brown-bricked façade of the *Harville Sentinel's* two-storied building. A few cars were unevenly parked at the open-air lot in the back. I joined them.

Then I went inside and introduced myself to Lionel Perkins, Sam's editor friend. Red-faced, heavy, and sweating, he'd merely grunted a greeting and handed me over to Apri, who'd walked me over to a corner desk in the small, cluttered office.

Where I sat now, the teenager handing me the print-out a page at a time. And complaining about the rigors of dating, as well as an ongoing conflict with her parents about her going away to college.

"Like I wanna stay *here*, and end up folding sweaters all day at Banana Republic."

Finally Perkins called her away and I had the desk to myself. Only a faint whiff of her scent—part perfume, part sour-apple jawbreaker—remained.

I spread all of Sam's materials on the desk. Then, for clarity's sake, began arranging the old newspaper clips in chronological order.

First came a number of stories about Harrisburg's own Evan McCloskey, and the growing success of his new law firm. The posed press photo accompanying one of the articles revealed a prematurely gray-haired, pale WASP type in a conservative suit standing in front of a stereotypically impressive shelf of law books. He looked like a million other guys in positions like his, in firms like his.

I kept reading. When he and his team won the case for Consolidated Feed and Grain, it made headlines in most of the national papers. Then came the announcement that Singer and Ganz had been promoted to full partners, though it was understood that McCloskey was still the head honcho. The "invisible face" of the firm, as one legal pundit observed in a *New York Times* Op-Ed from some years back.

Despite opening offices in other cities across the country, McCloskey kept the home office in Harrisburg. He lived in town with his wife and children, but often spent weekends at his sprawling estate in nearby Harville. As I learned from a feature spread in the Sunday *Sentinel,* displaying photos of the impressive building and its broad, manicured gardens.

Then the tone of the stories changed. A number of articles from national papers, as well as the state's major dailies, covered the arrival in Harrisburg of a Federal Trade Commission investigator named Henry Stubbs. He'd been called in from Washington at the request of the state attorney general to uncover evidence of malfeasance and fraud, long rumored to be rife at the prestigious firm.

Three articles later, Henry Stubbs is being quoted extensively as to the result of his investigation. He asserts that the firm's been cleared of any wrong-doing, and that the FTC has ended the investigation. There were also quotes from Evan McCloskey, stating how gratified he was by the FTC's decision.

Not two months later, the *Style* section of the paper ran a story about Henry Stubbs' decision to stay in Harville, "and make it my home." He goes on to explain that during the course of his work he "fell in love with the place," and that he was tired of big-city life. After all, he'd grown up in a small town in Montana and was still "a country boy at heart," despite his years in Washington. He was happy to report that he was retiring from government work, and would be using his pension to buy a nice home in the area.

The next article Sam had pulled up for me detailed Stubbs' decision to run for Sheriff of Harville and his subsequent victory. Apparently the voters were impressed by those "big-city" credentials, in addition to his obvious affinity for their town. He did well enough in the job to run unopposed for a second term.

I sat back from the desk and stared at the last piece of material April had printed out for me. It was a front-page story, complete with photo, about Stubbs' swearing-in ceremony. He stood tall and lanky, jacket unbuttoned, with a trimmed mustache. A real urban cowboy, but with a cop's glint to his eyes. Flanking him stood the Mayor, some city council members, and a number of campaign contributors. One of whom, smiling broadly, was Evan McCloskey.

I got to my feet and stretched. Then, bending to gather up all the hard copies, I called over to Perkins, thanking him. He didn't glance up from his own cluttered desk.

As I headed out of the office, I waved my thanks to an equally-oblivious April, who was flirtatiously playing with a handsome fellow intern's shirt collar as they bent over some paperwork.

Billy's jacket had been thrown over a nearby chair.

Chapter Forty-one

I called Henry Stubbs at the number Sam had provided.

The phone rang ten or eleven times. Nobody picked up. No answering machine. No voice mail.

I'd be arriving uninvited.

I drove the Buick out of town and turned onto a dusty, two-lane blacktop. I'd gotten directions from an attendant at the local liquor store, a retired Sears employee who still remembered Stubbs' house as "the old Stafford place." He also warned me that finding the residence in such densely-forested woodlands wouldn't be easy.

He was right. I drove past the dirt access road twice before spotting the tell-tale elm tree. Its lightning-split trunk rose up like a gnarled tuning fork against the pale azure sky.

As soon as I started down the rutted, serpentine road, I was plunged into a kind of semidarkness. The tree canopy blocked most of the sun, and the woods on either side of the road faded into gray-black streaks, like an Impressionist's brush-strokes.

After about five miles of twisting, bouncing road, I made out a barbed-wire fence to my right. I quickly pulled over, raising a curving tail of dust, and got out.

Peering through flitting curtains of shadow, I moved cautiously along the fence as it trailed off the access road and cut into a grove of trees. Overhead, broad gaps in the interlocking branches allowed some sunlight through, and now it glinted and danced off verdant clusters of foliage on either side of me. With every other step, I heard a rustling of movement in the thick undergrowth. Lizards, ground quail, perhaps a startled garter snake.

Finally, this stretch of wire fence led to a thick, squat concrete pillar, atop which was a pitted tin sign. In deep scratches, as though carved with a nail, were written the words "Keep Out."

Is this guy kidding? I thought. What's next, a snarling German shepherd, straining at the leash?

I wasn't that lucky.

The tin sign in front of me literally exploded as a bullet ripped through and whistled past my shoulder.

I hit the ground hard, clutching the dirt, as another shot fired. This one chipped a half-inch divot off the near edge of the concrete pillar.

Without knowing from which direction the shots were coming, I rolled instinctively toward the fence and began pushing my way under the razor-sharp wire. The barbed twists raked my back, shredding my shirt and finding skin, as I struggled to get through to the other side.

Two more shots echoed like cannon-fire, shaking dust from the trees, as I finally squeezed under the wire and rolled again, this time toward the shelter of an ancient, upended wheelbarrow rusting in the tall grass. I scurried around to its far side, hunching down as far as possible.

I must have been seen. The next bullet pinged off the edge of the wheelbarrow, inches above my hairline, shearing off flecks of rust. *Christ!*

I knew I was pinned down. The nearest cover was a stand of maples, fifteen or twenty yards away.

I'd never make it.

As I crouched there, breathing hard, I heard the sound of an engine revving, then a clutch down-shifting. I raised myself up enough to see the old, pitted chassis of a John Deere tractor rumbling across the field toward me.

Sitting behind the wheel, steering with one hand while the other held an upraised Remington rifle, was an older man in crisp denim and a cap.

As he got closer, I recognized the squint in the sharp eyes sunken into folds of tanned, mottled skin. And the mustache— now white, but still neatly trimmed.

Slowly, I got to my feet.

Henry Stubbs braked to a stop about ten yards from where I now stood behind the wheelbarrow. He leaned forward across the steering wheel, using it to brace his forearms as he aimed the rifle directly at my head.

And smiled.

"If you're here to kill me, son, you went about it all wrong. 'Cause I'm just about to shoot you where you stand."

"No, I'm not here to kill you. Just to talk."

"Ever hear of the telephone?"

"Sure. You ever hear of answering it?"

He clucked his tongue. "Well, there's that, I guess. You a cop? Private eye?"

"No. I'm a consultant with the Pittsburgh police."

"Consultant? What's that mean?"

"Depends. I'm a psychologist, and sometimes I advise them on cases. Right now, though, I'm working with Sam Weiss. The reporter you contacted."

"Is that a fact?"

"He got held up at the airport. Some work thing. But he'll be here as soon as he can. He sent me along to make sure you didn't think he wasn't gonna show."

"So you people are takin' me seriously, eh?"

I paused. "Sam is. He says you're a credible source."

"And what do *you* think?"

"I don't know what to think. I don't know you. I guess I'd have to ask you some questions."

He shifted position, as though easing some stiffened joints, then refocused on aiming down the line of the rifle barrel. Its black eye stared at me, unblinking.

"Questions, eh?" he said at last. "Like what?"

I took a breath and made my pitch. "We know about your connection to Evan McCloskey, Sheriff. Why you came to Harville, and why you ended up staying. And, frankly, I don't care about any of that. McCloskey's probably a prick, given the kind of people he represents. Personally, I hope you took him for a fortune. I just need to hear what he has to do with Leland Sinclair, if anything."

Stubbs gave a kind of snort. "Well, mister, you got marble stones, I'll give you that. Not that I got the slightest idea what you're talkin' about."

"Sure you do. You know exactly what I'm talking about. You also know that if anybody wanted to bust you for taking bribes, this place would be swarming with cops right now."

He considered this. "You know, son, if you're lyin' to me, I'm gonna have to go with my original plan and put one right between your eyes."

"I don't think so. I think you want to tell me your story. Tell *somebody.* Or else you would've shot me already."

A long pause.

"Well, I guess that's true enough," he said finally, a strange resignation in his voice. Lowering the rifle, resting its butt on the top of his knee.

He sat back, lost in thought. A deliberate stillness emanated from him, as though he were posing for a portrait.

Then, just as abruptly, he stirred, and gunned the tractor's engine. Plumes of black smoke rose from the sputtering exhaust pipe.

"Okay, then, mister," he said. "Get in. I got some liquor back at the house. I figure I'm gonna need it."

I walked across the high grass and swung up onto the seat next to him. As he turned the tractor around and headed back across the field, Stubbs shouted to me over the engine's roar.

"Psychologist, eh? Well, it ain't a priest, but I guess it's close enough. I sorta thought the same thing about that reporter fella."

"Close enough for what?"

"For confession."

I must have stared, because he broke into a raw laugh.

"Damn, maybe you ain't as smart as I thought. Truth is, I don't give a shit about McCloskey. *Or* Sinclair. But I'm fixin' to spill my guts about all this to somebody. And it sure as hell better be soon. 'Cause, mister, I'm dying."

Chapter Forty-two

"Non-Hodgkins lymphoma," Stubbs said, pouring a fourth of a bottle of Stoli vodka into the pitcher of lemonade. "They figure I got six months. Maybe less."

We were on the front porch of his rambling, two-storied house, all burnt brick and timber, intersected by wide, floor-to-ceiling windows.

When we'd stepped up onto the wide, railing–enclosed porch, the first thing I noticed was the oval cedar table with twin match-ing chairs. On a woven placemat in the table's center was a large glass pitcher of freshly-made lemonade. The dozen sun-melted ice cubes bobbing on the surface had diluted its rich golden hue.

"My mother's recipe." Stubbs indicated the pitcher, its curved glass bowl beaded with condensation. "Not too much sugar, and you leave the lemons in, outside in the sun. Been out here since noon. Really deepens the flavor."

Then, with a weary smile, he'd reached under the table for a half-empty bottle of vodka.

"Of course, every recipe needs modifyin' once in a while." After which he'd unscrewed the cap and began his modifications.

As he poured us each a generous glass, I reflected on what I'd seen as we'd walked up the winding driveway to the front porch.

Nestled in a stand of poplars, with views of the valley and surrounding hills, the house must have cost a fortune. Yet there were signs of recent neglect. Tree branches scraped the roof, the

gutters choked with leaves. Dirt and dust and skeins of old web-
bing clung like unwanted memories to every corner, every niche.

Henry Stubbs was dying, I thought, and he was letting his
home die with him.

"And don't worry, we got the place to ourselves." He pointed
the bottle's nose at the dim, spacious rooms on the other side of
the window. "I only got one girl workin' for me now, and I send
her home before the cocktail hour. If you know what I mean."

Stubbs put the vodka down next to the pitcher. Then he took
his drink and leaned against a porch railing. I stood across from
him, my back to the unlit house within.

Just past Stubbs' shoulder stood a weathered barn, half the size
of the house and at least twice as old. Its opened doors revealed
a sawdust floor, cords of firewood, and a rack of long-unused
farming tools. Rakes, shovels, a hand mower. Relics.

"I know what you're thinkin'," Stubbs said with a pained
smile. "What did I do with all the money?"

"I assume a lot of it's here. In the land. And in the house."

"Yeah, but most of it ain't. It's in trust funds my kids have
been livin' off for years. Grown men now, but neither one of 'em
worth a damn. I guess I gotta take most of the blame for that.
They were just babies when I left their mother."

"You were still with the FTC then?"

"Yep. In DC. The divorce was turning into a nightmare, so
when my supervisor asked me to come up here and investigate
McCloskey's firm, I jumped at the chance."

"The concerns about unethical practices…"

His mouth turned down. "I always laugh when people get their
shorts in a twist over legal ethics. I mean, shit, how do you think
big law firms get so big? By sweatin' the ethics? It's just a word,
son, like any other. After a while, it don't even mean anything."

"But what about McCloskey's firm? What did you find?"

"Pretty much every violation in the book. From illegal wire-
taps and blackmail to over-charging clients. Had a judge or two
on the payroll, too."

"So you definitely had the goods on Evan McCloskey. Only instead of busting him, you went to him with a deal: Your silence for a healthy piece of the proceeds."

Again, that pained smile. "I figured, what the hell, there was nothin' for me back in DC. And I hated my damn job. Paperwork. Bureaucracy. All that bullshit. So me and McCloskey came to an understanding…"

"What kind of understanding?"

He looked down at the drink in his hand. "Well, I guess I was plain greedy. I told him I was gonna go public with the evidence about his firm's illegal practices. Then I said I wanted ten million dollars to keep what I knew to myself. And, by God, I got it."

"Pretty dangerous game to play, wasn't it?"

"Not really. I've investigated guys like McCloskey all my life. White collar criminals, they call 'em. And for good reason. They'll happily rob widows and orphans of their pensions, or steal intellectual property from their rivals. But they ain't gonna kill nobody. They don't got the stomach for it. Or the knack. Truth is, when things finally go belly-up, ain't unusual for a lot of 'em to put a gun in their mouths. Or jump out the window of their fancy corner office."

"Still, ten million's a lot of money."

Stubbs laughed bitterly. "Not for McCloskey. Based on what I uncovered, his firm's paid more'n that in bribes to government officials. Or to get a competitor's top guy to give 'em some inside info. Hell, afterwards, I realized I shoulda hit him up for more."

He grimaced suddenly, holding his stomach.

"Not that I give a shit anymore about the money," he went on, with difficulty. "Soon as I got it, I set up anonymous trust funds for my kids—they think it's from some distant rich relative. So, to answer your question, that's where the money went. My ex-wife died soon after I settled here, so there was nothin' much I could do for her. But I wanted to provide for my sons. Bums, like I said, but I figured they got a bum father first."

He finished the rest of his drink. Then, slumping, he fell silent, haggard face half-hidden beneath his cap.

"But why stay in Harville?" I asked. "You could've taken the money and gone anywhere."

He turned his head, glanced out at the sloping hills fading behind lengthening afternoon shadows.

"I liked it here," he said. "It's quiet."

"So why not settle down and live a life of leisure? Why run for sheriff?"

"Tell ya the truth, after a while I got kinda bored. Even with this nice house and all. Plus I was shackin' up with this beautician at the time. Big red-head. Tits out to here. Life was good. But I was goin' nuts."

Stubbs drained his glass. "I figured McCloskey'd be only too happy to have the local law in his pocket, so I went to him and suggested he stake me for a run during the next election. I guess he saw some merit to the idea, 'cause he went along with it and helped elect me sheriff of Harville." He pointed his glass at me. "And, listen, I was a damn good sheriff. I always liked catching the bad guys."

"Except for the one you were blackmailing."

Stubbs gave a short, angry laugh. "See, it's that kinda remark that makes me wanna get out my rifle again."

He reached for the pitcher of spiked lemonade and refilled his glass, while I silently cursed myself. I'd counted on a kind of brash, "no bullshit" directness as being the best way to keep Stubbs talking. But I'd overplayed it.

Stubbs was the one who'd used the word "confession," because as his days grew short he *wanted* to confess. But I had to be smart enough to let him disclose his sins in his own time, and in his own self-satisfied fashion.

"But this was all many years ago, right?" I went on carefully. "What's the connection with Sinclair? With the campaign going on now?"

He sipped his drink, wincing as it sluiced down his gullet. "I'm gonna be needing my pain medicine soon. Can't go too many hours without it nowadays."

I took a step toward him. Insistent, but not crowding him. "Are you still keeping tabs on McCloskey somehow?"

"Maybe. Maybe I got someone on the inside at the firm. Over in Harrisburg. Just in case I'm not as good a judge of character as I think."

This took me by surprise, but I didn't let it show.

Tried not to, anyway.

"Sam Weiss said you'd heard something incriminating. Something McCloskey said about buying Sinclair."

"You bet I did. Heard a couple interesting conversations. On a real nifty digital recording."

"Made by someone in the firm? Someone close to Evan McCloskey?"

He stroked his mustache. "What do they call those guys in all the spy movies? 'Moles.' You might say I have a mole inside McCloskey, Singer, and Ganz."

"Who is it? One of the other partners? Some junior associate?"

"Now I can't tell you that, and you don't need to know. The important thing is the recording, which I got. Or which I *had*, before I destroyed it."

"What?"

"Don't worry, I transferred it to a CD first. Easier to hide." He paused. "I made a copy, too. Got it stashed somewhere far away from here. Just in case."

"Okay. But what's on it, exactly?"

"Enough. McCloskey's firm represents some of the biggest companies in the country. Financial groups. Manufacturers. Software giants. People who have a vested interest in how tax laws are being written. How employment practices are overseen. People who'd like a governor in their pocket, to make sure they have a path cleared for expanding their businesses in that state."

A mocking smile. "I sure hope I'm not shocking you with all this, son."

"No. To quote a friend of mine, politics is a dirty business."

"It sure as hell is—*if* you're doin' it right. I spent enough years in DC to learn that. Anyway, on one part of the CD, McCloskey tells some corporate client of his that Sinclair is in the bag. That once he became governor, the state was going to be very accommodating. Very partial to this particular client's interests."

I didn't risk glancing at my watch, but I could tell from the spreading shadows that it must've been close to six by now. Where the hell was Sam?

"This mole of yours," I said casually. "Why is he helping you? What's in it for him? Or her, I guess."

"Money, that's what. It's why most people do most things, son. Thought a professional man like yourself would've figured that out by now. He's doing it for the money. A *lot* of money, I admit. But I can afford it."

I took a last swallow of my drink, which he noticed. But I waved away his offer to refill it.

"But what about *you*, Stubbs? Why contact Sam Weiss? Surely you don't care whether or not Sinclair wins."

"I told you, I don't give a damn about some bullshit election. I just want the truth about McCloskey to come out. I want to die with my conscience clean. Or as clean as I can make it."

My voice hardened. "Then we'll need to hear what's on that CD. Sam won't run the story without hard evidence."

"I know that. And I'm gonna give it to him. When he gets here. *Him*, not you."

Stubbs and I exchanged wary looks. I knew better than to push him, but I was suddenly having trouble figuring out what to say next. My thoughts seemed scattered. Unfocused.

I took a long breath, to steady myself. Put out my hand and gripped the porch railing.

A hawk circled overhead, shadow flitting against the light vanishing over the hills.

Stubbs was reaching for the bottle again, but I stopped him. He looked at me for a moment, as though about to argue, when another spasm of pain bent him over.

"Look," I said, "where do you keep your medication?"

"Bedroom," he gasped, as I helped him to one of the two cedar chairs. "On the bureau."

His head lolled a bit, as if he too were having a hard time concentrating. Unless it was just the pain, growing in intensity. Spreading its tendrils.

My own head spinning, I pressed my thumbs to my temples. Tried to collect myself.

Taking quick, shallow breaths, I went into the house. Fumbling in the dark, it took me half a minute to find a light switch. Then, another thirty seconds to make my way to the nearest bedroom, to find the right medicine among a dozen similar prescription bottles.

The print on the bottle was small and fine. Blurring now, as I stared at it. What the hell was wrong with me?

Suddenly, I heard a loud thump come from the direction of the porch.

Shit. I knew I had to hurry back. Stubbs must have passed out, fallen from the chair.

I turned from the bureau, prescription bottle in hand. Heading for the door. Trying to. But my feet wouldn't move. My legs were wobbling, suddenly. Folding under me.

Too late, I realized what was happening. That I'd been drugged. That Stubbs and I had both—

And then the whole world seemed to spin in a whirl of dark, formless images. Turning, dissolving.

And then was gone.

Chapter Forty-three

I was vaguely conscious of a sound. High-pitched, rhythmic. A steady creaking. Like a rocking chair on a hardwood floor.

Dust swirled in front of my eyes as I forced them open. At first all I saw were dim, blurred shapes. Then, slowly, definition. The dull edge of a weed scythe, propped against a wall. The curve of a bucket. Hay bales.

I was in the barn.

I raised my head, blinked into wakefulness. My eyes burned in the harsh white glare of two flood-lights clamped to a nearby saw-horse.

The creaking sound seemed louder now, closer. It was in front of me, and just above. I looked up.

Henry Stubbs was hanging by the neck from the topmost rafter. Swaying gently. The thick noose knotted at his throat distorted one side of his face, compressed it, while the rest of his body hung limply, almost languidly. He looked oddly, hideously, at peace.

No, I thought. *Pretty bullshit. Solace for the living. He just looked dead.*

It was then that I realized I was sitting down. On the hard, sawdust-covered floor. With my hands tied firmly behind my back. Just as I had been before, in the OR at Pittsburgh Memorial. Only this time, I was held by some kind of thick rope. And my feet had been left unbound.

I squeezed my eyes shut, as if I could somehow will away the dulling effects of the drug in my brain.

Then, drawing a deep breath, I tried to move, to wriggle free of the rope. But got nowhere.

"One thing they teach you at Blackwater," a voice behind me said, "is how to tie a knot. You ain't goin' nowhere, Doc."

I recognized his voice before he stepped in front of me, back-lit by the floods. Tall, broad-shouldered, he eclipsed the light with his bulk.

Wheeler Roarke.

He took a step toward me, raising his good right arm. A .357 Magnum gripped in his hand. Which didn't make sense. I couldn't imagine where he'd gotten hold of one.

Then, favoring the bandaged arm curled at his side, he bent down, peered at me with a kind of dull curiosity.

"Life's funny, ain't it?" He scratched his nose with the gun barrel. "I mean, imagine my surprise when I see you in town earlier today. Just as I'm on my way to pay ol' Sheriff Henry here a visit myself."

He smiled coolly and straightened up. Rolled his shoulders. No longer wearing the torn and bloodied security guard's shirt, he'd changed into an extra-large work shirt. Probably to give his injured arm better mobility. Smart.

Which Roarke obviously was. Able to improvise in the field. Think on his feet.

But, as I'd learned at the hospital, also easy to dope out. He liked to think of himself as imposing. Needed to see the fear in his captive's eyes.

And I'd be damned if I'd give him any.

Roarke side-stepped a little, gestured toward the body of Henry Stubbs. Its remorseless swaying sent sharp-angled shadows scurrying around the interior of the barn.

"Now the key to rigging a hanging," he said, "is to make sure the guy's unconscious first, before you string him up. Otherwise, it's a bitch gettin' his head into the noose, what with him clawin' and fightin' you the whole time. Not to mention all the forensics that leaves behind."

I squinted up at him. "Any decent M.E. will spot the residue of drugs in his system."

"Maybe, but I doubt it. Stubbs was takin' so many meds, it'd be a bitch sortin' 'em all out. Especially given what we used. Great stuff. Tasteless, odorless. Barely detectable. One of my favorite souvenirs from Iraq."

"How'd you do it? Slipped it into the lemonade? It's been sitting out on the porch since noon, Stubbs told me. Maybe when he was away from the house…"

Roarke smiled. "Outstanding, Doc. While Sheriff Henry was takin' pot shots at you out on the north forty or whatever the fuck you call it, I was here spikin' the lemonade. I just waited till the housekeeper left and went up on the porch. Easy as pie."

I glanced past Roarke to look again at the hanged man.

"Slam dunk." Roarke went on. "Guy's in despair 'cause he's gonna die a slow, painful death from cancer. Takes the easy way out. See the overturned stepladder nearby?"

"But why kill him now? After all this time? Unless…"

Roarke pointed the gun at me and winked. "You guessed it, Doc. We know about the recording."

"Which means Stubbs' mole was found out. And talked."

"I couldn't say. Not my department. The way chain of command works, everything's on a 'need to know' basis. My job was just to get the damned thing and arrange the sheriff's untimely demise."

"No loose ends."

"Clear mission parameters, Doc. That's all."

"Something else you picked up in Iraq?"

"I'm a quick study. Always have been. Hell, back in Chicago PD, I coulda made chief if I wanted."

"Except for the fact that you're a murdering psycho." I managed a smile. "In my clinical opinion."

"Well, there's that, I guess. Plus the hours woulda sucked."

He feigned a yawn, enjoying himself.

I risked turning my head. Faint slivers of light bled through the cracked barn walls. It was almost dusk.

And what about Sam? Was he being held somewhere else on the property? Was he okay? Unless he'd never shown up at all…

A sudden muffled ringing drew my eyes back to Roarke.

It was a cell phone, in his pocket. He took a long step toward me and put the muzzle of his gun hard against my right temple. Then, using his bad arm, gingerly pulled out the phone.

Listened intently. Grinned. Hung up.

Then he lowered the gun from my head, took a few steps back. I could almost feel the tension leaving his body. His palpable relief.

"Well, that's that. We found the sucker. On a CD, in a box of other discs. Hidin' in plain sight, like they say. Stubbs musta thought he was bein' clever."

"Not as clever as you, turns out. You and your old Blackwater buddy, Ronny Baxter."

Roarke did his best to hide his surprise.

"That *was* Ronny on the phone, right?" I said sharply. "Your partner in crime."

So the cops had been right. When Roarke escaped from the hospital, with those squad cars in pursuit, he must've contacted Baxter using that trucker's stolen cell phone. Arranged for Baxter to be waiting to pick him up at the construction site.

It was Baxter who'd helped Roarke hide out. Get a change of clothes. And another gun.

It also explained how Stubbs ended up swinging from the rafters. Even when the victim's unconscious, hoisting a body up into a noose is a two-man job. Especially when one of the men has a badly injured arm.

"You got it all wrong, Doc." Roarke glared down at me, drawing himself up again to his full height. Trying to re-establish dominance. "Ronny and me ain't partners."

"You're not bank robbers, either, that's for damn sure." Speaking with a bravado I didn't feel. "That whole thing at the bank. The so-called robbery attempt. That was all bullshit, wasn't it?"

"If you say so."

"It's connected with all this, isn't it? The computer disc. Killing Stubbs. It's all about protecting McCloskey. Keeping your boss safe. In the clear."

"My boss?"

"Evan McCloskey. The prick you're working for. The guy pulling the strings."

Then I saw it. The blank, puzzled look on his face.

An involuntary reaction. He'd no time to bluff, to cover. Every instinct I had told me his response was genuine.

Wheeler Roarke had no idea who—or what—I was talking about.

Chapter Forty-four

Now it was my turn to be surprised.

But if it *wasn't* McCloskey—then who was Roarke working for? And why?

Not that I had the luxury to puzzle things out at that moment. Not with Roarke's gaze gleaming with malice. I'd seen that look in his eyes before, back at the hospital. Right before he'd calmly shot that police officer.

Time was definitely not on my side…

It was then that I registered it. Not ten feet to my left. The wall-length rack of farm tools I'd seen from the house. Those relics.

"Listen, Roarke," I said. "Much as I enjoy shooting the breeze with you, I'm wondering why you're still here. You got the CD. Stubbs isn't going to get any deader."

He spread his hands. "You said it yourself. Who needs loose ends? Once all the files in Stubbs' computer back at the house get down-loaded—just in case—we're outta here."

I stirred, shifting against my bonds, which made Roarke peer hard at me again.

"You ain't thinkin' about *tryin'* anything, are ya, Doc?" He rubbed his jaw. "Ya know, I had the feelin' you were sizin' me up back at the hospital. Man, if so, you got 'way too high an opinion of yourself."

"Maybe. But I'd get in a few good shots before I went down. I don't give a fuck how tough you think you are. You'd be in a world of hurt. Guaranteed."

Roarke laughed.

"What is this, some kind of psych-out crap? Tryin' to bait me?" He pointed a thick finger. "Shit, you think you can outwit a guy like me?"

"No, usually I prefer a challenge."

He laughed again, before aiming a vicious kick into my ribs. "You fuck," he said evenly, as I doubled over, jack-knifed, on the floor. I tasted my blood.

"Know why you ain't dead, asshole?" Roarke was pacing in front of me, livid. "Huh, genius? You know why you still got a pulse?"

I found my voice. "'Cause killing me isn't within mission parameters. You can't make the big decisions."

He strode over and drove his size twelve foot into my ribs again. I stifled a cry, as my body shuddered from the pain. And I rolled a few more feet to my left.

Roarke wiped his mouth with his sleeve, face burning with rage. He stepped back again, raising his gun to point at me—when the back of his head bumped against Stubbs' dangling legs.

"Fuck!" Roarke batted his gun-hand at the swinging body, which sent it revolving, and then swaying again in a zigzag arc.

All I needed. I scrambled to my feet and started running toward the tool rack. Roarke ducked away from Stubbs' corpse, gun jumping in his hand like a live thing as he fired.

I drove myself into the ground, chin-first, as the bullet whizzed over my head. I kept going, aching arms bent behind me as I crawled as fast as I could toward the saw-horse. And the lights fixed to it.

Roarke fired again. Gasping, I threw myself headlong into the inverted V of its legs, knocking the saw-horse over. The flood-lights plumed up toward the ceiling, plunging the barn floor into darkness.

"Goddam it!" Roarke bellowed. I could hear the dry rasp of his feet on the sawdust floor as he turned this way and that, looking for me. "God-fucking-dammit!"

I knew he'd find me soon enough. I rolled on my back, exhaling hard and tucking in as I brought my knees up. Within seconds, I'd wriggled my bound hands past my calves, then over my shoes.

Then I leapt to my feet, hands now tied in front of me. Better, but not by much.

Roarke's gun flared in the darkness. Another shot whistled nearby. His breathing grew louder as he made slow circles, expanding his search radius.

I tried to hold on to my mental picture of the barn layout as I moved in a crouch along the side wall. Only the faintest light came through cracks in the rough-hewn wood, but I got lucky and saw the outline of the rack. Maybe five or six yards away.

There were more tools there than I'd thought. A heavy shovel, pitted with rust. A block-and-tackle, its thick ropes coiled around a set of pulleys.

Then I heard a loud scraping noise behind me, and suddenly I was caught in the streaming light of the floods. Roarke had found the saw-horse and righted it, turning it in my direction.

I froze where I stood, bound hands still in front of me. Out of the corner of my eye, I saw his massive silhouette just beyond the circle of bright light.

"Nice move, Doc." His voice boomed out of the darkness. "Now just stand there, where I can see you. Remember back at the hospital? I'm still thinkin' belly shot. Takes forever to bleed out, and hurts like hell the whole time."

He laughed easily, and then calmly marched into the light. We weren't more than three feet apart.

With my back to him.

"Now, for this to work, you're gonna have to turn around," Roarke said reasonably.

I readied myself. It would have to be done in one smooth motion. Pivot. Grab the shovel.

I'd have one chance.

The shovel handle in its hook was about eighteen inches away. At about eye level.

"I *mean* it, Doc," Roarke growled. "Turn your ass around. Unless you wanna get it in the b—"

I turned on one foot and reached with bound hands for the shovel and kept turning. Raising my arms as somewhere beyond my field of vision Roarke was raising his, shouting and lining up a shot.

I swung around with the shovel and clipped him right at the shoulder, hard, knocking his gun away as it fired. Sending him spinning. He stumbled backwards, arms flailing, struggling to keep his feet.

As I came out of my swing, still clutching the shovel, I saw him fall backwards. Out of the light.

Then I heard a crash from the darkness, and his choked cry of surprise.

I took a step, then braced myself, shovel upraised. I saw Roarke stagger out of the shadows. His face screwed up in agony, his outstretched hands clutching the empty air. His voice was a strangled gasp.

The bloodied tip of a scythe's blade protruded from his chest.

His gaze found mine. Something unreadable burned in his eyes, and then the life went out of them.

Roarke pitched forward into the sawdust, and I saw that the scythe was buried to the hilt in his back. He must have fallen against it when I—

I threw down the shovel and crouched next to his body. Felt for his pulse, just to be sure. Nothing.

I sat back, breathing hard. Using my teeth, I pulled at the rope around my wrists until I got enough slack. Then I twisted my fingers down and started untying the knots, as the adrenaline shakes subsided.

Suddenly, I heard a voice calling out. High, panicked. From the house. Footsteps, pounding off the porch.

Ronny Baxter. He must have heard the shots and come running...

And he'd be armed.

I took off, pulling the rope free.

Chapter Forty-five

By the time I got back to my rental car, I was out of breath from the hard run across the fields.

Luckily, I'd managed to get out of the barn before Baxter reached it, and had bolted for the tree-shrouded barbed wire that bordered the property.

But I'd risked a last look back. Saw the smallish figure, swathed in deep shadow, crouching as it approached the opened barn doors. Even from this distance, I could also see the glint of a gun in an upraised hand.

Then I'd turned and started off, using the barbed-wire fence as a kind of guide line. Feeling my way along its taut length, gasping from the pain in my side, it took me ten long minutes to find the dirt access road, where I'd parked the rental.

I squinted in the gloom. The light was almost gone, and the darkness seemed to sprout now from behind every tree, shrub, scalloped hill.

I gave myself a moment to catch my breath, then got behind the wheel and started the engine. At the same time fumbling in my pants pocket for my cell phone. As I drove with one hand back the way I'd come on the unlit, treacherous road, I punched in Sam's number.

Nothing. Battery was dead.

Cursing, I tossed it on the passenger seat and focused on finding my way back to the on-ramp for Interstate 76.

At least I'd cleared up one thing that had been troubling me: why Sam hadn't called.

I hadn't driven a quarter mile when I spotted a gray Range Rover parked under an elm at the side of the road. Roarke's car. Or, more likely, Baxter's. Had to be.

I floored it. Barreled down the dark, unpaved road.

I tried to calm myself, but I was in some kind of primal state—half in shock, half pumped with adrenaline.

Two men, dead. A third one, armed, perhaps climbing into the Range Rover right now, soon to be on my tail.

Every instinct told me to just get out of there. Keep driving on into the night, and never stop.

But I knew I had to find a phone, call the police.

A real man don't lose his shit, my old man used to say. So I'd spent my life trying to figure out exactly what a real man *did* do. And how. And when.

Is that what all this was? The violence and death of the past week. Just another life lesson, like the ones my father used to deliver with the back of his hand?…

I smiled, as I felt the familiar, cleansing anger. *Thanks, Dad.* No problems now. Back in the saddle.

I peered into the night, looking for signs.

◇◇◇

An hour later, I pulled into a Denny's just outside Harrisburg. I hurried through the noisy dinner crowd to the rear of the restaurant, where the pay phones were. Ignoring the stunned looks of the other patrons. Not that I blamed them. My clothes were torn and caked with dirt. The back of my shirt, where it had been raked by barbed wire, looked like a bear had clawed it.

A sweating, heavy-set guy who was probably the manager came warily toward me, but I merely gestured at the bank of phones in the back. Which seemed to mollify him. At least I wasn't going to ask for a window table.

I'd thought things over during the drive here. After I got in touch with Sam, my next call would be to the local cops. Then another to Eleanor Lowrey or Harry Polk, filling them in on what'd happened at the Stubbs house. Especially what had happened to Wheeler Roarke.

At least, that was the plan.

As I neared the alcove housing the phones, I glanced over at the counter that ran half the length of the place. A waitress and some patrons were staring in silence at the huge flat-screen TV suspended from the wall.

I made my way over. On-screen, a wind-blown female reporter was doing a live remote, as a harrowing fire blazed in the background. The graphic along the bottom of the screen read, "Breaking News. Farmhouse Fire."

The reporter was shouting into her mike over the noise of the firefighters on scene, working frantically behind her. As the camera pulled back, you could see the fire was totally out of control.

"We're live at the home of retired Harville sheriff Henry Stubbs. According to authorities here, the size and ferocity of the fire may indicate arson. And while we don't know for sure at this time, firefighters concede it's unlikely anyone could survive this. Now let's talk to—"

I turned away and sat on a stool at the far end of the counter. Ronny Baxter must have discovered Roarke's body, with no sign of me anywhere. He had to figure I'd go to the cops.

Also, like Roarke, he hadn't wanted any loose ends. Maybe he'd taken the time to cut Stubbs down, or pull the scythe blade from Roarke's body. No sense leaving anything funny for the cops to find. Then he'd doused the place with kerosene, or maybe a can of gasoline he'd found in the barn, and torched it. Old dry wood structure like that would go up fast as flash-paper.

I looked across at the screen again, far enough away not to have to hear the audio. Whether Baxter intended it or not, the fire had spread to the house as well. It would take firefighters most of the night to put it down.

In the morning, all they'd find were the remains of two people in the barn, burned beyond recognition. Dental records would probably confirm their hunch that one of the bodies was Henry

Stubbs. My guess was it would be harder to trace the identity of the second corpse. Until I told the Pittsburgh Police who it was, and they told the FBI.

Which would just leave Ronny Baxter, the second gunman at the bank, at large. Armed and dangerous. And, moreover, still in possession of Stubbs' CD. The only hard evidence of McCloskey's attempt to influence the policies of the presumptive next governor. Of his claim that he had Leland Sinclair on the pad.

But did I believe it? Without the CD, there was only Henry Stubbs' word. Yet why would a dying man lie? Besides, he'd offered to turn the CD over, no strings attached. And despite his earlier crimes, his collusion with Evan McCloskey, I had to agree with Sam: Stubbs seemed credible.

I leaned forward, elbows on the slick Formica counter. I didn't know what to think. Or else I just couldn't. My mind was still hazy from the lingering effects of the drug.

Rousing myself, I pushed off from the stool and headed back to the row of pay phones. Dug some coins out of my pocket and dialed Sam's cell. He picked up half-way through the first ring.

"Danny! Jesus Christ, where are you? I'm in a bar watching the news and—"

"Yeah, I know. Stubbs' farm. Roarke's partner Ronny Baxter torched it."

"What?"

"Long story. Edited version: Stubbs is dead, and so is Roarke. And the CD is gone."

"What CD?"

"The one containing the evidence linking McCloskey's firm to Sinclair. Audio of a conversation between McCloskey and one of his clients. McCloskey claims Sinclair's been bought. That, as governor, his support for the client's interests is in the bag."

"Holy shit! That's—wait a minute, what do you mean, the CD is gone?"

"Baxter has it. And God knows where he is by now. Stubbs said he'd made a back-up, but he never told me where he'd hidden it. Could be halfway around the world."

"But without that CD—"

"You got squat."

Silence on his end of the line.

"By the way, Sam, where the hell are you? How come you never made it out to Stubbs' place?"

"You kiddin'? I tried calling you a dozen times but couldn't get through. I'm still here at the airport. Took longer than I thought to pull together that story on the Gordon brothers. Not to mention the screaming matches with the copy editor. Some Princeton grad who thinks he's H.L. Mencken. We had to parse every goddam word. Made the press deadline, but just barely. Meanwhile, my boss blames *me*. Chews my ass out."

"You're breakin' my heart. I still would've preferred your afternoon to mine."

His tone softened. "Yeah, I know. Sorry, Danny. I didn't mean to leave you hanging."

Poor choice of words, I thought. Though I didn't say it. Didn't want to get into all the details. Not at the moment.

"So," I said instead, "is it too late for us to fly back to Pittsburgh?"

"In the Cessna? In the dark? I'm not cleared for night flying, and I wouldn't do it if I were. I figured I'd book us a late flight on US Air. Just pay some local fly-boy to pilot the Cessna back to Gold Star Aviation tomorrow. Pad what's left of my expense account."

"Okay. I'll meet you at the ticket counter. Say a couple hours? I've gotta get cleaned up, buy a change of clothes. No way airport security would let me on a plane looking like this."

"Damn. Must be one helluva story. Good thing I get the exclusive, right?"

"Jesus…"

"Yeah, yeah. But, Danny, one more thing."

"What?"

"Do you believe him? I mean, Henry Stubbs. Do you believe what he said about McCloskey, that Sinclair is bought and paid for?"

I paused, but only for a moment. Surprised by my words as they came out of my mouth.

"Yeah, Sam. I think I do."

Chapter Forty-six

After hanging up, I pushed some more coins in the slot and called Eleanor Lowrey on her cell. I'd realized after seeing the story on TV about the fire that I didn't need to call the local cops. The authorities were already crawling all over the scene.

Eleanor was still in her office at the precinct when she picked up. Before she could get two words in, I gave her the details of my day's outing in rural Pennsylvania. Accompanying Sam Weiss by air to interview a possible source for a story he was doing about Sinclair. Henry Stubbs' contention that the District Attorney was dirty, based on a secret recording he'd heard.

Then I told her that Wheeler Roarke had shown up in Harville to kill Stubbs and get the evidence. But that it was Roarke who'd ended up dead, while his partner Ronny Baxter escaped with the CD containing the incriminating audio.

To her credit, she listened to my entire narrative without interrupting me. Instead, she merely asked one question.

"So there's no solid evidence that anything this Stubbs guy told you is true?"

"It's supposedly on the CD that Baxter has with him. He'd found it over at the house while Roarke was figuring out the most entertaining way to kill me."

Her long pause spoke volumes.

"Look, Eleanor, I know what you're thinking…"

"Then you know better than to try to defend yourself. I mean, what the hell did you think you were doing?"

"I was curious about Sinclair. Helping out my friend Sam Weiss. Getting to fly in a ridiculously small plane. Pick one."

"Don't get cute with me, Danny. You could've been killed. Roarke was no guy to fuck around with."

"Hey, it's not like I had a choice. It was him or me, Detective."

"Well, I guess I'm glad it was you. But I'm starting to think Harry's right about you. You're crazy."

"Whatever. The important thing is, Roarke's dead. The FBI's gotta intensify their search for Ronny Baxter."

"Don't worry, soon as we hang up I'm telling Biegler about what happened to Roarke. He'll kick it upstairs to the Chief and Alcott at the Bureau. They'll probably get in touch with the local blues in Harville and start piecing the scene together. Meanwhile, Ronny Baxter can't have gotten far. Not yet, anyway. That'll help the FBI in tracking him down."

"What about the Sinclair connection?"

"What connection? Some blackmailing hick sheriff says he heard an incriminating recording? Only we don't know who inside McCloskey's firm made it, and Stubbs himself is dead. Which makes him a tough interview. Hell, how do you know this so-called CD even exists? Right now, these allegations against Sinclair are just that—allegations. If your friend the reporter wants to break that story, let the ax fall on *his* head. Not ours."

"Sam won't run with anything without proof."

"Smart man. Now get your ass back here, Danny. You know we'll need a complete statement from you about today's events. You're a material witness to a homicide and arson."

"Or maybe a suspect…?"

"I seriously doubt it. But it'd serve you right. So when are you coming home?"

"Sam and I are flying back tonight."

"Good."

Another, longer pause. Then, hesitantly: "Look, Danny, I was wondering if you could tell me how Treva's doing. I know some Victims' Services people went over to her place today, but I didn't follow up with them. I didn't want it to seem like… well, like I was intruding. Checking up on her. She obviously doesn't want that."

"Well, I told her I'd call her tonight. I hope to get a better sense of her emotional state then."

"Thanks, Dan. For staying in touch with her."

I weighed my next words carefully.

"Listen, Treva told me yesterday that the only reason she's reluctant to see you is because she feels guilty. For having hurt you so badly. But that's just how she's feeling now. That could change."

"Maybe."

"Remember, too, the intensity of what's happened to her… what she's gone through these past two days. I think she just doesn't believe she can handle it. Seeing you again after all these years. Especially bearing the guilt she's carried with her since then. I could be wrong, but—"

"No, that makes sense. I just wish…"

I let the silence hang in the air between us.

◇◇◇

I'd run out of change, so I had to ask the counter waitress to break a few singles. After a furtive glance at the manager, who'd nodded gravely, she handed over eight quarters and quickly made her way to the other end of the counter. To wash her hands, probably.

Back in the phone alcove, I dialed Treva's home number and listened to its steady ring. Finally, she picked up.

"Sorry, Dr. Rinaldi. I was in the bathroom. It's the only time I get out of bed."

"Sounds like you're taking good care of yourself. Getting lots of rest."

"That's for sure. Total slug mode."

"Do you need anything? I understand the Victims' Services people came by…"

"They sure did. They rang my doorbell a bunch of times. They even left a message on my phone."

"Wait a minute, Treva. Are you saying you didn't let them in?"

"Don't be mad at me, okay? Besides, I called them right back. I'm not rude. I told them very politely that I didn't want to see anybody. Remember what I said to you? That I just wanted to shut out the world."

"Yes, but—"

Her voice grew thin, tentative. "I just couldn't deal with those people today. I couldn't bear to have to answer a lot of well-meaning questions. To let them make me herbal tea and tell me everything was going to be all right. Can you understand that?"

"Perfectly." And I did.

Then, abruptly, her tone brightened. "I know I'm being an awful patient. You should probably fire me."

"I'm afraid it doesn't work that way."

"Funny thing is, I'm feeling a lot better just talking to you. Like I might actually get out of bed and make something to eat."

"Glad to hear it. Even awful patients deserve a decent meal once in a while. But, seriously, I do think we should get together soon. We need to explore your feelings about everything that's happened. At least, begin the process."

"Yes. I know you're right. In fact, we could meet now, if you want. It's not too late, and God knows I've had my fill of sleep."

"Now?"

"Sure. You could come by here—unless that's too weird or against the rules or something. Or we could meet some place closer to you."

"I'd like to, Treva, but the truth is, I'm out of town. In Harrisburg. I won't be getting back till much later tonight."

"Oh."

The disappointment in her voice seemed genuine, which saddened me as well. This was the first time she'd even entertained the idea of letting me help her. Of starting the arduous psychological journey that lay ahead of her. And I was half a state away.

"I'm sorry, Treva. But let's meet tomorrow. Anywhere you want. My office. Or some coffee shop."

"Okay. But if we're going to meet somewhere else, I'll have to wear a disguise."

"A disguise?"

"So I can sneak past those Victims' Services people. They'll probably be camped out downstairs in the lobby."

I couldn't tell whether her humor was a hopeful sign of a real connection between us—that she was indeed ready to work— or else just another attempt to slip back into denial. Into that disarming, distracting fog behind which the traumatized often disappear.

"Okay," I said. "I'll call you tomorrow."

"And I'll answer. Promise."

Chapter Forty-seven

I left the phone alcove, waved good-bye to the obviously relieved restaurant manager, and went out to the parking lot. Across the street was a Motel 6, neon sign bright and buzzing. Next door was a sporting goods outlet store. Good. I wouldn't even have to move the car.

Ten minutes later I'd checked into a room, and was standing under a steaming shower. Afterwards, I sat on the bed and awkwardly wrapped the bandages I'd bought around my midsection. It felt like Roarke had cracked a few ribs.

Then I stood at the bureau mirror and awkwardly applied a new bandage to the back of my skull. Another war wound from the day before, courtesy of Wheeler Roarke.

I picked up the room phone to check my messages, but changed my mind. Tomorrow morning would be soon enough.

I'd already thrown my torn, dirty clothes into the trash can, and dressed now in the new jeans and shirt I'd bought at the outlet place.

Then, checking the time, I sprawled on the still-made bed. Closed my eyes and breathed deeply, slowly. But I could only allow myself a few moments' rest. I had to meet up with Sam at the US Air ticket counter by ten o'clock.

Back in the motel lobby, I grabbed a cup of coffee from the bubbling carafe near the front desk. Strong, bitter. Just what I needed.

I said good-bye to the kid behind the desk, but he didn't even glance up from the latest *Maxim* magazine. I guess having a guy who looked like the Unabomber's best friend book a room, change clothes, and then leave within an hour wasn't that unusual an event around here.

Or else the *Maxim* was a particularly hot issue.

◇◇◇

Sam and I sat next to each other near the rear of the US Air jet. We'd taxied out to the runway and were awaiting take-off. From my window seat, I could see the hills like rounded shoulders, hunched under the ink-black sky.

Been a helluva day. *Another* one.

Sam looked at his watch. "Eleven PM. Late flight, but it's the best I could do."

"Stop apologizing. You're not responsible for what happened out at Stubbs' place."

"I know, but still…" He scratched his tousled black hair. "Hell, it was *my* story. *My* source. I shouldn't have sent you out there alone."

"Forget it, will you? Though I'm sorry about Stubbs."

"Me, too. Now I just have to figure out how to verify his story. I mean, even without the CD, what he told you gives me lots of leads to follow. Confirms some of the stuff I've been thinking."

"Best thing would be for the FBI to track down Ronny Baxter. And the CD."

"If he still has it. He could've destroyed it by now. Or handed it over to whoever he and Roarke were working for." Sam gave me a sidelong look. "And you still think the bank robbery was part of all this?"

"Had to be. Roarke and Baxter try to rob a bank, kill a number of hostages, and manage to escape. Wanted for multiple homicides. Hunted by the FBI. So where do they go? Another state? Out of the country? No, they go to Henry Stubbs' farm in Harville, looking for some secret recording. With orders to kill Stubbs as well."

Sam pursed his lips. "You got a point, Danny."

The captain's voice boomed then over the intercom, announcing that passengers and crew should prepare for takeoff. Which we did.

Once airborne, I kept my head tilted against the window. Watched the blurred night roaring by.

Sam poked me in the ribs. I winced.

"Shit, man, sorry." He smiled sheepishly. "I forgot to tell you. We missed Sinclair's press conference tonight, but I can boot up my laptop once we land and we can find a link to it. In case you want to watch."

"Not if I don't have to."

"Well, as a reporter covering the campaign, *I* have to. Besides, we both know what he said. That he refuses to be intimated by the likes of Jimmy Gordon. Implying that he'd be equally strong and capable if elected governor."

"If he lives long enough to make the debate."

"Don't worry. I've been on the phone all day with my sources at headquarters. And the FBI. They've got every member of the Gordon family under wraps. Every known associate is being watched. Interviewed. Believe me, the good guys are on top of it."

The plane leveled off at 30,000 feet and most of the night-flying passengers around us settled in for the short ride to Pittsburgh International.

I did so as well, leaning my head gratefully against the seat cushion. Every muscle in my body ached, and the throbbing at the back of my skull had begun again.

I felt myself drifting, awake and yet not awake. In this half-doze, images of Henry Stubbs hanging from that barn rafter floated up in my mind. Swaying. Feet dangling. Moving in and out of the shadows, like a figure in a nightmare. Haunting. Surreal.

Then, unbidden, it morphed into another image. Andrew Parker, the patient at Ten Oaks. Andy the Android. Suddenly I was seeing him, too. Or at least how I imagined he'd looked, hanging from a bicycle chain in the clinic's tool shed…

With a violent start, I sat upright in my seat. Coming fully, vividly awake.

Because all of a sudden I saw how the pieces fit together. Or, rather, *didn't* fit. That remark Noah had made, about how Andy had "deactivated" himself. What Nancy Mendors had told me about finding Andy once on the floor of the kitchen, having stabbed himself with a screwdriver. What I'd read in those files she'd sent me about Andy's recent behavior.

As soon as we touched down, I'd call her to ask if the clinic's cleaning crew had gone into Andy's room yet. And, if not, tell her to make sure the room stayed untouched. And that I'd meet her at Ten Oaks in the morning.

Despite my fatigue, and the lingering effects of Roarke's drug, my mind was clear. And while I didn't know if I could prove it, I was sure I was right about what had happened to Andy the Android.

He'd hanged himself, yes. But it wasn't suicide.

It was murder.

Chapter Forty-eight

It was pretty damned crowded in Lt. Stu Biegler's office, especially at two in the morning. I was giving my statement about the previous day's and night's events to the cops. In addition to Biegler, who looked more annoyed and distracted than usual, there was Harry Polk, Eleanor Lowrey, and—most surprising of all—Assistant District Attorney Dave Parnelli.

None of whom seemed very happy with me. Especially Parnelli, whose comb-over glistened with sweat under the hot lights.

It took about forty minutes to tell it all, which I did. Everything. Despite Eleanor's earlier concerns that the Sinclair-McCloskey connection was mere allegation.

She wasn't alone.

When I'd finished talking, I leaned back in the sole chair opposite Biegler's desk and looked up expectantly. It was Parnelli who spoke up first.

"Are you seriously asking us to believe that this McCloskey guy—acting on behalf of some powerful corporate client—has his hooks in Lee Sinclair?"

"I told you, Stubbs seemed credible. At least it's worth looking into, right?"

"Based on what? You said this alleged CD is gone."

"Yes. Roarke's partner in the bank job, Ronny Baxter, found it in Stubbs' house. He got away with it, after torching the barn."

I sat forward. "C'mon, you've gotta see that there's some kind of connection between the robbery attempt and Stubbs' murder.

If Roarke and Baxter were just your run-of-the-mill bank robbers, they'd have skipped the country by now. Instead, with the cops and FBI on their trail, they decide on a day-trip to Harville, Pennsylvania, to kill a retired sheriff and retrieve some hidden recording. Evidence of a meeting between McCloskey and one of his clients, concerning Leland Sinclair."

"*Alleged* meeting." Parnelli sure liked that word.

Polk muttered something unintelligible, but Eleanor turned to the ADA. Her gaze frank, steady.

"There must be something to Dr. Rinaldi's story, sir. If not, then why did Roarke and Baxter go after Stubbs?"

"How do *I* know? This whole case has been a fuck-up from the beginning. Maybe Rinaldi's right. Or else maybe Stubbs was a wing-nut. Frankly, I'm not exactly bowled over by the unsubstantiated claims of an admitted blackmailer." He whirled on Biegler. "What do *you* think, Lieutenant?"

Biegler glanced up, startled, as though jerked back from an unpleasant daydream.

"Eh? Oh, yeah…I mean, this Stubbs mook. We oughtta know a lot more about him before we give any credence to anything he says. Especially about the DA."

Parnelli bobbed his head. "Agreed. Let's table that angle for now, and just concentrate on Baxter. With the brains of the outfit dead, little Ronny oughtta be easier to round up. And if he *does* have some kinda CD on him…"

"If he hasn't destroyed it by now," I said. "*Or* turned it over to his boss. Whoever *that* is."

"Those are always possibilities, too, Doctor. But from where I sit, you've already strayed way too far from your chosen field, in terms of this case."

"*That's* for goddam sure." It was Polk's first comment since I'd given my statement. He directed it at a spot on the wall over my shoulder, then cut his eyes at me.

"On the other hand," Parnelli said to me, "you *did* manage to find Wheeler Roarke. And kill him, for which we're all duly grateful…"

I climbed half out of my chair. "Wait a minute, that was self-defense—"

He gave me an indulgent smile. "Nobody here doubts that, Doctor. I, for one, am certainly unwilling to seek an indictment against you. Bottom line, there's one less stone killer walking around, plus the state's spared the expense of a long, drawn-out trial. It's a win-win, as far as justice is concerned."

Parnelli was laying the condescension on pretty thick, but I was too tired and sore to rise to the bait. By now, too, I figured I had his number. He had that abrasive, knowing sarcasm of a lot of high-echelon law enforcement types. Unlike cops—from rookie patrol officers to detectives first grade—guys like Parnelli and Sinclair saw themselves as standing above the messy personal dramas of ordinary citizens.

To them, it wasn't about murder or robbery, arson or fraud. It wasn't about perpetrators and victims. Trials were merely chess games to be won or loss. Convictions just stats on the ledger books, rungs on the ladder of upward mobility.

And in such a scenario, all that amateurs like me did was muck up the works.

After another twenty minutes of questioning, they released me. Biegler stayed behind, reaching into one of his desk drawers for a bottle of aspirin. Polk excused himself to visit the men's room. Eleanor, clicking on her cell, drifted off toward a maintenance door at the end of the corridor.

Leaving me and Dave Parnelli to walk together to the bank of elevators at the opposite end.

Hands in his pockets while we waited for the elevator car, Parnelli spoke to me without making eye contact.

"You stay out of trouble from now on, okay, Doc? I hear you're a valuable asset to the department. Be a damn shame if something happened to you."

"You get no argument from me. But do you mind if I ask you a question?"

"Depends."

"I just wondered why you went to the hospital the other day to okay Treva Williams' release. I mean, why you showed up personally."

He brought his head up like one of those big animals on nature documentaries. Half-turned. Eyes hooded.

"Interesting question. You always so direct?"

"Depends."

He grunted. "Look, this is an important case. I want hands-on involvement, that's all. You, if anyone, oughtta understand that."

"True enough."

"Speaking of hands-on, they've set the memorial for those bank victims for noon today. So that's where I'll be if you need me. Sinclair wants every person in the DA's office to attend the ceremony. From ADAs to secretaries."

"Big photo op for the candidate."

"Damn right. I learned a long time ago, life is politics and politics is life." He tugged on an earlobe. "Ya know, maybe you and me oughtta go have a drink sometime. Just kick back and shoot the shit."

Before I could answer, the elevator doors opened and Parnelli stepped inside. I stayed rooted in the corridor.

"Comin', Doc?"

"I'll catch the next one."

"Suit yourself. And let me know about that drink."

Parnelli smiled easily, as the doors closed on him with a hushed rumble.

◇◇◇

I turned and headed back the way we'd come. I'd wanted a word with Eleanor. Turns out, she wanted the same thing. As I walked up to her, she closed her cell and leaned back against the maintenance door. Eyebrows raised in greeting.

"Danny, I'm glad you haven't left yet. I just learned a couple hours ago that Treva's planning to attend the bank employees' memorial."

"She is?"

"I only found out about it when I called Victims' Services to check on how she's doing. They said she told them she wanted to go. They're sending a driver for her."

"Makes sense. Those people in the bank were her colleagues. Friends."

And *more* than friends, I thought. Though I didn't say. If Treva ever wanted Eleanor to know about her relationship with Bobby Marks, it was up to her to tell her.

Eleanor's brow creased with concern. "Poor Treva. It's gonna be so hard for her to be there, filled with guilt for having survived."

"Worse, for being the only one who did. Part of the trauma she'll have to work through. Treva's got a long road ahead of her, Eleanor."

"I know. And I'm glad she'll have you to help her."

An awkward silence.

"Well," she said finally, "I better get home and feed Luther. If he hasn't eaten the sofa by now. What is it—2:30, three in the morning?"

"Something like that. I feel like I've lost all track of time."

She hesitated for a moment, then laid her palm against the side of my face.

"You've done enough crime-busting for one night, Danny. You need to go home, too. Get some sleep."

Eleanor lifted her hand from my face. I took it. She looked at me with those deep violet eyes. As though asking me to read what was in them. Break the code.

Then, suddenly, she put her arms around me. Strong, insistent. Her full breasts pressed against my chest.

Without a thought, I brought my own arms up to encircle hers. Then, turning, I kicked open the door behind her and pulled us inside.

It was a small room, more like a closet. Crammed with mops, buckets. Airless. Stifling.

Our bodies merged, as though welded together. I felt the heat pulsing from her firm, flat belly, the urgent thrust of her pelvis against mine. I pulled her face close.

We kissed, hungrily. Her lips soft, pliant.

I felt my erection then, my aching need.

She felt it, too. She flushed, gasping. Kissing me again, hard, as though desperate for breath, for life.

Then, just as suddenly, she wriggled from my embrace. Pulled back, eyes averted.

My arms fell away. The sweet, pungent taste of her mouth still in mine.

"Eleanor…"

She looked at me at last, her expression unreadable.

"I'm sorry…" Voice oddly clipped. Parceling out the words. "I…I don't know why I did that."

"Do we have to know?"

"Jesus, Danny, we're…we work together, and—"

She took another step back. Then, flustered, she pushed past me and went out into the hallway again. I followed, but she kept her distance. Bristling.

"It's this damn case," she said sharply. "And Treva…Why the hell did *she* have to show up all of a sudden? I mean, I'm having a helluva time keeping my focus. Just working the case. Doing my job. That's who I am. This goddam job."

"It's not all you are, Eleanor."

"Yes, it is. That's why I'm so fucking good at it. I give everything to it, and it protects me. That's the deal. Don't you get it? That's the deal I make every day."

"Then it's a lousy deal. Lousy for you."

I gripped her arms. Fuck it, let her try to pull away.

"You can't lock yourself up behind some job, Eleanor. Believe me, I know. I've tried. It doesn't work."

Her gaze turned steely.

"Maybe not for you. But it does for me." A cool half-smile. Trying to regain herself. "Now let me go before I kick your ass up and down this hallway."

I didn't budge. Eyes on hers. I could do steely, too.

Finally, her smile thawed a bit. "Danny, please."

A long moment. Then, nodding dumbly, I let my hands drop.

"Thanks," she said. "Last thing I need is for Biegler to come out of his office and find us like this."

I couldn't argue with that. Especially since I didn't know what the hell was going on between us, either. If anything at all. Other than stress, grief, loneliness.

Maybe I should pursue this with her, I thought. Talk about it. But I didn't.

Instead, I said, "Don't worry about Biegler. From what I saw back there, he's got other things on his mind than us. Or the case, for that matter."

She managed a wry smile.

"Yeah, he's distracted, all right. His wife found out about LaWanda Collins, the policeman's friend. Her prints being in his unmarked. Rumor is, Biegler's moved into a hotel and his wife's talking to lawyers."

"Poor bastard. Never thought I'd say it, but…"

"Yeah, I know. Funny. I kinda feel the same way."

We exchanged a careful look. She lightly touched my jacket sleeve. Gave it a reassuring tug. Then she turned and headed for the elevator.

I held back, staying where I was. Letting her take the ride down to the garage alone.

As would I.

Chapter Forty-nine

It was nearing four when I got home and fell into bed. But I didn't sleep. Couldn't. Mind racing, I kept replaying the events of the past three days. Looking for connections that seemed achingly, tantalizingly out of reach.

As with a patient whose symptoms didn't quite add up, whose personal history was a jigsaw puzzle with pieces missing, I forced myself to look at things from a different angle. Tried to find a new, fresh perspective that my own involvement often made difficult to achieve.

To no avail. By five, frustrated and on edge, I dragged my weary butt down to the basement. Wrapped my hands in training tape and put on the gloves. Pounded the heavy bag until the sweat poured from me like rainwater sluicing off a steep roof.

By six, I'd shaved and showered, and was watching the morning news as I dressed. The death of Wheeler Roarke and the arson fire at Stubbs' farm was the lead, although, as the anchor reported, the facts surrounding these events were unclear. A brief statement from the chief's office merely asserted that with the wanted fugitive dead, perhaps at the hands of his partner in the bank robbery, the focus of the manhunt would now be on apprehending Ronny Baxter. The motive for the apparent murder of former Harville Sheriff Henry Stubbs was, as yet, unknown. But the investigation was in its early stages, and more information would be forthcoming soon.

Not bad, I thought. Just close enough to the truth to give the impression that the wheels of justice, however wobbly at times, were turning. Dangerous fugitive Wheeler Roarke was dead. His partner in crime had been identified and would undoubtedly be captured soon. The bloody carnage at the bank would be avenged.

As if to underscore the point, a companion story reminded viewers that a memorial for the slain bank employees was taking place at noon, and that the public was invited. Speaking at the event would be both gubernatorial candidates, Leland Sinclair and John Garrity, as well as the chief of police and the mayor.

Finally, the anchor mentioned the debate set for this coming Saturday, just two days away. Topics expected to be discussed included state-wide job loss and possible tax reform, as well as heated law-and-order issues. Both candidates would probably be asked their thoughts about Troy David Dowd, the Handyman, still awaiting execution. And, of course, their reaction to the deadly bank robbery.

Heavy news day. I clicked off the TV and reached for the land-line phone. First I checked my office voice mail, but thankfully had few messages of importance.

I did return one patient call. A formerly battered wife I'd referred to a women's shelter the week before had left a message saying she was settled in. Moreover, she'd finally gotten up the courage to call an attorney.

We spoke briefly and set an appointment for first thing Monday morning. Regardless of what the police said they wanted, I knew I had to be back in the office next week. Back doing my real job. Seeing patients.

Which reminded me to check in with Treva. We'd spoken about getting together sometime today. I wasn't surprised, given the early hour, that I got her answering machine. I left a message suggesting that, since she was attending the victims memorial at noon, we schedule a meeting somewhere nearby at two. I gave her the address of a Starbucks I knew in the area and asked that she leave me a confirming message when she woke up.

Then I checked the locks on the doors, left the house, and went out to my car. Before getting behind the wheel, I gratefully breathed in the clear morning air. Though the sun was up, it was giving off more light than heat. At least so far.

I'd just turned the key in the ignition when I had a sudden thought. Letting the engine idle, I took out my cell and punched in Angie Villanova's number.

She picked up after two rings.

"Danny. Don't tell me, you want a favor. And I haven't even finished my friggin' coffee yet."

"I'm glad we communicate on such a deep, intuitive level, Angie. Must be in the blood."

"Yank my other one. What do ya want and who do I have to sleep with to get it? Not that I'm averse to the idea."

"Don't worry, your virtue is secured. All I need is some info on ADA Dave Parnelli."

"Yeah. Parnelli. I've met him. Kind of a prick."

"Kind of. Could you get me some background on him?"

"Why don'tcha just Google him like everybody else?"

"I was hoping for something other than his résumé. Something deeper. Maybe you could ask around the DA's office. Get a feel for the guy."

She clucked her tongue. "Okay, tell you what. I'll see what I can find out, and you agree to come to dinner a week from this Sunday. I'm making ravioli. My mother's sauce."

"It's a deal."

"I mean it, Danny. No excuses. No patient emergencies. None of your usual bullshit."

"Is Sonny gonna be there?" Her racist, opinionated husband and I rarely got along.

"Like I got a choice. I married the bastard, right? He gets to eat here. So, you comin' or what?"

"I'll be there. Just get back to me about Parnelli."

"Yeah, yeah. Love you, too. Asshole."

◇◇◇

An hour later, having braved crushing midtown traffic, I walked across the unusually crowded detectives floor at robbery/homicide. Crowded because, due to the intensity of the ongoing joint police-FBI investigation, the demarcation between day and night shifts had blurred.

Which meant more bleary-eyed cops, swilling more bad coffee, following more useless leads. A weary, overworked, overextended police department feeling the strain of a long, grueling siege. With an impatient City Hall always bringing greater pressure, increased demands for results.

I passed a row of opened doors, nodding at the few detectives I knew—if only by sight—until I found Polk's office. I'd come bearing gifts. Hot coffee and Danish. The good stuff, from the Italian bakery around the corner.

"Nothing but the best for my old pal Harry," I said, placing the white paper bag on his desk.

Polk looked like hell. At least I'd gotten to go home, grab a shave and a shower. He'd obviously been here all night, since the 2 AM meeting in Biegler's office.

At first, he didn't react to the bag on his desk. Didn't even acknowledge me. Just kept shuffling papers on the messy, food-stained blotter. Then he adjusted his pale blue tie. Then he scribbled a note on the back of a crumpled business card.

Finally, he looked up at me with one bleary, blood-shot eye. "Okay, Doc. What the fuck do you want?"

I told him.

Chapter Fifty

For some reason, Polk remembered where Ten Oaks was, though I assumed it had been a year since he'd last been here. Yet, when I rolled to a stop on the curving driveway fronting the red-bricked, gable-roofed building, I saw his unmarked Ford sedan already parked in the side lot. I pulled in beside him.

At just after ten, the sun was already a flare-like blur in the cloudless sky. I could feel the heat coming up off the gravel beneath my feet as I went up to the large, gilt-framed double front doors.

As I crossed the opulent reception area—silent testimony to the exclusivity and expense of the private psychiatric clinic—I glanced up at the circular skylight, its curved glass glazed by the morning's sun, like icing on a cake.

Flashing my hospital ID badge at the girl behind the desk, I pushed through the doors just behind it and entered the facility proper. Walked down the familiar pea-green-walled corridors. Past the patient quarters, staff lounge, conference room. The haunts of my internship, my initial training as a therapist. Sights, smells, and sounds forever etched in my memory.

Though one thing was new. For the first time, I was going to see Nancy Mendors sitting in the Clinic Director's office.

Polk was waiting there when I arrived, standing uncomfortably by the wide rear window. Looking out at the recreation field with his usual skeptical demeanor.

Nancy came out from behind the desk, gave me a brief hug, then stepped back. Arms folded. With a look even more skeptical than Polk's.

"Are you sure about this?" Her first and only words since I'd walked in the door.

"Hell, no," I answered. "Ready?"

Polk turned from the window, cast a baleful glance in my direction, then gestured toward the corridor.

"It's *your* party, Doc."

As Nancy fiddled with the cuffs of her white hospital coat, I noticed what I took to be her new engagement ring. Nice, tasteful diamond. Gleaming off the light from the office windows.

If she saw me registering it, she didn't give any indication. Merely straightened, then led us out into the hallway.

And to Andy's room.

After we'd finished there, some twenty minutes later, Nancy told an intern to go ask Victoria Tolan to join us at the rear doors. We waited only a few more minutes, and then the pale, achingly slender young woman appeared. She stood nervously in her oversized blouse and jeans, compulsively twisting her long auburn hair between bone-thin fingers.

After Nancy had explained what was going to happen, she asked Victoria if she felt up to accompanying us.

"I want to," she said. "More than anything."

◇◇◇

"Hey, what's this all about?"

Stan Willis was standing alone in a corner of the clinic's rec yard, shaded from the sun by high, sculpted hedges. He'd been lazily tossing a baseball into the air, then catching it in a worn fielder's glove.

Until he saw us approaching from the rear of the main building. Crossing the generous expanse of short, fresh-cut grass. His eyes riveted on us as the last ball he'd thrown fell with a dull thud on the ground at his feet.

"Could we talk to you, Stan?" Nancy Mendors was the first to reach the slim, brown-haired man. We'd thought it best to let her do so.

"Is something wrong?"

Though he addressed his question to Nancy, Willis' eyes darted past her to where I stood, just a few feet behind her. Along with Victoria Tolan and Harry Polk.

Willis must've been outside a lot since I'd first seen him two days before. His tan had deepened, become a painful-looking burn.

"We'd like you to come with us." Nancy's voice stayed cool, noncommittal. A practiced clinician, though I doubted many psychiatrists had much practice handling a situation like this.

Willis was wary, but acquiescent. He even favored Victoria with a sly smile, but her returning look was marble-cold. Not much had changed, I realized, since Andy's funeral.

"Sure," he said at last. "If you want."

Polk made a face, squinting unhappily in the sun. "You folks want to move this thing along?"

I touched Nancy's elbow. "Let's go, Doctor."

Taking the lead again, Nancy turned and headed toward the wood-framed tool shed on the other side of the field.

An odd, tense procession. None of us speaking as we made the trek across the clipped, dry grass.

We arrived at the shed and Nancy took a ring of keys from her coat pocket. Opened the rough-hewn door. Again, in silence, we marched in a line inside.

The small, single room was stifling.

Nancy flipped on the overhead light, though it wasn't really necessary. The shed's splintered wood walls let in a constant, diffused sunlight. Enough to illuminate the racks of power tools, lawn equipment. A wide workbench covered with old hammers, screwdrivers, pliers. Boxes of nails, screws. A dusty, long-unused band-saw was bolted to the far end of the table.

"What are we doing in here?" Willis rubbed his hands nervously on his jeans. "I don't wanna be in here."

"I'm not surprised," I replied. A glance at Polk told me he was willing to let me take point on this. *My* party, as he'd said.

Willis turned to me, face going pale under the scarlet blush of his tan. "What do you mean? Who are you?"

"Dr. Daniel Rinaldi. And you know damn well what I mean, Stan."

He kept rubbing his hands on his jeans. Gaze darting from me to Nancy Mendors, then back again.

"Do I gotta talk to this guy, Dr. Mendors?"

"I'm afraid you do, Stan."

"Why?"

"Because," I said quietly, "you killed Andrew Parker. Andy the Android."

"*What?* No I didn't. Andy killed himself. He hanged himself with a bicycle chain. Right here in the shed."

"I know. But it wasn't suicide. Not really." Willis blinked, trying to compose himself. Even let a thin smile crease his face.

"*Not really?* What does that mean? This is crazy. *Andy* was crazy. Everybody knew that."

"And nobody knew that better than you. Which is why you were so furious that Victoria liked him. Liked being with him. Liked him and didn't like you."

He tried to look smug. Or maybe offended, I couldn't tell. Though his mouth twitched, and a thin veil of perspiration sheened his forehead.

"Isn't that right, Victoria?" I didn't take my eyes off Willis. "Isn't it true?"

The girl stood in a corner of the shed, fingers curling the ends of her hair. Eyes wide, frightened.

"Yes." A hushed, urgent whisper.

Willis stared at her, betrayed. Anger rising.

"This is bullshit! Andy killed himself 'cause he was crazy. He thought he wasn't human. He always said—"

I moved closer to him, crowding his space. He tried to back-step, but bumped against the edge of the work table. Tools rattled. Shifted on the sawdust-coated surface.

"That's right, Stan. Andy thought he was an android. A machine. Which got me to wondering—if he believed he wasn't a human being, what made him think he could kill himself by hanging?"

I took another measured step. Reached into my pocket and showed him what was in my palm.

"See these, Stan? Know what they are?"

Twitching more violently, he peered at the pills in my hand. Shook his head.

"They're Andy's pills. His medication. I found them hidden between the mattresses in his room. He hadn't been taking his meds. Not for weeks. Which was why his delusion had re-emerged. Why he was back to believing he wasn't human. Other people here at Ten Oaks noticed the change. I learned from my friend Noah that they were afraid he was getting worse. But nobody could understand it. Couldn't figure out why the meds weren't working. Because nobody knew that Andy had stopped taking them."

"So?" Willis swallowed hard. Clamped his hands on the table behind him to steady himself. Control the twitching. "What's that got to do with me?"

"Maybe nothing. Unless you talked him into hiding his pills. Unless you convinced him that he was doing so well, he didn't need to keep taking them."

"That's a lie! I didn't do that! That's a lie!"

"I guess we'll never know. What I *do* know is that by now he was fully in the grip of his delusion. Convinced he was a machine. Not a human being."

I looked across at Nancy, who stood quite still.

"And that's the important thing to remember. That's why something Noah said once got me thinking. He said that Andy had 'deactivated himself.' And the word stuck with me ever since. Because someone who thinks he's a machine *would* envision deactivating himself. *Human beings* die. Machines get deactivated. Shut off."

Nancy took a breath. "Oh, my God."

"You see it now, don't you? Remember what's in Andy's files? The ones you emailed me? When in full delusion, he disavowed being organic at all. Refused to eat. Even referred to his own mind as his CPS."

Polk stirred. "What the hell does *that* mean?"

"It stands for Cranial Processing Software. You see how perfectly consistent his delusion was? Human beings have minds, brains. Machines have cognition software."

Polk sighed heavily. "Christ…"

I ignored him. "That's also why his previous suicide attempts always involved stabbing himself in the abdomen. Or in the neck. Using *tools*. He was looking for the 'off' switch."

"Like when I found him that time," Nancy said, "on the kitchen floor. He'd jabbed himself repeatedly in the stomach."

"Yes. Directly in his navel. With a screwdriver he'd stolen from the tool shed. But why a screwdriver? He was in the kitchen, for Christ's sake. There were dozens of sharp objects he could've found there. Knives, whatever. But instead he takes a screwdriver—a tool—from the shed."

Polk looked unconvinced. "But why bring it to the kitchen to do it? If he was already in the damn shed…"

"My guess is, he wasn't alone in the shed at the time. Maybe some staffer was there, or another patient. Somebody who might try to stop him. So he pocketed the screwdriver and went to the kitchen, which happened to be empty. Found a quiet corner and tried—again—to shut himself off. And if Nancy hadn't found him, purely by chance, he might have succeeded."

By now, Stan Willis had calmed himself. The twitching had ceased, and his eyes had narrowed. Their gaze steady.

"Again—what does all that have to do with *me*?"

I took a long moment before answering. As the airless heat of the wood shed clung like drying clay.

"If Andy wanted to commit suicide—or, as he probably thought of it, shut himself off—he wouldn't try hanging himself. I don't think he'd believe it would actually work. Besides, he'd never tried it before."

"So what do you think happened?" Nancy said.

"I think Stan wanted Andy out of the picture, so he could make his play for Victoria. I think he got Andy alone here in the tool shed, on his thirtieth birthday, and challenged him about his delusion."

"Meaning what?" Polk said.

"Meaning, no matter how much Andy insisted that he was an android, a machine, Stan argued with him. Belittled him. Called him crazy. Doing the one thing you must never do with a delusional person—force him to prove that his delusion is real."

Polk scratched his jaw. "You mean, like, if some head-case thinks he can fly, you don't dare him to jump off the roof. 'Cause he might go ahead and do it."

"Exactly. Which is what I think Stan did. At some point, after mocking him, tormenting him, I think Stan convinced Andy to try hanging himself. After all, if Andy was truly an android, hanging himself by a chain wouldn't harm him at all. So, to prove Stan wrong—to prove that he really *was* an android—Andy wound a bicycle chain around his neck, tied it to that crossbeam, and hanged himself in front of his tormenter."

I paused, suddenly spent. Feeling not the flush of triumph, but a slow, deepening sorrow. The realization that, even if I was right, it didn't do one goddam thing for Andrew Parker. Didn't bring him back.

The numbed silence that had fallen over the small room was broken by Victoria's short, wrenching sobs. Nancy went over to hold her, but the girl didn't let herself fold into the embrace. Instead, choking back tears, she merely looked at Stan Willis.

Meanwhile, her would-be suitor stood stiffly, back against the table edge. Breathing slowly and deeply.

It was Harry Polk who broke the silence.

"This is fuckin' nuts." He squinted at me. "You're tellin' me this is all over some teenage love triangle? That *this* nut-job talked the *other* nut-job into hangin' himself so he could get chummy with his girlfriend?"

I nodded. "Believe me, I've seen patients feud endlessly over *pets*. Over what they perceived as dirty looks. I've seen delusional hatreds simmer for years. But premeditated murder? *That*, I admit, I've never seen."

I stared at Stan Willis. "Till now."

The young man's face hardened, as though a dark mask. Unreadable. Unmoving. Only his jaw working.

"This is so—"

He never finished his sentence. Never intended to.

Instead, with a guttural howl, he pushed past me and ran out of the shed.

Chapter Fifty-one

He didn't get far.

Willis hadn't made it across the threshold of the door before Harry Polk was on him. The burly detective threw himself at Willis, arms outstretched, barreling low. He tackled him hard at the knees, both men spilling onto the grass just outside the shed.

By the time the rest of us had clambered out into the blazing sun, Polk had Willis face-down on the ground, hands behind his back. Snapping on the cuffs.

With an angry grunt, Polk hauled his suspect up to his feet. Willis, the wind apparently knocked out of him, stood on wobbly legs. Bent at the waist.

Polk shook him like a rag doll.

"Fuck, I hate when they run." He leaned down, face at the same level as Willis'. "You hear me, asshole? Do it again, I won't be responsible for my actions. Got it?"

Willis, still gasping, managed a quick nod.

I went up to Polk. "Sorry I let him get past me, Harry."

"Yeah, well, ya don't look sorry enough."

A gruff, reluctant smile. Bagging a killer does a lot for a policeman's day. Especially when the rest of the week's news has been relentlessly bad. Polk probably figured a win is a win, even one whose circumstances were as bizarre as this.

As he dutifully read Willis his Miranda rights, Nancy Mendors joined us. "I...I can't believe it."

"*I* can."

It was Victoria Tolan, standing off to one side. Her face translucently pale in the bright sun. "I know it's true. I knew it the moment Dr. Rinaldi started to explain what happened."

She risked a careful step toward Stan Willis, who'd finally straightened. "You killed Andy. It was you."

Willis allowed himself a tight smile.

"Maybe I did. Maybe it happened the way Rinaldi says. But if so, I'm not guilty of anything."

Polk snorted. "What the—?"

"Get real, will ya? Not guilty by reason of mental defect. That's how this'll go down. I watch *Law and Order*. I know my rights."

He swiveled his head toward Victoria.

"Okay, so I gotta let them say I'm crazy. Fine. I can live with that. But at least I know I'm human. Shit, I may be crazy, but Andy Parker was crazier. Why couldn't you see that, you stupid bitch?"

For the first time, I saw something take hold in the young woman. A calm, sober strength. A clarity.

"No," she said. Quietly but firmly. "Andy *was* human, after all. Unlike you."

Willis stared back at her, at a loss, but Victoria had already turned to Nancy. Voice still calm. Measured.

"May I return to my room now, Dr. Mendors?"

"Of course."

Nancy took Victoria's arm and led her back the way we'd come, toward the main building. Neither woman looked back at Polk, his prisoner, or me.

◇◇◇

I skipped the memorial to the slain bank employees. I couldn't bear the thought of listening to Sinclair and Garrity speak to the assembled crowd. Mourners and media. Supporters and handlers.

I didn't want to hear the candidates take turns being outraged at this heinous crime, showing empathy to the bereaved loved ones, calling on God to gather these four innocent souls into His loving bosom.

I didn't want to see the grieving families and their attorneys. Nor watch eager print and broadcast reporters shove microphones in their faces to get their reactions to the memorial. The extent of their loss, what good they hoped might come from this tragedy. How much they thought Sinclair and Garrity really, truly felt their pain.

Maybe I just didn't want to see how far Mrs. George Vickers had proceeded with her makeover for the cameras. Or put it down to a growing cynicism about political opportunism, public displays of carefully-crafted emotion.

Regardless, instead of joining hundreds of others on folding chairs at Point State Park, I was sitting at a quiet midtown Starbucks. Sipping strong black coffee, waiting for Treva Williams to appear. A few blocks from the memorial site, I'd picked a meeting place within walking distance for her.

What was it like, I wondered, to be sitting in the front row, facing the dais. The only one who'd survived the bloody massacre that had taken her friends and colleagues. As well as Bobby Marks, the man she loved.

I was about to find out. Just as I was finishing my coffee, I saw Treva Williams step through the doorway from the busy sidewalk. Glancing shyly to her left and right.

I rose from my seat and waved her over.

"Dr. Rinaldi. How good to see you."

Her face was red from the sun, and her eyes, though moist from recent tears, were unusually animated. She wore a somber gray skirt and blouse under a black blazer. As when I'd first met her, her make-up was muted, nails unpainted. But despite her obvious sorrow, appropriate to the occasion, she seemed less fragile, less emotionally depleted than before. I thought this a good sign.

"Can I get you something? Iced coffee, maybe?"

She shook her head and we sat opposite each other at the table.

"I can only stay a few minutes," she said quickly, as though a clock were actually ticking. "My driver from Victims' Services is waiting for me at Point State Park. I had to beg him to let me come and see you, before he drove me home." A rueful grin. "He says he's on a tight schedule. Must be a lot of victims out there to take care of."

"Too many, I'm afraid. How was the service?"

Her chin lowered. "It was a nice ceremony. But really hard…I kept thinking about Bobby and everything. But everyone was quite nice…"

"I'm glad. I was worried that Sinclair and Garrity would just use it to make speeches…"

"Well, they did, I guess…but it wasn't obnoxious, you know? It was okay. And Brian Fletcher was very sweet to me. He sat right next to me the whole time."

That didn't surprise me much, though I said nothing.

"After it was over," Treva went on, "he said that Leland Sinclair wanted me to attend the debate tomorrow night. To be in the audience."

"The debate?"

"They've invited me to sit with some other special guests. With the families and friends."

"You don't have to go, Treva. Not unless you want to."

"I think I do, Dr. Rinaldi. Mr. Sinclair is going ahead with the debate to show that he wasn't scared by that man who shot at him."

"Jimmy Gordon."

"Yes. I mean, it's not like I've decided absolutely that I'm going. I'm thinking about it, that's all. Since Mr. Fletcher asked me and everything."

Her cheeks flushed, and she involuntarily lowered her eyes. I was reminded suddenly of something Treva mentioned to me once. About how flattered she'd been when her boss at the bank, James Franconi, had said she was good at her job. That she had a flair. I realized that Treva had probably spent a lifelong yearning to be truly *seen*, appreciated. To be taken seriously. To be noticed.

We chatted amiably for a few more minutes, mostly about the memorial service. The other victims' families. Then, finally, I steered the conversation back to her. And the work I felt she needed to do. I suggested that we set up a regular appointment schedule, in my office, starting next week.

To my surprise, she readily agreed.

"I know there's a lot I have to talk about. To work through. Everything I saw and heard. Plus Bobby…"

Here her lower lip trembled. Eyes blurring with tears. Then, blinking, she looked at her wrist watch.

"Oh, geez…I really have to go. My driver is waiting for me." She rose suddenly, straightening her skirt with her small hands.

I got to my feet as well.

"Dr. Rinaldi, are you going to the debate, too?"

"I'm planning to."

Her smile seemed more relieved than pleased.

"Good. I was hoping—I mean, I'm glad you'll be there. Just in case."

"In case of what?"

The smile melted from her face, replaced by a look of grim expectation. A seriousness of purpose.

"You *do* remember your promise to me, don't you?"

"Yes I do, Treva. But what do you mean? Are you afraid someone will try to hurt Sinclair again? And that *you'll* get hurt or—"

She shook her head. Vehemently. Almost angrily.

"No! Nothing like that."

"Then, what, Treva?"

Treva pressed her palms against her forehead. Hard. As though to keep it from exploding. Suddenly, she turned on her heel and ran out the open door.

Stunned for a moment, I took off after her. Bumping right into a middle-aged couple coming into the coffee shop. By the time I'd side-stepped them, hurried through the doorway, and made my way onto the crowded pavement, she was gone.

◇◇◇

I went back inside and sat at the same table, just as my cell abruptly buzzed. It was Angie Villanova.

"What is it, Angie? I'm kinda in the middle of something."

"Shit, do a guy a favor and what do ya get? Attitude."

"Sorry. Been a weird day."

"So I heard. Somebody told me about Harry Polk's collar earlier today. Some kid from that mental clinic."

"Stan Willis."

"Right. Though I gotta tell ya, they'll never make it stick. For one thing, the kid's family has hired some pricey defense lawyer. And now Willis is denying everything. There's not a shred of proof against him."

"Yeah. It was pretty much all conjecture on my part. Polk came along to put some teeth in it."

"Point is, you and I know what's gonna happen here. Willis is just gonna end up in another psych ward."

"Probably. We expect it. Is that why you called?"

"No, Mr. Charming. I called because you asked me to nose around about Dave Parnelli."

"Jesus, that's right. I'm sorry, Angie. Really."

"Turns out, there's not much to tell. Parnelli's from Brooklyn. Worked for the public defender's office for years. Divorced, with a kid. Ex and kid still live there."

"So he relocated down here alone?"

"Looks like. I put my ear to the ground, like you asked, but came up squat. Nothing special about him since he started with the DA's office. His coworkers think he's arrogant, but what Italian male isn't? Word is, he drinks too much, and flirts too much with the female staff, but stops short of sexual harassment."

"What about his record with the public defender's office in New York? Anything there?"

"*Nada*. Journeyman mouthpiece. Got his share of creeps and scum-bags off, and then got sick of it."

"So he moved straight to the Steel City and the side of the angels."

"Not exactly. After leaving the PD's office, he spent a year in private practice. Some law firm in Harrisburg."

My heart stopped. "Which law firm?"

"Outfit called McCloskey, Singer, and Ganz. Why, you know them?"

Chapter Fifty-two

The rooftop lounge at the downtown Hilton was nearly empty, so Parnelli and I managed to grab a window seat. It was just sunset, and streaks of red, yellow, and purple crossed the sky, their reflections dancing on the waters of the Monongahela River below.

Iron City in hand, I leaned my shoulder against the cool window glass. Sipped my beer. Looked and listened. Sparse river traffic, the mournful sound of a lone tugboat. The streets emptying of cars and pedestrians. The hum of drive-time vehicles on the Parkway, heading for home. The scattered glow of lamps coming on behind office windows. The city gathering itself up for the evening, as the day gathered up its light.

I swallowed a sigh. My favorite time of day, right before darkness falls, and I was spending it at a window table with ADA Dave Parnelli.

"Glad you took me up on that drink, Dan." Parnelli was on his third Scotch. His tie was askew, his sweat-dotted comb-over curling at the ends. "Though this is a bit early. Even for me."

Somehow I doubted that.

Parnelli pointed the rim of his glass at me.

"Plus, I usually don't get to work banker's hours. It's a twelve hour slog most days for this dedicated, under-appreciated public servant. But not today, with the victims' memorial. Not to mention another big fund-raiser in Squirrel Hill."

He drained his glass. "That's one of the perks of havin' a boss runnin' for high office. He's never at his desk. So when the cat's away, et cetera. Another one?"

I shook my head and raised my beer.

"I'm good."

"At this rate, Danny, you'll never catch up."

He laughed and signaled for our waitress to come to the table. She was a real beauty. Young, Mediterranean features. Large breasts rising like creamy smooth mounds in a scoop-necked blouse.

Parnelli ordered another Scotch, gave the girl a leering smile, and sent her on her way.

He leaned back in his chair.

"Smart girl. The bigger the tits, the bigger the tips. It's the way of the world."

Parnelli eyed me carefully.

"You don't say much, do ya?"

"I'm a therapist. I mostly listen."

"Uh-huh. Though I get the feelin' you have somethin' on your mind."

"I do. I'm wondering about what you did after leaving New York. And before coming to Pittsburgh."

"No big secret. I worked at McCloskey, Singer."

"Funny you didn't mention that before. Like when we were talking about Stubbs having the goods on McCloskey."

"*You* were talking about it. Truth is, I didn't think it was relevant. Like I said, it's not like it's a secret."

I let that pass. "How long were you there?"

"Just over a year."

"Not long. Why'd you leave?"

"I don't think private practice is in my DNA, to be honest. Whether I'm keepin' people outta jail or tryin' to put 'em in, I'm a public servant to the core. Probably 'cause my old man was a quasi-Socialist. Give him a soapbox and he'd climb up on the damn thing and start rantin' about the big shots keepin' the little guys down."

I took another pull of my beer. The same one I'd been nursing for an hour.

"Then what the hell were you doing at McCloskey's firm? Trying the good life on for size?"

He grinned. "Score one for the shrink. Exactly right. I thought, hell, since I'm leavin' the PD's office, why not make some real money for a change? Hang out with the country club crowd. Screw some rich WASP divorcees and help keep rock stars and CEO's out of jail."

"Well? What happened?"

"My old man's voice in my head's what happened. My goddam DNA's what happened."

He looked up as our waitress returned with his Scotch. When she placed the glass on a napkin in front of him, Parnelli put his fingers lightly on her wrist.

"You have beautiful hands, young lady. Anybody ever tell you that?"

She shrugged. "That's not usually the first thing most people comment on."

He shook his head. "That's because most people are shallow. Unlike me. I'm more of a poet, see? I appreciate the little things, the subtle aspects of beauty."

The waitress turned to me.

"Don't let him drive, okay?" she said dryly. Then she walked away.

"Smooth," I said to him.

"Never fear, Danny. The best things in life take time to develop. And the night is young. Now, where were we?"

"You were telling me about Evan McCloskey."

He took a large swallow of Scotch, carefully replaced the glass, and leaned forward. Elbows on either side of his drink, hands laced together.

"Let me put it this way. Back in New York, I had this case. Well, two cases, really. One was defending this crack whore who'd thrown her baby out the window of her tenement apartment. Baby was cryin'. Starvin', probably. But Mom just needed her junk, didn't care about nothin' else. So the kid screamin' and cryin' is really settin' her nerves on edge, right? So out the window goes the kid. Baby hits the ground, nobody says nothin'. Nobody comes outta their little holes to check up on the infant. So it just lies there, in the dirt between two tall apartment buildings. Maybe dead, maybe dyin'. And then the night comes…and the dogs. And there ain't no hungrier dogs than ghetto dogs."

Parnelli lifted his glass, took another swallow.

"The next day, cops come. Take what's left of the kid away. M.E. says there's no way to even tell if the baby was male or female. That's how little there was left."

He raised a forefinger.

"That's case number one. My second client was this Russian day-laborer. Did construction, odd jobs, whatever. Fresh off the boat from Minsk or wherever the fuck, right? Old world values, this specimen. His idea of a good time is to take his pay, get drunk, and beat up hookers. Doesn't *fuck* 'em, you understand. They're too old. He saves his man juice for his twin ten-year-old nieces. His brother's kids. Which the brother—another real piece of work—rents to him on an hourly basis. Just to supplement the family income. Anyway, where was I? Oh, yeah. Like I said, my client likes to beat up on prostitutes. I mean, beat 'em real bad. Like, they-don't-walk-so-good-again bad. Like the-docs-can-maybe-save-an-eye bad, ya know? But the girls, they don't say nothin'. Don't press charges. 'Cause they know their pimps will only beat 'em worse."

Parnelli turned his head, looked out at the darkening sky. As though an answer lay out there somewhere.

"Now, by the time I get this Russian guy as a client, he's upped the ante. Maybe it was an accident, maybe not. But one of the hookers he beats the shit out of suddenly dies. Heart stops, whatever. So now he's got a dead hooker on his hands. So he goes to his brother—these fuckin' Ruskies, it's all about family, ya know? Kinda touchin'. Anyway, he goes to the brother and says, hey, I got a dead hooker in the trunk of my car. Brother says, what am I supposed to do about it? My guy says, well, let's not waste an opportunity here. Which, bein' enterprisin' young men, they don't. So here's what they do: they sell tickets to guys in the neighborhood, who take turns pissing on the dead girl in the trunk. Then they hold a raffle, winner gets to pour gasoline in the trunk and light it up. A nice little bonfire in the back of a Chevy Impala. One of the eyewitnesses said it smelled like burnt pork. Stupid bastard thought someone was havin' a barbeque. Brought some beer down from his apartment. Imagine his disappointment."

I'd said nothing throughout Parnelli's narrative. Just watched his eyes as they grew dark and cold and sad.

He took a breath, finished the rest of his drink. Leaned in again, eyes flattening to narrow slits.

"So, here's the thing: you take those two cases, those two clients. The crack-whore momma and the Russian psycho. Hell, throw in the psycho's brother. Put all these folks together and stick 'em in one room. Just you and these fuckin' monsters. And guess what?"

"What?"

"I'd still rather spend a whole night in that room than one hour with Evan McCloskey in his corner office. The one with the windows overlooking the state capitol."

"Jesus Christ. Why? He's that bad? That violent?"

"Hell, no. He wouldn't hurt a fly. Probably faint at the sight of blood, his or anyone else's. I mean, the guy's a deacon of his church. And faithful to his wife, I hear."

"Then what is it? About McCloskey?"

"He's *loyal.* To his clients. To the money they spend with his firm. To the things that money buys. The lifestyle it supports. For himself and his family. He's loyal. Not to truth, or honor, or the facts. Not to the law. Loyal to himself and his kind. What they've built. What they represent. Who they are in the scheme of things. And in the name of that loyalty, he'll rip off competitors, bribe government officials, blackmail his clients' enemies. He'll pay off judges and support political candidates who share his agenda. He's the *paterfamilias* of corporate law. The sentinel protecting his interests against all comers."

Parnelli gave me a slow smile.

"He's the devil, Danny. One of 'em, anyway. And we got a lot of 'em now. See, guys like him run the whole show. Where government and business and law and Wall Street all mix together, one big stew of corporate greed. The power elite, you might call 'em. And it's as removed from the world you and I live in as Paris is removed from Calcutta."

I frowned. "I hate to interrupt, Parnelli, but you're starting to sound like a conspiracy theorist."

"Bullshit, there's no conspiracy. Nothing dark and sinister. It's just the way it is. Always has been. You think it mattered who the king was when the Medicis were in power? Think of it this way: there are basically two groups. There're the guys who run things, and then there's everybody else. Let's say McCloskey is in that first group, okay? And leave it at that."

"And that's why you left the firm?"

"Yep. And I never saw one dishonest, illegal act take place. Never was asked to participate in anything criminal. I just read the tea leaves. Smelled it on the wind. Pick your fuckin' metaphor. All I know is, every time I passed Evan McCloskey in the hall, the little hairs on my forearms stood straight up."

I let everything he'd said sink in. It was a lot to digest. More importantly, putting aside the "corporate overlords" paranoia, I had to ask myself if I believed him. If Evan McCloskey was indeed this behind-the-scenes power-broker, as Henry Stubbs had maintained as well, could I believe that Dave Parnelli had never been a part of it? That he'd intuited the true nature of the firm and decided he couldn't stay?

"I know what you're thinking." Parnelli pondered his empty glass as though it were Yorik's skull. "And, yes, you can believe me. I can't prove a thing, but McCloskey, Singer is corrupt to its core, and I couldn't in good conscience stay in its employ. Maybe all big private firms are like that. I wouldn't know. As I say, I think I'm destined to be a public employee for life. Seed of my poor old man, the quasi-Socialist. God rest his soul."

He grew quiet. Sullen. Maybe thinking about his late father. Or the choices he'd made in life. Maybe thinking about nothing at all.

Regardless, I had two questions to ask.

"Do you know the name Henry Stubbs? Worked for the Federal Trade Commission?"

"Never heard of him."

That had been the easy one. Next question was riskier. "You mentioned that McCloskey's firm often threw its support, financial and otherwise, behind friendly political candidates. People who could be bought. Ever hear anything in that regard about Lee Sinclair?"

"Not a peep." He looked at me askance. "What kinda crap are you still tryin' to sell?"

"I'm not selling anything. Just asked a question."

"Yeah? Well, watch your goddam mouth, that's my boss you're talkin' about. And probably the future governor." He tapped his empty glass on the table, agitation mounting. "Christ, Rinaldi, what are you gettin' at here?"

"Not sure. I'm just wondering—"

"Wonderin' *what*? You tryin' to get me in the shitter with Sinclair? Get me jammed up or somethin'? What's with all these questions, all of a sudden?"

"Jesus, Parnelli, get a grip—"

But he just grew more belligerent. A drunk's outrage. "Listen, asshole, do you have somethin' on Sinclair—somethin' *real*—or are you just shootin' off your mouth? I mean, everybody *knows* there's bad blood between you two—"

I grabbed his forearm, forced it down on the table.

"I said, chill out. *Now*."

"What the fuck—?"

He stared, taken aback. Unsure of his next move. Or even if there was any to make.

He let out a long, slow breath. Calming himself.

"Let go of my goddam arm, will ya?"

I kept my grip on his arm. At the same time, I was suddenly aware of the few other customers in the lounge. All looking our way. Embarrassed. Concerned.

Parnelli noisily cleared his throat.

"Enough already, okay, Rinaldi? End of rant."

I hesitated.

"I mean it, Danny. I'll chill out."

I nodded finally. Let my hand fall away from his arm.

Parnelli pulled it back, rubbing it where I'd held it. Offering me a wounded, indignant look. Followed, strangely enough, by a broad wink.

Then he swiveled in his seat, gaze sweeping the room. As though challenging our onlookers to say anything.

"That's it for tonight's entertainment, ladies and gentlemen." Voice booming. "Show's over. Feel free to go back to your meaningless little lives."

Ignoring a few audible grumbles from the other side of the room, Parnelli turned back around and gave me a boozy, satisfied grin.

"I assume this impromptu meeting is adjourned?"

"Oh yeah."

"Cool." Raising his voice again. "Now where the fuck is that big-titted bitch with the smart mouth? A guy could die of thirst around here."

Chapter Fifty-three

Ten minutes later, I said good-bye to Parnelli. I took the elevator down to the parking lot, got my car from the valet, and rolled into sluggish night-time traffic. I'd just cranked up a "best-of" Nancy Wilson CD when my cell rang. Eleanor Lowrey. Upset.

"Danny, thank God I got a hold of you." I heard an urgent, contentious swell of voices in the background.

"What is it?"

"It's Harry. We're all here at the Federal Building. Biegler, Alcott, and the rest of the task force leaders. Even the Assistant Chief. Everybody but Harry. Biegler's goin' nuts."

"I thought Harry squared things with Biegler. Said he had his act together now…"

"He did. Which is why Biegler's so pissed. Look, it's crazy here. We've got units gearing up for the debate tomorrow night, a whole tactical operation underway. Plus the teams still assisting the FBI in the hunt for Ronny Baxter. Meanwhile, the Mayor's screaming at us to find the prick and bring him in. Like yesterday."

"Rotten time for Harry to pull a no-show. Again."

"I know. Now listen…" Her voice fell to a whisper. I heard a door softly close, the murmur of voices fading. "I tried calling Harry on his cell, but he set it to switch over to his home phone. Who'd guess he even knew how to do that? Anyway, I left a couple messages on his answering machine, but never heard back. Then I tried the bar."

I knew she was referring to the Spent Cartridge, a venerable cop bar off Liberty Avenue.

"Was Harry there?"

"Yes. Looks like he still is. The bartender answered the phone, told me Harry was sitting alone at the end of the bar. On his fourth beer."

"Christ."

"Look, Danny, I can't leave here and go get him. But I have a bad feeling about this. I hate to ask, but…"

I hesitated only a moment.

"I'm on my way. Must be my night for angry drunks."

"What?"

"Nevermind. I'll go round up Harry."

"Thanks. I owe you, Danny."

◇◇◇

The Spent Cartridge was a relic of an earlier time, and had the cramped, weary look to prove it. Huddled between two new high-rises, its darkwood facade, frosted window glass, and buzzing neon beer signs seemed a defiant rebuttal to the urban renovations surrounding it.

As I recalled from my visits the year before, the interior wasn't much different. Though I wouldn't get the chance to find out tonight.

I'd just pulled around the corner and begun peering past oncoming headlights for a parking space when I saw Harry Polk step unsteadily out of the bar. I slowed down, watching him make his way down the street to where his blue unmarked sedan was parked. From my vantage point, I could see him fumbling with his car keys. It took him a few tries to get the door open. Then he slumped behind the wheel.

I picked up speed, figuring I'd pull up next to his car and call to him. No way could I let him drive in that condition. But before I reached him, a truck came barreling around the corner, heading in my direction. Horn honking. Spinning the wheel, I pulled hard to the right, nearly hitting a parked BMW, as the truck roared past me.

Shit! By the time I'd gotten back in my lane, Harry had already pulled out of his spot and headed into traffic. Now all I could do was follow him.

Keeping a good four car lengths behind, I managed to stay on his tail as Harry wove through busy, night-veiled streets. He seemed to be heading for Shadyside.

Five minutes later, I was proven right. He'd just turned onto a gridlocked Walnut Street, its array of shops, art galleries and restaurants packed with Friday night revelers. Every parking space was filled, so Harry ended up circling back two more times.

Finally, giving up, he pulled out of traffic and swung into a narrow side street. Lined on either side by brownstone apartment buildings and townhouses, the residential area was lit by a row of sodium lamps whose intense glow threaded through the tangled tree canopy.

Polk found a parking spot under one of those high lamps. I slowed to a stop half a block down from him, waited till he'd moved away from his car, then parked myself. Stepped out into the warm night air.

Giving Polk a good thirty yards distance, I followed carefully as he walked to the corner and turned back onto Walnut. I hurried then to catch up, afraid I might lose him in the crowd moving four-deep along the sidewalk.

I'd just turned the corner onto the busy street when I stopped suddenly. Stepped back. Then I poked my head out, peered down the block.

Harry Polk was leaning against an SUV, smoking a cigarette. Casually, as though he owned the vehicle. His eyes were riveted on the small, elegant café just opposite. Its outdoor patio boasted a dozen guest tables, all occupied by chatting couples. Drinking wine. Laughing. A few holding hands.

I followed Harry's gaze. He was watching one couple, whose table was at such an angle that only their backs were visible to anyone on the sidewalk. The man had just stood up and tossed some bills on the table. Then he was helping the woman to her feet.

As they headed to the sidewalk, their bodies touched. Heads tilted together. An easy intimacy.

Until, suddenly, the woman looked up. Eyes darkening. She was in her late forties. Big hair. Red-painted lips.

"Harry!" Her voice as sharp-edged as a blade.

Her companion started, bland face going pale. He was well-dressed, a bit more polished than the woman. Monied.

Polk stepped awkwardly away from the SUV. Tossed his cigarette to the curb.

"You know who this guy *is,* Maddie?" Polk stared at the well-dressed man. "What he does for a living?"

Maddie came storming up to Harry, her forefinger raised as though a weapon. Her anger brought a deep scarlet blush to her cheeks. Made her whole body quiver.

"Who I see is none of your business, Harry! *None,* you crazy piece o' shit! Or didn't you get the divorce papers?"

"I got 'em, all right. I use 'em to wipe my ass!"

Before she could respond, Polk had pushed past the woman and confronted her companion. The stunned guy stood rooted to the pavement, mouth dropping open.

"And *you,* you sleazy prick! Stay the fuck away from my wife or I'll rip your lungs out through your throat!"

Maddie whirled on her heel. "I'm *not* your wife, Harry! Not anymore! If you don't get that through your thick skull, I'm gettin' a restraining order. I swear to Christ, I'll *do* it!"

But Polk seemed not to be listening. Instead, he took another menacing step toward his ex-wife's date.

By now, onlookers were pointing and talking, or else giggling nervously. Others were slinking away, scared. And for good reason. So I hurried down the pavement and put my hand on Polk's arm. Spun him around.

I don't know which surprised him more—that somebody had grabbed him from behind in the middle of the sidewalk. Or that that somebody was me.

"Rinaldi?! What th—"

"Gotta save you from yourself, Harry. God knows, you're too damned drunk to do it."

He bristled, pulled himself out of my grasp. Back-stepped on the pavement. Almost losing his balance.

"Look at him! The guy's totally shit-faced!"

These were the first words uttered by Maddie's date. Apparently emboldened by my arrival, he'd sidled over to stand indignantly next to her.

I put my hand on Harry's shoulder again. A firmer grip this time. "Harry, you're a good cop. I'm not gonna let you throw your career away."

Maddie put her hands on her hips.

"That's right, Harry. You crazy bastard! What do ya think the department's gonna do, once they find out you been *stalkin'* your ex-wife? Huh? They're gonna toss you out on your ass, that's what they're gonna do!"

"No shit?" A strange smile appeared on Polk's face. Then he walked calmly over to Maddie and her companion. Deliberately crowded the man's space.

"What did you tell Maddie, eh, pal? That you were some kind of investment banker? Some crap like that?"

The man's eyes narrowed, even as he stiffly crossed his arms. Feigning indignation.

Maddie grabbed Polk's elbow. "What the hell are you talkin' about, Harry? Martin *is* a banker—"

"Yeah? And I'm Elvis Presley. He's a con, Maddie."

The other man started. "Now, listen—"

"No, *you* listen, asshole. After you and Maddie left that bar in Market Square last night, I snuck in and lifted your drinking glass. Had a buddy of mine in the lab run your prints."

Maddie stared at him. "Are you shittin' me, Harry?"

"'Fraid not, Maddie. Lover boy here's got a sheet as long as my dick. He's wanted in a half-dozen states for fraud, check-kiting, you name it. His specialty is gettin' his girlfriends to invest in real estate development."

"What?"

Polk grabbed his ex by her shoulders. "Jesus, Maddie, his name ain't even Martin. It's Louis Blakely. And when he ain't bangin' *you*, he's doin' some widow named Esther Franklin, over in Highland Park. I oughtta know—I been followin' the prick all over town. Him *and* you."

Maddie squirmed in Polk's grasp. "Let me go!"

But he merely swiveled his head to stare at the man.

"So how's it comin' with poor Esther, Blakely? She fork over any of her dead husband's insurance money yet? Or are ya still workin' her?"

I watched beads of sweat appear on Blakely's forehead. I also saw his manicured hands clench at his sides.

But I knew it was just reflex. Blakely trying to get a grip on his nerves. He was no fighter.

Meanwhile, Maddie had finally wriggled free from Polk and stepped back on the pavement, eyes going back and forth from Blakely to her ex. Her whole body trembling.

"This ain't true, is it, Marty?"

Blakely's grin was sickly. "Look, honey, you can't believe this lunatic. He's just jealous. Can't stand to see you happy. I—"

But Maddie merely stared at him. Unblinking. As the truth inevitably dawned.

Polk turned again to Blakely. "Now say good-bye to the nice lady, Louis. 'Cause I'm runnin' you in."

"But...but I haven't done anything yet—"

Maddie gasped. "*Yet?* You lyin' sack o' shit!"

Suddenly, before either Polk or I could react, Blakely turned and bolted down the sidewalk. Shouting, shoving people aside as he disappeared in the thick of the crowd.

Laughing, Polk called after him.

"That's right, Louis. Run!"

I stepped up beside him. "You're letting him go?"

"I'm homicide, Doc. Not bunco. Penny ante bullshit. Besides, where can he go? He's got warrants out on him all over the country. Sooner or later, some lucky uniform will collar his sorry ass at a bus station somewhere."

Polk turned then, smiled at his ex-wife.

"Sorry about that, Maddie. Honest. I was just lookin' out for you."

"So who asked ya to?" She showed her teeth. "I don't care why ya did it. Hell, maybe Blakely was right, and it was just because you can't stand to see me happy."

"That's not true, honey. I—"

"We're *done*, Harry. Finished. Now leave me alone to have a life. Or better yet, why don'tcha get one yourself?"

Harry froze then, and looked at her with a naked longing that took me by surprise. Her, too, I thought.

"You *were* my life, Maddie." Voice barely audible.

She took a breath. Then, with a sad smile, she turned to me.

"If you're his friend, mister, get him the hell away from me. And keep him away, okay?"

By now, whatever audience we'd had on the sidewalk had dispersed. Nothing more interesting was going to happen, like on a reality show. No more street drama.

Maddie gave Polk a long, last look. Then she pushed her shoulders back and walked off down the sidewalk.

Leaving me standing with a spent, shame-faced Harry Polk. Shoulders slumped. Eyes moist with banked tears.

"God, I hate her," he said. "The stupid cunt."

"I know."

"And I love her."

"I know that, too."

He paused for a long moment. Wiped his eyes with his jacket sleeve. Sighed heavily.

"You ain't gonna tell Lowrey, are ya, Doc? I mean, about what I've been doin'?"

"I keep secrets for a living, Harry. Remember?"

◇◇◇

By the time I got Polk buckled into the passenger seat of my car, he was lucid enough to give me directions to his place. Then we drove in silence to this squat, ugly apartment complex in

Wilkinsburg. Classic housing for singles, the elderly, and the recently divorced.

At his insistence, I deposited him at the curb. He was unwilling to let me walk him to the front door, nor to accompany him up to his apartment.

"It's bad enough I hadda get a ride home with you."

He leaned into the car through the open passenger side window. Aimed a stubby forefinger in my direction.

"And don't go gettin' any stupid ideas about you an' me. We ain't never gonna be best buddies or nothin' like that. Hell, I still think you got no business stickin' your nose into police work."

"Duly noted."

"Yeah, whatever. Now I'm goin' upstairs and get some shut-eye. First thing in the mornin', I gotta go in and kiss Biegler's ass. Plus the whole damn force is gonna be ramped up, with that bullshit debate and all." He looked off at the black, star-swept sky. "Shit, I got the feelin' tomorrow's gonna be a killer of a day."

Harry Polk had no idea how right he was.

Chapter Fifty-four

That day began eight hours later, at dawn on Saturday morning, with Sam Weiss having breakfast with me at a family-owned diner in Squirrel Hill.

Talking about the death of a man I'd never heard of.

Sam had awakened me from a deep sleep while it was still dark outside, urging me to turn on the TV news. And then to join him at his local coffee joint. Groggy and irritable, I grudgingly did both things he asked.

But not before grabbing a quick shave and shower, and then removing the bandage from the back of my head. I figured the bruise had healed enough. I was right. Driving down from Mt. Washington with the windows open, the predawn air felt good moving freely through my hair.

Now, our breakfast finished, and oblivious to the murmur of voices and clatter of dishware around us, Sam shoved some plates aside on the table and pointed to his laptop screen.

He'd pulled up a video from CNN, covering the apparent suicide last night of a junior attorney at McCloskey, Singer, and Ganz. Howard Gould, married and the father of three, had been found in his office at the New York branch of the law firm. Dead of a self-inflicted gunshot wound. Though he'd left no note, family and friends confided to police that Gould had been troubled by mounting gambling debts. Behind on house payments and private school tuition, as well as losing a hoped-for promotion at work, Gould had grown increasingly despondent.

The report ended with a statement from a spokesman at the renowned firm, expressing shock at the tragic loss of one of its valued employees and offering its condolences to Gould's family.

Sam clicked off the video and gave me a sober look.

"Are you thinking what I'm thinking?"

I nodded. "Howard Gould was Henry Stubbs' mole inside the firm. The guy who'd recorded that conversation between McCloskey and one of his clients. About Sinclair. With all his debts, Gould probably felt he had no choice but to work for Stubbs. He needed the money."

"Then, somehow, Gould was exposed. He must've admitted to working for Stubbs. Even told them about the recording."

"Which is why Roarke and Baxter were sent to Harville. To kill Stubbs and retrieve it."

Sam snapped the laptop lid closed and reached for his coffee. His eyes were lidded, heavy from lack of sleep. He'd been working on the Gould suicide since the story broke in the middle of the night.

"Once Gould was found out," he said, "God knows the pressure he was under. I guess he saw only one way out."

"Any doubts about the suicide?"

"None. Cops found no evidence of foul play."

I leaned back as our waitress approached, giving her room to refill my own coffee mug. Though I was beginning to think there wasn't enough caffeine in the world. Not for how woolly-headed I was feeling.

After she'd moved on, Sam folded his hands under his chin. "So, we're still figuring McCloskey is behind all this? That once he found out about Gould, he sent Roarke and Baxter into action?"

I sipped the hot coffee without tasting it.

"That's the thing, Sam. I was with Roarke in the barn when I mentioned McCloskey. Looking right at him. I swear, he had no idea who I was talking about."

"Meaning what?"

"Meaning, I don't think he got his marching orders from Evan McCloskey."

"Then from who? Or *whom*. I never get that straight…"

"I have no idea. Just like I don't understand the bank robbery. I mean, I know it's part of all this. I just don't know how…or why."

Sam favored me with that crooked smile of his. "That's why God invented the police department, Danny. Maybe you oughtta let *them* figure it out for a change. I know it's a crazy idea, but…"

I said nothing. Draining my coffee in one gulp. As I watched the smile fade from Sam's lips.

"You realize, of course, that we could be all wrong about Gould. He could just be another poor bastard who got in over his head financially and cracked under the strain. With no connection to Stubbs. The fact that he happened to work for McCloskey, Singer is just a weird coincidence. They're a big firm, with a hundred guys like Gould on the payroll. A hundred junior lawyers.

"The truth is," he went on, "we've got nothing. No proof. Henry Stubbs is dead. Gould is dead. Any recording—if it ever existed—is gone. Probably destroyed. Which means all my theories about McCloskey and his sinister plans are…well, just that. Theories."

He rubbed his eyes wearily. "Maybe he's exactly what he seems to be. Just another filthy rich lawyer in a world full of filthy rich lawyers. Maybe everything I've come up with is pure fantasy. Or else I just dreamed it all. Hell, maybe I'm dreaming *now*."

"You're not dreaming, Sam. If you were, you'd be having breakfast with Angelina Jolie. Not me."

He laughed sourly. "True enough. Though it's funny… whether or not I'm right about all this, looks like Lee Sinclair's going to win the election. I was checking out yesterday's poll numbers online before you got here. He's moved way ahead of Garrity. Six, seven points."

"That ought to make Brian Fletcher happy."

"Ecstatic. You oughtta see the press release the campaign put out an hour ago. I guess Fletcher wanted to make sure everyone knew which way the wind was blowing before the debate tonight."

"To suggest that a Sinclair victory in November is a foregone conclusion, no matter how the debate turns out."

"You got it, Danny. Politics 101. Act like you already won and the voters will follow suit." That crooked smile returned. "Everybody wants to back a winner. Right?"

◇◇◇

I was heading out of Squirrel Hill, the sun low and at my back, when my cell rang. The dash clock read 8:00 AM.

"Danny, it's Eleanor."

"Hey, I was just going to call you. Did Harry—?"

"Whatever you said to him last night did the trick. He was in this morning before I was. Did a huge *mea culpa* in Biegler's office. Even brought the lieutenant coffee and bagels. I think he's officially out of the dog-house. For now, at least."

"Good."

"But that's not why I called. We need you at the Federal Building in an hour."

"Who's 'we'?"

"The brass, that's who. There's some new info that's just being processed. Some background stuff we're still putting together. And we're going to need your input. About how to talk to Treva about it."

"Treva? What's this all about, anyway?"

"Bobby Marks, the assistant bank manager."

"What about him?"

"Just get your ass down here, okay, Danny? Everything's coming to a head, and I don't have time to explain it all now. See you in an hour."

◇◇◇

I found a shaded parking space near the construction site at the Point and cut the motor. I had a few calls to make myself.

First I checked my office voice mail. Again, nothing urgent. Quiet week, at least in terms of my practice. As Angie Villanova would say, "Thank God for small favors."

Then I checked in with Nancy Mendors. She was already in her office at Ten Oaks and picked up on the first ring.

"I just wanted to see how Victoria Tolan was holding up," I said. "More importantly, how *you* are."

"Victoria's fine, Danny. And she's decided to stay on here at Ten Oaks." I heard a warmth enter her voice. "And *I'm* fine, too. Still a little stunned by what Stan Willis did, but glad that it's all over. Thanks to you."

"No need to thank me. Once in a while I get lucky, that's all."

"Yeah, right. Anyway, now that the real story about Andy's death has come out, a few patients have even asked if they could have his room. I think that's a good sign. Like it means things are getting back to normal around here. Or at least what passes for normal."

She took a breath. I knew what was coming.

"Look, Danny, I really think it's time you and Warren met. You'll like him, I promise. And he'll like you."

"You know I'm going to think he's not good enough for you, right?"

"You kidding? I'm counting on it."

I nodded at the phone, as though she could see it. But she'd already hung up.

◇◇◇

My last call was to Noah Frye. He picked up from the phone next to the cash register at his bar. I could tell from the clink of glassware, which he compulsively arranged and rearranged in the overhead rack as we talked.

"You're starting work early, Noah. You okay?"

"I'm fine. Couldn't sleep, that's all. Too wired. We did an extra set last night for a group of dentists in town for a convention. Real jazz nuts. Lousy tippers, though."

"Where's Charlene?"

"I'm lettin' her sleep in. Poor kid, works her fingers to the bone around here."

"You take your meds when you got up?"

"Yes, Warden. And I cleaned all the porn out of my cell. Now I'll get my harmonica and play a melancholy jail tune."

"I just want you to stay on top of things, man."

"Bullshit. You want to know if I heard what really happened to Andy the Android, and how it wasn't because his meds stopped working. It was because he stopped *takin'* 'em, the stupid jerk."

"It's true, Noah. He'd stopped for a week or more."

"I get it, okay? As a matter of fact, I did take my head candy this morning. With my orange juice and fiber pills. This way, not only am I rational, I'm regular, too. Any other personal info you need, Danny? My blood pressure? Religious affiliation? Favorite sex toy?"

"No, I'm good. Glad to hear you are, too. Say hello to Charlene for me, okay? And Thelonius."

"Charlene? Sure. Though the cat and I ain't currently on speaking terms. Don't ask me why, it's a long story."

So I didn't.

◇◇◇

The parking lot at the Federal Building was nearly full, which was unusual for a Saturday. But not for today. Not with the debate only eight hours away and law enforcement on high alert.

On the radio driving here, the lead story detailed the tight security planned for tonight's political event at Hilman Library on the Pitt campus. Most divisions of the Pittsburgh Police, as well as a contingent of FBI agents drawn from the tri-state area, were being deployed. Streets would be blocked off, traffic diverted.

"Despite these precautions," the reporter intoned, "tensions are running high. After all, who can forget Jimmy Gordon's chilling words—even as police hauled him away—about District Attorney Leland Sinclair? 'He won't make it to the debate alive.'"

I frowned and clicked off the radio. Not Gordon's exact words, but close enough. Certainly the kind of quote that gets news directors salivating.

I finally found a spot at the west end of the Federal Building lot and went in the main entrance. Grateful for the blast of air conditioning, since the sun—even at this early hour—was already baking the Steel City. According to the weather report I'd heard, officials were expecting a record high today. Maybe 105, if not higher.

The guy at the desk checked my name and sent me up to the top floor conference room. When I got there, I found the double doors not only closed, but locked.

I knocked, loudly.

Chapter Fifty-five

I hadn't finished shaking hands with Neal Alcott, the local FBI agent in charge, before he was complaining about the fact that I was there.

"Biegler here tells me the department needs Treva Williams as a witness." Alcott turned back to take his seat at the conference table. "And that they need *you* to keep her from going off the deep end."

I said nothing as I took the only remaining empty seat. The conference room was wood-paneled, igloo-cold, deliberately impersonal. Classic FBI décor: stoic, no-nonsense, purely functional.

Alcott leaned back in his swivel chair, hands locked behind his head. A bit thinner than he'd looked on TV, he still displayed wide shoulders in his tailored suit. And the burred hair of a former jock.

"Personally, though, I don't like using civilians in any law enforcement capacity. Dilutes the gene pool, if you know what I mean."

Stu Biegler stirred, grinning. "You and I are on the same page there, Agent Alcott."

"No need to pucker up just yet, Lieutenant. There'll be plenty of time for that after this fiasco is contained."

An embarrassed silence, as Biegler ducked his head down over the files fanned out on the table in front of him. Everybody else, glancing down at the duplicate materials in front of them, pretended to do the same. This included Harry Polk, ADA Parnelli, and Eleanor Lowrey.

Since a similar packet of files hadn't been left on the table for me, I was free to keep my attention focused on Neal Alcott. Watching the color drain from his smooth, telegenic features as I stared. Smiling.

Finally, offering me a weak smile in return, Alcott put his palms down on the table. "Obviously, Doctor, it's nothing personal against you. I assume that if you weren't an asset to the department, you wouldn't be here."

"Assume whatever you want, Agent Alcott. Especially since I have no idea what's going on. Except that it concerns Bobby Marks."

Alcott flipped open a slim manila folder.

"Before we begin, I should mention that I've already briefed the assistant chief on most of what we have so far. He and I have agreed that we'll need more clarification on some crucial aspects of this case before sending our conclusions further up the food chain."

"Meaning the Cchief, the DA, the mayor…" Biegler stating the obvious in a desultory, still-wounded voice.

Which Alcott studiously ignored, as he looked at me.

"First of all, Dr. Rinaldi, Detective Lowrey shared with us your suggestion that the bank robbery wasn't exactly what it appeared to be."

"And…?"

"Apparently, you were right. There are a lot of puzzle pieces still missing, but we're fairly convinced the bank job was a cover for something else. Namely, the murder of Bobby Marks, the assistant bank manager."

I let this sink in. "You mean, Marks was the intended victim all along?"

"It appears so, yes. But I'll get to that."

I turned to Harry Polk. "What about James Franconi, the bank manager at First Allegheny? Did you ever figure out whether or not he was involved?"

"He's clean as a whistle, far as we can tell." Polk rubbed his broad, ruddy brow. "He really did have a bad cold the day of the robbery. Plus he's got no priors, not even a parking ticket. Solid gold rep. Friends and family swear he's a fuckin' paragon of virtue."

"Moreover," Alcott continued, "it was Franconi who set everything in motion…whether he meant to or not."

"What do you mean?" I said.

"We just found out yesterday that Franconi had suspected for some time that Bobby Marks was involved in shady financial doings. So he approached the SEC a few months ago and they began an investigation into Marks' activities. Let their forensic accountants loose on him. Turns out, Marks has been using the bank's resources to funnel large funds through various dummy corporations into the Cayman Islands. Some of these funds were traced back to a number of PACs—political action committees, who work to help specific candidates get elected."

"I know what PACs are," I said. "Now let me guess: one of the PACs is affiliated with Leland Sinclair."

Dave Parnelli spoke up quickly. "That's right, though in itself that fact proves nothing. Not a goddam thing."

"We're all aware of that, Mr. Parnelli," Alcott said evenly. "But it's certainly suggestive…"

"Of what? Shit, as evidence of wrong-doing it doesn't even pass the laugh test."

Alcott raised his hand, palm out. "Relax, will you? We're nowhere near making any connections to your boss yet. But one thing is clear: Bobby Marks was the target all along. It's the only thing that makes sense. Roarke and Baxter never even tried to open the bank vault. Then, with the whole Bureau on their tail, instead of heading for the border ASAP, they go after this Henry Stubbs. These two murders have to be connected."

Eleanor glanced over at me. "Which is the same notion Dr. Rinaldi came up with. A couple days ago."

Alcott ignored this. "The point is, whoever Marks was working for got nervous for some reason, and—"

"You know *exactly* what the reason was," I said. "Evan McCloskey found out his conversation about having Sinclair in his pocket had been recorded. Because Henry Stubbs had been paying somebody to spy for him inside the firm. My friend Sam Weiss, from the *Post-Gazette*, thinks the spy was some poor guy named Howard Gould."

Harry Polk smirked. "You mean, that loser in New York, on the news? Ate his gun last night in his office?"

Alcott peered at me. "Oh, yes. This obsession of yours about some big-shot lawyer named Evan McCloskey. We've heard about that, too. As I understand it, you believe he's been pulling strings to help Sinclair win the election. So that he can leverage this influence to get the newly-elected governor to play ball with one of his firm's major clients. That's the gist of your theory, right?"

I held his gaze. "I don't think it's a theory. I think McCloskey paid Bobby Marks to hide illegal funds used to bankroll Sinclair's PAC…and who knows how many other candidates' campaigns? But once he discovered that Howard Gould had sent an incriminating recording to Henry Stubbs, both Gould and Stubbs had to go. As well as Bobby Marks."

"But why kill Marks?" Eleanor asked.

"Because McCloskey didn't want any loose ends. Marks might talk, if pressured. Maybe McCloskey had even gotten wind of the SEC investigation and figured it was only a matter of time before Marks was exposed."

"So Roarke and Baxter were sent to get rid of Marks, but to make it look like he'd been killed as a result of a bank hold-up gone wrong."

I nodded. "Which was why Roarke didn't care about killing the only guy who knew the codes to open the vault. They were never there for the money. They were only there to silence Marks."

"I'm bettin' Marks was probably supposed to be the only victim," Polk added, "but when Baxter panicked and skipped out, Roarke freaked, too. Figured he'd lost control of the situation. Started shootin'."

"Better than that," Eleanor mused, "killing the other bank employees helped disguise the fact that Bobby Marks had been the target all along."

Polk rubbed his chin. "Then, after Roarke escapes from the hospital and drives to the construction site, his old buddy Baxter is there to pick him up. Next stop: Harville, PA, to finish off Henry Stubbs and get the recording."

"Which Stubbs had converted to a CD and tried to hide," I added. "Unsuccessfully."

Neal Alcott had listened in stony silence as this narrative was laid out. Then, sighing heavily, he closed his manila file and folded his hands on top of it.

"So," he said to the room, "we're assuming Roarke and Baxter were trigger men for this Evan McCloskey guy? That the senior partner of a well known, highly respected law firm is behind all this? Ordered all these murders?"

"Looks that way," Biegler muttered, almost to himself. "Of course, there's not enough to connect any of it to Lee Sinclair…"

"That's for damn sure," Parnelli growled. "Or, may I point out, enough to move against *anyone*! I mean, I worked for Evan McCloskey. God knows, he gave me the willies. But last time I checked, that's not an indictable offense. Face it, people—there's no credible evidence to support any of these allegations. Certainly nothing linking him to Roarke and Baxter."

"Exactly." Alcott's voice sharpened. "That's why bringing in Ronny Baxter is our number one priority. We need him to connect the dots."

"Even then," Eleanor said, "we've gotta hope he hasn't destroyed that CD."

Polk laughed. "Lotsa luck with that. As the man says, 'it ain't the despair that kills ya, it's the hope.'"

"On that optimistic note," Alcott said coolly, "let's move on. We still have to coordinate the security protocols for tonight's debate."

He turned to me. "Which means, Doctor, you're excused. You have the relevant information on Bobby Marks. How you plan to deal with his girlfriend once the news becomes public is your department."

Eleanor put her hand on my forearm. "We can probably keep a lid on it until Baxter is brought in. But after that, there's no way Treva won't hear about Marks. That he was crooked. That Roarke and Baxter were sent to kill him."

"Which means that if it weren't for him," I said, "those other people in the bank would still be alive. Once the reality of *that* hits her…"

Polk winced. "Christ. Talk about survivor guilt. Sure glad it's *you* havin' to deal with her, Doc. And not me."

Chapter Fifty-six

At four that afternoon, one of the cleaning crew prepping the main floor of Hilman Library found an old, grimy backpack stuffed in a men's room trash can.

Not ten minutes later, the bomb squad was on the scene, as well as half the Department's Oakland division. Campus security was reduced to emptying the building of its few Saturday visitors, diverting traffic from Forbes Avenue, and keeping pedestrian onlookers from interfering with law enforcement.

I saw all this on the TV news, as I stood at the ironing board in my living room. I was in my underwear, sipping a Jack Daniels, trying to take the creases out of my last remaining dress shirt in the house.

I put down my drink and shut off the iron. Watched in disbelief as news cameras came in close on techs in heavy armor shuffling awkwardly into the low-slung, gray-walled building. An on-scene reporter, her face gleaming red in the unrelenting sun, moved along the sidewalk in front of the library. Shoving her mike in the general direction of anyone in a uniform, wearing a badge, or who looked even tangentially involved in the police operation.

The report cut back to the TV station, where the anchor kept repeating what few facts they had. No information yet on the contents of the mysterious backpack, nor official word from either gubernatorial campaign about whether the debate would be rescheduled.

I pulled my semi-ironed shirt off the board and slipped it on. Its warmth made it cling to my arms and chest. Then I went into the bedroom to finish dressing. I was adjusting my tie when my cell rang. Eleanor Lowrey.

"Tell me you're watching the news, Danny."

"Oh, yeah."

"Well, so was Treva. She was waiting at her place for one of Sinclair's campaign staffers to pick her up. Brian Fletcher invited her to sit in the front row at the debate, so Sinclair can introduce her from the podium before they start."

"I know. Total sop to the cameras. The sole survivor from the bank massacre, there to support the candidate."

"Whatever. The point is, by the time the driver got to her place, Treva was in hysterics. The bomb threat. You can imagine her reaction…"

I could indeed. "Where is she now?"

"Still at home. The driver called Sinclair's campaign head-quarters to ask for instructions, and apparently they told him to stay with her and sit tight."

"Why?"

"They're trying to find another venue for the debate."

"Tonight? Won't be easy on such short notice."

"Tell me. Rumor is they're pulling strings to get that big conference hall at the Burgoyne again. Wouldn't take long to prep the room for the cameras and stuff."

"Where are you getting all this?"

"Biegler. He's been on the phone for the past hour with Sinclair and Fletcher. They need the Department's help to pull this off."

True enough. The logistics alone would be a nightmare.

"Wait a minute," I said. "What about the audience? Weren't they expecting a couple hundred people?"

She chuckled. "Way I hear it, they've got everyone in both campaigns—from high-level staffers to student volunteers—call-ing all the ticketed attendees. Telling them to show up at the Burgoyne instead."

"I'll bet the bomb scare at Hilman keeps a lot of those folks away from the hotel, too. Why take chances?"

"That's the concern, all right. No matter where the debate is held, no matter what the precautions, people know somebody out there wants Sinclair dead. It could really cut into the size of the live audience."

"Though it'll probably triple the debate's TV ratings. And give Sinclair another bump in the polls."

"Whatever." Her tone softened. "Anyway, if Treva *does* end up attending…"

"Don't worry, Ell. I'll be there."

◇◇◇

Before leaving the house, I checked the TV news report again to see if there'd been any developments. There had.

The same on-scene reporter was standing next to a black bomb squad vehicle, its opened rear doors spread out like condor wings. Two bomb techs were carefully loading what looked like a dirty denim rug into the truck. It was the backpack, now wrapped in a plastic evidence bag.

The reporter explained that the techs had examined the backpack thoroughly and found nothing dangerous inside. Just some balled-up old newspapers.

"A prank?" She looked sternly at the camera. "Or some deluded individual's idea of a political statement? At this juncture, the police don't know.

"However, we just received this statement from Leland Sinclair, at his campaign headquarters—"

The report cut to a video of an exhausted-seeming Sinclair, looking defiantly at the camera.

"As I've said before, I will not be intimidated by threats or scare tactics. My debate with Councilman John Garrity will take place tonight. The issues that matter to the people of this great state will be addressed in that forum, as has been the case since the nation's founding. And no criminal or lunatic fringe will interfere with that noble tradition."

Then, cutting back to the on-scene reporter: "You just heard from District Attorney Sinclair. We look for something similar from John Garrity's camp. Now, back to the newsroom…"

I clicked off the TV and hurried out to my car.

◇◇◇

Embedded in typical Saturday night traffic crossing the Fort Pitt Bridge, I kept turning my mind to the events of the past four days. But whether as a result of fatigue, stress or the soul-sapping heat, nothing came together. Made sense. As though, if there *was* some pattern, it was hidden behind a veil. Just out of sight…

The ringing of my cell made me start. I grabbed it up.

"Danny? Dave Parnelli here. Your new best friend."

"How's your head?"

"Fine, fuck you very much. I guess you're headin' down to the Burgoyne Plaza? I mean, how 'bout that bomb threat at the library? Now *there's* publicity money can't buy."

"I doubt the candidates see it that way."

"True. I bet Garrity's still shittin' his pants. Not that Lee's probably holdin' up much better."

"I guess we'll find out tonight. At the debate."

A sour laugh. "Yeah, I can't wait."

"You in your car, Parnelli?"

"Just about to get behind the wheel. Why?"

"Why not take a cab, okay? That way, you give our city's poor pedestrians a chance to get through the evening in one piece. You sound like you've had a few."

Another, deeper laugh. "Ya know, Rinaldi, I still haven't made up my mind whether I like you or not. Believe me, shitty comments like that don't help."

Like I cared. I clicked off.

◇◇◇

The sky had grown charcoal-black by the time I turned into the parking entrance at the Burgoyne. A sign indicated that the underground garage was full, so I had to take a spot in the open-air spillover lot across the street.

I'd just cut the engine when my cell rang again. To my surprise, it was Harry Polk.

"Harry? You okay?"

"I'm fine, Doc. Why wouldn't I be?"

I didn't have time to answer that one.

"So what is it, Harry?"

"Lowrey asked me to call. She's in with Biegler. But we got some big news. For some reason, she likes keepin' you in the loop. Me, I don't get it."

"What news?"

"The FBI. They found Ronny Baxter."

I felt myself gripping the phone tighter.

"They found Baxter? Where?"

He told me.

After we hung up, I took a slow, very deep breath.

And stared out at the black, implacable night.

Chapter Fifty-seven

As I strode across the ornate lobby of the Burgoyne Plaza, it occurred to me that I had no idea what was about to happen.

I had a plan, if you could call it that. But the clock was ticking. If the debate turned out the way most people expected, Sinclair's lead would be insurmountable. He was going to be the state's next governor.

McCloskey's governor.

I reached the curving, carpeted stairway that led to the mezzanine and headed up, taking two steps at a time.

Fueled by adrenaline. And a deep, inchoate anger.

Because the pattern had finally come into focus. Clear. Hard-edged. Obvious.

At least, it should have been. But there'd be time to curse myself later. Right now, I had to—

The same young man and woman who'd stood outside the conference hall, checking off names for Sinclair's fundraiser, were there now. Though both were dressed much less formally. Neither managed that same dazzling smile as before, either. There was instead a real air of tension, of barely contained anxiety, in both our greeters and the other grim-faced attendees joining me in entering the room.

After I was waved in, I headed directly down a middle aisle formed by two long phalanxes of folding chairs, many already occupied. Though, as I'd guessed, the number of empty seats indicated how many of the anticipated audience had been scared off by the bomb threat earlier.

At the far end of the room, a similar dais as before had been erected. Two wood-grained podiums stood at either end of the platform, facing out to the audience.

Neither Sinclair nor Garrity had arrived yet to take their places at the podiums. However, sitting at a long table on the floor directly in front of the dais, were three local journalists—I recognized one of them from the TV news—all poring over their notes for the debate. Readying their questions for the candidates.

Right behind them, a TV crew was positioning cameras, setting lights, and unspooling microphone cords. Prepping for the live broadcast.

I registered all of this in a vague, distracted way, as I did the murmur of the audience and the familiar sight of dark-suited security people stationed at points around the room. I also noted the heavy police presence, the dozen plainclothes officers leaning against the back walls.

This included Harry Polk and Eleanor Lowrey, as well as Lt. Biegler and Agent Alcott. The latter standing near one of the side exits, talking importantly into his cell.

With no time to lose, I gave Polk and Lowrey a quick nod and kept moving down the middle aisle toward the dais. My focus narrowed to the front row of seats, where I found ADA Dave Parnelli, the chief of police, and a half-dozen other city dignitaries. At the far end of the row sat Brian Fletcher and the campaign's special guest, Treva Williams.

As I drew near, she smiled brightly up at me and patted the empty seat on her other side.

"Dr. Rinaldi!" In her simple skirt and blouse, she looked quite pretty. Well rested. "We've saved you a seat."

At the same moment, Brian Fletcher rose and put out both his hands to clasp my right one.

"I was afraid you weren't going to make it, Doc." An easy smile beneath the trim mustache. He wore a new Armani suit, accented by those same gold cufflinks.

No question, this was his night—or at least his candidate's night—to shine.

"Wouldn't miss it, Brian." Taking my seat next to Treva. I leaned in to her, my voice low.

"How are you doing, Treva? I was concerned about you, after the incident at Hilman Library."

She paled, but only slightly.

"It…well, I admit, I was a little freaked out at first. But I'm fine now. And so glad you're here with me."

I nodded and squeezed her hand.

Just then, Dave Parnelli reached across behind two chair backs and tapped me on the shoulder.

"Here I am, Danny. Without leaving a single dead body on the road."

Even from this distance between us, I smelled the liquor on his breath. So, I could tell, did Fletcher, who leaned back in his seat, flinching.

I spoke across the campaign manager's body.

"Before you give yourself a medal, Parnelli, let's see how the rest of the evening turns out."

Parnelli grinned, flipped me his middle finger, and sat back in his chair. Loosened his tie.

Then Treva touched my forearm, bringing my attention back to her. She peered up at the dais.

"I think they're about to start."

I followed her gaze to the curtain at the back of the stage. A crew guy wearing a headset stepped through the heavy fabric. Motioned urgently to the camera operators.

"Looks like you're right, Treva." I smiled at her. "But before they do, I just need to talk to Brian for a moment."

I turned in my chair and took Fletcher's elbow.

"There's something we need to talk about. Privately."

"What?" His brow tightened. "*Now?* This thing's starting in five minutes."

But I was already standing. "Don't worry, it won't take that long. C'mon."

Before he could really protest, I tightened my grip on his elbow and pulled him to his feet.

His eyes narrowed to tiny points. But he kept his voice down. A clipped whisper.

"What the hell are you doing, Rinaldi?"

I gave him a tug, pulling him slightly off-balance.

"Just two guys, walking over to a quiet corner to have a private conversation. Okay?"

I didn't give him time to respond. Moving quickly, my hand still firmly on his elbow, I walked us both over to the service door. The one I recalled from the night of the fundraiser. The door leading to the kitchen.

I pulled him through the door, and then kept us moving across the kitchen. Startled kitchen workers in stained white aprons and wilted chefs' hats stepped awkwardly out of the way as we passed.

"Goddam it, Rinaldi, this is—"

But we'd already crossed the kitchen floor to where the service elevator stood. With my free hand I pushed the button. The scuffed metal door opened and I pulled us into the small, cramped car.

By now, Fletcher had recovered himself enough to shake himself free of my grip. He straightened, pulling down on his shirt cuffs. Eyes ablaze with anger.

"Listen, Rinaldi, I don't know what the hell you think you're doing—"

"What am I *doing?* I'm ending this, is what I'm doing."

"What?"

I put my hands on his shoulders, and slammed him hard against the opposite wall of the car.

Chapter Fifty-eight

Brian Fletcher struggled to get free, his jacket lapels bunched tight in my fists. I widened my stance, leaned in. Pressing him back against the wall.

Frustrated, all he could do was sputter angrily in my face. "You're out of your mind—!"

"Always a possibility. Still, two things have been bothering me since the night Jimmy Gordon took a shot at Sinclair. Two big questions."

Fletcher glowered at me, but kept silent.

"I kept thinking about what Parnelli had said later that night. He couldn't understand, with all that security, how Jimmy managed to get into the fundraiser with a gun. To disguise himself as a waiter and get past the security check earlier that day."

Fletcher said nothing.

"Then there was Jimmy's threat, the one he made as the cops were hauling him away. He said that Sinclair would never make it to Saturday's debate alive. Yet how did Jimmy know about the debate? That there was even going to *be* one that coming Saturday? When you were with Detective Lowrey and me, right before the shooting, you told us that you'd just nailed down the details of the debate. That you'd reached an agreement about the rules and venue with Garrity's people less than an hour before. So how could Jimmy Gordon, working as part of the kitchen staff since that afternoon, have known about it? Unless *you* told him. He wouldn't have access to anyone else in the know."

Still, Fletcher said nothing.

"Know what, Brian? I think you were right when you called it political theater. Because that's what it was. You sought out Jimmy Gordon and paid him to pretend to try to shoot Sinclair. Because of his public threats against the DA, he made a very plausible assassin. But you never intended for him to kill Sinclair. It was all staged."

Which finally roused him to speak.

"Why the fuck would I do that?"

"To foster sympathy for your candidate. Better than that, it allowed him to appear brave in the face of that failed attempt. Unwilling to be intimidated. It reinforced the image of him as a tough law-and-order man, willing to risk standing up to criminals."

"If you say so. By the way, when this little party is over, I'm pressing charges. Assault. Kidnapping."

"Knock yourself out. But, hell, I have to hand it to you: your plan worked. Sinclair's poll numbers have been rising, especially among those blue-collar voters you've been so worried about. Though I think planting that backpack today at the library might have been overkill. I guess we'll have to see when the latest polls come in."

"I guess we will." A trace of pride in his handiwork slipping into his voice. I knew then I was right.

Fletcher let his shoulders go slack then, as he collected himself. Tried to regain some composure.

I moved on. "Once I realized that you'd staged the attempt on Sinclair's life, everything else kinda fell into place. It was you all along. Had to be. That's why Wheeler Roarke didn't know who I was talking about when I mentioned Evan McCloskey. Roarke didn't work for McCloskey. Never even heard of him. He worked for *you*."

"Who's this Evan McCloskey?"

"The money man. Maybe you work for him, maybe you're partners. I don't know. But he bankrolls everything. He wanted to have a Governor Leland Sinclair in his pocket. A nice perk he could provide for one of his big corporate clients. Though we'll probably never know which one."

I took a breath. Watched the sweat beading Fletcher's forehead as the small, airless elevator car grew even closer from our body heat. Felt the drops of my own sweat stinging my eyes. My grip on him slipped.

"Bobby Marks was your inside man at First Allegheny, using the bank's resources to launder the PAC money. So when McCloskey learned there was a mole in his firm and told you about the potential danger of exposure, you hired Roarke to kill Marks. Using a bank robbery as a cover.

"Then, when Roarke escaped from the hospital and went to the construction site, it was *you* he called. Not his partner. It was you who met him there and helped him elude the police. It was you who sent him to kill Henry Stubbs. McCloskey had told you who the mole was working for, and where he was. He knew Stubbs from years before. Knew where to find him."

Fletcher managed a wry smile then, and glanced at his Rolex watch. "You know, Doc, as interesting as all this is, we're missing the debate. In fact, I bet Lee and the others are starting to wonder where we are."

"Then let 'em come find us. I'm going to turn you in to the cops now and let *them* sort it all out."

"You do that. 'Cause no one's gonna believe you."

"Maybe not at first. But once the cops start digging into your background, your financials…once they connect you to Wheeler Roarke or Bobby Marks…I mean, you *found* these people. *Paid* them. Money leaves a trail. Sooner or later, somebody always finds it. And then *you go down*."

He tilted his chin up, as though about to say something. But then a sharp hiss slit the thick silence.

Fletcher and I both turned, caught off guard.

The elevator door rumbled open.

Treva Williams, lips trembling, stood in the doorway.

"Dr. Rinaldi?"

I took a step toward her.

"Treva! No—"

"I saw you both go in the service door. But then I got worried, so I followed you in and—"

Suddenly, Fletcher reached past me and grabbed Treva's arm. Dragged her roughly inside the elevator car.

I whirled to face him.

And found myself staring at the barrel of a small, ugly revolver he'd slipped from his jacket. A revolver he held at her head.

"Don't move, Rinaldi. Not a goddam muscle."

I froze. "Security let you keep a gun on you?"

"It's licensed. For personal protection. And like you pointed out, they work for *me*. If I vouch for a guy—like I did with Jimmy Gordon—he gets a pass. No questions asked."

Then he shifted his body, moving Treva with him, and punched one of the elevator buttons with his elbow. With a metallic shudder, the car began to descend.

Treva, eyes white with terror, stared at his grim, determined face. "Where are we going?"

Only then did he smile.

"To hell."

Chapter Fifty-nine

If it wasn't hell, it was close enough.

When the service elevator doors slid open, Brian Fletcher waved his gun, motioning Treva and me to step out in front of him.

Into the windowless, concrete-enclosed underground maintenance bay, one level beneath the bottom floor parking garage. A sprawling, low-ceilinged expanse barely lit by flickering fluorescents hanging by chains above our heads.

"Oh, my God…" Treva's voice. Faint, all breath.

Fletcher grunted. "Nice ambiance, eh? I scoped this place out with the security detail before the fundraiser. Made kind of an impression on me."

He pressed the gun in the small of my back.

"Now *move*. Both of you."

We did. Slowly, haltingly. Within seconds, Treva was gasping, hands to her throat. The air was acrid, superheated. Thick as cotton wool.

I felt it, too. Oppressive waves of heat, moving like something slithering and alive from the huge, shuttered vents on either side us. Tendrils of steam, rising.

We walked through a cavernous chamber cloaked in semi-darkness, whose other-worldliness was intensified by the incessant, low-decibel throb of massive equipment. Huge AC units, multifunneled furnaces. Glass-enclosed rows of digital displays. The humming mechanical heart of the glittering hotel above us.

Fletcher stayed right behind me, footsteps echoing mine. I could almost feel his breath.

"I can't let you fuck things up for me, Rinaldi. Not after all the work I've put into Lee Sinclair. All the shit I've taken from that pompous, arrogant prick."

"I get it, Brian. McCloskey wants influence, you want power. And Sinclair, oblivious, was the horse you were both riding on. You hope to ride him all the way to the White House someday, don't you?"

I heard his sharp laugh at my ear. "It's the one real secret of politics, man. If you're gonna dream, dream big."

"Meanwhile, with Sinclair as governor and you as his trusted chief of staff, you'd be in a position to steer state policies McCloskey's way. Though I'm not sure you'll get Sinclair to play along. He can be a real hard-ass."

"So can I. I just have to threaten to go public about his affairs. Usually with women at work. Lee could never take the scandal. Trust me, he'll do what I tell him."

Out of the corner of my eye, I could see Treva's feet dragging. Her gait listless, unsteady.

With an angry growl, Fletcher gave Treva a push with the flat of his free hand, sending her stumbling on the rough concrete. With an effort, she righted herself.

"Keep moving." His voice a sharp hiss that sliced through the constant mechanical hum.

Treva quickened her pace so that we were side by side as we moved through the shadowed maw. Past huge banks of pressure valves, voltage meters, panels arrayed with winking lights. Under and around long, twisting aluminum tubes, coiled like giant anacondas. The veins and arteries leading out from the pulsing, ever-pumping heart of the building. Carrying heat and refrigerated air and steam and water, the life-giving nutrients of the gilded rooms above.

Treva grabbed my hand then. Squeezed it with the same desperate strength I remembered from that day in the hospital. I turned, met her wide, tear-blurred gaze.

Remembered too that promise she drew from me. The raw, aching fear behind it. My solemn promise to protect her, no matter what happened.

Fletcher was tapping my shoulder with the gun muzzle.

"Turn down here. Now."

Still grasping her hand, I steered Treva in the direction he'd indicated. A smaller, concave tunnel, lit along its cracked, flaking ceiling by huge magnesium bulbs encased in wire mesh.

I glanced at a temperature gauge bolted into the near wall: 112 degrees. As we walked still deeper into the gloom, past carelessly discarded machine parts, scattered piles of cinder blocks. Further down the length of that nightmarish tunnel…

My mind racing, I tried to stall for time. To keep Fletcher talking. Until I could think of…something.

"So what's the plan, Brian?" Keeping my own voice strong, measured. Or at least trying to. "You figure you'll just shoot us and leave us down here?"

Fletcher laughed again. Something in the timbre of that sound, it's easy assurance, made my heart pound harder.

"Actually, I *am* gonna shoot you, Rinaldi. Then I'm gonna wrap Treva's hand around this gun and put it up against her head and pull the trigger again."

I stopped in my tracks, turned to face him. Treva let go of my hand, back-stepped awkwardly on the uneven floor.

Fletcher ignored her, his gun now pointed at my gut.

"See, I gotta assume people saw you and me leave the conference hall through the service door. Probably to have a private conversation. Then those same people saw Treva follow us. Problem is, her recent ordeal has sent the poor girl around the bend."

"You're kidding."

"Hell, no. Check it out: Unhinged girl is obsessed with her therapist. Wants a personal relationship with her big hero. When he rebuffs her, she manages to slip my gun out of my jacket pocket. Before I can react, she shoots the unlucky bastard. Then turns the gun on herself. A real tragedy. Stunned, I stagger back upstairs to get help."

"No one is gonna buy that, Fletcher."

A serene, knowing smile. "You'd be surprised what people will buy."

Again, Treva's stricken face tilted up to mine. Skin flushed, burning. I felt my own perspiration pour in rivulets down my neck, into my shirt collar.

But it was the panic in her eyes that riveted me. The glaze of white, nameless fear.

Suddenly, a pressure gauge near Fletcher's shoulder beeped loudly. Startled him. Drew his glance away—

All I needed. I grabbed for the gun in his hand with both of mine. Pushed it up and to the side.

But, with a surprising strength, he held fast to the gun. We both did. Struggling. Gulping thick, stinging air. Banging against the machinery on either side of us.

Finally, I found my footing and drove his gun hand against the side of a barrel-wide aluminum tube. Hard.

Too hard.

With a deafening roar, the gun went off, puncturing the tube. Releasing a white-hot geyser of steam. Rushing, screeching. Exploding into the narrow tunnel.

From somewhere behind me, I heard Treva scream.

And then another, more horrifying scream rent the air. Dwarfed hers.

The force of the escaping steam pushed me back against the opposite wall. Knocking the wind from my lungs. I stumbled, choking, gasping for breath.

As I struggled to keep my balance, I saw Brian Fletcher step like a wraith out of the billowing, expanding clouds of steam filling the tunnel.

He was still screaming, a long, agonizing wail that seemed to come from his very core. As he staggered toward me, I caught sight of his face in the harsh lights.

What was left of it. The white-hot steam had seared half away, leaving only shards of skin and exposed bone, muscle. What skin remained was a scalded mass of pulped, blistered tissue.

I rolled away as he lurched toward me, hands twitching spasmodically. As hissing steam poured out of the aluminum tubing, filling the tunnel, crowding out the air.

Within seconds, the entire area was suffused with billowing clouds of stinging, translucent white. Obscuring everything. Every shape, every form.

I crawled quickly across the floor, eyes burning, calling out for Treva. Suffocating. My bearings lost. As though snow-blind, in a blizzard of scalding white heat.

Panic rose in my chest. I crawled faster, staying low to the ground. My hands baking on the scorched concrete floor. Feeling around me desperately for Fletcher's gun. I thought I'd heard it skitter away on the concrete after going off…

Finally, reaching out my hands in sweeping arcs of motion, I did feel something. The curved edge of the tunnel wall. Hot to the touch, beaded with moisture.

Moisture…which meant the steam was cooling. And, soon, rising.

I crouched against the wall, trying to breathe. To gather myself. Vision still blurred, hazy.

But I was right. The steam was lifting, dissipating.

Maybe a safety valve in the machinery had been triggered. Or else the full force of the pressure venting the steam had begun to diminish.

I leaned my head back against the wet stone wall. Gulped air that tasted like hot embers into my lungs. Coughed. Called out for Treva again. And again.

And then I saw, under the rising billow of steam, a figure advancing on me. Its shape coming more into focus with every second. Emerging out of the swirling, milk-white eddies encircling him.

It was Brian Fletcher, his one good eye livid. Burning with hatred. A mindless fury.

He held something in both hands. Something heavy. Held high, over his head. A thick cinder block. Dust from its sides drifting down on his scarred, heat-ravaged face.

I saw him weaving under the block's weight. Looming over me. I was still crouched in the corner. Trapped.

"You…" A rasp, threaded with pain. "You…"

He raised the cinder block a few inches higher, ready to bring it down on me with all his strength.

I closed my eyes. Hands involuntarily up, as though I could ward off what was coming. Stop it. *Live.*

Suddenly, a gunshot echoed. Loud, high-pitched. More like a shriek in the confines of the narrow tunnel.

I peered up, in time to see the astonished look on Fletcher's ruined face. As the strength went out from him, and the cinder block fell from his grasp, and the bullet hole in his chest welled black and bloody…

And then he collapsed, like a sail in dead calm, and fell to the floor in front of me.

I hunched forward, felt his neck for a pulse. Nothing.

Fletcher was dead.

Another set of footsteps. Slow, tentative.

As the last remaining spirals of steam evaporated, I saw her. Treva Williams. Her small, slim body quivering. Holding Brian Fletcher's revolver.

Chapter Sixty

Treva took another careful step forward. Stared down at Fletcher's body on the concrete. The blood beginning to pool beneath him.

"He…He was going to…I *had* to…"

"I know."

By now, the tunnel had almost entirely cleared of steam. Though rivulets of moisture streaked the walls, the metallic skins of the still-throbbing machinery.

An incessant hum whose echo would stay in my memory, I knew even then, for a long, long time…

Finally, as though just now aware of it, she glanced at the smoking revolver in her grasp. Let her hands drop slowly, deliberately, still molded around the gun.

Bracing against the wall, I pulled myself to my feet. Legs stiff and wobbly beneath me.

Glassy-eyed, she looked at me.

"It's funny, how things turned out. How I ended up protecting *you*…"

"Yes, you did. And I'm grateful."

But my words sounded hollow, even to me. False.

I sighed heavily, let myself lean against the wall. Feeling its wetness stain the back of my shirt.

"But you were also protecting yourself, Treva. I know that now."

She frowned. "What do you mean?"

"With Brian Fletcher dead, no one can connect him to you. No one will ever know that you were working for him. *With* him. From the very beginning."

Her mouth opened, but it took her a long moment to speak. "But I hardly knew Brian Fletcher, and—"

"Jesus, you're good, Treva. You're very good. You fooled me..."

"But I don't—"

I rubbed my eyes. Suddenly weary. Spent.

"Though it wasn't all a lie. I realize that now, too. You *did* love Bobby Marks, and after seeing Roarke kill him in the bank, you really *were* traumatized. Believe it or not, I can imagine how you felt. I've felt it myself."

By now, her face had grown tight. Harder, somehow. But tears dotted the edges of her eyes.

"No, you can't. I loved Bobby with all my heart. And I didn't—I had no idea what Roarke was going to do..."

"I believe you. But that's *all* I believe. Because everything else was a lie. You and Bobby both worked for Fletcher. Maybe Bobby recruited you, maybe it was the other way around. I don't care. But you helped him at the bank. Helped funnel those PAC funds through dummy corporations."

Treva said nothing. Merely stared at me.

I went on quietly. "There was no second robber at the bank. No partner. Wheeler Roarke came in alone, then shot out the video cameras. Then he killed Bobby. Right in front of you."

She nodded again. Slowly.

"He...Roarke said..."

"I can guess what happened next. He threatened you. Said the same thing would happen to *you* if you didn't cooperate. So when SWAT started assembling outside the bank, Roarke sent you out. As a released hostage. He told you what story to tell. That there were *two* robbers. That Bobby had been shot for apparently disobeying their orders not to move. That his death was just a terrible result of panicked, trigger-happy gunmen."

It was only then that Treva glanced down at the gun still gripped in her two small hands. The gun she was slowly bringing up again. To point at me.

"Don't you understand?" She sniffed. "I saw what Roarke did to Bobby. If I didn't do what he said, the same thing would happen to me. I…I was terrified."

"I know. I saw that fear when I was tied up next to you at Pittsburgh Memorial. When he made Dr. Holloway tend to his wound. You must have been horrified when Roarke showed up in your room at the ICU. When he forced you and the doctor downstairs to the OR."

"Yes. I thought he was going to kill me right there. After he got fixed up by the doctor."

"Maybe he would have. Luckily for you, I volunteered to be his hostage instead."

Treva moved closer to me. The gun shaking.

"Look, I…I don't want to hurt you. I just want to get away. Far away. You know yourself I didn't mean for all these bad things to happen…"

"Maybe not. Not at first. But then why keep helping Roarke? Unless he contacted you after he'd escaped from the hospital. Threatened you again…"

Her face paled. "How did you know…?"

"It's the only thing that makes sense. It was Roarke who told you to leave your apartment the next day. To get out of there before the Victims' Services people came to call. It was Roarke who told you to fly to Harville. Hell, maybe you flew together. Took the same flight early that day. Arriving just before I did."

Treva was shaking her head.

"No…that's…that's wrong. You *know* that. It was even on the news. Roarke and his friend Ronny Baxter were at that farmhouse in Harville. It was Ronny who—"

"Stop it, Treva!"

I pushed off from the wall. Anger rising in my throat.

"It was *you* at Stubbs' place. While Roarke and I were in the barn, you were in the farm house, looking for the CD. When you finally found it, you called and told him. I saw him take the call myself."

I risked another step.

"Just as it was you who helped Roarke get the drugged Henry Stubbs up into that noose. With his wounded arm, I knew he needed help doing it. "

"How could *I* have helped? I'm not strong enough to—"

"You didn't have to be. I saw that block-and-tackle set under the tool rack. All you and Roarke had to do was loop it over the rafter, and use the pulleys to hoist Stubbs up. It compensates for the weight."

She bit her lip. Blinking.

I pressed on. "When I was running away, after Roarke died, I looked back and saw a small figure moving toward the barn. In the darkness, I couldn't make out who it was. I just assumed it was Ronny Baxter. Running toward the barn, carrying a gun." My tone sharpened. "Tell me, Treva. If you *had* found me there, would you have used it?"

Her voice rose. "I swear to you, that wasn't me. It was Ronny Baxter. He—"

"Goddammit, it wasn't Baxter and you know it. Ronny Baxter is dead! The FBI found him in the county morgue in El Paso, Texas. He'd been dead over a week. Killed in some drunken bar fight. Days before the bank robbery. Before any of this."

I moved closer, crowding her. "No, Treva, it was you with Roarke in Harville. You who ran in the barn after I got out. Who found Roarke's body and torched the place."

She was blinking furiously now. Hands shaking more noticeably, as she tried to steady the gun.

"No…I wasn't there. I was *here*, in town. At my apartment, remember? You *called* me there. I even asked you to meet. To get together someplace and talk."

"Yes, you did. And that threw me at first. Till I realized that you'd set your phone to take incoming calls and reroute them to your cell. When I called you from that restaurant outside Harrisburg, I thought I'd reached you at home. On your home line. But that whole time, you were talking to me on your cell. Probably from that rented Range Rover near Stubbs' farm.

"Which is also why Victims' Services got no answer when they went to your place that day. You weren't there."

She pressed her lips together. A thin, tight line. I could tell she was trying to focus. To keep the gun straight and level. Trained on me.

"You *are* very good, Treva. You knew I was in Harville. So when I called you, you came up with the idea of inviting me to meet you somewhere, establishing your alibi. That you were still in town, at your apartment. Knowing full well I couldn't accept the invitation."

I took a long breath.

"I'm right, aren't I? For once, Treva, tell me the goddam truth—"

"Yes!" A sudden shout. Choked, as though wrenched from her. "Yes. I…everything you said. I did it. I…"

I nodded. "After that, all you had to do was book a late flight back to Pittsburgh—as I did—and go home. And continue playing the distraught, emotionally needy victim. Or, in my opinion, actually *being* the distraught, emotionally needy victim. Traumatized by everything she'd seen. And done."

She didn't answer. Couldn't.

"It's true, isn't it, Treva? You're feeling it right now. Fragmented, lost. Terrified. And yet some part of you, some self-protective part, keeps pushing you on. It's why you followed Fletcher and me out of the conference hall. You needed to know what we were talking about. Whether I'd guessed the truth and was confronting Fletcher. Whether he'd reveal that you and he had been working together. That after all you'd been through, it would still come out."

Again that slow, glassy-eyed nod. Panic giving way to shock. Disorientation.

"And now it will, Treva. All of it."

I reached into my pocket and withdrew a small digital recorder. With wireless transmitter attached.

"That was the plan all along. To get Fletcher alone, get him to admit his guilt. Before Sinclair's victory became a done deal." I nodded at the sleek device in my hand. "With what's on this, McCloskey's hold on the campaign is over. At least I hope so."

At last, she found her voice.

"You...you were recording Fletcher...?"

"*And* transmitting to the cops. Which means I have *your* admission, too."

She just stared at the recorder, numb.

I pocketed it again and approached her, my palm outstretched. "Give me the gun, okay, Treva? You aren't going to shoot me. You know you aren't."

She grew agitated. Conflicted.

"I...I can't..."

Suddenly, another voice—sharp, commanding—filled the narrow space between us.

"Then give it to *me*, Treva! Now!"

As though slapped, Treva jerked her head back. Stared in the direction of this new voice.

I turned as well, just as Eleanor Lowrey stepped into view, bathed in harsh light from the ceiling lamps. Coming quickly toward us from the mouth of the tunnel. Service weapon upraised.

"I said, give me the gun!"

I faded back as Eleanor approached, her eyes narrowed with purpose. And visible pain.

Treva stood frozen, rooted to the spot. Until slowly, reluctantly, she made a half-turn and faced her former lover. For the first time in many years.

Then, without a word, without a sound, Treva handed the revolver over to Eleanor. She pocketed it.

Without taking her eyes from the younger woman, Eleanor spoke to me.

"You okay?"

"I'm fine. How much did you hear?"

"Enough." She tapped the receiver hooked behind her left ear. "Fletcher *and* Treva."

"But where the hell were you? I thought the plan was to give me five minutes alone with Fletcher, then the cavalry comes in—"

"Right. Till Treva followed you out the service door, and Fletcher brought you two down here. Then we just hauled ass after you, but—"

"But we got lost in a crap-load of steam foggin' the whole place up." It was a flustered Harry Polk, lumbering toward us. Breathing hard. "Plus we went down the wrong goddam tunnel. Regular fun-house, this place."

With his trademark scowl, he surveyed the scene. Took in the two women, the dead body on the ground. Me.

"What *is* it with you, anyway?" he said at last. "Every goddam crime scene in town, you're there."

"It's a gift."

He snorted. "Look, not that I give a shit, but our two candidates upstairs wanna get things started. Crowd's gettin' restless, too. They want their show."

I smiled over at Eleanor. "Late or not, I'm glad you guys made it."

But she was looking at Treva. "Me, I'm not so glad."

A long, uncomfortable silence.

Harry gave me a puzzled look, but I merely shrugged. Then we both watched as Eleanor drew a pair of cuffs from her jeans pocket. Went briskly over to where Treva Williams slumped, forlorn, against the wall. Fingers twisting in front of her.

"I'll need you to turn around, Ms. Williams."

Treva peered up at Eleanor with a child's countenance.

"If I confess, will that make things easier for me? I mean, since you already heard—"

"I can't promise anything."

"Damn right, you can't." Polk shuffled over and read Treva her rights. But she barely seemed to listen. Her gaze was riveted on Eleanor's taut face.

"I'm so sorry, Ell. I really am. About everything."

Eleanor paused. But only for a moment.

"I know."

Their eyes locked. Something unreadable passed between them, something private and unfathomable.

And then, her hand on Treva's shoulder, Eleanor Lowrey turned the younger woman around and brusquely snapped on the cuffs.

Chapter Sixty-one

On Sunday, the heat broke.

It wasn't exactly a cold snap, but as the afternoon unspooled into evening—with the thermometer never getting above eighty—most people felt a palpable relief.

At least, that's what the TV reporter claimed, as he walked along Walnut Street in Shadyside, mike in hand, canvassing the passers-by. Couples and families happy to be out for the day, sipping cold drinks and licking ice cream cones. Walking big long-haired dogs who, for the first time in weeks, didn't seem about to fall prostrate in the street from the unremitting heat.

"God knows *I'm* ready for winter." Noah's gaze was riveted to the TV screen as he casually slid my Iron City across the bar. He looked pretty good today. Relaxed.

"Me, too." Taking a long, grateful pull.

"Besides, Charlene says she can't wait to get me up on the slopes. She thinks I'll really dig skiing. Personally, *I* think she's hopin' I'll crash into some big-ass tree so she can collect the insurance money."

"*What* insurance money?" Charlene's cheerful bellow came from behind the kitchen doors.

Noah grinned, gave me an exaggerated wink, and shuffled off to serve another customer. As he did, I caught sight of Thelonius, leaning against the cash register, cleaning his paws. Still a member of the family.

I took my beer and slid off the bar stool. Walked through the rear door onto the outdoor patio where the wooden floor slats smelled of brine and fish oil. The sun was just going down, its waning rays riding the slow-moving crests of the dark river. Sending off sparkling divots of light.

There were only a few Happy Hour regulars out here on the deck, so I easily found a quiet table and pulled up a chair. Sat breathing in the Monongahela's particularly pungent aroma, sipping my beer, and watching some river birds scavenging the bank below.

I'd had enough of the news for one day. And there'd been a lot of it, especially for a Sunday.

Naturally, the lead story was the death of Brian Fletcher, and the revelations about his orchestrating the fake attempts on Sinclair's life. These were easily confirmed when Jimmy Gordon, not an hour after learning of the campaign manager's death, hastily confessed to his part in the ruse. Of course, he was adamant that he never really planned to kill the district attorney. He was just supposed to shoot wildly and miss. All part of Fletcher's plan to help Sinclair in the polls. When asked why he agreed to work for Fletcher, Gordon was quoted as saying he needed the money.

I took another swallow of my beer and smiled to myself. Recalling what philosopher Hannah Arendt had said about the banality of evil. How guys like Jimmy Gordon proved her point every day of the week.

Even bigger than the Fletcher story was the sudden announcement, just this morning, that Leland Sinclair was pulling out of the gubernatorial race. Though police were confident he'd had no knowledge of, nor any participation in, Brian Fletcher's criminal activities, it seemed obvious that a win in November was unlikely.

In his short press conference, Sinclair took no questions. Instead, he read a prepared statement expressing his dismay at how his campaign manager had duped him—*and* the public— and that he felt it was in the best interests of the state that he withdraw from the race. Moreover, since he had two more years to serve in office as district attorney, he'd have plenty to keep him busy. Safeguarding the lives and property of the great citizens of Pittsburgh. At the end, he wished John Garrity—his only serious rival in the campaign—all the best of luck.

Poor Sinclair, I thought. This had to be a stunning blow. Especially since most pundits agreed that he looked to be the probable victor in the election. Which, these same commentators agreed, also practically guaranteed he'd make another run for the governor's mansion in four years. Knowing Lee Sinclair, I didn't doubt it.

As the sun dipped further behind the old hills, and shadows lengthened across the sluggish waters below me, I finished my beer and got up. Stretched.

It had been another long day, beginning with the three hours spent this morning giving my statement about the previous night's events to the cops.

I'd sat with Harry Polk in one of the interview rooms at the Old County Building, nearly deserted on a Sunday morning, and gone over everything. Twice.

Until, apparently satisfied, Harry leaned across the table between us and shut off the tape recorder. Which meant I could finally ask the only question I cared about.

"What's going to happen to Treva Williams?"

Polk grimaced. "Well, for starters, nothin' she confessed to you is admissible. Though I don't think she knew that. Not that it matters, since she was Mirandized right after. Sang like a bird to Lowrey all the way down to the station."

"Guilt can do that to a person."

"On the other hand, she's already lawyered up. The guy's sayin' she was a helpless victim of powerful men. Terrified of both Fletcher *and* Roarke. According to him, she had no knowledge of Bobby Marks' criminal activities at the bank. She and Marks were just lovers, and she was traumatized by his murder. Not in her right mind when she helped Roarke at the Stubbs place."

He gave me a thin, dark smile. "Geez, Doc, looks like he's workin' *your* line."

"And he could be right. About all of it."

Polk gathered some papers up from the table.

"Won't do him any good, though. ADA Parnelli says he's willin' to take a plea, but not for less than eight to ten years."

"That's hard time."

"My heart bleeds. Hell, she's lucky. Given her crimes, I'm kinda surprised Parnelli's settlin' for a deal."

"I'm not. He probably figures she'll look like a deer in the headlights to a jury. They might go easy on her."

I ought to know, I thought.

Polk clambered to his feet.

"Now get the hell outta here, will ya? I talked to Angie Villanova this morning and you've been released from your obligations to the Department. For now, at least. Go back to stealin' your patients' money."

I rose, too. Held out my hand.

"Looking forward to it. See you around, Harry."

"Christ, I hope not."

But he was grinning.

◇◇◇

As previously arranged, Sam Weiss and I grabbed a quick lunch at Primanti Brothers on the Strip. Usual weekend crowd. Blue collars and white. All big eaters.

The reporter spoke above the din, chewing on his double-stacked steak sandwich. "You realize, of course, that with Fletcher dead, there's nothing to connect any of this with Evan McCloskey. And I mean *nothing*."

"Yeah. That's why the cops agreed to let me confront him at the Burgoyne. I felt sure I could rattle him enough to admit what he did. We knew that even if I got Fletcher's confession, it wouldn't be admissible, but they figured they could use it to get him to roll on McCloskey. But, now, without Fletcher's testimony…"

Sam groaned. "Tell me about it."

"But what about Stubbs' story? And the CD?"

"No way to substantiate anything Stubbs said, either. Even if Howard Gould *was* his mole in McCloskey's firm, he's no longer around to verify it. As for the CD…" He took another generous bite of his sandwich. "*If* it existed, I'm guessing Treva Williams destroyed it. Threw it on the fire she set at the barn."

I mulled this over. "Well, I understand they're still sifting through the ashes over there. Maybe it'll turn up."

"If it does, it'll be too fried to do us any good." Sam tossed the scant remains of his sandwich on his plate. "Face it, Danny. We got nothin'."

Then, as if to emphasize the point, he pulled his laptop up onto the table. Booted it up and found the video he was looking for. Turned the screen toward me.

"Here. Check this out."

It was a news story—covered by a local TV station in upstate New York—about the home-town funeral of Howard Gould, junior attorney at McCloskey, Singer, and Ganz. Standing at the gravesite, next to the lawyer's grieving family, were the senior partners at the firm.

I leaned in for a closer look. Saw Evan McCloskey's bland, sober face. Watched as he gingerly squeezed the hand of Gould's widow, weeping at his side.

I was struck, as I'd been before, at how ordinary he looked. How almost indistinguishable he was from the other lawyers. The other middle-aged white men in suits.

I sat back in my seat. "So that's that, eh, Sam?"

"Not necessarily." He mustered that familiar, crooked smile. "Remember what Stubbs told you? He made a copy of that CD and stashed it somewhere. Maybe it's with some friend or colleague back in New York. Or in a locked safe in some other out-of-state law firm. With Stubbs dead, the damn thing may just turn up…"

He stood up, stretched. "Meanwhile, I still got all my notes. So, hell, maybe someday…I mean, ya never know. Right?"

◇◇◇

"You hear what happened with Biegler and his wife?"

It was Eleanor Lowrey. I'd just pulled away from the Strip, heading toward Noah's Ark, when my cell rang. She'd blurted out the question before I could even say hello.

"No. Though I'm almost afraid to ask."

"Well, the lieutenant is still bunking at the hotel, but looks like they're going into couples counseling."

"I don't envy their therapist."

"But here's the kicker: to make this happen, Biegler had to pony up some cash and convince LaWanda Collins to relocate. As in, get outta town. Rumor is, she'll soon be working the mean streets of Braddock, PA."

I could hear Eleanor trying to keep her voice light, humorous. But I was also aware of what lay beneath it.

"Look, Ell," I said at last. "I was going to call you myself today…"

"I'm…I'm doing okay, Danny. I mean, I'm worried about Treva. She's looking at real jail time…"

"Listen. If I've learned nothing else about Treva, she's a survivor. She's damaged, sure. Like we all are, I guess, one way or another. But *you're* the one I'm concerned about."

"I told you, I'm fine. Or *will* be. Soon enough."

"Just know that I'm here, all right?"

A long beat of silence.

"Look, Danny…about you and me…"

"Is there a 'you and me'?"

"Maybe. I don't know." A wry smile returned to her voice. "I mean, if you're really lucky…"

"Well, one thing I *do* know. We never got around to working out together. To see if I could keep up."

"You're right, we never did. Let me get back to you on that, okay?"

"You have my number."

"In more ways than one, Danny. Believe me."

◇◇◇

The day ended with me sitting on the rear deck of my house, second Scotch in hand, looking down onto the lights of the city. The glistening Three Rivers joining at the Point. The night sounds of traffic on the bridges, working boats on the water, the occasional jet roaring overhead, out of Pittsburgh International.

The Steel City on a Sunday night, about to settle itself down. Ready itself for the week ahead.

I had the kitchen window behind me opened up full, to better hear the sounds of Ahmad Jamal's piano coming from the radio. I was readying myself, too. For the work week ahead. For Mary Lewicki and the other patients like her. For things to get back to normal.

I'd also just gotten off the phone with Angie Villanova, confirming—under pain of death—my appearance at her place for dinner next Sunday.

That call had followed a similar phone conversation with Nancy Mendors, agreeing to another dinner next week. To meet and get to know her fiancé, Warren.

Now, sipping my drink under the blackening night sky, I realized how unenthusiastic I was about each upcoming occasion. How, due either to irritation or jealousy, all I felt was a sense of obligation. Bearing witness, as I often did, to the unfolding lives of others. Whether they were friends or patients. Acquaintances or colleagues.

Jesus, I thought, what self-pitying bullshit. Or else a sober assessment of the life I'd created for myself. One thing I knew for sure. After a couple Scotches, a week's worth of inadequate sleep, and a brush or two with imminent death, the last thing I should be doing at that moment was making any judgments. About anything.

So instead I got up, finished my drink, and went back inside the house. Shut off the music, killed the lights, and checked the locks. Grateful suddenly for the easy sameness, the unvarying routine.

Then I undressed, climbed into bed, and fell into a long, dreamless sleep.